THE MONSTERS OF

ST MARK

DAMAGED GODS

NEW YORK TIMES BESTSELLING AUTHOR **JA HUSS** WRITING AS

KC CROSS

Damaged Gods – The Monsters of Saint Mark's

DAMAGED GODS
THE MONSTERS OF ST. MARK'S
JA HUSS WRITING AS KC CROSS

Copyright © 2021 by JA Huss writing as KC Cross
ISBN: 978-1-950232-69-7

Edited by RJ Locksley
Cover Design by JA Huss

ABOUT THE BOOK

When I answered an ad for a caretaker at Saint Mark's Sanctuary I thought I'd be dusting chandeliers and polishing floors. I didn't expect to be tricked into a curse, going in debt to a monster, and being forced to take a self-paced "Let's Learn Magic" course so I can fix a two-thousand-year-old problem.

And that monster?
Not your ordinary, everyday beast.
He has hooves, and horns, and fur on his legs.
But ya know where he doesn't have fur?
Yup. *There.*
Which is fine.
Except he doesn't wear *pants.*

Nothing at Saint Mark's is exactly what it seems.
The entire inside is magic, the hallways upstairs are nothing but parties from the past, and the super-hot guy who lives in the dungeon?
Yeah.
Not *human.*

My name is Pie and all I want is to be a normal girl with an average life.
I refuse to get stuck in this curse.
I refuse to learn magic to break it.
And there is no way in hell I will fall in love with a monster.
Famous.
Last.
Words.

CHAPTER ONE – PIE

The smudgy filth on the gas station mirror isn't enough to hide the girl looking back.

Someone is pounding on the restroom door, but I only half hear it because I'm staring intently at myself, wondering how it got this bad.

I have never been a hundred percent on board with the girl I am, but I've come to accept her.

Until today.

Today... *today* I am questioning everything.

Especially my outfit.

"What the hell was I thinking last night?" I mutter this to the girl in the mirror, but it's Pia who answers me.

"Stop it." Her tiny voice is a bit muffled because she's hiding in my flannel pocket, but it's clear enough to hear her judgment. She hates it when I start with the self-loathing.

"It's ten AM in the morning, Pia. I woke up in a cave at Mount Aloysius College thirty minutes ago. An angry nun hit me with a stick and called me a Babylonian whore." That might not be right. I was pretty out of it when I woke up in that cave place. It might've been Roman whore. "Then," I continue, "I got a ticket for illegally parking at the chapel last night and I just did the walk of shame through a rest-stop gas station in my Halloween costume."

This outfit seemed like a really good idea yesterday afternoon. I was driving through rural PA and saw the kids from the college celebrating when I was at a red light in their sleepy little town. One thing led to another, blah, blah, blah… and then I was doing Jell-O shots with the cool kids dressed like this.

Is there any other way to attend a Halloween party at the private Catholic college without being a naughty schoolgirl? Am I right? I'm totally right.

Pia pokes her head out of my pocket, just enough so I can see her crown of red feathers. Her little beady eyes peer up at me as she speaks. "That wasn't a cave. It was the Grotto Our Lady of Lourdes. Miracles happened there."

"What language are you speaking?"

"A grotto is a cave with water and the miracles happened in Lourdes."

"Well, trust me. There are no miracles happening in this part of PA. It's nothing but hills and the people who live in them."

I screw up my face in the mirror and try to force the outfit from my mind. It made so much sense yesterday. The red and black tartan schoolgirl skirt— in micro-mini version—the ripped, black fishnet stockings, and the red, strapless leather bustier. The flannel came later. After I pulled my head out of my ass and escaped from Sister Judge-y. Why didn't I bring clothes into the bathroom with me? I have trash bags full of them in the back of my Jeep. Then I could've avoided the walk of shame out of here.

"The combat boots really pull it together," Pia offers.

I appreciate her optimism. She's always ready with a compliment to boost me back up when I'm flailing.

More pounding on the door.

"Why must people pound on doors!" I say it loud enough so the asshole on the other side gets the hint. Then I sigh and add, to Pia, "I have a raging hangover."

"I warned you about that last round of Jell-O shots."

I point at her in the mirror. "That you did." I wet a paper towel and pat down my face.

Pia's warm, sparrow body squirms inside my flannel pocket, trying to climb out. She is under strict orders not to speak to me in public, but it's OK right now, since we're in the bathroom. "Blaming yourself won't change anything." She manages to claw her way up onto my shoulder and even though she can't weigh any more than a few ounces, her presence is much bigger than her size. I find this comforting.

Which is both sad and… well, just sad.

Because she's not real.

No one can see her or hear her except me. And even though I spent the better part of my childhood insisting she *was* real, that was a losing battle and always ended up in the same place. Me being called crazy and confined to institutions.

So. Fine. I've accepted it.

She is just my imagination.

She is my imaginary friend.

My personal hallucination.

I snort at my smudgy face in the mirror as the person outside continues to pound on the door.

"For fuck's sake!" I turn towards the pounding and yell back. "What part of 'occupied' don't you understand?"

I throw the door open and come face to face with a small girl. Maybe eight. She is pinching her legs together and squirming, like she's about to pee herself, and if I didn't already feel bad enough, now I feel worse.

Karma, man. It fucking hates me.

"I'm so sorry." I step out of the way and wave a hand at the thoroughly disgusting gas station restroom. "It's all yours."

I linger in the hallway crowded with unopened boxes and a bucket of filthy water with a mop sticking out, because this place is super busy and I don't want to repeat my walk of shame just yet. This costume is a losing battle. I'm either a petulant, overgrown teenager who just recently became obsessed with the movie *The Craft*, or... this is my Halloween costume and I didn't go home last night.

Not that I have a home. I don't. I was on my way to Ohio to crash with a former foster sister when I got caught up in the whole 'spirit of Halloween party' thing.

Note to self. Never show your face at Mount Aloysius College again.

The most ironic thing about this costume—these are my actual clothes. I pulled them right out of those trash bags in the back of my Jeep.

I lean against the dirty wall and casually browse the bulletin board across the aisle. There are lot of business cards pinned to it, plus a few advertisements for kittens, a poster for a missing dog from last year, and a help-wanted flyer.

I pull the flyer down and study the picture. It's a sketch of an old church-like building somewhere in a town called Sanctuary, which I've never heard of, but no one's heard of anything in this part of PA. It's all very rural.

"What's it say?" Pia asks.

I always found it interesting that Pia can't read. I mean, she can talk. Why wouldn't I give her reading capabilities?

"It's a help-wanted ad. For a live-in caretaker at some place called Saint Mark's Sanctuary."

A guy about my age is walking out of the men's room and shoots me a funny look, wondering who I'm talking to. I lift my hair away from my ear and point to the bud.

He looks away, satisfied that I'm not nuts, just being rude by having a phone conversation in public.

I learned that trick early. I mean, as soon as they came out with Bluetooth, I was all over that shit. The perfect excuse if one is perpetually talking to her imaginary friend.

Pia doesn't offer up an opinion on the job, so I read the rest of the flyer to myself. It could be promising. The building looks nice, but why use a sketch instead of a photograph?

It's a red flag.

The building looks super old and it's probably infested with rats or something. And there's no picture of what the live-in situation really entails. Is it a room in this institution? Because I might rather be homeless than live in another institution. I've had enough of those for ten lifetimes.

It doesn't say anything about a salary, either. In fact, it says very little. A couple of sentences extolling the virtues of the grounds and the history of the building, most of which has to be a lie because it says the main building was erected in 1685 and as far as I know, this part of PA was nothing but forest in 1685.

Pia sighs on my shoulder. She is me, after all. And I'm feeling particularly weary right now.

"Maybe I should apply?" I say. "It can't hurt."

The truth is, I'm tired of living in my car. And I already know that this trip to Toledo to stay with Jacqueline is gonna be a disaster. We haven't seen each other in six years. The last time we talked she told me she had four kids and was working three jobs. If she actually lets me stay more than one night, I'll probably end up her babysitter.

And it's not like I would mind helping her out, especially if she let me stay, but...

But I had grand plans once.

Caretaker.

It's better than babysitter. No kids.

I don't know what a caretaker does, but I imagine cleaning and stuff like that. They probably have a whole crew of cleaners. I could meet new people, learn my way around a new town, and start a whole new life. And besides, I wouldn't have to stay there if the room isn't nice. I could rent a little house in the woods. Rent is super cheap in this part of PA. Back in Philly, where I come from, people my age can't afford to live on their own anymore. It's all about how many roommates you can get along with while paying seven hundred dollars a month for a room the size of a closet.

Pia climbs back down my shirt and disappears into my front pocket, her tiny heartbeat galloping against my chest.

And that's it, I guess.

I do my walk of shame with my head high (and my sunglasses on), fill up my tank, get back into my Jeep, and then go south towards the town called Sanctuary.

The sun is setting by the time I drive along the massive brick wall until I find an equally huge iron gate in front of the building sketched out in the flyer. There is no parking lot, just a small pull-in space in front.

I put the Jeep in park and peer up at the old brick building. It's not crumbling. In fact, it looks to be well cared for. The grounds are neat, not a single leaf on the grass, which is still quite green, even though it's November first.

"Is it closed?" I'm not really asking Pia. Just trying to sort out how I get inside the sanctuary.

I get out of the Jeep and walk up to the gate. It's a very nice gate. Something custom and old. *Very* old. Maybe even as old as this building claims to be because it's got a patina. Mostly it's black with some rust spots, but there are words engraved over the arch of the top and those are aged-copper green. *A horn, a hoof, an eye, a bone. A man, a girl, a place of stone. A tick of time, a last mistake, keep them safe behind the gate.* These words are separated by a relief image between 'a bone' and 'a man'. It's a… symbol. Some kind of simple mark. I search my brain for the word I'm looking for. Not a logo. Not a crest. More like a… sigil.

Yeah. I think. I'm not really sure what a sigil is, but that word pops into my head and it feels right so I go with it.

I peek through the wrought-iron bars. There is no one on the grounds in front. There is no intercom to buzz and ask for guidance, but there is a skinny walking gate on one side, and when I try the old iron handle, it turns with a squeak. "It's not locked," I say. "Maybe we should just walk up and knock on the door?"

"We should leave," Pia says, flying over to land on my shoulder. "I don't like this place, Pie."

"Well, I do." I'm annoyed with her and it comes out in my tone. Because Pia is the whole reason why my life is crap and people think I'm crazy.

I am the girl with the imaginary friend.

I am the girl who talks to herself.

I am the girl who hallucinates.

And I have always stuck up for her, insisting that she is real. So can she just be supportive? Please? Right?

Pia is why my mother left me in foster care when I was nine. I was dragged to dozens of free, Medicaid-approved psychiatrists when I refused to say that Pia was fake. They diagnosed me with schizophrenia when I was six. Put me on all kinds of drugs. Made me go to therapy and finally, when I was about twelve, I figured out how to play their stupid game.

Lie. Just lie.

So I became a liar.

And it worked.

They stopped the drugs, they stopped the therapy, and they stopped calling me crazy.

But that was a lie too, because I don't care what anyone says. Pia is *real*.

She has to be real. Otherwise I really am crazy.

"I want to check it out," I tell her. "And if you wanna stay here, then stay. In fact, I think you should stay here. The last thing I need is you distracting me and blowing this opportunity. Or… killing my hope. Because right now, this place has potential. It's got no chance of being a home, but I could do worse when it comes to a temporary way station to regroup and rest after running away from my worthless crap of a life back in Philly. It's got to be better than Jacqueline's couch. She doesn't even know I'm coming yet, by the way. So. Yeah. I'm checking this place out."

Pia doesn't respond. Just snuggles back into my pocket.

And that's that. I'm doing this.

So I suck in a deep breath and walk through the gate.

There is a little bit of fog rolling in as the sun begins to dip behind the tall trees, and I shiver. This is when I once again take notice of what I'm wearing.

I should've changed, at least. No one is gonna hire me looking like this. So I turn, and in that moment, I'm convinced this is a terrible idea. I don't know what I was thinking, coming here looking like a Halloween leftover. No one wants to be a stupid caretaker anyway. And I'm just about to push that walking gate open and leave when a man calls out.

"Hello!"

I whirl around. "Hello?" I don't see anyone.

"Up here."

I look up to the second floor of the main building and see a young man, about my age, wearing—well, from my vantage point, he's not wearing much at all, actually. I can't see if he has pants on—I'm going to assume he does—because the brick balcony is in the way. But he definitely has no shirt on. Because I can see every freaking muscle in his upper body.

I dip my sunglasses down so I can see him better. "Well. Hello back."

He stares down at me for a few moments, smiling.

And wow. That's a nice smile. *Please, please, please, God. You owe me. Please make this man my boss.* I cross my fingers behind my back to give that prayer a little extra.

"Are you here for the *job*?"

"Um." I look down at my clothes and just say, *Fuck it.* I'm inappropriate at all times. If these people are going to hire me, might as well get that out of the way up front. So I look back up at him and nod. "Yep. I'm here for the caretaker job."

He clasps his hands in front of his chest like he's praying, awkwardly pauses, then finally says, "That's. Amazing."

Just like that. Two sentences. Like it truly is a miracle.

And I agree. He's amazing. So I let out a breath, smile at him, and say, "Yes. And…" I look over at the massive front door to the… not church, but sanctuary. "Should I meet you inside?"

"Indeed! I will meet you inside, young lady."

Young lady. I kinda swoon at that. He's not that much older than me. Definitely not thirty yet. But I like his manners. Oh, my God. What if all the boys out here in the woodsy part of PA are like this? All hot and cut, but with manners. "Perfect," I call out just as he disappears from view.

I pull my pocket open and throw Pia a thumbs up. "We're in."

"We should go back."

"Fuck that, Pia. We're here. There's a hot dude with no shirt acting all polite and shit. I like this place already." I bite my lip. "I hope he's not the caretaker who's leaving. Because that would suck. But…" I brighten. "Generally speaking, hot men hang out together. There's bound to be more of them, right?"

Pia doesn't answer me. But it's better that way so I let her silence go. I'm just talking to myself anyway. Pia is, and always will be, just a hallucination.

I walk up the long, red cobblestone walkway and then up a set of seven wide brick steps until I'm standing inside an elaborate portico and in front of the biggest set of wooden double doors I've ever seen.

Everything about this place feels massive and, standing there, waiting for the hot guy to let me in, I feel suddenly small.

Several minutes go by and no one comes to the door.

I look up. And again, there is that poem. *A horn, a hoof…* blah, blah, blah. There is also a very large, round, iron doorknocker with a Green Man face on it, but it's like seven feet from the ground and there is no way in hell I can reach it. So I knock with my knuckles, and call, "Helloooo? I'm the girl outside. Here for the caretaker job." And then pause, wait, and listen for footsteps with my ear pressed against the door.

Nothing.

Just silence.

Did they come to their senses and decide that a girl like me doesn't deserve this amazing fresh start? Doesn't even deserve to interview for it?

I let out a long breath, suddenly depressed again. Then I look over my shoulder at the Jeep, thinking maybe I should just be on my way to Toledo after all. But I can't even see it. The fog has rolled in thick.

"Don't lose your nerve now, Pie," I chastise myself quietly. "You're here. You showed up. That's half the battle. And people who quit when they're halfway there are just... dumb."

So I square my shoulders, tip my head up, ignore my stale costume and the fact that I can still taste Jell-O shots in my mouth, and try the door handles—which are a pair of brass plates with intricate carvings of vines and creatures, and are not a proper doorknob that locks or turns. Just the kind you pull and the door opens.

So I pull and the door opens.

It creaks like no one has opened this door for a thousand years and I suddenly feel like I'm in some dark fairy tale and this is the moment when it all goes wrong.

"Nope. Nope, nope, nope. This is the moment when it all goes right, Pie." I suck in a breath, mutter, "Get a hold of yourself now. Your future is waiting." And then I step through.

It's dark inside. But there's a bit of sun shining through a large stained-glass window on the far side of the gigantic entrance hall.

For a moment I just stand there thinking, *This is kinda creepy,* when the sunlight flashes against the stained glass and illuminates a little bird in the design. A little tree sparrow with a red-topped head that looks so much like my Pia, I take another step forward. Then another. Trying to understand what I'm seeing.

Because what are the chances that this place has a bird like my bird in their glass window?

It's weird. I take a few more steps, and then the heavy wooden door slams closed behind me.

Immediately, the entire interior goes dark. Like the sun just… disappeared. And I'm about to turn around and leave when I hear footsteps echoing through some distant hallway.

"I'm coming! I'm coming!"

It's a young man's voice. Not the same voice from outside, but deeper and out of breath.

"OK!" I call back, then feel dumb for doing that.

His footsteps get closer and his breathing is labored when he bursts into the room. In fact, he's breathing so hard he needs to hold up a finger—the universal sign for 'give me a moment'—as he doubles over, huffing and puffing, trying to recover from his apparent sprint.

"I'm sorry," he finally manages. "I was all the way across the campus." He has to stop there and just breathe again. "When the"—he breathes—"bell"—breathe—"rang."

He seems pretty out of shape. Though he's not overweight. Very tall, very skinny, and very young. Maybe even younger than me. I'd peg him at maybe twenty-one? Twenty-two?

I'm not sure what to do or say, so I fall back on manners. "If this is a bad time, I can just… come back tomorrow?"

At this he stops breathing. Literally holds his breath as he straightens up and stares into my eyes like he's… what? I don't know. A deer in headlights?

"Noooooo." It comes out as one long, low tone. Almost a moan. "No," he says again.

13

Then he smiles. Super big. And I've been around enough people who didn't like me, or want me around, to recognize a fake smile. Which is like weird thing number seventy-five since I pulled that flyer off the gas-station bulletin board, but I continue to pretend it's all good because I might want this job. It's got perks.

"Don't be silly." He has recovered now, his breathing under control and the fake smile just a tiny bit more authentic than it was a few seconds ago. "Don't be sil-ly," he repeats. "You're here. I'm here. We're here. So…" His smile falters. "Why are you here?"

"Uh." Yeah. I don't know. This guy is acting bizarre. And he's definitely not as hot as the hot dude. He's skinny and he's got a nerd vibe to him. "The job?" I finally say.

"Right! Right! Right! The job. You're here for the *job*. The caretaker job." He whispers that last part like he just remembered that there was a job.

"Yep. Caretaker. But…" I look over my shoulder. "Maybe I should just come back tomorrow." Or never. "It's late and—"

"Let me give you the tour real quick. Then you can decide if this is for you and if not, you don't need to bother coming back tomorrow."

This is the first reasonable thing he's said, so I don't have a polite way to get out of it. "OK. Sure. Show me around." I pretend to look at a watch that I am not wearing and add, "But I've only got ten minutes. My friend is expecting me and it's a long drive, so—"

He looks up at the faint glimmer of leftover sunset still shining through the stained-glass window and then nods. "Ten minutes is plenty of time. Follow me. I'll show you the grounds first. Then the caretaker cottage."

"Cottage?" I was picturing a room. A bland, institutional room that could double as a patient bedroom in one of the many psychiatric hospitals I've been in over the years. Not a cottage.

Just the word 'cottage' conjures up images of roaring fires and… I don't know. Wooden cupboards. Maybe a tea pot on an old stove. And shutters. Lots of windows with shutters.

"Yes." He beams at me. "The cottage comes with the job. And it's completely private. And secure," he adds, holding up a finger. "Inside the walls."

"Oh. Nice. What did you say your name was again?"

"We're going to go down this way. Watch your step, now. These stairs are old. Not up to code. People tend to trip on them because they are shallow and you can take three or four in one stride, but it's best to be careful and only take them one at a time."

"Gotcha."

I follow him down the stairs, which truly are baby steps. And there are like a thousand and one of them. There are no lights on in the open room at the bottom, but there are lots of them outside in the… what do I call it? Sanctuary backyard? The windows go from floor to ceiling and that is at least thirty feet, so there is lots of glass for that light to leak through.

I don't exactly know what a sanctuary is supposed to look like, but the first word that comes to mind as I gaze around, taking it all in, is… *cathedral.*

"Oh, yes," the boy-man says. "It's impressive, isn't it? I remember the first time I saw this place too. I was so stunned, I couldn't think straight."

"Yeah," I absently agree as I try to see it all at once. There is so much stained glass in front of me, there might be an entire story up on the windows. There is also a second grand staircase, much like the one we just came down, but off to the left. Then a third one, off to the right.

"This place must be huge," I say. Then I start to worry about the job. Taking care of a cathedral feels like a very big thing. "How many caretakers do you have?"

"Just you." He beams. "It's all yours."

"Well, not yet." I laugh.

He plays with a silver ring on his finger as he pauses in front of a large door that leads outside. "Right. First things first." He opens the door for me and waves me forward. I pass through and find myself in front of the most beautiful gardens I've ever seen. And the lights? They are lampposts, but they are gas. Like... the olden-days kind of shit you see in Williamsburg.

I'm just about to comment on the gas—I do not know how to take care of gas lights—when I notice this isn't actually a garden. "Is this a... cemetery?"

"We prefer to call it a sanctuary. Come. The cottage is this way. Let's pick up the pace."

He hurries up a pea-pebble pathway that leads to a top of a hill, and then we go down, towards the back wall of the grounds. I look around as I try to keep up, because he's practically running again. Huffing and puffing his breaths. Very, *very* focused on his mission to show me the cottage.

This means I can't really study the sanctuary. But I can tell this place is not like any cemetery I've ever seen before. All the graves are huge. They are all like little houses. Like... tombs.

Right. Like tombs, you idiot.

Soon enough, we reach a small building. It's not exactly the cottage I pictured up in the cathedral. There is no thatched roof, no shutters, and no window boxes with bright-red geraniums poking up. But it's quaint. A small brick building—maybe a carriage house back in the day—that has four very tall, very skinny windows facing the front, two on each side of the entrance.

"Here we are." My guide stops and nods his head at the door as he once again fidgets with the silver ring on his pinky finger.

The door is obviously made of the same old, heavy wood the front doors were. And there is that poem again. *A horn, a hoof, an eye, a bone. A man, a girl, a place of stone. A tick of time, a last mistake, keep them safe behind the gate.*

"Why don't you go inside? Take a look around while I take care of something just on the other side of the wall before it gets too dark."

I look at the door. Then back at him. Then all the way back to the main building, which feels very far away at the moment.

This guy is up to something. I'm not sure what, but he's gotten me out here, with no one around. No one even knows I'm here except Pia, and... Oh, wait. That hot guy who greeted me out front. "Hey, where's that guy I saw out front? Is he the current caretaker?"

"Uh... guy?"

"The shirtless hot guy on the second-floor balcony?"

"Oh. That's Tomas."

"Tomas." I whisper his name before I can stop myself. "Nice name."

"Yeah. Uh, no. He's not the caretaker. I'm the current caretaker."

"So he's not leaving?"

"Oh, no." Caretaker guy laughs. "He's not going anywhere."

I nod, smile—try not to smile too big, actually—then say, "OK. I'll take a look around."

He lets out a breath, then smiles, turns on his heel, and walk-runs his way around a towering green hedge.

Yeah. He's weird. But he's leaving. So who cares, right?

Plus, now that he's gone, I feel better. About everything.

Life is gonna get better.

I can just feel it.

CHAPTER TWO – PIE

When I turn back to the door, I feel drawn to it. Like a moth to a flame.

And like the doors out front, the design is intricate. Vines engraved into the antique brass wind their way around the knob and down the plate. This motif even continues onto the aged, dark wood of the door.

When I open the door, I step into a dark room that smells faintly of cinnamon.

"Hmm. Lights. Where would the lights be?"

I feel along the wall, find a switch, and two dim sconces flicker on, filling the small space with a warm, amber glow. But it's literally a flicker.

Gas lamps inside? That's weird, right? I mean, I can see the whole ambiance thing for outdoor lighting. But in your house? Isn't that a fire hazard?

I'd like to consider this more, but then I actually *see* the room. "Wow." I pause in the tiny foyer and let my eyes wander across the space and then I say it again. "Wow." Only this time it comes out as a whisper.

Because this room is everything I imagined. Like almost in every detail. Two overstuffed loveseats with a quaint French-country floral pattern face each other. An oval, wooden coffee table stands between them with a full tea service set up on a vintage silver tray. Beyond the seating area is a small dining nook with a distressed white table and chair set, and just off to the side is a galley kitchen with a vintage stove and farm sink in white enamel.

I turn and look at the tall, skinny windows lining the front and actually gasp when I see real distressed wooden shutters—mounted on the inside—that will close off the outside world.

Pia pokes her head up from my pocket. "This is weird."

"Weird? There's nothing weird about this. It's adorable. It's everything. I freaking love it."

"That's my point." She squirms her way out of my pocket, then flies off and lands on the kitchen counter. "If this is the caretaker's cottage, and the current caretaker is a man your age, then why does it look like this?"

I shrug. "He's got good taste?"

Pia's response is the bird equivalent of a snort. Then she morphs into a moth, but just as quickly, she flickers back into a sparrow. She doesn't flicker much anymore, but when I was young, she spent more time as a moth than she did as a sparrow. Usually when I was up to no good and she was trying to make herself as small as possible so as not to be noticed. Which is dumb. No one can see her. But whatever. The point is, this flickering feels judge-y.

Everything about this room is perfect so I decide to ignore Pia and just enjoy my moment. The kitchen cupboards are all painted white and have glass fronts, so I have a clear view of the most adorable painted dishes I've ever seen. There are decorative tiles on the wall behind the stove. Whimsical Pennsylvania Dutch designs in bright colors. And the rug and hand towels even match. It's all very comfy. And so far, the life I've been living hasn't had much comfy in it. Who in their right mind says no to comfy?

I walk over to the spiral staircase, place one hand on the wrought iron, and climb, trying to get a peek at what's above me. But it's dark up here, and I have to slide my hand along the plaster walls for almost a minute before I find the switch.

Again, the light is a warm glowing amber coming from two small sconces on either side of the bed. And the bed…

"Holy shit, Pia. You gotta come up and see this bed!" It's not overly large, maybe a double. But it has weight. It has presence. There is a canopy with lavender velvet curtains pulled back, making the bed look almost like a tent. The bedding is white. And when I drag my fingertips over the duvet, it's soft, well-worn cotton. The pillow cases are detailed in white eyelet lace and have a delicate lavender flower pattern on them.

Pia flies up and lands on my shoulder.

"It is perfect," Pia admits. "For you, anyway. But don't you think it's a little too perfect? That other caretaker is obviously not living in this den of feminine frills. So why is it here? And why isn't it covered in dust if he's the only caretaker?"

They are good questions. I will admit that. But I don't have an answer. "What are you thinking?"

"I'm thinking this place is not what it seems."

I'm just about to open my mouth and ask what she means by that when we hear someone cussing outside. "What the hell?"

Pia flies over to the window and slips through the closed curtains. "You better come look at this."

I cross the room, throw the curtain aside, and stare down at a small walkway paved with red brick. The caretaker is down below, carrying a wooden crate that seems to be filled with clothes and books. "He never did tell me his name," I whisper absently, watching him balance the crate on his hip as he messes with that ring on his finger. He throws the ring down and it rolls along the bricks, the silver catching a glint of light as it stops near the edge of the path.

He laughs. No. That was a cackle. Then reaches for the door of the wooden gate and slips through, disappearing from view.

"Over here." Pia flies over to another window on the other wall.

I pull the curtains aside and look down. "What…? Who is *that*?"

"That's *him*."

"Him who?" The man down below is old. Like hunchback old. He's wearing a tattered-brown coat that drags on the damp gravel of a parking lot.

"The caretaker," Pia says.

I snort. "That's not the caretaker. He's my age and this man is… ancient."

"He *was* your age. And then he passed through that gate and turned into this old man."

I scoff and crane my head to the side, trying to see around the corner where the young man must surely be.

"It's him," Pia insists. "I watched him turn into that old geezer right before my eyes."

"That's ridiculous." My attention is back on the old man. He's shoving his crate of clothes and books into the front seat of an old yellow-green El Camino.

He looks up at the window and laughs, then slips inside to the driver's seat, starts the engine, backs out of the parking lot with a spray of stones, and takes off down a dirt lane that winds around a lake.

I just watch his glowing orange-red taillights until they disappear into the woods. "What the hell was that?"

"That was *him*."

"That wasn't him, Pia. You've lost your mind."

"Then where is he?"

"I don't know. Outside, I guess."

"Let's go look." She flies down the stairs, but I don't follow. Instead I flip the light on in the bathroom and resume my tour.

It's super small, but that's OK. There's an old tub with a shower, a small vanity, and a very nice antique mirror. I finger the towels hanging off a rack absently, kind of admitting that this *is* a little weird.

Pia is right. The cottage looks very much lived in, but there are no personal items—no hairbrushes, toothbrushes, no clothes on the floor or anything like that. But someone has to live here. It's all too... taken care of. And it cannot be the young caretaker giving me the tour.

Unless French countryside is just his style? But honestly, I don't think that's it.

"You better come down here and look," Pia chirps.

I flip the lights off and go back down the stairs. The cottage door is still open, so I walk through it, assuming she's already outside.

This cottage is a little bit downhill from the main cathedral. So even though I can see the top of the building and the glow of the gas lights, there are no actual lights down here. Just the leftover shimmer of amber filtering through the cottage windows.

"Pia?" I call into the encroaching darkness.

"Over here."

I slip around the corner to a little walkway, and then look up to find the window Pia and I were looking out just a couple minutes ago. Yep, this is the place.

"Where is he?" I look around, but there's absolutely no one here but us.

"He went through the gate. I told you. That old man was the young caretaker."

I just roll my eyes at her, walk down the path, grab the handle of the wooden gate, and pull on it so I can look in the parking lot.

But… it doesn't open.

"Shit. It's locked."

Pia lands on my shoulder. "I think we need to leave. Right now. Something is wrong here. Something is very, very wrong here."

I pull on the gate one more time—still locked— then turn around and spy the silver ring on the edge of the path. I walk over to it and I'm just about to pick it up when Pia says, "Don't touch it!"

I straighten. "Why not?"

"It's magic."

"Oh, my God. Why are you so stupid today?" I pick up the ring and look at it in the dim light of the moon. There's an engraving on the outside, but it's too dark to make out. It's similar to the design on the cottage doorknob, leaves and a face. Maybe that

Green Man guy, but I can't be sure because there's not enough light.

"Don't put it on," Pia warns.

"I'm not gonna put it on, you weirdo. I'm going to find the caretaker and give it to him. That old guy was probably his grandfather or something."

Pia climbs over my shoulder, and slips inside the front pocket of my flannel. Burrowing into my chest.

Her warm body is a comforting feeling that I have grown used to over the years and more than once I have found myself hoping that she never goes away. Even if it means I really am crazy.

I slip the ring into my front pocket with Pia and start back up the walkway, irritated with the caretaker. Because what the hell?

My annoyance doesn't last long. I'm too enthralled with this place and I find myself thinking about the cottage instead. It's so nice in there. So homey, and warm, and comfy. I really could see myself living there. I mean, not permanently or anything. But I can picture this life. The secluded woods. The old buildings. All that stained glass to stare at on the daily. How hard could caretaking be?

I get to the top of the gently sloping hill and the cathedral comes into full view. It looks a lot smaller on the outside. So much smaller, I pause on the path to consider this. In fact, the front of this place and the back of it don't look anything alike.

The atrium—that's what I'm calling that back room that leads out into the cemetery—is clearly visible from here. It's a wide half circle. And if I squint, I can see the grand staircase of stone steps that we came down through the massive windows. But there is no way there can be two equally grand stone staircases on either side of it.

It's just not possible. The building isn't even that wide.

"Huh."

I expect Pia to say something. Ask me what I'm thinking, at least. She's reliably nosey in almost all situations. But she doesn't even poke her head up out of curiosity.

"It must be a trick of the light," I mutter, continuing on my way.

The stone tombs on either side of the walkway are a lot creepier now that the sun has set. Light filters down the lawn from the cathedral and back patio, making weird, dark shadows on the grass all around me. And there are so many tombs out there. I didn't quite understand that before. They are packed together. Almost on top of each other.

It's kinda creepy after dark and I'm suddenly having second thoughts about that cottage.

I look over my shoulder, but the top of the slightly sloping hill I'm now walking down has hidden it from view.

If I get this job, I would be living out there all alone.

"Oh!" I say, more to myself than Pia. "Maybe we should find that Tomas guy? He wasn't creepy at all. I liked him. And the caretaker said he was staying. So who cares if that guy makes us shiver? Right? He's leaving. We don't need to bother thinking about him at all."

This line of questioning should get Pia's attention. But she keeps quiet.

I hurry past all the eerie tombs and enter the cathedral once more. Then pause to take in the two staircases on either side of the main one. I go back outside, just to make sure I'm getting this.

Nope. There is no possible way that those staircases exist.

Except… when I walk inside, there they are.

OK. Maybe Pia is right. This place might actually be more than we think.

She's still huddled inside my flannel pocket. Quiet. Unmoving. This is not like her. Not like her at all.

Well, not entirely true. She hides like this—goes all quiet and still—when she thinks I'm in danger and I should not be distracted.

She went still and quiet when we got arrested for stealing soup when I was seventeen.

She went still and quiet when my mother dropped me off at child protective services when I was nine and never came back.

A chill runs up my spine.

Pia is right. Something *is* wrong.

I run towards the stairs and take them three and four at a time. A minute later I'm rushing out into the main hall, aiming for the massive double doors through the dark shadows. I grab the handle, fully expecting to find it locked, but it opens easily, and with that same familiar creak.

Then I'm through, and out, and running across the well-manicured lawn in a thick fog, towards the walking gate.

But… it's not there.

The fog curls around my legs like a snake. But I keep going. Until there is so much fog, I can't see anything in front of me and I have to stretch my arms out, feeling around for the cold iron. "It has to be here," I whisper, out of breath from running and panic. "It has to. Gates don't just disappear."

And young men don't turn into old grandpas before your eyes, either.

But that's just what Pia said happened. I didn't actually see that.

"Pia." I don't know why I'm whispering. There's no one out here. But I do it again. "Pia?" My voice is more urgent this time.

Her tiny body is still huddled inside my pocket, but she's not moving.

I stop in the fog, reach into my pocket, and pull her out. She is limp.

"Pia?" I gasp. I put her up to my cheek and she's still warm, but she's… lifeless. Which is kind of ironic, because she's not even real, but there's a clear difference in how she feels right now and how she should feel if nothing were wrong.

I pet her back and wings, keeping her pressed up to my cheek. "What is going on?"

And where the hell is my Jeep? I keep walking. The fog lifts just a little, just enough so that I can tell the difference between where I'm at and where I'm going, but I can't make out anything else but *depth*. No trees, no grass, no street, no gate. And when I look over my shoulder, I can't see the cathedral, either.

For a moment I stop and just stand there. Afraid to go forward and also afraid to turn around.

As unlikely as it seems, there is clearly nothing in front of me.

But if I turn, I might get lost. I have no landmarks to orient my way.

"Hello!" I yell. "Can anyone hear me?"

I pause, hoping for a reply, but there is nothing. Literally nothing. Like I'm in some kind of blank space. Some kind of in-between.

And for some reason, the word that comes to mind is... *purgatory*.

"Hello?"

Nothing.

"Pia. Wake up, Pia. Why are you doing this? What's happening?" I sound pathetic and small, and this kind of pisses me off. Because that's *not* who I am.

I'm fearless, and snarky, and most of the time, I'm downright bitchy.

I am not afraid, or weak, or fragile. Not usually, at least. But right now, I feel like all of those things have taken over my body. And then I truly do panic. My heart starts racing. My chest feels tight, like I'm about to have a heart attack. I can't seem to get enough breath into my lungs. It's all ragged gasping. I collapse to my knees, still holding Pia protectively in my cupped hand.

"Help." It's not a call this time. Just a sad, weak whisper of a plea.

"Hello?" A deep voice cuts through the fog. "Where are you?"

"I'm here!" I say, getting to my feet. "Where are you?"

"Follow my voice. You're in the gray."

"I don't think I can. I can't tell where you are!"

"Just follow my voice. You can do it. I'll keep talking."

I take a step and then another, unsure if I'm going in the right direction. But then he says, "Keep coming. I think I see you."

So I keep walking until the shape of the hot dude who called out to me from the second-floor balcony comes into view. Tomas. That's what the caretaker guy called him. "You. Where did you go?" I ask. Which is an odd first question to a complete stranger. But he should've met me at the door, not that creepy kid.

"Oh. Sorry." He frowns, his dark eyes drooping a bit with his mouth. "I was stuck upstairs."

"Who *are* you? Where's my Jeep? Why is there no gate?"

Tomas hesitantly stretches out his hand. Like he's not sure if he wants to really offer it. "We have to go back. You can't be out here. It's very easy to get lost."

"But where is *here*?"

"We can talk about it later. Just… try to take my hand."

And there's nothing else for me to do but what he's asking. I place my hand in his and immediately my entire body becomes warm and the fear that was so acute just a moment ago ebbs and then… disappears.

Suddenly we are walking on grass again. And then the cathedral comes into view. Pia begins squirming in my hand, like she's waking up from a bad dream.

"Pia! You're OK!" I hold her close to my heart. She chirps, but no words come out of her mouth. Just bird talk, which I do not speak. "Why are you talking like that?"

"Talking like what?" Tomas asks me.

Shit. He can't see her. Of course he can't see her. But he can't hear her little bird chirps either, so now it looks like I'm talking to myself.

Again.

And he will think I'm crazy, just like everyone else. And that's… I sigh. Pretty much the story of my life.

"Never mind," I say, suddenly very tired, my feet very heavy, like I'm walking with lead shoes.

We trudge up the steps and we're just about to enter the cathedral when I turn and look over my shoulder. Surely the gate is still there. My Jeep is still there. The road… all of it has to *be* there.

But it isn't.

There is nothing but the hazy gray fog. It's so close to the building now, I get a chill and a wave of claustrophobia shudders through me.

I follow Tomas into the sanctuary and he shuts the massive wooden door behind me.

"There," he says. "It's OK now. But…" He stops, looking past me. And when I turn to see what he's focused on, I find him staring intently at the staircase.

"Who are you? What is this place? Where is my fucking Jeep!" My voice starts soft, but by the last demand, it's loud and echoing up in the high ceilings.

"Shhh!" He hushes me with a firm hand over my mouth. Then he pauses, looking down into my eyes as I gaze up at his. I don't know what happens, but we have some kind of *moment*.

The silent moment is broken by a peculiar clip-clop sound that reverberates up from the bottom of the stairs.

I rip his hand from my mouth and turn. "What the hell is that?" I don't completely understand the panic in my voice, and if asked, I wouldn't be able to articulate it. But it's there.

His hand quickly covers my mouth again. "Do not say another word." Tomas looks down at me. He's still shirtless. Still cut and handsome. But he's not confident. He's not… comfortable. And he holds my gaze long enough for me to discern all the different colors of brown in his eyes. Rings of light brown—almost a wheat color—circle his irises. There are blurry blotches of green too, and some dark parts. His eyes are like a kaleidoscope of all the hues in the woods.

The clip-clop continues on the stairs and I find myself leaning that way, trying to see what's coming, even though every bone in my body is screaming at me to run.

This makes no sense. But that gray fog outside didn't make any sense either, and nothing about this place seems to be logical.

The clip-clops become louder. Almost thumping. No, thundering with each footfall, because now I understand what it is I am hearing.

They are footsteps.

But not feet. Not of a human. Human feet don't clip-clop. Horses clip-clop. Goats. Bulls. Cows. Deer, maybe, but not humans.

So it should come as no surprise to me that the creature—no, the *monster*—that appears at the top of the stairs isn't human. And I am so focused on the footsteps, that's where I'm looking when the feet finally come into view.

But of course, they are not feet. They are *hooves.*

A horn, a hoof, an eye, a bone…

My gaze wanders up the monster's legs, covered in thick, light brown fur that matches the wheat-colored rings in Tomas's eyes. He still has his hand over my mouth.

They are not human legs. They are the legs of a goat, or a deer, or a bull.

I look up and find a bare chest. The chest of a man. The neck of a man. The arms and hands of a man, except for the claws. And when my eyes track to the beast's face, and meet his gaze, I hope for the eyes of a man too, but that's not what I find staring back at me.

"What the fuck is that thing!" Even though Tomas's hand is still clasped tightly over my mouth, I scream these words out. And then I bite him, forcing him to let me go. I run to the door, ready to pull it open and take my chances in the gray nothingness, but the thundering, thumping sound of hooves follows me, and I am abruptly pulled back—flying through the air and looking up at a magnificent painted ceiling— before I *fall*.

And then three things happen all at once:

Pia flies up out of my hand and turns into a moth.

Tomas yells, "No! He's gone, Pell! He's gone! We need her!"

And I hit the ground and everything goes black.

CHAPTER THREE – PELL

When you are cursed, you know it.

No one has to tell you. No one has to explain it to you. It's just… there. Like your hand always was.

And when a curse breaks, that realization rushes in.

This is how I wake up this evening. With the abrupt realization that Grant is gone.

Not gone, like he went to the store without me. Not gone, like he took the car in for an oil change. But capital-letter-G gone, as in his curse has been lifted.

And there's a moment—there's always that fucking moment—when I think, *Hell yeah. We're done. We're finally free.*

But then… *Reality check, Pell.*

He's gone.

I'm still here.

I just had that moment and now I am standing in the middle of the cemetery, surrounded on all sides by lifeless, lost souls, watching the form of an unfamiliar shadow as it runs into the cathedral.

I turn that direction, then sniff the air and turn back towards the unused slave cottage.

Because someone has been here.

Someone who is not Tomas, who is not Grant, who is not me. And there is no one else. Hasn't been anyone else in more than half a century.

Except now there is.

I look back at the cathedral, wondering about my shadow intruder. But I am drawn back to the scent coming from the opposite direction.

It's conflicting. It's a mixture. I can discern it now. Grant and someone else. But Grant's scent is different somehow. Nothing I can immediately understand, I just know that something has gone wrong here tonight.

So instead of following the shadow, I follow Grant. Slowly at first, my joints aching from the day's inactivity. But then I am running down the hill and it's so much stronger down here, the scent of *wrong*, that I slide to a stop in the wet grass and sniff again, trying to separate out the scents.

Grant.

Not Grant, but close.

And the third scent is definitely not Grant at all.

This is when the situation really sinks in.

Grant has left the sanctuary.

This is not completely unusual because he leaves all the time. The grocery store, the oil change place, what have you. But he never leaves without the ring on his finger and that ring is still here. I can feel it.

I turn and look back at the cathedral. The shadow took the ring and Grant is gone. He left behind his magical scent and slipped into a brand-new one.

No.

Not a new one, an *old* one.

The one he came here with fifty years ago.

A rage builds inside me. It starts in my chest and radiates out, pulsing and undulating through my muscles. A hatred. A malice with a nice dose of malevolence mixed in with bitterness and spite.

Who does he think he is? Who gave him permission to walk away from this prison?

But I already know the answer. The new scent. Female. Young. Uncorrupted by the curse of an unrelenting punishment.

I approach the cottage, acutely aware of the way her scent triggers the monster inside me when I swing the door open and track her through the rooms, up the stairs, to the window. And the missing car.

She watched him leave.

She… is the *reason* he left.

Because she does not *belong* here.

He does.

I jump down the stairs, pass through the open door, gallop up the hill and into the atrium. I pause at the bottom of the stairs, sniffing. She is so close, her scent so strong, I almost become intoxicated from it.

And I can hear her. A soft voice.

Then Tomas. Cautioning her. Warning her.

I take the steps seven at a time. There are at least a hundred, so in sixteen strides I am in the grand entrance. And there she is.

Tomas's arms around her. One hand held firmly over her mouth.

Her eyes track up my body, starting with my hooves and land on my narrowed eyes.

The look she gives me is pure terror. She pulls the hand from her mouth and screams, "What the fuck is that thing!"

Thing.

Thing.

Thing.

It echoes in my head.

She breaks free of Tomas, runs for the door, and even though I know she can't escape—she is part of the curse now, and there is no way around that—I go after her, prey instinct triggered like a wild beast, jaws grinding, teeth gnashing, fingers reaching, claws... snagging.

I pull her back so hard, she flies up in the air.

"No!" Tomas yells. "He's gone, Pell! He's gone! We *need* her!"

I already know this. I don't need the rules explained to me. I have lived within the boundaries of my curse for two *thousand* years.

But it's too late.

I am nothing but rage and hate.

And I want to take the full wrath of my fury out on this young human woman for daring to walk into my sanctuary. The one place on this godforsaken earth where I am *permitted to exist.*

For daring to change my world.

For daring to make me change with it.

And now I blame it on her. I put it all on her.

It is now her fault that I'm here. Because she let the only man who could set me free from this wretched curse walk out.

Because now I have to start over from the beginning.

Because there is no way this stupid girl will be able to match the skills of Grant.

Grant. In my mind I sneer his name. "He left!" My words come out as a ferocious growl.

The woman hits the ground less than a moment later. Her head smacks hard on the polished marble floor, the air in her lungs escapes with a grunt, and she slides for a good distance before her body goes still.

"You fucking idiot!" Tomas yells. "You fucking idiot! We *need* her!"

I turn and pace down the length of the entrance hall, my hooves clomping, my breath heavy with leftover anger. My chest rises and falls at a pace that leaves no room for doubt that I am *pissed*.

I turn back to Tomas and direct all this rage at him. Point at him. Accuse him. I can't accuse the woman again, because she is unconscious, so Tomas is my new target. I pin it all on him now. "Where did he go! Why did you let him leave?"

"I have no control over Grant! You know that!" But in this same moment, he bends down to the woman and places a hand on her cheek. Then he gently slaps her, trying to bring her around. "Hello? Can you hear me? Can you open your eyes?"

And this is new. And weird. And disconcerting. Because Tomas should not be able to *touch* this woman. "What the—"

But he cuts me off. "Don't just stand there, you disgusting monster! Help me get her into the apothecary so I can find something to wake her up!"

I look over my shoulder at the apothecary at the north end of the great hall. The massive wooden door is framed by an intricately carved, Gothic arch with images of… me. Monster me. Raging me. Killing-machine me. And of course, that stupid fucking poem that practically sits above every single door in this place.

"Never mind," Tomas growls. "I'll do it myself."

JA Huss writing as KC Cross

He grips the woman under her arms and begins dragging her body across the polished marble. I just stand there and watch him, curious. He pauses at the door, balances her with just one arm as he maneuvers the lock, then pulls and props the door open with his hip.

A moment later, the woman's legs disappear from view as Tomas drags her into the apothecary.

"Huh." I scratch my chin. Some of the anger dissipates inside me as I consider the strange turn of events with Tomas.

But this curiosity doesn't last. It's not enough to distract me from the reality of *my* new situation.

I turn towards the staircase, fully intending on going back out to my tomb, when I hear the woman moan. I pause.

Tomas hushes her from inside the room. "Shhh. Just lie still. I'm sure Grant has something in these bottles that can help." She groans again, and again Tomas gently admonishes her.

I let out a long, angry sigh. Because he's not allowed to do these things. This woman is mine. She is here for me and me only.

Tomas has no power here. He is trapped here. He is nothing here.

So he should not be talking to my woman, or consoling my woman, or helping my woman.

He should get his filthy fucking hands *off* my woman.

And then the rage is back.

I stomp over to the apothecary door, push it open so hard it bangs against the stone walls and shakes hundreds of glass bottles on tens of dozens of shelves, and I just stand there under the arch and watch Tomas as I seethe.

"Fuck you," Tomas spits. Because after two thousand years, he can practically read my mind. "Do you see?" he taunts me. "Do you see what's happening here?"

I do. And I don't like it one bit. "She is mine. You know this. Don't you touch her. Don't you—"

"Fuck. You. *Monster*," Tomas sneers. He's pulling potions off the shelves, quickly reading labels, then putting them back and moving on. "Looks like this one's different. And I've been here, under your thumb for far, *far* too long." He laughs out that last bit and then he finds the potion bottle he's looking for, turns towards me, and snarls, "It ends now."

He has placed the woman on a lounger, and he sits next to her, the potion bottle in one hand. The other slips around under her head and gently lifts it up as he pulls the cork from the bottle, spits it out in my direction, and then places the lip of the bottle up to her mouth. "Drink," he whispers. "This will bring you back."

I squint my eyes at the bottle, trying to read the label. There was a time, many, *many* decades ago, when I was interested in what Grant did in here.

I was hopeful, and he was a competent alchemist, so I let him soothe me with all those false promises. But I never trusted him so the shiny newness wore off quicker than most of the other caretakers I've had. It became apparent that Grant was not truly working on a way to lift my curse, just biding his time until he could escape his.

And today, he did escape.

I didn't even care that he was making no progress. He was stuck in the curse with me. And he would spend eternity here if he couldn't find a way to break it.

But today—the miracle he had been waiting for happened.

This woman walked into *my* sanctuary and Grant walked out.

The woman sputters, choking on the glowing lavender liquid. "That's it," Tomas soothes. "Sit up a little. It will be easier."

The woman is not really responsive. Her choking is but an instinct. But Tomas helps her sit up and props her back against the cushions, hovering so close to her, for a moment I imagine he might try to kiss her.

A low growl builds in my throat.

Tomas doesn't even look at me. But he does swipe a lock of hair away from her face and whisper, "Don't worry about him. You have *me* now. *I* will take care of you."

"Fuck," I mutter, then turn and walk towards the door. "Go to hell, Tomas. Oh"—I pause and look over my shoulder as I scoff—"I forgot. You're already here."

"Go jerk yourself, Pell."

I walk out and seventeen leaps later I'm at the bottom of the grand staircase.

I cross the hall and go outside. The moon is dark tonight. New. Fitting.

But I have only one thing on my mind at the moment, and that's Grant.

His scent lingers in the cemetery. It's everywhere, and this just makes the anger inside me build once again.

But it's mixed with pheromones tonight. Fear, mostly.

And he should be afraid. He should be very afraid. Because if I ever see him again, I will tear his head right off his body.

But that's not that part that pisses me off. Because mixed in with the fear is a dose of excited anxiety.

That growl in my throat is back again. Deeper now. Rage. Hate.

Because he left this place with expectations.

He left this place with *hope*.

I tilt my head up to the black sky and roar out my rage. Then I gather myself, walk down the path, down the hill, up to the wooden gate that separates us from the outside world, and peek over.

His car—El Camino, he named it—is gone.

He is gone.

I take many deep breaths as I force myself to come to terms with what has just occurred.

This woman is magical. That's a given. The ability to enter Saint Mark's Sanctuary without invitation is a skill that runs in the blood. It skips two generations and is only passed on if both parents have a recessive gene for sight.

Or so Grant said.

But how would I know? I have not been schooled in the knowledge of alchemy. Almost anyone can work spells, but I'm not an alchemist. And I only have a few innate powers. None of which are particularly helpful or have anything to do with the curse of Saint Mark's.

My head is thumping to the beat of my heart, that's how angry I am right now.

Calm down, Pell. You must think clearly.

It was a nice ride with Grant. It has been easy for more than fifty years. Predictable. But he never did anything for you. This girl is a fresh start.

Here's my problem. I don't like the fresh start. I prefer the predictable. I enjoy the easy. And maybe I am whining a little bit—only internally, of course—but the easy is gone now. Grant has left and in his place is this woman.

Woman? Hardly. I have not spent a lot of time outside the gates of Saint Mark's because Grant had to escort me, like a fucking babysitter, whenever I wanted to go somewhere. But I have kept up with the times. I think. So I have a cursory understanding that in this day and age, the woman in the apothecary is considered to be *young*. Early twenties. A girl. Barely more than a child.

In my day, a woman her age might already have a daughter who was having daughters. She would be wise to the ways of the world. She would've been practicing her craft for well over a decade. She would have discovered things. New things. Important things. She would have ideas about potions, and herbs, and she would not only have opinions about how things inside the sanctuary apothecary worked, she would be plotting ways to make the potions and herbs stronger and more effective.

She would be an asset. But this *girl?* I scoff into the night, my breath creating a stream of white steam across the blackness.

She will know nothing. She will be useless. She will be a millstone around my neck for decades, possibly even centuries. And maybe I didn't have a lot of hope that one day I might break this curse, but at least Grant knew what the fuck he was doing.

And now this new thing with Tomas. Surely he is also considering his change in fortune. He is also plotting a way to lift *his* curse. If that's what it is.

And he is planning on using *my* woman to do that.

I place the tips of my fingers up against my forehead and make little circles.

This is more than I can take.

Well, do something about it, Pell. You left him alone with your new woman. He could be telling her things. Things about you. Things Tomas has no right to divulge.

I whirl around and gaze back up the hill at the cathedral. And then I'm running. I will stop him. She is mine. He will not use my slave to fulfill his needs or gain his freedom.

I burst through the doors, leap up the stairs, and then I'm huffing with anger under the arch of the apothecary door.

"Take your hands off her!"

Tomas sneers at me. But I'm not focused on him. I'm focused on her. She turns her head and I already know what's coming before the scream leaves her mouth.

I turn back around because I'm tired of it. I didn't bring her here. I didn't put this curse on her. She did this to herself. She and her family—her bloodline—they are the entire reason I'm stuck here. So she doesn't get to look at me like I'm the monster when *she* is the reason I'm cursed.

"Get away from me! Stay back!" She screams this as she scoots to the furthest end of the lounger.

And Tomas is spewing his threats. "I have *this*," he says, holding up a flask filled with bright green liquid. "I have *this*, Pell. And I swear to fucking God, I will use it if you come any closer!"

I'm not afraid of Tomas's little potion bottle. That's stupid. But the look on this girl's face right now?

It's more than terror as she gapes at me. At my monster body.

It's… disgust. It's hostility. It might even be hate.

And fuck that. She has no right. So I turn and leave, slamming the heavy wooden door with all my might, so hard the doorframe cracks a little.

Good. Let it crumble. It was carved by an asshole called Antonius who spent ninety years with me almost a millennium ago. He didn't even get the story straight. But did he care that he was carving lies all over my home?

No.

Antonius never did a single thing to make my life easier. I was actually happy when his replacement showed up and he got to leave. He died in the back gardens—this was when the sanctuary was still located across the ocean in the Old World. He lived five minutes outside the walls after his spell was broken.

More than he deserved.

I walk out to the center of the grand reception hall and breathe deeply, trying to calm myself. But my mind is still hyper-focused on what is happening in the apothecary when a flutter of wings up in the ceiling makes me look up.

A tiny sparrow is in my grand hall.

"Huh." I rub a hand over my face as I consider this. I have never seen a bird in the sanctuary. Not even outside. They can't get in here. They can't get past the magic. Everything that enters needs an invitation, including this bird.

So how did it get here?

Obviously, it came with the girl.

Wonderful. Pets. Now we have *pets*.

What else will this girl bring?

I forget about the bird and go back down the stairs, telling myself the entire way that this is why I stay out of the cathedral. I don't like what happens in here. I don't like the people in here and I don't need to be reminded of my story, thank you. I lived it.

At the bottom of the stairs, I push through the doors and wander into the cemetery, picking my way around the hundreds and hundreds of tombs.

The cursed. This is the only place on the property where I truly feel I belong.

They like to keep us all together in one place, I suppose. Cuts down on the need for dozens of magical bloodlines to keep us all contained.

I go first to Tarq. I visit him each night. I like to keep him up to date on things. He can't respond, obviously. He's a fucking statue. But I like to imagine that he can hear me and that he appreciates my visits.

There are dozens of pathways that weave through all the tombs in the cemetery, but finding Tarq's is easy because he's smack in the middle of the west lawn.

At nearly eight feet tall in statue form, Tarq is incredibly imposing. But even back in his real-life body he was a big monster. Built like a warrior with broad shoulders and well-muscled arms and thighs as thick as tree trunks. We never fought each other, so it's unknown who would win that fight if one ever took place, but most people would put their money on Tarq just due to his massive bulk.

In statue form he doesn't just look dangerous, he looks... *evil.*

He is made of black marble that is so detailed, you want to run your hand down the slick rock just to test it out and see if that stone is made of hide. His fur, in real life, is slick, jet black like his long hair on his head. His skin is a light shade of brown and he has welted brands declaring him the property of the god Saturn on both biceps.

My legs are much the same, but they more resemble a ram's than a bull's, and they are covered in fur the color of wheat straw. I have the branded markings of an owner as well, but much to Saturn's dismay, I never belonged to him. I was the property of the goddess Juno.

We, the monsters, we were all made by the infamous alchemist Ostanes for the gods to play with. But even though they are gods, they are not perfect. Far from it, in fact.

The gods I knew were petty, jealous creatures. Always competing with each other. Doesn't matter what, they always needed to compete. Saturn and Juno were the most powerful. Mates at times. But their pairing was only out of necessity to keep their bloodlines going. They birthed the rest of the gods and then everyone went their separate ways. You can't trust the gods. Even the gods don't trust the gods. This is why they needed us. The monsters. We were their children. They lived through us. They used us.

This is how the curse starts. The killing of Ostanes, the alchemist in charge of making monsters.

No one knows how the curse ends, obviously. Since it's still in place.

I exhale loudly and look back up at Tarq. His horns are minotaur-like in appearance, with the dark color of the water buffalo, while mine are more corkscrew in nature and belong on the head of a kudu.

We are chimera. Half god, half monster with fur, horns, hooves, and, in the case of myself and Tarq, we are *well-endowed* because we were originally part of an ancient monster-breeding program of satyrs.

At least I have that going for me.

The smile that begins to creep up my face cannot be stopped and eventually it turns into a grin.

What do you get when you cross a nymph with a satyr-minotaur hybrid?

Some very tall, very strong, very handsome evil-looking motherfuckers.

Us. That's what you get.

"Tarq." I lean on him. "You're not going to believe this fucking night. Grant is gone, some new woman is here. She looks pathetic. Any hope we had for a reunion seems…" I shake my head. "Well, very far away."

He says nothing back, of course. So I wander over to his tomb, slide my back down a wide, weather-stained, Corinthian column, and stare up at his stone face.

It has been two thousand years since I've seen him in the flesh. And they have been long years. "You probably hate me by now, don't you? I mean, I'm stuck in this place, just like you. But at least I can come and go from my tomb. You're just… here. And if there was a way, brother, I'd fix that. I would get you out of there. I do not care that you carry the markings of Saturn on your flesh. We are blood."

I would love to have my friend back. This life is so pointless without friends. And Tomas doesn't count. He's... not one of us. Not really. More of a lingering mistake than anything else.

Two thousand years. And none of the caretakers have been able to break our curse.

"It pains me to say this, friend. I have never given up hope, but losing Grant is a blow I do not think I can recover from. Grant was competent so I kept hoping that one day he would produce the words, and the potions, and the herbs to turn back time and get us out of this miserable existence."

Was it stupid? That dream? That we could beat this if we just tried long enough? Worked hard enough? If we just kept going?

I don't know. But I don't like to depress Tarq. If he can hear me, then I want to lift his spirits, not crush them. So I continue with the update.

"He was making progress. He had that spell that would allow me to leave the sanctuary in the form of a man for a few hours at a time. And yes, I hated the fact that I had to be within an arm's length of Grant to keep the glamour strong enough to disguise my true form, but it was better than nothing. Wasn't it? I had a tiny taste of freedom. And maybe you're not capable of being happy for me—hell, if I were you, I wouldn't be happy for me—but I really thought that we'd get there, ya know? I really thought that we were just a decade or so away from the answer. From the *cure*. And Grant took all that progress with him."

It's coming out a little whiny. So I stop talking and try to work the rage back up.

I look back towards the cathedral and yep. There it is. My rage.

That girl.

That *baby*.

That good-for-nothing substitute.

I want to hunt Grant down and kill him for leaving me here to rot.

But then my mind wanders to the apothecary room with the hundreds upon hundreds of potions and herbs lining the floor to ceiling shelves. And the books. Grant kept notebooks. He was a meticulous record-keeper.

So maybe…

I get to my feet and start walking back towards the cathedral.

Maybe he wrote down his progress. He couldn't take the books with him—they are magical. They are part of this curse. They belong to Saint Mark's Sanctuary, not him.

Which means they now belong to the girl.

All of Grant's progress now belongs to the girl.

There is no doubt she comes from Grant's bloodline. That's how she got in. That's how he got out. So she has the magic inside her. And even if she has no idea it's there, it can be coaxed out.

I've done it a few times before with ignorant slaves of the past. But it wasn't very productive.

Still. I can only work with what I have.

I enter the cathedral, feeling like I've made more trips to this stupid building in the last hour of darkness than I have in the past decade, and once more climb the long staircase.

The apothecary door is slightly ajar—like I slammed it too hard and it didn't quite close when I stormed off—so when I approach, I can hear talking inside.

"—but why?" the girl says.

"Because you can't help him. No one can."

What? I lean closer. The fake rage I had mustered up to stop my whining is becoming very real again.

I have never trusted Tomas but I never imagined he was working *against* me. And now that he has this new power—this new ability to touch my slave—he might need to be dealt with. He is not supposed to be able to touch them. He couldn't touch Grant. He couldn't touch any of them.

So why now?

Why this girl?

"These books," the girl continues.

"Don't even bother. Grant wrote everything in code."

He did? No. That's fucking bullshit. I've seen the books. I don't understand the books, but I've seen them. They are written in the common language.

I push the door open and storm in. I reach out towards a table covered in dozens of vials and bottles with various levels of herbs, and salts, and liquids inside them, and I swipe them all onto the floor with a resounding crash to announce my arrival.

It's all drama. I know that. But I'm feeling dramatic.

The girl stands up, screaming and fearful, while Tomas yells at me. "You fucking beast! What the hell is your problem!"

My problem? He wants to know my problem? "You," I growl. "You were the reason Grant never broke the curse. You poisoned his mind, didn't you? You are the one who told him to leave me tonight!"

"Fuck off, you goddamned freak!" Tomas exclaims.

I pick up the nearest potion bottle and throw it at his face.

Bright green liquid hits him and in that same instant he disappears.

So now… I turn to the girl.

CHAPTER FOUR – PIE

I am backing into a corner, hand over my face, mouth open in a scream of fright, when the monster throws the potion bottle at Tomas's face. And when the bright green liquid hits Tomas, he just vanishes. Poof. Gone.

I panic and start stumbling towards the door, ready to make a run for it. Tomas told me a little bit about the monster of Saint Mark's. He's an angry beast. He is vengeful, and cruel, and petty.

And as far as I can tell, Tomas was right.

"Where do you think you're going?" the beast growls at me.

My breath hitches in a gasp. That sinking feeling you get when something is about to go terribly wrong is real and heavy in my gut at the mere sound of his voice.

I turn to face him. Well, not really to face him. Just to try to ward him off as I take steps backwards. "Stay away from me!" I thrust my palms at him. "Do you hear me? Stay away!"

His eyes go from yellow to orange to red. And I make a run for it, acutely aware that I cannot outrun this thing. His legs—oh, God, those legs! Like a goat's, or a bull's, or a horse's—I'm not sure, but they are powerful and long. And he has already demonstrated how quickly he can snatch me up when I bolt.

But I do it anyway. The only alternative is to just freeze and hope for the best and I've done that plenty of times in my life, so I know it never turns out well.

Better to die trying.

"Stop!" he commands.

And even though in my mind I have every intention of absolutely *not* stopping—I freeze. The exact thing I just said I would not do.

He laughs, amused at my sudden paralysis. "You slaves," he grunts. "You always think you hold all the power here. But it's not true. You hold power over Saint Mark's, yes, but I'm the one who holds the power over you. And the sooner you realize that, the better off you'll be."

And he's right. Because my entire body feels like it's been filled with cement. My feet are stuck to the floor, my arms reaching out in the direction of the door. Stiff. My eyes are motionless. I can't even blink.

His steps are loud, his hooves clacking on the marble floors, but they are also slow. It takes an agonizingly long time for him to reach me. To be right up next to me. So close that I can feel the heat coming off his body. And he is so big—so utterly massive—that when he comes around to my front I am face to face with the middle of his bare human chest.

Which… I'm not gonna lie, it might even be better than Tomas's chest. And if Pia were here, and I could talk, I would make a joke about being right. Hot men do hang out together. Even if they're monsters.

The beast reaches out and takes a strand of my blonde hair in his fingertips as I concentrate on the hard, corded muscles of his body. I want to shudder at his touch. This is an invasion of my private space, but I cannot move.

He drops my hair and turns, walks a few paces forward before turning again.

I am still staring straight ahead, but his full body is now in view.

Half human, half beast. The lower half is covered in straw-colored fur, shaggy in some parts, but not shaggy enough to fully hide his genitals because he is not wearing clothes. His hooves are black with squiggly bands of cream running vertically. His face—while not fully in my view because I can't look up—is serious and hard in my peripheral vision, a bit of a blond beard covering his chin and upper lip, and his hair is cropped too short to discern the color, but it's probably blond too.

"Don't worry." His gruff voice is deep and penetrating. "You'll be seeing a lot more of me from this point on, slave."

I don't know what he means by that, but I don't like the sound of that word 'slave.' I'm one hundred percent sure the flyer said 'caretaker.' Not 'slave.'

"You don't need to get all your looks in now. Did he explain it to you?" His voice is softer now. But I can hear the lie in his milder tone. I can hear the malice lurking underneath. He nods his head in the direction where Tomas used to be. "Did he tell you what you stumbled into tonight?"

Tomas talked quite a bit, actually. His freaking mouth was moving like he had a million years to catch me up on. But almost none of it penetrated into my brain for comprehension. I mean, when someone starts explaining how you have been cursed and your life as you know it is now over, you tend to stop listening to the embellishments and just focus on the facts.

So that's what I did. I shut down. I stopped listening. My mind was a whirlwind of confusion, trying to piece together the flyer, the gate, the boy who turned into an old man, the loss of Pia—where the hell is Pia?—and then the sudden appearance of the beast and my subsequent trip into unconsciousness.

"Let me explain it clearly," the beast says. "So that we're on the same page. You belong to me. You are my slave. You are part of my curse and you will remain here, with me, until such time that another one of your bloodline stumbles into *our* sanctuary." He pauses to chuckle. "And I know what you're thinking. 'Well, if I stumbled into this curse, surely someone else will too.' But it almost never happens. Grant was here for over fifty years."

If I could gasp in this moment, I would. I don't even know how I'm breathing. I don't think I am breathing.

Focus, Pie.

Fifty. Years.

That's why the caretaker—Grant—that's why he looked like a young man when I met him, and then turned old and sickly when he left. All of those fifty-plus years he spent here caught up with him in an instant and he was suddenly old. And he must've known this was how it would end. He must've known that when he left, his life would be nearly over.

And yet he left anyway.

"And the one before him?" the beast continues. "He was here for two *hundred*."

I am so fucked.

"But listen carefully, slave girl. I do not care what Tomas told you, there *is* a way out of this. If you break my curse, you break your curse as well. So it would behoove you to work diligently on that task from this moment forward."

I, of course, am unable to answer him. But if I could, I would protest mightily.

I do not break curses. I don't know anything about this place. And I am not from Grant's bloodline. That's not possible. My mother was an only child. I am an only child. And even though I don't know who my father was, I doubt he has any relation to the boy who was here before me.

I mean, how could I be related to these caretaker people?

Grant was younger than me when we met. Surely, there was no way for him to already have had children before he got stuck in his curse.

"Now," the beast says, "I'm going to let you go, but you will stand still." He doesn't wait for me to answer him or agree to his command, of course, but says, "Proceed."

In that moment, my body is no longer cement, my feet no longer heavy. I fall forward and the marble floor is rushing up to meet me when his powerful, clawed hands grab my flannel. I stop—just for a moment—but then the flannel rips and I crash the rest of the way to the floor.

Luckily, it was only a few inches, so while my nose does hit hard enough to make it bleed, it's not as bad as it could've been.

I breathe hard and heavy for a few moments, trying to catch my breath as I study the thin gray veins in the black marble slabs.

I don't know that I was really expecting the beast to help me up, but it doesn't matter. He does not. He stands in front of me and I stare at his hooves for a moment, just blinking. Trying to force myself to make sense of my new reality.

When he moves away my view changes to the open doorway where I can see Tomas walking quickly towards us. He's not even halfway across the grand entrance hall when the apothecary door slams shut of its own accord.

I roll over in time to find the beast with a hand raised, like he just commanded the door to close with his fingers.

Tomas pounds on the door, yelling to be let in. But his voice is muffled and his exact words unclear.

The beast snorts, but it's a sound of satisfaction. Presumably he is happy about Tomas's banishment. His attention abruptly turns to me. "Get up." Then he crosses the room to a very messy desk near a tall, stained-glass window and picks up a notebook. He spends a moment thumbing through it, then, apparently satisfied that this was what he was looking for, he tosses it onto the floor in front of me. It lands with a loud thump. "I said get up."

I get my feet underneath me and rise, one hand covering my bloody nose, the other grabbing for the book. But this is not a one-handed kind of book. It's thick, and wide, and feels like it contains a million years of information within those pages. I have to use both hands to pick it up, so my nose drips blood onto the cover until I can shuffle it around and hold it tight to my chest and use my other hand to cover my face.

The beast points at the book. "That is where Grant left off. You will pick up there."

I put the book down on a black stone counter, take off my flannel, and bunch it up so I can use it to stop my nosebleed.

When I look over at the beast, he's staring at my perky breasts because I am wearing a scarlet-red bustier that looked very sexy and cool last night, on Halloween, but is getting more and more ridiculous as this day progresses. I glance over at the beast and when I look down, I find him…

"Oh. My God." I cover my eyeballs, then nod at his semi-hard, male appendage and glance up at his face. "That's gross. Put on some *pants*, for fuck's sake."

He doesn't even blink. But his eyes do migrate upward from my breasts and meet my gaze. "Do you understand me, witch?"

I close my eyes and shake my head, trying to banish the image of his beastly dick from my brain, and turn back to the notebook. Again, it is a very hefty book bound with glue, and cloth, and leather with studs pounded into it. And when I open it, the paper is thick and has a coarse texture. One quick glance at the pages is all I need. I will be disappointing the beast tonight, because… "I do not speak Latin."

"What?" I look over my shoulder and find him sneering. "You're speaking Latin right now. It's the common tongue."

I turn all the way around to face the monster. He is intimidating. But facts are facts. And I don't have very many to work with at the moment, so I feel like taking a stand on the language we're both speaking. "It is not the common tongue. It is a dead language. Even I know that, and I failed three history classes in my high-school career. And no, sir, I'm not speaking Latin right now, I'm speaking English and so are you. This?" I pick up the notebook and drop it onto the counter with a dramatic thump. "Is not something I can help you with, even if I did speak Latin. Which, once again, I do not. I am not a…" I pause to choose the correct word. "I am not a *witch*. So I won't be breaking any curses, or conjuring up any spells, or whatever. I live in *reality*, thank you. And these are the *facts*."

He blinks at me.

And for some unknown reason, I burst out laughing. A proper guffaw. Because I *don't* live in reality. I have *never* lived in reality. Because my one and only friend in this world is a talking bird. And she's not a parrot, or a mynah bird, or a starling, or any other kind of bird that mimics talking.

She is an invisible sparrow.

The beast scowls at me and I just laugh harder. He ignores my outburst and continues to boss me around. "You will stay out of the cemetery, do you understand?"

I laugh again. Not as loud. It's more like… one of those stifled giggles you see people do in public places at the most inappropriate times.

"You will spend your days in here. In this room. Reading those books—because you *can* read them, and you *can* speak and understand Latin, and you *will* find the cure."

This time I don't even bother laughing. I breathe out the word, "Ohhhhhh," then suck in air through my teeth. "Here you go. Here's what I'm gonna say. Are you ready? OK. Fine. No problem. I will pretend to read your books and learn how to break your curse. But if you honestly expect me to be of any help to you, you will be disappointed. So you should seriously consider getting yourself another... witch. Or whatever. Because the longer I stay here, the more behind you'll be."

He ignores my words. "You will put the ring on, you will—"

"Whoa, whoa, whoa. What? Did you say ring?"

"You will put it on. You will do as you're told. And as far as that *pet* goes? I don't want to see it. And if it shits on my floors—"

"What the fuck are you talking about?" And then it hits me. "Pia, you mean?" Can he see her?

"—you will clean it up immediately," he continues like I'm not even talking. "If I see one speck of bird shit on anything I will—"

"Where is she?"

"—punish you," he finishes.

I look up. Then at the door. "Where *is* she?" I throw my flannel down—my nose bleed under control now—and start walking for the door. Tomas is still pounding on it, still spewing threats at the beast. But when I try to open it up, it doesn't budge.

"You do not walk away from me, *girl*. You are *mine*. I command you. And I'm in the process of commanding you to listen to me explain your role here."

I turn, flip him off, and say, "Fuck you. Where is she? Pia?" I call, shouting up at the ceiling, even though it's pretty clear she's not in here. "Pia!" I shout it.

"She's out there."

I look over my shoulder at the beast and he's pointing at the door. "Open the door right now so I can go find her."

"You need to find the ring and put it on. Then you can find your pet."

"She's not a pet, you idiot. She's *me*. And I already have the ring." I walk over to my flannel, pull the ring out of my pocket, and hold it up in the light. "It's right here. But I'm not putting it on. It's got creepy writing on it."

"It's the charm that lets you leave."

"What?" I blink at him. "Did you just say *leave*?"

"Yes." My hope builds. "Temporarily," he adds. "For a few hours at a time so you can run errands for me."

I snort. Like, literally snort. "Run *errands* for you?"

"Put it on."

"No. I'm not putting it on. This ring feels like a trap. Like once I put it on, that seals the deal. I've seen enough movies to understand how it works. You need to bind me here somehow and this ring is how you do that."

"You will put it on."

"I will not."

"Trust me." And for the first time since we met, the beast smiles at me. But it's not a friendly smile, it's a snarky one. And it comes with fangs. It would be easy to forget what this thing is if you're only looking at his face. I mean, the shock of the horns has worn off and I'm not looking at his lower half ever again until he learns what pants are. But when he smiles, he shows me his teeth. They are the teeth of a beast and this smile says, *I've got you. There is no way out now.* "You will put that ring on," he continues. "You will need to leave the sanctuary. We will run out of food in a matter of days. Grant's weekly grocery trip is tomorrow."

"Grocery trip? The *fuck*?"

"Put it on," he snarls again.

I'm not going to put it on, but before I can object again, the door bursts open and Tomas comes tumbling through.

"Get out!" the beast immediately roars. "You are not allowed to break through my magic!"

Tomas gets to his feet, dusts off his hands, and then points to the beast. "Fuck you, Pell. In case you haven't noticed, things have changed around here with the new girl. Looks like you're losing control. Maybe there was a limit on the number of caretakers you were allotted? Or maybe the gods are just bored with you and have decided to hand things over to someone else."

"Someone like you?"

"Yeah. Someone like *me*. Someone who can get shit done."

The monster—Pell—scoffs.

"Come on," Tomas says. He extends his hand to me. "Come with me. I'll show you around."

I hesitate. And I don't really know why I do it because Tomas has a certain look to him. A look that says, *I've seen things. I know things. I can do things.* And I don't know what that whole conversation was really about, but I'm pretty sure about one thing and one thing only.

Tomas is not the one in charge here. Has never been the one in charge here.

So even though I want to go with him—I would feel safer with him—I can't.

Because this is a moment that will decide things and I need to think this through.

If I leave with Tomas, we will be split clearly into two camps. And I have a feeling that eventually Tomas will end up on the losing side. He's big, and muscular, and he's strong-willed and loud, but he's up against a beast. A monster who is nearly seven feet tall. A monster who can freeze me in place and slam heavy wooden doors with the wave of his finger. A monster who just explained that we are cursed and our curses are tied together.

Is this curse thing real?

I don't know.

Is Pia real?

To me, she is. And if my talking alter-ego is real, this curse thing might be too. I don't know. I need time to process. And maybe I'm not all up on the whole Saint Mark's curse and everything, but it doesn't take a genius to understand that siding *against* the beast in charge isn't in my best interest.

On the other hand, if I'm truly stuck here, I don't want to alienate Tomas. So there is just one thing left to do. "No," I tell Tomas.

"No?"

I look over my shoulder at Pell. "No to you as well. I don't know what's going on here. Perhaps I'm just dreaming and in a little bit I will wake up and laugh at the absurdity of it all. But then again, maybe not. It wouldn't be the first time the gods have frowned upon me. All I know is…" I pause and look the beast straight in the eyes. "I don't *need* you. You need *me*."

Then I turn my head and look at Tomas. "And I like you, Tomas. I think you might be a good man and you're kinda hot—but while I'd love to trust you, I've learned a thing or two about trusting attractive, charismatic men who take an instant interest in me. So I don't need you, either. I don't either of you. I've been traveling through this life on my own, with just my *pet* at my side"—I sneer the word at the monster—"since I was nine. And that's how it's gonna stay. So you can tell me where Pia is"—I point at the beast—"or not. She is me, and I am her, and I will find her with or without you."

The beast called Pell straightens. And this makes his absurdly large male appendage straighten as well. "For fuck's sake," I mutter, turning my head to the side. "Can you *please* put on some pants?"

I turn on my heel, push past Tomas, and walk out into the grand entrance hall. Unsure of where I'm going, just very sure I need to get out of that room and away from that beast.

"She's up there," the beast calls. And when I look back at him, he's pushing past Tomas too. Then he points to the ceiling. "She's up there. I saw her earlier."

I eye him with suspicion. Because his tone has changed once again and this time, the softness doesn't feel like a lie. But it still could be. He's probably just being helpful to make Tomas mad. But right now, I'll take any assistance I can get if it helps me find Pia.

So I squint up at the ceiling. It's a very beautiful ceiling. Like the Sistine Chapel, almost. But with beasts and monsters instead of angels or whatever.

"Pia!" I call. Is she scared? Is that why she flew off? Why isn't she calling for me? The last time I remember talking to her, we were outside that gate near the cottage. I picked up the ring and... oh, fuck. I wilt a little.

It's the ring. I put in my pocket and she crawled in there and when the beast threw me up in the air, she flew out of my pocket and disappeared.

But the monster said he saw her and he said *bird*. But when she flew away, she was a moth, not a bird. I turn to the beast. "What did she look like?" He and Tomas are both staring at me. They are side by side, the monster towering over Tomas, who is well over six feet tall himself. "Hello? I asked you a question. What did the bird look like?"

The beast shrugs with his hands. "A bird."

"That's not helpful. Maybe it's not my bird? Maybe it's some other bird?"

"There are no birds here," Tomas explains. "No animals at all." Then he hooks a thumb towards the monster at his side. "Well, except for him."

"Fuck you," the beast snarls back.

A flutter of wings high up in the ceiling draws all our eyes upward.

"There," the beast says. "That's her."

And maybe it is. I hope it is. But even if I squint, I cannot see that high up. "It's too dark in here," I say. "Where are the lights?"

"We don't have lights in the cathedral," the beast says. "We have sunshine."

"And sconces," Tomas adds, nodding to the sconces on the stone walls, which I hadn't really noticed before this moment. "But we don't have electricity in here. So. No lights. Everything runs on gas."

"Everything?" This can't be right. "Where does it come from? Who pays the bill?"

"None of that matters," the beast says. "There is no electricity here, so if you are not used to cooking with fire, you should grab a book on it when you go to the store tomorrow."

I don't even know how to process that sentence. "What the fuck are you talking about?"

"Cooking," Tomas explains.

"I don't cook." And did he just change sides? Because he's acting like I will be cooking for them in the near future. And I don't even cook for myself, I am certainly not cooking for these cursed people.

"You're a woman," Tomas says.

"Women cook," the beast adds. Like this is a logical sequence of critical thinking.

I snort. So that's where we are? Some monster version of the good woman at home? I snort again. "I am not the maid."

"Technically…" Tomas holds up a finger of protest.

"Whose side are you on?" I blurt.

"There is only one side here," Pell says. "Mine."

For fuck's sake. *If there is a god, please, please, please wake me up from this nightmare. Soon.* I turn away from them and mutter, "This isn't real. This cannot be real."

"It is real," the beast says. "And I was explaining the facts of the curse to you for a reason. If you want out, you must get *me* out first. I wasn't talking to hear myself. I was explaining—"

"Yeah, yeah, yeah," Tomas interrupts. He walks over to me. "Listen, your bird is fine. She probably can't leave the sanctuary. Not without you, anyway. No one can leave without you." He pauses. "Well, I can't ever leave. But Pell can. You won't mind the errands. It will get you out of the house. That's what Grant used to say."

"The rules," the beast says. "I'm going to make this easy for you." He turns to Tomas. "Where's the rulebook?"

Tomas nods his head to a massive three-story bookshelf just inside the apothecary that has a precarious ladder attached to slide rails. Above the ladder is a small catwalk that lines the perimeter of the room with another, even more suspect, ladder, presumably so you can search for books on the second floor. This goes on for yet another level and if one were actually inclined to search for books three stories up using those deathtraps, they would find themselves a good forty feet in the air.

There are thousands of books and the thought of going through them all to find answers about a curse suddenly makes me weary.

The beast walks into the room and over to the bookshelf. He scans it for several long, silent moments, and then plucks a book off the shelf and turns back to me.

I'm already shaking my head. "Nut-uh. Nope. That is not the rulebook. It's like two thousand pages long. There cannot possibly be that many rules."

The beast is not deterred. He walks over to me, thrusts the book at me, and waits. Expecting me to take it.

I salute him with my middle finger. Then I turn on my heel, walk down the staircase, through the doors, outside into the night, down the hill and past his stupid cemetery, and go inside my cursed cottage.

CHAPTER FIVE – PELL

"I don't think I like her." I pace back and forth across the room, trying to force this night to make sense. I am not prepared for this change. Fifty years is a long time for Grant to be stuck here with me, but if he'd just held on for another ten, he wouldn't have been able to walk out. There would be no escape because there would be no life waiting for him beyond the walls of Saint Mark's.

"That feeling seems to be mutual." Tomas says this absently. He's stretched out on the lounger flipping through one of Grant's notebooks. "I like Pie though. And I'm pretty sure she likes me too."

"Pie?"

"That's her name."

"Meat pie? Shepherd's pie? Fruit pie? What kind of pie is she? And why is she named after pie when she refuses to cook?"

Tomas ignores all of my questions. "How far do you think Grant got?"

"What?"

"I bet we could find him."

I'm failing to see the logic here. "Why would we want to find Grant? He left. He's not coming back. Why the hell would he?"

Tomas thinks about this for a moment. "I think he will want to talk to me. He didn't get to say goodbye."

"Hold on a moment." I put up one clawed hand to halt this train of thought. Because Tomas needs to be set straight. His kind are dangerous when you let them run with a delusion too long. "Where were you when he left?"

"What do you mean?"

"Were you missing? Were you lost in the forest? Were you locked in a tower?"

"What the hell are you going on about? I was here. Working out on the second-story balcony." He flexes his biceps at me. "I got a little lost in the hallways coming downstairs so he left before he could say goodbye."

"Where did the girl come from? The back gate?"

"No. She came in the front gate. Grant met her out in the hall."

"So he was here, she was here, you were here. But he didn't say goodbye to you?"

"I just told you. I got lost. I was late."

"Did he leave you a note?"

"No." Tomas hesitates. His delusion falters for a moment. I can see it on his face. But he rallies—he *always* rallies—and then he smiles. And poof. That delusion is firmly back in place.

Grant hated Tomas. He hated me more, so there's that. But Grant gives no fucks about Tomas.

I consider how far I want to push this line of questioning. It's been a while since Tomas and I talked this much. We don't usually cross paths here on the grounds of Saint Mark's. He stays here in the main cathedral and I prefer my own space out in the cemetery. And I would not call my feelings towards Tomas caring or anything close to that. But I don't want him focused on some goodbye he never got from Grant.

Tomas has gone quiet though, so there is no need to prolong this conversation.

I turn my back to him and walk out.

I leave the cathedral and begin walking in the direction of Tarq's tomb with the idea that I might continue our one-way conversation. But when I get to the top of the hill, I catch a glimpse of the little cottage house down below, near the back wall. Gas lamps glowing on both floors.

Grant didn't like that place. So it has not been occupied for all these decades. But she is down there now. Her scent trail leads right to the door.

I sit down on a nearby tomb base, wondering just how much life will change now that there is a girl here.

It has been a long time since I had the opportunity to be around a woman. And while she is not my type—I have my own preferences and she is not it—she is… *here.*

I won't be able to compel her to like me, but I can compel her to do lots of other things.

I shake my head, pushing thoughts of that out of my mind so I can concentrate on what's really important.

The curse.

I struggle with it now. Have been struggling with it for about a hundred and fifty years, actually. That's when things really started to change in the outside world. I haven't left the sanctuary for nearly three years, but Grant would bring things back. Phones, for one. The kind that fit in your pocket. They didn't work here, of course. Not for calling people. But about a decade ago, these phones were no longer just phones. And Grant did a lot of other things with them.

The slave before Grant was into science and he actually hooked up a bunch of wires about eighty years ago. He strung them everywhere and then he hooked up a phone. The old-fashioned kind. He even got a connection once. Just once though. It was like the curse didn't understand what he was doing and it took a moment to figure out this phone line—like electricity—was unacceptable. He did manage to get the gas lights working though. So there's that.

But the outside world is not something I understand.

Everything about it feels like magic and magic is always a trap.

Then, now, and always.

I go back to Tarq's tomb and stop at the front. There is a door, but there is no door. Not for me. I have been banished from the tombs since the beginning. Every single tomb door has been glamoured with ancient spells. I know they're there and I have the key to open them, which is me. But I can't *see* them. And the caretaker slave can see them, but not *open* them.

If you're going to be cursed it's actually quite nice to have a partner. That's what my slave caretaker is supposed to be. They get the sight, I get the key. It should be a simple thing. But when we're together, the slave caretaker cannot see the tomb doors.

When the great alchemist Ostanes made this place to keep her secrets safe, the gods panicked. The entire curse was created through a flurry of magical moves and countermoves by Saturn and Juno. But in

74

a way that made everything more complicated, not less. So not much about Saint Mark's makes sense. Especially the magic that governs it.

And this is how it goes.

One step forward, two steps back.

There is another way to open the doors. But I have never told anyone about that. If I were the one who could enter the tombs I'd be partying with Tarq right now. But it's not me who can get in, it's the caretaker.

I have never told the caretakers about that other way because I don't trust them

The slave caretaker and I are bound to each other. We're supposed to be powerful. But it has never worked. We were made enemies, but forced to be together. And the caretaker has certain duties. They are supposed to make me happy.

They just never do. Even when they perform the tasks I assign them.

It's like a cruel joke.

The ring does work for leaving the grounds. As long as the slave caretaker has the ring on, he can walk through the gates. And as long as I'm with the slave caretaker, I can walk through those gates too.

I can't stay away long. Grant and I did many experiments on this back when he was new and eager. Four hours is about the limit. And fifty miles. Anything further away or longer in duration and I just disappear and end back in my tomb like I never left.

The nearest town is Granite Springs, and that's as far as I've gone in almost thirty years. There is no point in venturing further. And I'm not really interested in the wider world. I want the curse lifted, but I am a creature of another time. What happens to me if I do escape?

I didn't think about this much until Grant came along. The world is always changing, but the events and discoveries of the past fifty years have been something like a fiction.

And every time I think about what's happening out there, the word 'magic' comes to mind.

Two thousand years I've been in this world and only the last fifty or so have been able to stun me silent.

I place my hand on Tarq's tomb where the door should be. "Open," I command it.

But, of course, it does not respond.

I sigh and look around at the other tombs nearby. I don't know any of the monsters in this cemetery. And new tombs pop up all the time. Who is putting them here, I have no idea.

Are they dead? Do they see me out here? Can they hear me?

I would like to think they can. I would like to think that Tarq waits for me to come and tell him the news.

But it's unlikely.

Even if I do get the tombs open, there's probably nothing in there but bones. Or worse, they are empty.

I look down the hill at the flickering lights of the cottage. I like it, I decide. The look of it being used. It's depressing to look around and see nothing but darkness down there. Sometimes, when the moon is full, I can make out the shimmer of light on the surface of the lake that lies just beyond the walls.

But tonight, there is no moon so if that girl was not in the cottage, it would be dark and depressing.

I sigh again, then pat Tarq's arm. "I have a lot to tell you, friend. But not tonight."

Then I turn away from him and start walking towards my own tomb, ready to go inside and go back to sleep. But I catch sight of the cathedral out of the corner of my eye and turn that direction instead.

When I get inside, I go up the stairs and right back into the apothecary room. Tomas is asleep on the lounger, an open book lying over his chest like he was reading it.

It's Grant's last notebook.

I pick up the book and leave the apothecary. But I don't know where to go. There are no lights in my tomb, so that's out of the question. Across the great hall is the greenhouse. Not a place one reads, so I strike that off the list.

There are some benches around the perimeter, but they are made of stone. And why should I stay in this room? This cathedral is as big as a palace. Hundreds of rooms tucked away down long hallways or up hidden staircases.

They are all magical, of course. All cursed, right along with me. You never know what you're going to find when you explore the hidden interior of Saint Mark's Sanctuary.

But at least you know none of it can kill you since the curse won't let you die. So I walk down the stairs one more time, but instead of going outside, I turn and look behind me. There are three staircases. The center staircase leads up to the great hall. But it's the other two I'm interested in.

I've been up both before but it's been long enough that I don't have much recollection of either.

I choose the one on the right.

CHAPTER SIX –PIE

Despite being cursed, losing my best friend, and getting a lecture on how to be a good slave by a monster with horns and hooves, I slept pretty good in the little cottage.

In fact, I slept so well, I wonder if the water is drugged. But it's a well. There is a pump over the sink in the kitchen, so unless someone is drugging the water under the ground, that's not it.

I don't want to admit that it might just be the comfy, cozy nature of the place because I fully intend on getting the fuck out of here today. I will not be putting on that ring, that's for sure. I think there's a loophole in this curse as long as the deal isn't sealed. So I'm gonna find it.

My first disappointment of the day is the realization that there is no hot water. Why would a place have a bathroom with no hot water? Also, who the hell would I call to fix a plumbing issue?

Never mind, Pie. You're not gonna be here that long.

I go down to the kitchen—ha. I should've looked harder at this last night. There is a wood stove to cook on, but no electricity, so no refrigerator. Also, no food in any of the cupboards. So the monster was probably telling the truth when he said we would need groceries.

But again. Not gonna be here that long. If I have to fast for a day, I can deal.

Unfortunate thing number three this morning is that I don't have clothes. Just this stupid schoolgirl uniform from two days ago.

There is a closet, and it even has clothes in it, but a whole flock of moths fly out the moment I opened the door.

So. No outfit change.

I pump some water into a bowl and finger-scrub my teeth, then take a deep breath and walk out of the cottage to go find Tomas. I hurry up the hill, trying my best not to look at the cemetery. The statues in the daylight are horrifying. Just monster after monster after monster. And the tombs are just as creepy. Each one of them has a door. No, door is the wrong word. They are gaping black holes in the stone walls.

I can't see past the blackness—thank God—but I don't need to see what's inside those things to understand I need to stay away from them. I direct my eyes back to the cathedral and walk faster.

The grounds are eerily silent as I make my way up to the double doors that lead into the bottom-level entry hall. No birds, no wind, no rustling. Just silence.

Inside I face a moment of indecision when I come face to face with the three staircases. I know the middle one leads up to the top entrance hall I'm familiar with, but the other two are a mystery. And they are obviously part of the magic of this place because I've already established that this cathedral— while impressive and tall, from the back side, at least— is not wide enough to accommodate the interior of this space.

A flutter high up in the ceiling draws my attention away from my choices to where it should be.

"Pia?" I call up to the sound, then sigh when my friend fails to appear.

Either that's not her or she's not mine anymore.

Both of those realizations make my stomach sick so I push it away for now and climb up the center staircase. It feels like a very long walk this morning. Yesterday I went up and down this thing a few times without thinking about how many steps there actually are, but I don't have that same adrenaline rush right now.

Once up at the top I head straight to the apothecary room. The door is ajar so I just push it the rest of the way open and take a step inside. "Hello?" I say it softly. Like this place is a church. I'm pretty sure it's not a church since it's filled with cursed things, but there is an expectation of reverence lingering in the air in here.

No one answers me, and when I take a good look around, I realize that's because no one is here. It's just me, and the books, and a sense of bad luck and foreboding.

I go back out to the upper entrance hall and look around. Up, actually. Hoping for a glimpse of the bird that may or may not be Pia. I miss her. Even though I have always understood that life would've been a whole lot easier if she wasn't here, I never imagined myself without her. I just made plans to cope with life *with* her.

So now I feel… lost. Unbalanced, even.

I want Pia back. I want to leave this place. I want to get in my Jeep and go to stupid Toledo so I can overstay my welcome on Jacqueline's couch and then beg her to let me be her babysitter forever and ever.

My eyes gravitate to the massive front door and then, without thinking, I'm walking towards it. Pulling it open. Stepping out onto the front steps.

The gray is still there, the fog rolling around at the edge of things. But it's sentient or something. Like it can sense me. Because it begins rolling my way, trying to make me reconsider the idea that I might be able to walk out of here. I might be able to find that gate and get back to the real world.

"Good morning."

I startle and turn to find Tomas standing next to me holding a cup of coffee. He stretches his neck and back, like any person would when they first wake up and take stock of the day before them. And he's shirtless again, wearing only a pair of pinstriped pajama pants. I get caught up in his in body—it's hard not to. It's… very nice—but then I look up at his face. He's yawning.

I sigh.

His next words come out with the tail end of his yawn. "So what's the plan for today?"

"Plan?" I scoff a little. "The plan is to get the hell out of this creepy place, Tomas. That's the plan."

He nods as he sips his coffee. "Perfect. So you're gonna put the ring on?"

"No. No. I'm not putting the ring on. That seals the deal. Right now I'm in some kind of… in-between. I have not committed to this yet. There's still a chance I can get out of it."

Tomas makes a face. It's an adorable face that says, *Yeah. No. Maybe you're a little crazy.* "I don't think that's how it works, sunshine. You came through the gate. Grant left. You're stuck here. The only choice left is to decide how you will be stuck here. With that surrounding you all day and night?" He nods to the fog. "Or the real world on the other side? And if I may make a suggestion? I'd go with option two. *Truuuust* me. I've been there, done that. They all say the same thing on the first day. 'I'm not gonna put on the ring. I will not take part in this curse.' But after a few days of the creepy fog, they give in. You should save yourself the trouble and do it now."

I shake my head as I watch the fog. It's still coming for me. "No. There has to be a way out."

"There is," Tomas agrees. "Free Pell and you're free too."

"Another way," I huff. "One that doesn't involve unleashing a monster on the world."

Tomas takes another sip of his coffee and lets out a long, "Ahhh," after he swallows. Which is so annoying. Then he turns to me—"Well. Good luck with that"—and goes back inside.

Meanwhile, the fog is coming up the steps and the edges of it are starting to take on the appearance of tendrils. So I follow him.

And to my delight, who is coming up the stairs? The monster responsible for all this crap.

I shield my eyes. "For fuck's sake. Can you please put on some pants?" I don't wait for him to answer, I hurry over to the apothecary room and slip inside before he can freeze me again and force me to stare at his enormous package.

I close the door, sending a hint that I would like some alone time to think about things, but the monster just comes in after me anyway, apparently unable to read a room.

I turn my back to him. I'm not looking. I refuse to look at him.

"Where's breakfast?" he growls.

"You tell me. I don't live here."

"You're in charge of breakfast and I'm hungry, slave."

"First of all"—I hold up a finger, my back to him—"I'm not your slave. I did not put on the ring. I will never be putting on the ring. But even if I did put it on, I would still not be your slave. I answered an ad for a caretaker."

"An ad?" Tomas says. He's standing behind the beast called Pell. "That's… interesting."

"Caretakers make breakfast," Pell says.

"There is no food in my cottage… so…"

"Oh, there's a kitchen," Tomas offers brightly.

I turn to him, still keeping my back to the beast, and shoot him a look. *Whose side are you on?*

He just shrugs. "I'll show you where it is. What's today? Sunday?" He cocks his head at me. "We usually have pancakes and bacon on Sundays. And I'm fucking starving. I feel like I haven't eaten in centuries." He rubs his hands together. "So let's do this."

"I would like to be served in the dining hall," the beast adds.

"Listen." I point my finger at Tomas. "You're a traitor. And you"—I hook my thumb over my shoulder at the monster—"can get your own damn breakfast. I'm staying right in this room so I can look for the out clause."

I turn my back to both of them now and walk over to the nearest bookshelf to peruse the titles.

There's a moment of awkward silence and even though I don't turn to check, I imagine they are sending each other looks. Unspoken-word looks. They are having a whole conversation about how to 'manage' me behind my back.

Finally, the beast says, "Perhaps we should start this day with the rules."

"Fuck your rules," I mutter. "You and your rules—"

But that's as far as I get. Because he puts that freeze spell on me again.

My hand is reaching for a thick volume on the shelf in front of me when this happens. There is not enough room for the beast to maneuver into my line of sight, but he does it anyway, his hard, muscular stomach pressing against my chest. Then he places his fingertips under my chin and forces my head to look up at him.

There is nothing I can do.

I must obey. I can't even close my eyes. I have to see him.

He makes me stand there, frozen in silence, for several more seconds before he speaks again. "I'm only going to say this one more time, slave. You are here at my pleasure. I'm going to give you the benefit of the doubt and thoroughly go over the rules with you. Then you will make us breakfast, you will put on that ring, and you will go into town and purchase our essentials. Now I'm going to let you go, but when I do, I expect you to agree immediately. I will not tolerate your insolence."

And then I am unfrozen. I stumble forward, just like I did yesterday. But the bookshelf catches me before I fall.

The beast growls. "Do you understand me?"

I turn. I force myself to look him in the eye. And then I say, "Put. On. Some. Pants."

CHAPTER SEVEN – PELL

I growl at her. "Satyr chimera do not wear *pants*."

"Well, the sight of said satyr chimera's *package* is disgusting. And I refuse to talk to you until you put. On. Pants."

"Package?" I mutter more to myself than to her.

But she answers me through clenched teeth. "Your *dick*."

"My cock?"

"Yes." She's fuming now.

But I'm enjoying myself. I like her flustered because when she's flustered, she's tolerable. Amusing, even. "Does the sight of a man's sex parts make you… tremble?"

"Tremble? No." She points to my lower body and waves it her finger around in a circle. "This whole thing… I can't. OK? I just can't this morning. Just… cover it up."

I look down at my *package*, then back up at the girl called *Pie*. "What's wrong with it? None of the women I've pleasured have ever had any complaints."

She scoffs. "Were they human?"

"I've had thousands of human women. Always satisfied."

"Gross."

She has still not looked down again. I could order her. I could wait until she slips and then freeze her. Make her stare at it for hours. But I'm hungry. And this is a tantalizing opportunity for another time. This slave is going to take months to train. And now that I know that my natural supererotic state makes her blush like a virgin on the eve of Ostara, I will want to use this to my full advantage.

So instead, I turn and look at Tomas. He's got his hand over his mouth like he's hiding a smirk, quite enjoying our little interaction. But I'm not sure if he's happy about her dismissal of me, or the way her cheeks went bright pink the moment she said 'pants.' "Show her where the kitchen is, Tomas. I must excuse myself to go find *pants*." I shoot her a look, but she's turned her back to me. And that pisses me off. She has no right to judge me. She is a slave. "You will have breakfast ready in one hour. And after that, we will go over every rule. I will explain my expectations in detail, so there is no misunderstanding. And then you will put on that ring and go into town to run my errands like a good slave caretaker should."

Her shoulders go stiff when I say the word 'slave.' And that is enough to satisfy me.

I turn, push past Tomas and his smirk, and exit the apothecary.

I spent last night exploring the hidden floors of the upper levels. And I did actually find a room filled with satyr clothes. Centuries ago, when I was paired with a particularly adept slave caretaker who could sew, we threw parties in the sanctuary and I wore this finery. This was back in the old world when humans barely needed to be drunk to accept a satyr chimera in their midst.

I sigh as I climb the magic staircase and enter the maze of hallways. I miss the old world.

Sometimes the rooms move and you can't ever find the one you need when you need it. But today, I am in luck because I find the closet room easily. The clothes are magic, so they have not rotted and the colors have not faded. They are as bright and fine as the day they were made.

I will wear pants for this girl. But it's not going to be enough to hide my *package*, as she puts it. Because the pants are tight. They were not made to hide the shape of me. They were made to accentuate it.

I draw the line at shirts. And she didn't ask for a shirt, so if it's a shirt she requires to be comfortable during her first years here, she is out of luck. And she will learn her lesson. If you're going to ask a monster for a favor, you had better be specific.

The breeches are a rich, green velvet. The color of the forest. And they make me look like the woodsy monster-thing I am. Something akin to Pan himself. All I need is a pipe flute and I could be the wood god incarnate. Though my horns are much nicer than his ever dreamed of being.

I take my time returning to the lower levels. The kitchen here at the sanctuary is a thing to get used to. It took Grant months to perfect the art of cooking over a wood stove, so I am not expecting much when I arrive at the dining table. But to my surprise, she has prepared a feast.

"What is this?" I ask Tomas as I approach. He's already eating. Which is rude. And before this girl came, Tomas, in this form, anyway, wasn't real. Not corporeal. Not of any *substance*.

He was a ghost. Sort of.

But he wasn't able to touch my slave either. And it seems he can now do both of these things.

Interesting.

"Mmm." He's still chewing. "Isn't this great? We used the last of the bacon. And I ate most of it already. Fucking bacon. Mmm." He points to the plate with his fork, which has two meager pieces left. "But there's pancakes. We're out of syrup though." He shrugs like this can't be helped, and continues chewing.

"She did not make this."

"I did so." And there she is, leaning against the wall leading into the kitchen, her arms crossed. This is when I fully notice her ridiculous attire. It's strange, I believe. Even with my limited experience of recent events on the outside, I know this outfit is out of place. The very short skirt that shows off all of her legs and leaves almost nothing to the imagination. Plus a corset top. Her ample breasts practically spill out of the scarlet-red leather.

There is no way she made this food. It's magic left over from Grant. Tomas probably knew about the spell. And now I am left wondering how much of Grant was actually real, and how much was glamoured?

He was a talented alchemist. He could make potions to do just about anything.

Except break this curse, of course.

I had assumed he just morphed into a talented cook over the decades. But what if everything he got better at was just magic?

"Tomas," I roar. "Bring us the rulebook. This is a working breakfast." I figure if he's real now, I might as well put him to work.

"Is he a slave too?" the girl asks.

I glare at Tomas, even though he wasn't the one who asked. "Get me. The rulebook."

He gets up and goes.

"You're rude. You know that?" Then she sneers in the direction of my pants. "And those? Not helping."

"You said pants. I put on pants. It is not my fault that my cock is huge and your eyes are virgin."

She snorts. "Right. You wish."

"And you're one to talk about appropriate dress. If that corset were any smaller, your nipples would pop out."

She makes a face. Then crosses her arms tighter.

Tomas appears with the rulebook and plops it down on the table, then helps himself to the last two pieces of bacon and sits back down, shoving them into his mouth before I can protest.

"Sit," I command the girl. Then I point to the chair where the book is. "And begin reading on page one."

She exhales loudly, but obeys, scraping her chair on the marble floor as she pushes herself in.

I sit across from her, not touching the food even though my stomach is growling. If I had known that Grant was glamouring my meals, I would've punished him for that. And I would not have eaten them. Just the thought of how much of his magic I have ingested over the decades makes me ill.

"Read," I growl. "We are not wasting this day. After we're done here you will throw out every bit of food we have in the pantries and root cellars, and then you will put the ring on, go into town, and buy all new provisions. And the next time you prepare a meal for me, you will not use magic recipes."

I'm angry about the food. There is no telling what kind of magic Grant was working on me over the last few decades. And I'm beginning to feel like Grant knew things. Lots of things. Up to and including how to break this curse.

But he didn't break it.

Why?

For the reason the girl stated? She will not unleash a monster on humanity?

Maybe. But doubtful.

The girl opens the book with a loud sigh. "It's in Latin! I do not read Latin!"

I point at Tomas and bark, "Tomas, read the book."

Tomas swallows his bacon, dabs his mouth with a napkin, then slides the book in front of him. "'Rule number one. The slave caretaker will wash the hooves of the guardian monster daily.'"

"Oh, hell no. Hell the fuck no. I am not washing your feet every day! That's gross!"

I shrug. She will come to understand. "Please refrain from commenting. We have a lot to do today."

"'Rule number two,'" Tomas continues. "'You will feed the monster three times a day. Rule number three. You will bathe—'" Tomas pauses to look at Pie when she squeaks. She grits her teeth and looks at me, shaking her head.

Tomas reads, "'You will bathe the monster each night.'"

And again, she whispers her objections. "Fuck this. Just fuck this."

"Keep going, Tomas," I growl.

"'Rule number four. You will study alchemy, herbology, and spellcasting. Rule number five. You will attempt to break the curse at least once a month until it is done.'"

Pie sighs and bows her head, her shoulders slouching in defeat. "I can't do any of that. I don't know why I'm here, but"—she looks up at me, meets my gaze—"you've got the wrong girl."

I raise my eyebrows at her. "And yet you came in here with a magical bird?"

She lets out a long breath. "Magic? Um. For your information I have been locked in several psychiatric hospitals over the years. I'm not magic, I'm just… insane. Delusional. I hallucinate. I'm most likely just a very high-functioning schizophrenic."

"Keep reading, Tomas."

Pie deflates even more when I don't show her any sympathy.

"'Rule number six. You will take care of the greenhouse and collect herbs as necessary. Rule number seven. You will run errands for the monster and keep the kitchen stocked with fresh food.'"

"I hope you have money for this," Pie says. "Because I don't have any."

"Oh, don't worry about that," Tomas says. "We have magic money. You just write down the word 'money' on a piece of paper and hand it to them."

"Them?" She's confused. "Them who?"

"The people in town," I clarify. "Any piece of paper will do. Simply write down the word 'money' and they will accept it."

She ponders this for a moment while Tomas and I exchange a look. I wait for him to tell her the rest, but he keeps quiet.

Maybe he is on my side?

"Wait." The girl points at me, then Tomas. "What's that look you two are doing?"

"What look?" Tomas asks, feigning ignorance.

The girl squints her eyes at him. She knows something is up, but she's not sure what.

"Keep reading," I command.

She exhales with frustration and anger. Tomas continues. "'Rule number eight. You will pleasure the—'"

She snorts before Tomas can even finish. "Fuck you. Just fuck you, beast. *Pleasure you*? What the hell does that even mean?"

I shrug. "Lots of things give me pleasure. We'll figure it out."

She looks at Tomas for help. But he's already standing up, wiping his mouth with a paper napkin. "I gotta go, sunshine." He reaches over, brushes his fingertips against her cheek, and then winks at her. "But I'll be around if you need help with anything." Then he waves his fingers at her playfully and walks out of the dining room.

The girl looks at me. "Nope. Nope. If you think I'm going to sexually satisfy you—"

I bellow out a laugh and point at her. "Wow. Well. We know where your mind is." I stand up, fist my cock through my skin-tight pants. "Still on my package, I see. Why am I wearing these pants again?"

"What?"

"Sexually pleasure me?" I glare at her. "What the hell is wrong with you?"

"Me?" She points to her chest. "You're the one who needs to have your feet washed every morning and to be bathed every night. Like you can't do that shit yourself?"

"You're my slave. I'm the Monster of Saint Mark's. The only sex between you and I will happen in your dreams!"

She stands up, flips me off, and is walking towards the hallway where Tomas disappeared when Tomas is suddenly there again.

"We have a problem." He's looking at me. Not her.

"What is it?"

"Well." Now he does look at Pie. "Your car just got a ticket."

The girl just looks at him, like she's not understanding. "What?"

"Yep." Tomas twirls a finger in the air. "The sheriff is out front. Flashing lights and everything."

I smirk. I can't help it.

"What do you mean? There's nothing out front but fog!" She's in complete denial. About all of it.

"No," Tomas says. "Listen. This is how it works. Most of the time people can't see the sanctuary. It's hidden in the trees, this road we're on is private, there's no mail delivery, et cet-cet-cetera. So it's practically invisible even without magic. But if they do notice us—for instance… a car is abandoned on the side of a country road—someone calls it in to the local sheriff. The sheriff comes out to take a look, so now the building, which was always here, just slightly, magically sorta hidden, is now visible to anyone who cares to look in our direction. So they can see us and we can see them."

"But the fog?"

This poor girl. She's slow. Not very bright at all. "The fog is only there because you have not put on the ring," I explain. "And it will stay there until you do. But now that your car has been noticed—"

"Oh"—Tomas laughs—"it's been *more* than noticed. They are towing it."

"What?" She's starting to panic. "They can't tow my Jeep!"

"Agreed," I say. "We need that car to get groceries."

"Fuck your groceries! That Jeep is the only thing I own! They can't tow it! I can't get it out! I don't have impound money! And I can't even leave here."

I hold up a finger. "You *can* leave here. Remember?"

"*If* I put on the ring."

"Exactly." I smile, satisfied. "If. You put on the ring."

She glares at me. And her face goes dark as I watch her. "You did this." Her voice is low. Growly. "You did this, didn't you? You got the sheriff out here to tow my Jeep so I'd be forced to put that stupid ring on."

"Woman, how the hell would I get the sheriff out here? There is no phone. I can't leave unless I'm with you. You're losing your fucking mind because you know you have to put that ring on and there is no way out. And let's get this straight right now—I'm not the one fucking up your life. You're the one fucking up *my* life. You're here and no one trapped you. You came of your own accord. So do you want that car or not? Because if you don't go take care of this, you'll be walking into town for groceries and it's a nineteen-mile hike."

She narrows her eyes at me. "I hate you."

"Back atcha."

"OK, OK, OK." Tomas slides between us, one palm pointed at me, one palm pointed at her. "We're all we've got, kids. We don't hate each other. But Pie, seriously. You do need your car."

"No shit," she scoffs.

"So…" Tomas pauses. Like she's about to turn into a reasonable person before his eyes and realize she needs to put the ring on.

He's always been a dreamer.

"So? So what?" she snaps.

"So…" he tries again. "Put the ring on, Pie. Go out there, tell him it's your car, and handle this shit."

She purses her lips. Taps her boot on the marble floor. Puts her hands on her hips. Huffs. "We'll see," she says. Then she turns, momentarily gets confused as to how to leave the dining room, then picks a direction—

"Not that way," Tomas calls.

I just shake my head and look skyward, asking for patience.

"Come on." Tomas takes her hand. "I'll show you how to get back to the great hall. It's tricky," he says as he leads her out. "The hallways…" Then his voice trails off.

I follow, reluctantly. But it's not like I have anything better to do. Tomas is getting very hands-y with this girl. I'm sure he's enjoying her immensely and I am starting to get the feeling that Tomas thinks that he and this girl will have something special.

Good. Good for him. If he wants to cozy up to her, fine with me. She's not my type at all.

When we get back to the main hall, Tomas and the girl are looking out one of the tall skinny windows that face front.

I join them and all three of us watch as a sketchy-looking tow-truck driver slides under her car to hook it up.

"Better get that ring on quick," I taunt. "You're about to lose everything."

Her head turns to the side. "You're an asshole. And I don't need to put the ring on. I can have this conversation through the gate."

And with that, she turns to the door. Pulls it open and walks out.

Tomas and I look at each other, smirking.

He sighs. "She's…"

"Insane? Dumb? Obstinate?"

"I was going to say… eternally hopeful." He snickers. "But she'll learn."

"They always do." I cross my arms and wait for her illumination to happen before my eyes.

CHAPTER EIGHT – PIE

I walk out the door and the sunshine hits me in the face. I feel like I've been cloistered away for decades and it's only been one night. I want to believe that this is all a bad dream, and I was holding out hope this morning, but this isn't a delusion. And even if it is, while I'm living the delusion, I need to outsmart it. I need to be one step ahead. Hell, ten steps. I need to make good decisions and weigh every one of them carefully. Because it's all a trap. I can just feel it.

The sheriff hasn't noticed me yet and the tow truck driver is too busy hooking my Jeep up to a very questionable truck. Maybe my Jeep is nothing special, but it's my baby. And picturing it rattling behind that clunker is giving me heart palpitations.

Once I'm halfway down the path I call out, "Hello! You can stop now. I'm here."

None of them turn to look at me.

"Hey!" I call out, louder now. "I said you can stop. That's my Jeep. I live… here." That was hard to say. "Hello?"

They don't even look at me.

In fact, it's like they don't even see me.

"No," I whisper. "No, no, no, no, no. This is not happening." Am I invisible? "Hey! Dickface sheriff! You're an ugly—" I stop. It's very apparent that I do not exist without that ring on my finger. But aside from that, I was going to call the sheriff ugly. And... he's not ugly. Like. At all. He's... "Wow." He's fucking hot.

"Huh." I plant my hands on my hips. "Maybe my theory about hot dudes was true?"

Tomas is a looker. Like... mmm. That kind of looker.

And even though the beast is a monster and he has horns, and hooves, and fur... he's got a nice face. And that scruff of blond beard? Mm-hm.

I shake my head and snap out of it. Because the tow truck driver is lifting my Jeep up now. Like he's about to pull away.

I turn, run back to the sanctuary, fling the door open, and screech to a halt. Because the monster is standing right there, palm out, ring in the center of it. "Forget something?" He smirks at me.

I snatch up the ring. "Fuck you." He might have a nice face, but he's the reason I'm stuck here. And he's a dick.

"You're gonna have to put it on, sweetheart."

I sigh up at Tomas. "Give me a minute."

"You don't have a minute," the beast says. "Your car is about to pull away."

"What?" I look out the window, and sure enough, the driver is getting into his truck. I spin around, go back out, run down the walkway, and slip the fucking ring on my finger just before I call out, "Hey! Stop! That's my Jeep!" A repeat of what just happened two minutes ago, but with real fear in my voice this time.

The tow truck driver just pulls away. Either he didn't hear me, or didn't care.

But the sheriff has definitely noticed. He turns in my direction, flashes me a brilliant smile, lifts his sunglasses up to his forehead to reveal the greenest eyes I've ever seen, and he says, "Well, well, well. Would you get a look at this."

I stop at the gate and frown at him. "Get a look at what?" And that's when I realize… I'm still wearing my slutty schoolgirl outfit from Halloween night.

The sheriff actually leers at me, looking me up and down but *good*. And I'm still trying to decide if I'm offended or not when he adds, "You, little darling, are a vision in plaid."

I want to be offended. I really do. But wow. He's so hot. Like… supernaturally hot. He's tall. And lean, but not skinny. I can see the definition of his biceps through his khaki-colored button-down shirt. And those already-mentioned eyes. Not to mention his accent. It's just the right amount of rural Pennsylvania hick.

I smile at him, even though his comment was pretty sexist. I don't care. Besides, I have to sweet-talk this guy. He just had my Jeep towed and I need it back. *Without* paying for it. "Hi," I say. "I'm… Pie—"

"Pie?" He chuckles. "You're *Pie*? That's…" He licks his lips. "Adorable."

"Well. Thank you. Um. And. Yeah. What I'm here to say is—" *Holy hell, Pie. Get a hold of yourself. You're acting like a schoolgirl.* This almost makes me snort. "Anyway. I'm sorry to bother you, but that was my Jeep." I point down the road where it disappeared. "Do you think you could call the driver and have him bring it back?"

I do a flirty thing here. I bat my eyelashes at him and kinda swivel a little as I wrap a long strand of blonde hair around my finger and pucker my lips. I don't even know where this is all coming from, because I cannot recall a single time in my twenty-five years where I've ever been such a shameless flirt, but it makes the hot cop smile. So whatever.

"Well," hot cop says, "Pie." He licks his lips again. Like I might be delicious. Then his smile falters. "I'm sorry. But once the car is hooked up, the driver has to take it in. It's… procedure."

"Procedure." I keep smiling. I'm not giving up that easy. "But… procedures… they're subjective sometimes."

"No." And, unfortunately, hot cop seems pretty set in his ways about this no. "Rules are rules, *Pie*."

I look over my shoulder, picturing Tomas and the beast having a good laugh over this.

"But I'll tell you what," hot cop says. "I'll drive you into town and help you get it out of impound. How about that?"

"You will?"

"I will. I like to be helpful. Protect and serve and all that junk."

"All that junk." I giggle these words out and then… my eyes slide down to look at his junk. When I look up at him again, he's grinning wildly.

"I'm Sheriff Roth, Pie. Sheriff Russell Roth. But you can just call me Russ. Everyone does."

"Russ Roth," I whisper under my breath. "Sounds like a quarterback name. Did you play football in high school, Sheriff Russ Roth?"

"How did you know?" He winks at me as he walks over to the little gate, pulls it open, and says, "Come on, Pie. Let's get you to school."

And like an idiot, I laugh at this dumb joke that is both sexist *and* offensive.

It's weird. But also… I don't care. I'm completely enamored by former high-school quarterback Sheriff Russ Roth.

I walk through the gate and do not even look back.

To hell with the monster of Saint Mark's Sanctuary. And I like Tomas, but he's part of this whole curse thing. I'm out of here.

Sheriff Roth even opens the passenger door and lets me ride in front with him. I'm pretty sure this is against regulations. I mean he's got his rifle right there between the front seats.

"Don't worry." Russ slides into the car and pats his weapon. "I won't let it hurt you, Pie."

I shrug my shoulders up and grin. Damn. He's very nice to look at.

We pull away from Saint Mark's and he gets on his radio. "Eileen. I'm 10-8. Heading back to Granite Springs."

There's a crackling on the radio, then a female voice. Presumably Eileen. "Got it, Russ. See ya soon."

Russ picks up his radio again just as we turn back onto the main highway. "Dammit, Eileen. How many times do I have to tell you to use the 10 codes? Act like a professional. I have a passenger listening."

"Sorry, Russ," Eileen crackles back. "Understood." She clicks off, then clicks back. "I mean, 10-4, Russ. See ya soon."

He puts his radio away and sighs. "She's my cousin's wife-in-law's sister. Not the sharpest tack on the bulletin board, but she tries hard."

Cousin's wife-in-law's sister? I can't even begin to unravel those words so I just forget I ever heard them.

"So how long have you been out here at the cemetery?" Russ asks.

"Oh, it's not really a cemetery. It's a sanctuary."

He lifts an eyebrow at me and I realize I should shut up about Saint Mark's. If what Tomas and Pell said was true, then he only thinks about that place when it comes up. And I'm pretty sure that it's better for everyone if Saint Mark's doesn't come up.

"What's the difference?" he asks.

"I'm not sure." I wave a hand in the air. "Doesn't matter. So you're the sheriff, huh? That's a pretty big job."

He chuckles as we speed down the highway towards the town of Granite Springs. "Not really. We've got about five hundred people living in town. Maybe a couple dozen more running the farms on the outskirts. We're a quiet, sleepy little place, Pie. And can I say—that name of yours? It's…"

"Adorable?" I offer. Since he's already said that.

He points at me. "So. Damn. Adorable. Where are you from?"

"Philly."

"No. They don't have girls named Pie in Philly."

"Not anymore they don't." I laugh.

"So what kind of pie are you? Strawberry? Peach? *Cherry*?" And 'cherry' comes out as a whisper. Like it's something dirty.

I actually sigh over this. I don't know what it is about this man, but I like him. He's on the obtuse side as far as women go, but it comes off as more small-town cute than big-city insulting. "I don't know," I say. "I haven't ever thought much about it."

Which is a lie. People ask me this question all the time. And I always have an answer. But I'm enjoying Russ Roth's low-level flirting.

I watch the scenery as we drive. There is a thick forest on either side of the highway, so all I see is trees. But they are nice trees. Fall colors. Brilliant reds and fiery oranges, with a sprinkling of bright yellow. I am beginning to love rural PA. It's so damn pretty in the fall.

And even though we're complete strangers and this silence between us should be awkward, it's not awkward. I'm enjoying the ride and I'm actually disappointed when the quaint town of Granite Springs comes into view.

It's something out of *Gilmore Girls*. Only better, because Stars Hollow isn't real and Granite Springs is. There's an old downtown with dozens of shops lining the main street. A hardware store, a grocery store, a mechanic and tire place, the post office. Plus a slew of touristy places that sell things like candles and locally made goods like goats' milk soap. There's a big feed store next to the police station, but we don't turn in to the station. We go right on by to the outskirts of town where the tow yard is.

And that's where we stop.

He picks up his radio. "Eileen, I'm 10-6."

She crackles back, "Got it, Russ. I mean, 10-4, Russ. But Russ?"

"Yes, Eileen?"

"I'm gonna need you to go out to the old trailer park on 75. There's a scuffle happening."

Russ sighs, then looks apologetically at me. "I wish I could stay and iron this all out with you, Pie. But duty calls."

I salute him. "I can take it from here. Thank you for the ride in, I really appreciate it. And it was a pleasure meeting you, Sheriff Roth."

I smile stupidly at him. Damn, what is wrong with me? I don't flirt like this. There's just something about him that makes me *want* to capture his attention.

"How about…" He pauses. "I mean… this is wildly inappropriate, but…"

"How about what?" The eagerness in my voice almost feels like desperation. And I want to smack myself out of this stupor he's put me in.

"Would you like to have lunch with me? After you're all sorted and I take care of my scuffle?"

I'm nodding my head before he even stops talking. "I would love that, Russ."

"Great. Meet me at the Honey Bean in about two hours."

"Honey Bean?"

"It's the only diner in town. You can't miss it. It's right next to the Buffalo Nickel."

"Got it." I smile as I open my door and get out. But then I lean back in. "One hour, Russ."

He winks. "Don't be late, Pie."

I close the door grinning like a girl in love as he pulls away. But as I walk to the grungy office door of the tow yard shop, I suddenly feel like an idiot for the way I just behaved.

What the hell was I thinking?

I'm not dating the stupid sheriff of Granite Springs. I'm in the middle of a curse. A curse that involves a magic cathedral, a cemetery filled with stone monsters, and a real-life monster who expects me to wash his hooves and pleasure him daily as part of my duties.

I have more than enough going on. I do not need a love interest.

And the minute I walk through the shop door I decide I will break this date. Once I get my purse back from my car, I'll call up the station and let Eileen know that I will not be meeting Sheriff Russ Roth for lunch and have her relay the message.

"Can I help you?" The older woman behind the glass doesn't even look up at me as I approach. Just keeps typing on her keyboard.

"Yes. My Jeep was just towed in. I need to get it out."

"Name?"

"Pie Vita."

Now she does look up. She is late sixties, maybe. Pin-curled blue hair. That's old-lady blue, not hipster blue. She's got an elaborate pair of reading glasses perched on her nose. The frames are glittering with rhinestones and they are on an equally elaborate, sparkling silver chain. She pushes them down her nose. "I'm sorry, what language are you speaking?"

I sigh. I get this a lot. Sometimes, if people understand what the word 'vita' means, they even get the joke. Pie. Life. Pie is life. And I have to admit, it's a little bit cute.

Old-Lady Blue does not find me cute. She looks at my outfit, then me. And I see it all on her face.

Trash.

"First name Pie," I say calmly. "Last name Vita. Pie. Vita. My Jeep just came in and I want it back."

Her long fingernails click her keyboard as she scans her computer. "License plate?"

"Seriously? I don't have my purse. It's in the Jeep. I don't know the license plate. It literally just came in. It's that one."

She pushes her glasses down again. "Can you describe the Jeep?"

"Brown? Rusty? PA plates."

Her fingernails click again. "That's two hundred and twenty dollars."

"What? That's a joke, right?"

"Not a joke, *Pie*." She smiles as she says my name. "It was picked up quite far out of town. So there's mileage. Plus the hook-up fee, the drop-off fee, and the storage fee."

"Storage fee? It just came in. It hasn't been stored."

"There's a minimum three-day storage fee for our trouble."

"Fucking hell—"

"Mmm-mmm-mmm." She shakes her head at me. "Not today, Satan. We do not put up with the likes of that here at MoMack's Towin'."

I sigh. "I need to get my purse out of the Jeep. Can I at least do that?"

"Let me alert MoMack that you're here and he can help you out. One moment, please." She gets up and disappears through another grungy door.

"Two hundred and twenty dollars," I mutter under my breath. "That's highway robbery."

I only have fifty bucks left in credit on my card and like thirty in my checking, but maybe they will let me write them a bad check?

Then I see the sign. *No checks.*

Wonderful.

Oh. Then I remember what Tomas and the beast were saying this morning about how our money works.

Did I just say 'our money'? And did I make all that up? Or was it real?

One glance down at the silver ring on my finger clears up any lingering doubt about my new reality. And now that I'm looking at it in the light, there is no Green Man face on it. It looks like oak leaves and maybe a tiny acorn or two. I try to take it off and it doesn't budge… so yeah. It's all real.

I wish Russ Roth was still here. Maybe he was a little aphrodisiac-y, and that's a red flag when you're neck-deep in a magical curse, but I'll take that swoony feeling over this despairing one any day.

I reach through the little opening in the glass partition and grab a pen and piece of paper, then write down the word 'MONEY.'

This will never work. It can't work.

But then again, I'm wearing a cursed ring and I'm the new slave caretaker of a horned, hooved beast called Pell who comes with a rulebook that sounds suspiciously like a manual for a dominant-submissive sex club.

Old-Lady Blue comes back and plops down in her seat. "He'll meet you out back, Pie." She smiles at me when she says my name. But it's way too saccharine sweet, to be honest.

We'll see who's smug when I leave here with my Jeep and all you get in return is a piece of paper off your own notepad.

"Thanks," I say, my appreciation just as fake as her smile.

Out in the yard, MoMack is waiting for me by my Jeep. He has unhooked it and is holding my purse.

"Honey," he says, handing it over. "You don't have enough money in there to pay this bill."

"Don't you worry about it," I say, snagging my purse from him. "I'm good."

I go back inside and shove the piece of paper through the glass at Old-Lady Blue.

"What's this?"

"Huh?" Shit. Please, please, *please* tell me this is going to work.

"What is this paper?"

"Oh, sorry," I say, sliding it back towards me. "I thought you dropped it—"

"Two hundred and twenty dollars, sweetie Pie."

I point at her. "Clever. Never heard that one before." Then I proceed to dig in my purse, pretending to look for money. But really, I'm replaying that conversation back in my head. They told me to write down the word 'money' on a piece of paper. That's all I needed.

Obviously, they left out a detail or two, because it's not working.

"I really did think you were speaking another language," Old-Lady Blue says.

"Huh?" I look up at her without interest.

"When you came in here. Pie Vita. I thought you were speaking Latin or something. *Livin' la Vida Loca.*" She does a little shoulder shimmy. "Isn't that what the kids say?"

"That's a Ricky Martin song and he's Latino, but I'm pretty sure the similarities end there... ooo! *Latin!*" Of course! That must be it. I need the Latin word. Pell was insisting that we were speaking Latin even though we weren't. Welp, it can't hurt to try. "One more sec," I tell her, then grab my phone and do a search for the Latin word for money. I snatch the pen from the counter, cross out 'money,' and write '*moneta.*'

I pass the paper back.

Old-Lady Blue smiles. And this time it's real. "Thank you very much for your business, Pie Vita. We really do appreciate it. You have a good day now."

Holy fucking shit. It worked!

"You too, ma'am." I smile back. And my smile is real as well.

I have literally been given a blank check.

I can spend as much as I want.

I can buy *anything* I want.

The first thing I do is take the Jeep to the mechanic place because one of my tires is looking suspiciously low. The mechanic finds a nail in the wall of my back tire and tells me I should buy all new ones since they are mostly bald.

I get that sinking feeling of panic when I hear this. It's the kind of panic only people who don't have money for a full set of tires can appreciate.

But then I rally. Because I don't need money. "Sure," I tell the mechanic. "I'll take four brand-new tires. The big ones. You know, the kind that makes Jeeps look cool." Then I spy shiny chrome rims stacked on the one side of the waiting room. "And a set of those too. Give me the best ones you've got."

The mechanic looks at me like I'm stupid. Because my Jeep is a piece of shit and this purchase is probably worth more than the actual vehicle.

But I don't care.

Not my money.

Not money at all.

I snicker as I slide my key off my ring and give him my phone number so he can text me when it's ready.

Then I hit the shops. And I hit them hard.

So I totally forget that I planned on canceling my date with Russ Roth until he pulls up beside me as I'm walking down the main street, my hands filled with bags of clothes, and candles, and makeup, and all kinds of fancy shit I could never afford to buy before today.

Russ's window slides down. "Pie Vita. If I didn't know better, I would think you're trying to stand me up." Then he winks at me.

And yeah. There is no freaking way in hell I'm breaking this date.

This man does things to me. I can't explain the way he affects me, but affect me he does.

Russ doesn't even wait for me to answer. He gets out of his car, opens the back passenger door, takes all my packages and puts them inside, and says, "Get in, Pie. We're going on a date."

And that's exactly what I do.

CHAPTER NINE – PELL

"I cannot believe she just left like that." I'm pacing back and forth in front of the sanctuary, enjoying the sun on my bare back, but other than that, pretty pissed off that Pie left here. Without me. With that sheriff.

"Relax, will you? She'll be back." Tomas is sitting on the front steps of Saint Mark's sunning himself with a piece of foil-covered cardboard under his chin like he hasn't got a care in the world. "Just enjoy the sun. And the view. It's nice out here. I've missed it."

"Grant has only been gone one day, idiot. You didn't even have time to miss it."

He drops his foiled cardboard and looks at me. "I go nuts without the sun. It's the only thing keeping me going." We stare at each other for a moment. Long enough that I have time to wonder if there's some hidden meaning in that statement. But then he props his cardboard back up and closes his eyes.

I resume my pacing. "She's been gone for hours."

"Calm down. How long does it take to get into town?"

"I don't know," I grumble. "Twenty minutes."

"Exactly. That's forty minutes there and back. Plus, she had to get groceries—"

"She didn't even take my list!"

"She's a grown-up, Pell. She knows how to grocery-shop."

"I'm angry. I'm going to make her go back. She won't get my favorites."

"You're starting to sound like a child. You'll live without your Boo Berry cereal for one week."

I stop pacing with the sound of an approaching vehicle. Tomas gets up and tosses his cardboard. "See. She's back."

"Four hours later. What the hell was she doing for four hours?"

The Jeep pulls in and Pie honks at us, grinning from ear to ear.

"Oooooh, shit," Tomas says.

And at the same time, I say, "Fucking hell. Did we forget to tell her—"

"We did," Tomas says.

I actually laugh. "Well, that smile won't last long."

Tomas chuckles as well. "We didn't do it on purpose. She left abruptly."

I point at him. "Right? This is all her fault."

Tomas shakes his head. "She's gonna be so pissed."

"Maybe we shouldn't tell her?"

Tomas shoots me a look. I can't tell if it says *That's a dick move* or *You're brilliant, Pell.*

I'm going with dick move. Because it is.

"Hey, you good-for-nothing monsters!" Pie is yelling for us. "Get over here and unload the car."

"You can't park there," Tomas calls. "The sheriff will come back. You have to park in the back."

"Oh." Pie stops. Her hands are filled with bags that are *not* groceries. Yep. She's gonna be so angry at us when she figures out the caveat with the money.

There's always a 'but' when free money is involved. Everyone knows that.

Except our girl Pie here.

"Well, how do I get around to the back?" Pie calls.

I let out a long breath. Some of it is relief that she came back. Not that she ultimately has a choice, but the slave caretaker has more freedom than I do, that's for sure. All rules have loopholes. "I'll show you."

I'm not gonna lie—walking through that little gate feels good. It's been a long while since I went anywhere with Grant. He and I had been on the outs for close to two decades. The fun of trolling town with him wore off last century.

"Give me your keys," I say, palm out.

Pie snorts. "You're not driving my Jeep."

"Oh, I am. Give me the keys."

"You can't just bully your way into driving my Jeep." She looks down at my hooves. "It's a manual transmission. You don't have feet."

"Obviously I have feet because I'm walking."

"You're not driving my Jeep with hooves and that's the end of it. Get in the passenger side or don't come. How hard can it be to find my way around the block?"

I narrow my eyes at her. "Maybe I should let you try."

She's about to take me up on that, but she must sense there's more to finding the back gate than simply driving around the block, because she says, "Fine. But if you crash—"

"Woman, I've been driving for over a hundred years. I'm not gonna crash your piece-of-shit Jeep." I snatch the keys from her hand and point to the passenger side. "Get in."

She gets in, sneering at me as she fastens her seatbelt. "Why do you have to be such an asshole?"

I shake my head at her as I back up and pull out from the sanctuary. Tomas waves to us from the other side of the gate. Sometimes I feel bad for him. He has literally never left this place since he got here. "Why? I'll tell you why. Because Saint Mark's is my domain. I am the master there. You work for me. And yet you continuously question my authority."

"You're completely overreacting. I've been here one day."

"And yet you were still able to do it continuously."

"What do you want from me? It's not my fault I'm here. I was tricked."

"You weren't tricked. You saw an ad, you answered the ad. That was all you."

"It was a trick. If I had known that the job came with a curse, I wouldn't have bothered, obviously."

"You put the ring on. So now you have to own it, *Pie*. We're in this curse together and the sooner you realize that, the better off we'll both be."

"I'm not a witch. I can't break your stupid curse."

"You say that, but yet… here you are. How does that make sense?"

"I don't know. But I'm not a witch. I don't know any spells, I can't concoct any potions. And the breakfast doesn't count. Tomas told me how to do it. And it was just reciting words and waving my hand over raw food. I will not be helpful in any other capacity. So what we should do is—"

"Oh, you've been thinking about this, have you?"

"It was a quiet drive back, so yes, I had time to think. And I was thinking... we should just find another witch to help you."

I almost snort. "Should we? Should we do that?"

"Yes. One who does have some actual magic."

"What about your bird?"

"What about her?"

"She's not magic?"

"She a psychosis. My personal hallucination. So no. She's not magic."

"Then why can I see her?"

"You don't see her. That's not my bird up in the ceiling."

"Just some random bird, huh?"

"Yep. Just another random bird."

I sigh. She's just... not very quick, is she? "OK. Fine. She's not magic, you're not magic, but you've stumbled into a magical person in town?"

"Exactly!" She sits up straight and claps her hands. "Oh, my God. You're not going to believe this—"

"You're right, I'm not."

"—but that sheriff? He's your guy! Not me!"

I frown. "My guy?"

"Your magical guy. That flyer was meant for him. I'm sure of it. He opened the gate, Pell. The walking gate. Didn't you see it?"

"Hm."

"Yeah, hm. And that's not all. He's like... an aphrodisiac or something. He got me all hot and bothered while we were together. I mean, I don't normally kiss on the first date, but after I went shopping, we met for lunch, and the next thing I know, he was dropping me off at the garage to pick up my Jeep, and we made out in the front seat of his cop car. I'm talking, his tongue was like…" She sighs.

"Was what? His tongue was like what?"

"Practically crawling down my throat."

"That's disgusting."

"Mmmm." She hums, like she's thinking this over. "Nah. It wasn't. At all. It was fucking hot. Hot. Like totally—"

"I get it. It was hot. I cannot believe you were making out with the fucking sheriff of Granite Springs."

"See, this is my point."

"I'm failing to see any points in this conversation."

"He *did* that to me. I am not the kind of girl who just makes out with a total stranger on the first date."

"Date?"

"Lunch was our first date. But not the *official* first date. We decided that's tomorrow. We're going to dinner."

I pull the Jeep over and yank on the parking brake to make a point. "You are not dating the sheriff."

"Oh, I absolutely am. Because he's the magic you need. See? I'm doing it for you."

"Listen, Pie. Hear me. OK? I need you to hear me. You are not dating the sheriff. He is not taking your place in the curse. And from now on, you need my permission to leave the sanctuary."

She snorts at me. "No."

"Yes."

"No. I'm not agreeing. And you can't stop me from leaving. What are you gonna do? Chain me up in a dungeon?"

I consider this.

"You wouldn't dare chain me up in a dungeon."

"Wouldn't I?"

"Pell. If I have to be stuck here washing your fucking hooves while I sweet-talk the sheriff into taking my place, then you will let me enjoy myself."

"Does that mean you're going to follow the rules?"

"Not if you make me ask you permission to leave."

I wave my hand in the air, then release the parking brake and pull back on to the road. "Forget about the sheriff for now."

"I'm going on that date tomorrow night."

"Whatever. I have other things to explain."

"Can't it wait? Oh, hey!" She points to the lake. "I recognize this. That's the lake behind my cottage."

"Yep. Here we are." I pull the Jeep into the gravel parking lot and turn the engine off. "Now listen, about the shopping today."

"I didn't know what you like, but I bought a lot of meat. Like, the best steaks ever. Porterhouses, and ribeyes, and T-bones. Mmm. I'm gonna cook them tonight. I'm a decent griller. I don't need Grant's kitchen spells to help me do that."

I let out a long breath. She's gonna be so pissed.

Tomas's head appears at the top of the gate. He's waving and yelling. "Did you tell her the bad news?"

"What bad news?" Pie asks.

"That's what I was trying to say. And part of the reason your hot sheriff won't be taking your place any time soon."

Her face contorts into a look of pure confusion. "What are you talking about?"

"You see… the money? It's not free."

"What do you mean it's not free? You literally told me it was all free. And I used paper to pay for everything."

"Right. *Buuut*… the universe keeps accounts."

"Accounts?" She goes pale white.

"It keeps track of what you spend. So I hope you didn't spend too much today."

We both look at the back seat of the Jeep. It's piled high with shopping bags. And most of them are not groceries. They are from the cute boutiques on Main Street. She bought clothes, and shoes, and shit from that overpriced candle shop.

"But…" She's at a loss for words. I like this side of her. "But my tires."

We get out and look at her tires. "They look new," I say.

She bites her lip.

"New rims too, Pie?"

"What was I supposed to do? Those tires were bald! I needed them. For you!" She points at me. "For your stupid errands!"

"Mmm-hmm. I needed rims?"

"OK, OK, OK," Tomas says from the back gate. "We can work this all out later. Let's get the food inside."

Pie is happy to defer this conversation until later, but later isn't going to help her. She spent a lot today. And perhaps I should've warned her that everything she spends she will need to pay back, but fuck it. Every other slave caretaker, when told about the free money, asked what the catch was.

Every one of them but her.

She is like a small child.

She needs rules, and clear expectations, and there need to be consequences when she fucks up. Like this. This is a fuck-up. One I don't care much about because it's not my debt. I won't need to pay it back. And anyway, I'll be the one benefiting from this debt in the long run.

But she is apt to make other mistakes. Mistakes that *will* affect me.

Like this date with the sheriff?

No. That's not happening for many reasons.

First and foremost, she is mine. Not his. So if any dating happens around here, it will benefit me. Second, if he really is part of the bloodline, then he needs to stay far away from Saint Mark's. I cannot have the sheriff of Granite Springs as a slave caretaker. Third, I don't like the look of him. He's far too... well, everything about him is far too much.

She will not be dating the sheriff.

"Hello?" Tomas calls. "Let's get this show on the road."

I nod down at Pie. Her mouth is still open in shock and I think she's calculating up the price of all her goodies in the back of her Jeep. "What if I return them?" She looks up at me, hopeful. "Will that help?"

"Nope. It's a done deal. Once you hand the paper over, the debt is yours. Might as well keep the stuff. You paid for it. Now, bring in all the groceries and put them in your pantry. We'll be taking breakfast in your cottage from now on."

"What? Why?" She looks annoyed.

"Because you're not going to use Grant's spells. That's why. I'm sure they'll wear off in a decade or two. But until then—"

"Decade or two?" Pie scoffs. "Oh, fuck that. I will not be here for another two *days*, let alone another two decades."

"That's amazing," I deadpan. "I look forward to your imminent curse-breaking."

"Dick," she mutters.

"Put the groceries away in your cottage and meet me up in the pleasure room in half an hour."

"What? What *pleasure* room?"

I walk past her, push past Tomas at the gate, and call over my shoulder, "You're about to find out how you work that debt off, sugar Pie."

She sputters and gasps and Tomas does his best to soothe her. But soon, they are out of earshot and her whining fades. And as I make my way up the hill, and the cathedral comes into full view, I realize I feel pretty good today. Maybe it was the drive? It's been a while since I drove. Or maybe it's the scenery. The lake property in back of the sanctuary walls is amazing in the autumn.

Or maybe… *maybe* it's the fact that I've got her now.

She can protest all she wants. And it's possible she was right about that in-between time before she put on the ring and she did have a way out that didn't involve me or my curse. Anything is possible. That's something I've come to accept. But it's too late now. Not only did she put the ring on, she also took on some debt.

That's what I want to check before she comes back up the hill.

I need to know how deep of a hole she's dug so I know how far I can push her.

This thought makes me snicker with satisfaction when I enter the lower grand hall of the cathedral. And I'm still chuckling under my breath as I climb the stairs.

Once at the top, I enter the apothecary, scan the bookshelves until I find the Book of Debt, and then set it down on the counter and open it up to the last page.

There she is. Pie Vita.

Oh, that's adorable. *Pie is life.*

I think the universe might be fucking with me. But I like this joke.

And—"Holy fucking cow." I whistle under my breath. "Ten thousand, two hundred and seventy-five dollars in debt. On day *one*." I laugh out those last words.

This is amazing.

Out of curiosity I flip back a page to find Grant's name, but that's all the page says. Just his name. All his debt has been cancelled.

Yeah. I don't know how he pulled that off, but moving on.

I close the book, tuck it under my arm, and leave the apothecary, heading back towards the stairs. But instead of going down, I duck into a hallway on my left and follow the dark marble floor tiles past dozens of doors, two staircases, and an atrium before finally arriving at my pleasure room.

It's really just a natural hot spring. But it's nice and steamy and even though the water smells a little bit like brimstone, it always feels good to get in. I haven't been in here in decades. Grant never accepted the idea that he had to work off his debt, so he just flat-out refused to cooperate. But I'd grown tired of the steam cave long before Grant.

But Pie is no Grant. She is no Stewart, or Jonas, or Michael, or Ignacious, or Antonius, or Luther, or Milo, or Odo. The point is, she is not *male*.

And this might be the only perk about Grant's betrayal.

Getting a horn and foot massage from one of those jerks? Yeah. That's not fun.

But getting a horn and foot massage from Pie? Or any of the other numerous ways in which she will be working off that debt?

Fuck, yeah. I'm up for that.

I set the book down on a stone table, making sure to leave it open to Pie's accounting page, and look at the pool of spring water bubbling up from the surface of the cave.

My face sports a wild grin as I strip off my pants and jump into the eternal hot spring. I sigh with pleasure and contentment as I settle onto a familiar smooth ledge, my arms stretched out along the edge of the rocks, my head tilted back with my eyes closed, my body instantly relaxed.

I'm going to enjoy this day.

In fact, this one day is going to make up for the two thousand shitty years that came before it.

I am roused from a blissful sleep by the girl's voice. "Well, I'm here. Now what?"

I reluctantly open my eyes and sit up straighter, then sleepily direct my gaze at her. "We need to go over the Book of Debt so you know where you stand and then go over the rules of money."

"Do you think you should've explained this to me before you sent me out on errands?"

"We didn't send you out. You left. Without asking permission or even telling me. This is unacceptable. And that date you think you're having with the sheriff? I will say it one more time and that's it. You will not be alone with that sheriff at any point in time."

"Says you."

I stand up on the ledge, then step out of the pool, trailing streams of water down my shaggy legs.

"Pants!" she whines, shielding her eyes like a child.

"I'm not putting on pants. Satyr chimera do not wear pants. I'm all wet and you are in no position to make demands."

"Oh, right." She snorts. "I put on your stupid ring so now you think you own me. So your concern for my wishes, that was what, just platitudes? To make me think you are some kind of reasonable monster? Hah. What a joke."

I glance over at Tomas. He's cringing. He mouths, *Put on the pants.*

I ignore him and walk over to the Book of Debt, making puddles under my hooves, then tap the page with her name on it and her list of purchases. "There it is. Every time you use the money, the book records it."

Still shielding her eyes, she walks over to the stone table and looks down at the book. "But how does it work? How did it know? I mean, it's freaking *itemized.*"

I glance down at her list. "Fucking hell, Pie. You paid two hundred dollars for underwear?"

When I look up at her, she's no longer shielding her eyes since my exceptionally large package is now mostly hidden by the table. "It's lingerie, not just underwear. And…" She sighs. "Well, if I had known you would be invading my shopping privacy, I'd have used my own money." She bites her lip. And I know this is a lie. The lip-biting thing is one of her tells.

"It's magic. The entire curse is all based on magic. It doesn't need explanation."

"Well, that's dumb. Everything is explainable. Including this stupid book. Someone is controlling it. Who is it?"

"Obviously, it is the gods."

"What gods?" She shrugs with her hands. "Like, fricking Jesus Christ has time to keep an annotated list of my shopping habits?"

"Not Jesus Christ. For fuck's sake, Pie. The old gods."

"Specifically?" she asks.

"Specifically, Saturn, for sure." I sigh. I don't like thinking about him. "Juno. Mars. Jupiter. The whole lot of them, I guess."

She squints her eyes. "Old Roman gods, then."

"What other gods are there?"

"You tell me. You seem to be on a first-name basis with them."

"I just did. And this is beside the point. The point is, you have a debt."

She flips the page back without even asking for permission, and this girl's brazenness is really getting on my nerves. "What's this?" She taps the page with Grant's name on it.

"That is Grant's page."

"It's empty."

"You're very observant."

"Why is it empty? Didn't he spend money?"

"Oh, hell yes, he did," Tomas says, coming up next to us. "And he never worked any of it off."

"Well, good. I won't either."

"He paid for it," I say.

"In years," Tomas adds.

"Did you see him leave here?"

She makes a face at this question. "Kind of. I was peeking out the window of the cottage."

"And what did he look like?" Tomas asks.

Pie sighs. "He was young on this side of the gate and very old on the other."

"There you go. That's what happens when you break free of the curse with debt left behind. It steals your life."

"OK. Hold on." She blinks up at me. "If I work off the debt, then when I leave here, no matter how long I stay, I will be young still?"

"Correct," I say.

"Hmm."

"Still wanna be difficult?"

"I'm thinking. I'm considering my options."

"You don't have many," Tomas rightly points out. "You either work the debt off by taking care of Pell here, or you don't and leave this place the way Grant did."

"But if you stay here longer than your natural lifetime, you will just die the moment you take the ring off and walk through the gates if you still have debt."

"And," Tomas adds, "it's just better to keep up with it, Pie. Don't be like Grant. By the time he wanted to clear his debt, it was way too late. He would've had to give Pell here blowjobs twenty-four seven for ten years to clear that debt."

"What?" She looks at me, then down, then hurriedly looks back up and shields her eyes. "Blowjobs?"

I shoot Tomas a would-you-please-shut-the-fuck-up-now look and he quickly corrects himself. "I'm just messing with you," Tomas says.

Pie looks around, frowning, not really seeing the steam cave. Her wandering gaze is more of a demarcation, a clear line drawn in the air that separates her old life and her new one into two very different camps.

Finally, she turns back to me. "Hopefully the blowjob thing really was a joke. Because I'm not doing that. So what do you want me to do?"

"Look." I flip the pages in the book until I get to the beginning. "Here are all the tasks you can complete to make me happy. Each one comes with a payment. When you earn the payment, you erase part of your debt."

She turns the book towards her and starts to read.

I expect her to comment. I expect her to stomp her feet, and throw a tantrum, and walk out insisting that she will never do these things.

But she stays quiet.

She might even... wilt a little.

"Pie?" Tomas asks. "Are you OK?"

She sucks in a deep breath and on the exhale she says, "Do I look OK?" She points her gaze at him now. "I didn't ask for this. I just wanted a job, and a home, and a life that didn't involve begging to sleep on Jacqueline's couch and taking care of her kids in

Toledo. I have never asked for much. And fine, I went a little overboard in town today." She looks at me now. "But I did need the tires. And OK, I didn't need the lingerie, but I've never owned stuff like that. I've never had the means to walk into a grocery store and buy steaks. And I did get them for you. I didn't know what you eat."

She's almost pleading with me. Like if she could just win me over, I might delete her curse and her debt. But none of this is up to me.

"I didn't know. So I guessed…" She trails off and never picks up her train of thought.

Tomas and I stare at each other with what-do-we-do-now looks. He shrugs. "I do like steaks," I offer. Because I haven't seen this side to her yet and it's making me uncomfortable. An hour ago, she was a fierce, determined fighter and now she's… vulnerable.

"Look," Tomas says, "we don't need to do any of this today, right, Pell?"

I shrug. "Whatever. It's not like we're on a deadline."

"Great. So why don't you go take a bath or something, Pie? Change out of that outfit. Which is completely adorable, by the way. But you've been wearing it for days now."

At the mention of her clothes, Pie looks down at herself and frowns even deeper.

"And you have new clothes now," I add. "So. That's… nice."

She doesn't even look up at me. Just continues staring down at herself. "There's no hot water in the cottage. I can't take a bath."

"There is so," Tomas says. "Come on." He takes her hand. "I'll show you how it works."

And then he leads her out of the steam cave.

They leave me like that.

Like they are together and I am no one.

Just like always.

But I follow them. At least until I get to the cemetery.

Then I veer off and head back to my tomb where I belong.

CHAPTER TEN – PIE

It was stupid of me, really. To think that I might fall into some good luck. That's just not how my life works. I never get anything good. Everything that comes my way is terrible. Sometimes, it's borderline evil.

Like this. Being cursed with a monster. This is what I would consider borderline evil.

I'm sitting on the bed listening to Tomas mess with some water heater thing downstairs. You have to feed it wood. And he says it takes a while to get enough hot water for a bath, but it's worth it.

So he tells me.

I'm not arguing. I do need a bath. I didn't even notice how bad I smell and how my cute, completely-appropriate-for-Halloween schoolgirl costume now looks more like a three-day-bender, I-have-no-other-clothes outfit.

Tomas comes up the steps and walks into the room smiling. Then he frowns. "I thought you were gonna put your new clothes away?"

We both look at the piles of bags filled with new clothes. Then back at each other. I sigh and shrug. "It's not as fun now that I know it was a high price to pay. I would be better off getting a waitressing job in town to pay for what we need instead of using the free money."

"Can you do that?"

I perk up a little because he didn't immediately tell me it's against the rules. "I don't know. Can't I? I mean… if I came home every night it wouldn't be breaking the rules, right? And then I wouldn't have to go into debt and I could pay for all our food and stuff."

Tomas sits down next to me. He's been really nice to me today. "I don't think Pell would like that though."

"No," I say, feeling utterly defeated. "I suppose he wouldn't."

"But you could ask him. No one has ever come up with that idea before. It's a good one. It saves you, at least."

"But not him, right? I'm here to please him, and work for him, and break his curse."

"It's your curse too."

"Yeah." I don't need reminding.

"Come on." He stands up. "I'll help you put your new stuff away. Then you can take a bath and settle in, and I'll even make dinner tonight."

"Fuck. I forgot about dinner."

"I said I'd make it. You just relax."

I look up at him and man, this guy just gets better-looking by the second. He's still got the same roaring hot body. But he's a good guy too. And that's not usually how the hot ones come. "Thanks, Tomas. I really mean it. I don't know what I'd do if you weren't here to help me today."

"Believe it or not, Pell is a pretty good guy."

"Guy?" I make a face. "He's got horns, Tomas. And hooves. He's half-goat or something."

"He's actually half-minotaur." Then he pauses, like he wants to say something. But the pause goes on too long and even though he keeps talking, I just know that what comes out next wasn't what he was thinking about. "My point is, even if I wasn't here, you'd be OK. He's not *that* bad."

I shoot Tomas a look. "Did you see the list in that book?" He winces. "I'm not an idiot. I know what 'fellatio' means."

"No slave caretaker has ever—and I do mean *ever*—given Pell a fucking blowjob to pay a debt."

My eyebrows shoot up. "Did they do it to not pay a debt?"

"The point is, he's not gonna make you do any of it. Except for the foot wash and the horn polishing. He does like that shit. Especially the horns. So if you need to pay a debt off, you can't go wrong with the feet and the horns."

"Hoof washing." I sigh.

"It pays well. It's a win-win."

"Whatever. I don't want to think about any of it right now. I feel so... worthless. Like my life has no value at all. I'm just some *thing* to be used and discarded."

"That's not even true. You're worth a lot."

"What do you mean? The magic book is trying to steal everything from me. I didn't agree to anything, I'm not getting paid to do this job, and nothing is free. Not even room and board like the flyer promised."

"That's not really true. Your parents are getting paid."

I blink at him. Then snarl, "*What?*"

"Yeah. I mean, not directly. It's just… good luck. They'll wake up tomorrow and something good will come their way. Something fabulous. They win the lottery, they get left money in a will by some long-lost relative, their house is suddenly paid off."

I put up a hand. "Hold the fuck on. My *mother* is getting paid? Like… I was literally sold into slavery?"

"It's luck—"

"Fuck your luck! The woman who abandoned me with child protective services when I was nine because I refused to say that my Pia was imaginary—that bitch is gonna get *paid* with good-luck tokens while I'm stuck here being a monster's *slave?*"

"Um. Wow. I'm sorry she did that shit to you."

"And that reminds me. Where *is* Pia? This is not funny anymore." I feel like I'm on the verge of tears. "I want my friend back."

Tomas puts his hand on my shoulder. "Pie. Please, just don't think about any of it right now. We'll all work it out tomorrow. Maybe getting a job is a good idea. I'll tell Pell that it is, OK?"

I sniffle. "You will?"

He nods. "Just… don't cry. And relax a little. It's gonna work out, I promise."

He doesn't wait for me to answer, just gets up and starts pulling my things out of bags. I watch him. Let him put it all away anywhere he wants. And he does all that in silence.

Finally, he proclaims the tub ready for me and then excuses himself to go make dinner and check on Pell.

The hot water does feel wonderful and when I sink all the way up to my shoulders, I let out a long breath of relief. Nothing is better. I'm not sure anything will ever be better again. But… Tomas was right. The bath was a good idea. It helps.

There are some bottles of stuff. Shampoo, I guess. And some bars of soap. And when I wash my hair with it, it's surprisingly soft afterward. Maybe it's magic shampoo? That would be a small perk.

I soak in the tub for a long time, just thinking about my new life. How none of this would've happened if I hadn't stopped at that gas station to pee and wash my face.

I would still have Pia. I would be on my way to Toledo. I would still be me. And I would be free.

I don't even know how to make sense of this new life.

Tomas is nice. I like him a lot. And he's fun to look at. His wild, dark hair falls just to his shoulders, and it's thick. His eyes are dark too, like maybe he's Italian. If so, that makes sense because I'm pretty sure they come from ancient Rome. I wonder what it was like back then? I try to imagine living though all those two thousand years. All the changes. All the new inventions. Especially in the last century. Rovers on Mars, and self-driving cars, and cell phones.

I do have to admit, Pell could drive the Jeep. He didn't lean on the clutch or stall out or anything. He's been driving cars for a hundred years. That's what he said.

He's actually not that scary now that I've known him for two days. It's rather easy to unsee his monster parts. Except that dick of his. Holy hell. It's huge. And he has no shame about it dangling around all over the place. But he did put on pants for a few hours for my benefit.

I smile about that part. I was kinda bossy earlier. Before I realized I truly am a slave.

He's got nice eyes. They're yellow, and totally unnatural. But that just makes them interesting. And his hooves are really pretty. Those black and cream striations are unique.

And the horns. God, the horns. They aren't like a ram's, that's for sure. They're not circular that way. They are long, and don't grow upward, but downward and to the back. They have a little corkscrew twist in them too.

Now, that cemetery? I don't know what to make of that. I should probably just stay away from it, like Pell said. The cathedral though. Now that place is going to be a trip to figure out. I haven't been up those other staircases yet. It could be cool to explore.

The apothecary, on the other hand, won't be fun at all. There were so many jars. So many books. Too many potions and spells to think about. I'm never going to be able to break this curse, that's for sure.

The cathedral kitchen was massive. And when Tomas showed me Grant's magic recipe book and how to make the food prepare itself—well, that might've been the best part of my day.

I really did feel like I was doing magic, even if none of those spells were mine.

But Pell said no more. Now I have to prepare food here.

Then I remember Sheriff Russ Roth and sink a little further down into the tub. Now he was nice. He was the absolute best part of my day. And I am going on that date tomorrow night. Pell is mistaken if he thinks he can control my social life. If I have to be stuck here in this curse with him, the least he can do is let me have a little fun.

And I'm going to insist on that job.

There was a 'help wanted' sign in the Honey Bean window. I bet the sheriff could even put in a good word for me and then I'd be a shoo-in.

I could make it work. That's the point of all this thinking.

If I have a plan, I can make it work.

Eventually I have to get out and face my new world again. I do this reluctantly, not even sure if I should go downstairs. I can hear Tomas in the kitchen and if it wasn't for the smell of grilling steaks, I might skip dinner. But it's been a long day, and I was too consumed with the hot sheriff and my sudden influx of fake money to eat much at lunch, so I'm actually starving.

I put on a pair of soft sweatpants I got from the lingerie store, and a t-shirt, and I suddenly feel a thousand times better than I did an hour ago.

That schoolgirl costume needs to be burned. Three days I was wearing that stuff.

Crazy. Because I had actually forgotten I was wearing a costume.

Anyway, when I go downstairs Tomas is just buttering some of the fresh rolls I bought from the bakery today.

"This all smells delicious," I say, walking over to the table and taking in the spread. There's salad, and wine—I hit that liquor store pretty hard—and the steaks. "You're a great cook, Tomas. Maybe you should be in charge of feeding the beast? Speaking of him, where is Pell?"

"Sit," Tomas says, placing a roll on my plate. "He's in his tomb, I think. I went looking for him, but..." Tomas shrugs. "He's not around, so I'm assuming he has retired."

"Can't you go knock on the door?"

"The tombs don't have doors."

"Of course they do. They are creepy black holes that have a menacing vibe to them, but they all have doors."

Tomas just stares at me for a moment. "You can see the tomb doors?"

"Of course, can't you?"

"Hmm." He shakes his head. "No. I've never been in one. But the way Pell talks about his, it's like another world in there."

"What do you mean?"

"Like... you know when you're outside the cathedral and it's just a simple old building? But when you go inside and see all those staircases and high ceilings, it's huge, right?"

"Yeah. I've noticed that."

"I think that's how the tombs are. Really small on the outside, but inside they are like a whole other world."

"Literally another world?"

"You'd have to ask Pell. Before you came, he and I weren't exactly friends."

"No? He seems to like you."

"I guess. But really, losing Grant was a shock to us. I mean, we've always known it could happen. It just almost never does. So when you showed up, it was unexpected. We're still adjusting."

"Am I going to get punished with some kind of debt because he's not eating tonight? I don't understand how his wellbeing is my concern."

"You don't get punished. He's allowed to make his own decisions."

"Must be nice," I mumble.

"I will talk to him about the job, though. I promise. I bet he gives in. He doesn't like being here either. But he's been stuck in this curse for so long now, he has no clue what it would even be like to walk the earth as a free man anymore."

"He was human once?"

"Human? Who said anything about human?"

"You said 'a free man.' So I just assumed…"

Tomas shakes his head. "No. Well, yes. He's a man, for sure. We can all see his package dangling all over the place." I chuckle. Can't help it. "But no. He was made this way."

"How long have you been here, Tomas? And why are you cursed?"

"I don't even remember a life before here."

"What?"

Tomas lets out a long, tired sigh. "Yeah. I don't remember. I've just… always been here, I think. Well, not here specifically. We were in the Old World for thousands of years before they relocated the sanctuary to Pennsylvania in the late sixteen hundreds."

"Were you a priest? Or some kind of monk?"

He considers this for a moment, wearing a look of 'doubtful,' but says, "Maybe."

"Hmm. And you're not interested in finding out more of your story?"

"Where would I look?"

"There are so many books in that room. Maybe in there?"

"That's the apothecary. Those are spells, and potions, and dire warnings."

I try to laugh off the 'dire warnings' part, but I'm not sure I entirely succeed. So I just change the subject. "Doesn't this place have a library?"

"Somewhere, I'm sure. Up in those moving hallways."

"They move?"

"You could literally get lost here at Saint Mark's."

"Like, never find your way back lost?"

"Back where? You won't leave, not really. But those rooms up there, they're... how do I explain this? They're like memories."

"I don't get it. Memories?"

"Yeah. Like... days gone by. Somewhere up there are rooms that contain everything that's happened over the many thousands of years it's existed. This place is always growing. You'll see. Eventually there will be a room up there for this day. I don't know what the lag time is, so don't go looking for it or anything. But one day, this will be history." Tomas pans his hands wide at my new tiny cottage and then sighs. Like he's tired.

"Well, that's kind of amazing. So if you wanted to figure out your past, you could theoretically find the room from your first day here, and what? Go relive it?"

He shrugs. "Maybe. I don't know. Never tried."

"We should try, Tomas. I'll help you. This memory stuff might be the best thing about this place."

He doesn't agree or disagree, so I know he's not really interested. This is my cue to drop it and change the subject. The meal is over now and he'll be leaving. Then it will just be me in here and I'm not used to that. I'm used to always having my friend on my shoulder. I miss Pia terribly. And I want her here with me so bad, it makes my heart hurt.

I need to figure out what's happened to her. But until then, I'll have to settle for Tomas's company.

And as soon as I think that thought, he stands up and wipes his mouth with his napkin. A clear signal he's ready to leave.

"You know what would help?" Tomas says.

"With what?"

"Making Pell agree to the job in Granite Springs."

"Should I even ask?"

Tomas grins. "Hey, I'm not saying he's *not* an asshole. He is. But I was serious about the debt payoffs. He's not gonna make you do anything you don't agree to. He gives no fucks if you have debt, Pie."

"That's not helpful. What were you gonna say?"

"Come up with a spell."

I crinkle my face up at this. "I'm not a witch."

"You don't need to be a witch. It's not magic. Not really. It's just the laws of the universe, Pie. Learn to live within them. Learn how to ask for favors. That's all magic is. And you can do that. Hell, maybe even I could do that. And anyway, Grant left a shitload of spells, and potions, and instructions in that apothecary. Just like all the caretakers before him. There are literally thousands of years of knowledge in that room. Use it. Come up with a spell, or a potion, or a glamour that will make Pell happy. That will tell him that you're on his side and you will work hard to break his curse. That's all he wants. Just give him what he wants and he'll do the same for you."

"I hope he appreciates you. Because you're a good friend, Tomas."

He smiles at me. "Thanks." Then he looks over his shoulder. "I'm gonna go back to the cathedral."

"Wait, where do you stay up there? How do I find you if you're not around?"

"I'll find you." He winks at me. "Don't worry about that."

The next morning, I wake early. Or, I should say, I get up early. I'm not sure I actually slept. The first night here everything was overwhelming. I was exhausted and confused and sleep was necessary. But last night all this new stuff was swirling around in my head like a freaking whirlwind.

It's not even light out yet when I leave the cottage. I don't know what time breakfast is served and Tomas didn't show up to direct me—obviously, Pell didn't either. So I decide I'm going up to the cathedral to check out the apothecary myself.

Tomas's suggestion makes a lot of sense. Everything in this world runs on give and take so if I want Pell to be reasonable and give me something I want, I need to do that in return.

And how hard could it be, really? To mix up a potion? I mean, if there really are thousands of years of spells, and potions, then that's like having a recipe book. I'm not a great cook, but I can follow direction and that's mostly what cooking is. I might not be a master chef but I can scramble eggs.

Is spellcasting much different?

If I can find something to make Pell's life easier, he will be happy. Hell, this might even strike some debt off my page in the book.

I have nothing to lose and everything to gain by trying.

I hurry up the hill in the approaching dawn and do my best not to look at the tombs on either side of the path. But it's pretty hard not to notice those gaping black doorways. And inside some of them, I see movement. Like there really are monsters inside. I shudder and walk faster until I'm over the hill and the cathedral is looming before me.

I pause briefly in the lower great hall and look up the staircases on either side of the main one. I wonder what's lurking up there. Ghosts? Other monsters? Or just bits and pieces of time tucked away in rooms?

That poem above the doors comes back to me. Not the part about the horns and the hooves, but the part about time. *A tick of time, a last mistake. Keep them safe behind the gate.*

But I don't really know what it means. The gate— that's probably the gate out front. Or the gate in back. Or hell, who knows? Maybe there are dozens of gates to this place?

Again, I shudder, then go up the central staircase and enter the apothecary room and let out a long breath. There's a lot to unpack in here. And then I remember that it's all written in Latin, so I just slump down onto the couch and think.

How does this Latin thing work?

There's something there that I'm missing. Because Pell thinks we're all speaking Latin when we're not. Is it possible that there is a spell that allows him to understand foreign languages?

It makes sense to me. And it's a starting point. So I get up and start looking at the spines of the books for clues. There are too many for this plan to be practical, but the book Pell was showing me yesterday is still open on the stone counter, so I start there. These are Grant's notes. Pell and Tomas make him out to be, if not brilliant, at the very least competent, in the realm of spellworking.

I take it back over to the couch, sit down, and start paging through the book. I'm well into the middle of the thing before I find one I can read.

And boom. It's exactly what I was looking for.

Pia's words inside the cottage come back to me in this moment. *This is weird.*

She was right back then and it still holds true now. Because this spell is called *How to Read the Books in the Apothecary.*

I page ahead, looking for more spells I can understand, but the rest of the book is all in other languages, most of them not anything I recognize as letters—unusual symbols, and dots, and lines. Some of it even looks like music notes. But not exactly music notes.

And every single page in every other book I take off the shelves is written in another language.

One spell. That's what I have to work with.

Good thing it's exactly the spell I need.

I find an apron, tie my hair back, crack my knuckles, and get started.

Magic, here I come.

CHAPTER ELEVEN – PELL

I don't go to dinner and I don't show up for breakfast. So it's nearly lunchtime when I stroll out of my tomb and start making my way up the hill towards the cathedral.

I'm just... what is the best word for how I'm feeling?

Bitter? Angry? Jealous?

I'm gonna go with bitter. Because I am not jealous. That town sheriff is no one. Not a threat. Not in the least. And besides, the girl is mine. I have a hold of her entire life. The sheriff hasn't got a chance and neither does Tomas. Pie might like Tomas better than me, but he's unavailable. And eventually, Tomas won't be able to hide what he really is and she will see I truly am the only one in her life who matters.

So definitely not jealous.

And not angry, either. Nope. Anger is reserved for situations I cannot control. We are definitely not in anger territory yet, so I'm going to go with bitter.

I enter the lower great hall and start walking up the stairs, taking my time because this realm is mine. I rule this place. I am the fucking king.

And yet... they left me in the steam cave like I was no one. Like I didn't matter. Like it was them against me.

All right. Maybe I'm a little angry.

I blow it off.

And then, up in the ceiling, the little bird flutters and flaps. I pause on the stairs, looking up. What did she call that thing? "Pia," I say out loud. Like Pie, with an a.

I whistle to it.

It whistles back, mimicking me.

Hmm. I whistle again, and it reciprocates.

"Well"—I sigh, looking up at it—"I don't know what to make of you, little bird. But you're not my problem." So I continue up the steps and when I get to the top, I'm fully intending on making my way to the kitchen to fix my own damn meal when I catch the scent of something burning in the apothecary.

"Now what?" I stomp over there, throw the door open, and—"Holy fuck. What the hell is all this?"

I look around for Pie—because clearly this is her doing—and then spot her feet peeking out from behind a stone counter. "Shit." I rush over, bend down, and cradle her head in my arm. "Pie?" I growl in her ear. "Can you hear me?"

She moans, then she's slapping at me as she tries to sit up. "Stop it! Get away. Let me go."

I back off and stand up. "What the hell are you doing on the floor? And what's that awful smell?"

She breathes deeply and blinks several times before looking up at me. "Pell! Pants! How many times do I have to tell you to put on some fucking pants?"

"Satyr chimera don't wear pants. I'm never going to wear pants again. Get over it. And you didn't answer my question. What in the name of the gods are you doing in here?"

"I'm making potions so I can read the books." She struggles to get to her feet, shielding her eyes from my lower body, and while I have an overwhelming urge to help her, I refrain because clearly she doesn't want or need it.

Besides, I wouldn't want to scar her fragile sensibilities with my enormous package. So I turn away and scan the room. "Tomas! Where the hell is Tomas?"

"He hasn't shown up yet and I don't know where to find him."

When I turn back, she's wiping her hands on her apron. "Why were you on the floor?"

She haphazardly paws at her hair. It's a mess and kinda hanging in her face. "I think I passed out after I tried the last potion."

"You what? Wait. You're *trying* the potions…" I sigh and let the words trail off. "How stupid are you?"

"Shut up. And go away if you're just gonna be a dick. I'm busy here." She picks up a beaker, eyes the level of purple liquid inside, adds a pinch of something, pours it into a test tube, and then starts to put it up to her lips, like she's going to drink that shit.

I swat at her hand and the test tube goes flying across the room, shattering on the stone wall.

Pie looks at the wall, then the smashed bits of her potion, then directs her glare to me. "What the hell is your problem? Do you have any idea how long it took me to brew that?"

I almost have no words for this girl. "My problem? You're the dumbass drinking random potions!"

"They're not random. They came right out of Grant's book." She taps his notebook to make her point. "And I'm close. I can read the Greek and Babylonian books. Latin can't be far behind."

"Nothing you just said made a bit of sense."

"I'm cooking up a spell so I can read Latin."

I look down at the book, read the spell she's pointing to, and laugh.

"Laugh all you want, monster. I'm practically there. I'm trying to conjure up a spell that will make you happy so when I ask you for permission to get a job in town so I won't go into debt, you will say yes. But you seem to be dead set on blowing up my world at every turn. I spent all morning coming up with that potion to read the books and you just destroyed most of it! Every time I start to figure something out, you're there to kill my buzz!"

"First," I say, holding up a clawed finger, "thank you for thinking of me."

She inhales though her nose and forces out, "You're welcome."

"Second"—I raise another clawed finger—"you will not be getting a job. That's out of the question."

"Why not?" She's working herself up now. "That's totally not fair! You want me in debt to you so when I finally do leave here, I'll have lost my youth!"

"Third"—I add to the list—"I'm not blowing up your world, Pie. You're fighting it. And the harder you fight, the worse it will get. Just… accept it. You're here. Possibly forever."

"No. No!" She screams it. "I'm going to break that curse. You'll see. This magic? It's not magic. It's a fucking recipe. All I have to do is follow the recipes and it's all gonna work out. And it's not going to take forever. A few weeks, that's it. And I need to work off my debt so that when I leave here, I'm not some over-the-hill thirty-year old! And the only way to do that is to get a job so I can pay for the stuff we need with real money instead of magic money! And if you were any kind of compassionate *human being*, you'd understand this and want the best for me because what's best for me is best for *you*!"

I am actually a little bit touched at this. "You want a job to support us?"

"Exactly!"

I sigh. "It's not gonna take weeks, Pie. It's going to take decades."

"No." She shakes her head furiously. "No. I refuse to allow that to happen. I'm smart. Your boy, Grant, he was smart too. And he took excellent notes. I think he was hiding things from you."

I frown. "What things?"

"I think he had the answer. I found these books written in Babylonian and Greek. And they are all about how to break your curse." She pauses. "I think he was writing things down in weird languages so he could hide things from you."

I get up and walk over to the stone counter. "Let me see that." And sure as shit, that little fucker *was* hiding things from me. "What's it say?"

"Oh, you can't read it?" She's mocking me. "I thought you were the king here. The ruler, the—"

"What does it *say*?"

Her whole face brightens. In fact, she smiles at me. And it's a nice smile too. "Do you want the potion?"

"What potion?"

"The one I just invented to understand Babylonian, and Greek?" She nods her head at me. "It worked."

I look at her alchemy bench. It's a fucking mess of test tubes, and beakers, and open flames. There's jars and jars of herbs, and crystals, and powders. Some of this shit is glowing. Which I'm not sure about because from my experience, glowing potions are very powerful. And she's on day one of her self-paced Let's Do Magic course, so that's probably not a good thing.

"I dunno."

"Is the great big bull-god scared?"

"Yeah. You have no idea what you're doing."

"And yet I understand Babylonian, and Greek. And you can't even read this book." She taps the book to illustrate her point.

"Fine. Which of these many, many disgusting concoctions is it?"

"This one." She picks up a test tube of glowing purple goop and thrusts it at me. "Drink it."

"If this kills me—"

"If this kills you, you should thank me. Since you're immortal. That means your curse would be broken."

Well. She's got a point there. I put the test tube up to my lips, almost pass out from the horrible smell, then down it in one gulp. It hits my stomach with a burn.

"The burn passes," Pie says hurriedly. And she puts her hand on my arm, either faking compassion or really meaning it.

Her touch is warm too. And something about it does make me feel better. Soon, the burn is gone and in its place is a tingling feeling in my hands. Then a buzzing in my head.

"Did you get to the buzzing yet?" she asks. I nod. "Good. You're almost there. Now, while we're waiting for it to work, let's talk about this job."

"No." I put up a hand. "Not now."

"Yes. I need a job. Just a part-time one. The Honey Bean is looking for a waitress. I need that, Pell. And I will use all my money to buy what we need and then I won't have to go into debt."

"You don't get it. That won't work. The harder you fight the curse, the more it works against you. The less magic money you use, the more the curse will force you to use it. Bad things will happen. And that will force you to work harder to…" I pause, not really wanting to say the last bit.

"Harder to what?" she presses.

"Please me. The harder you'll have to work to please me with the debt book stuff."

She points a finger in my face. "I will not be blowing you. Just… FYI."

I cannot hide my laugh. "Good to know. And for the record, Pie, you're not my type."

She lifts her chin up in indignation like I just insulted her. "I'm not your *type*?"

"Nope."

"What kind of type do you like? Bull girls?"

"I'm not a bull."

"A satyr chimera girl?"

"There are no female satyr chimeras. We're all men."

"Then what is your type?" And now she's annoyed.

I shrug. "I've always been partial to the nymphs."

"Nymphs." She crinkles her nose like the thought of nymphs is distasteful. "Water fairies?"

"Not fairies. *Nymphs*. You know. Willowy girls with evil intentions lurking in the forest."

She laughs. A real laugh. "You like *bad* girls?"

"I do."

"I'm not *bad* enough for you?"

"Not even close."

"Hmmph." She's trying hard not to show it, but she's definitely taking exception to my preferences. Either that, or she fancies herself a bad girl and I just... what? Insulted her? Challenged her?

I hope it's the second one. Because even though she's completely ridiculous, Pie is... fun. And I could be on board with her being bad with me.

"Oh, for fuck's sake. Can you just put on an apron or something?" She's looking down at my... package. Which is growing due to the little bad-girl fantasy currently running through my head. "You're so gross. Why do you insist on flaunting your penis?"

I actually guffaw.

She's shielding her eyes with her hand as she walks around to the other side of her alchemy bench. Then she picks up an apron and throws it at me. "Put that on or get out."

I catch the apron, but don't put it on. "You've heard me say it a few times now, Pie. And you didn't ask, so maybe assuming that you're ignorant is being presumptuous, but... do you have any idea what a satyr actually *is*?"

"What do you mean?" She's doing her valiant best to not look down at my cock right now.

"You need to do some research. And if you still insist that I put on pants after you're done, I will no longer be assuming you're ignorant. I'll just classify you as stupid."

Her mouth falls open and I take a moment to notice that she has nice lips. She closes her mouth, perhaps noticing that I'm staring at it. And when my eyes dart up to meet hers, her little pink tongue slips out to wet her lower lip.

Fuck. She's really not my type. Way too cute. But… she's got an innocent kind of sexiness to her.

"For real," I say. Because our silence has suddenly become awkward and Tomas isn't here to break it up, so I guess it's on me. "Just look us up. And then you'll understand. Because we're just… horny. At all times. And we have perpetual erections. This?" I point down at my dick. "This is nothing. Just a little chubby in my world."

"Good God, you are *gross*."

"There's no way to stop it, so get over it, Pie. Because it's a part of me and I'm not going to hide it to please you."

Maybe it's something in my tone, or maybe she just has the good sense to recognize me being honest, because she looks properly embarrassed. "Sorry," she breathes. "I didn't mean it that way. It's just…" She sighs. "Never mind. I see your point."

"And I see yours as well." I put the apron on. "Things are much better around here when you don't fight it, Pie. I'm not an animal. I'm not human either, but I'm not an animal."

She blushes. "I didn't—"

"I know you didn't. You just don't know any better."

She has no idea what to say to that, so I take over and pull the book closer to me. "Oh, hey. It really did work. I can read it."

"Really?" Pie is delighted.

I decide I prefer her delighted. She's not *bad*. And she's not a bitch, so that's nice. In fact, she's got an aura of goodness around her. Not a bad girl. Not at all.

OK. Enough about Pie. Back to the issue at hand. I can read the book and now it is clear that Grant *was* hiding things from me. Why put his notes in a language I can't read?

"Here's the part that bothers me about this," I say. "He didn't *need* to hide this shit. I never looked." When I glance up at Pie, she's paying attention, her face serious again. "I never looked at any of it. I don't do magic."

"Wait." She puts up a hand. "But you do. You froze me. You slammed the door closed with your hand."

"I have abilities. But I don't do alchemy. The powers I have, they're just innate. You, for instance, couldn't learn how to do what I do the way you can learn alchemy. I was created with these powers. They can't be taken, destroyed, or borrowed. So I never bothered with the apothecary. Before you came, I literally hadn't been in here in…" I pause to think. "Decades. At least. I don't even remember the last time I came in here. So why would he go to so much trouble to hide this stuff from me?"

"I don't know, Pell."

"We'll have to keep that in mind and think on it. There's something there, I'm just not sure what yet."

She nods. Breathes deeply. "OK. So… the job?"

"Fine. You can get a job."

"I can?"

"Yes. I'm not trying to trap you. And regardless of what you think, I had nothing to do with you coming here. I don't know anything about how the caretakers are chosen other than it seems to follow a bloodline. I don't know how you were recruited or—"

"It was a flyer in a gas station. Advertising for a caretaker job at the sanctuary."

"Ah. It was magic. Bait. Charmed too. If you were able to see the flyer, you were of the bloodline." I shrug. "For what it's worth, I'm sorry you got stuck here with me. I get it. You want to live your life. You didn't expect it to be stolen from you."

"Yeah."

"So you can have the job. But the date—"

"I have to go on the date, Pell! I already said yes. If I don't show up, he'll come out here. And if he can open the walking gate, what's to stop him from coming through the front door?"

The thought of that sheriff being able to enter my sanctuary without an invitation is disturbing to say the least. I don't have a choice. "Fine. One date. But you need to end his curiosity with you and the sanctuary. It's dangerous for people to know about us. You get that, right?"

She nods at me. "I do. And I will. I'll cut it off. He's a little bit weird anyway."

I narrow my eyes at this. "Weird how?"

"I dunno. He's like an aphrodisiac or something. Whenever I've got his attention, or he's close to me, I'm…" She hesitates. And this pause goes on long enough for me to get impatient.

"You're *what*?"

"I don't really know how to explain it. I'm just… giddy around him. Or something. Stupid. Lovestruck."

"That's not possible."

"What's not possible?"

"Lovestruck? Are you sure?"

She nods. "I swear, I'm really not the kind of girl who kisses a man I just met a few hours ago. He makes me feel weird."

I let out a long, tired breath. Because what the hell? Why is everything suddenly so different around here?

"Hello?" Pie says. "Are you going to explain your frustration?"

"He's an eros. He has to be. That's a side effect of being around them."

"A what now?"

"A cupid."

"A fat baby with a bow and arrow?" She laughs.

I shoot her a look.

"What?" This look makes her nervous.

"You know what an eros is. You're one of them."

She laughs. Loud. "I am not one of them."

"You are, Pie. That's the only way you get inside the gates. You have to be an eros. You have to be from that bloodline. It's mandatory. That's literally where this curse starts."

She furrows her brow and shakes her head. "No. I would know this, right? Wouldn't I?"

"You should, but…" I shrug. "The sheriff doesn't seem to know either. So I dunno what's going on. I'm not in charge of any of this. I have one power and one power only."

"What power? Slamming doors? Freezing people?"

I hesitate. And she *must* be an eros. She must be using her charms on me right now. Because this hesitation is the beginning of an admission. I quickly come to my senses and say, "Yeah. Those are my powers."

"That's two."

"What?"

"You said one power. Then you admitted to two powers. So which is it?"

"Slamming doors isn't really a power, Pie. The freezing people. That's my one power."

"OK. So anyway. I'm not an eros. But if the sheriff is, then I need to know more about him. Tell me what you know."

She has to be an eros. She has to be. That's how she got in. But... I wasn't immediately attracted to her when she got here. I was kind of a dick, actually. And I hurt her. If she were an eros, would I have hurt her like that?

I was infatuated with Grant for almost a decade after he arrived. It took a good long time for his charms to wear off. The new caretaker should be intoxicating. And while Pie is kind of having that effect on Tomas, she did not have that effect on me.

I was angry when she came.

No. That wasn't it. I was angry that Grant *left*.

I could counter that argument and say, well, I like her now.

I like her because she's cute. She's kinda funny too. And pretty. Let's not forget pretty.

But I'm not *swooning* over her.

Still, she has to be an eros. That's how she got in here.

Isn't it?

"Well?" Pie taps her toe on the floor. "Are you gonna fill me in or what?"

"The eros are…" I shake my head. "Bad, *bad* news, Pie. You really need to get rid of him. Maybe I should come with you?"

"No. That's dumb. I can't glamour you like Grant could. It's too dangerous."

"Hmm. I wonder if he's using you to bait me?"

"What?"

"OK, you can't go—"

"Pell!"

"—unless… you come up with a protection spell. To counter his magic."

"How can I do that?"

"There has to be a spell here somewhere. I guess you had better get busy. I'll be back later to check your work."

And with that I turn and walk out of the apothecary. Maybe she comes up with a spell and maybe she doesn't. That's neither here nor there. The sheriff should not be able to get in here now. Pie's Jeep was moved to the back parking lot and all that property back there is charmed.

When Pie said she could find her way around the block to the back gate, she was mistaken. The entrance to this world is always glamoured. Without a map, she would've been lost.

This is good. It means that that the pesky sheriff will forget all about Saint Mark's Sanctuary until some new situation arises out front and grabs his attention as he's driving by.

With all other problems dealt with—at least temporarily—I turn my attention to the one on the back burner. Tomas.

Because he's not here. And that only means one thing.

He's having trouble.

Normally—i.e. before Grant left and Pie arrived—I would not even notice if Tomas was missing for a morning. But Grant did leave and Pie is here—and Tomas likes Pie. A lot more than he liked Grant because he can touch Pie. He can interact with Pie. He *needs* Pie. So he would not be missing this morning unless something else was up.

Which means something else is up and I need to find out what it is before things get out of hand.

I walk across the great hall, casually looking at the door that leads to the greenhouse as I pass. I will have to tell Pie about that later. It is her job now. I pass the dining room and enter a hallway that curves around in a spiral and descends into the variable lower levels.

This part of the cathedral changes at will. Sometimes the variable parts will stay the same for hundreds of years, only to completely disappear one morning as something else takes its place.

But Tomas's part of the cathedral hasn't ever disappeared and most of the changes are so minor, they're difficult to detect unless you're here on a regular basis. Which I am not, so it all looks the same to me—stone walls lit up with torches that spiral downward so far you get cold and then hot again. The *smell* begins somewhere in between. I try not to breathe through my nose as I descend. Time is weird down here. I never know if it takes minutes or hours to finally reach the bottom because it all looks the same.

Eventually I do reach the bottom and I grab a torch off the wall to light my way in the darkness ahead. "Tomas?" I say it softly, doing my best not to disturb things. But when he doesn't answer, I have to say it louder. "Tomas? Are you here?"

I keep walking. Slowly, since the cone of light in my hand only reaches a few feet in front of me. It's almost like the darkness swallows the light. Which isn't how things work. Light rules dark. Light needs only to exist to banish darkness.

The dark has no such power over light.

Except when it's not really darkness, but something else altogether.

"Tomas?" I call. Not loud, but not soft either. "Are you here?"

"Go back." Tomas's raspy voice is barely audible.

"I'm just checking on you. Do you need—"

"Get *out*!" He growls it this time and I feel the darkness that is not really darkness push against me. Warning me.

"OK. I'm leaving. But if you need anything—"

"Go. *Now.*"

I put up my hands. Not like I'm surrendering. Just letting him know I'm cool. "I'm going." I back up until I hit a wall. Then I turn, quickly retrace my steps to the spiral hallway, replace the torch on the wall, and do a full retreat.

When I finally come up into the stable sections of the cathedral, I let out a long breath.

Tomas has been wearing that human costume around me for so long, I had almost forgotten what he really is.

I won't make that mistake again.

CHAPTER TWELVE – PIE

By the time Pell returns to check on me, I've started two fires, blown up a small pile of powder, and inhaled fumes that made me temporarily forget who I was. None of which will be mentioned in any kind of update.

"Well?"

He's standing in the apothecary doorway. No pants.

I did look up satyrs. They are known for their sexual exploits, lewdness, and, yes—their exaggerated, ever-present erections.

Why me? It's a serious question.

"Well." I blow a piece of hair away from my face. "I think I've come up with something."

Pell takes a long look around the apothecary. It's a total mess. I'm talking dumpster-fire mess. There are powders all over the stone counters. Herb jars are open and lying on their sides, spilling leaves and roots and petals all over the place. And there are eleventy billion test tubes with the remnants of all my attempts at potions.

He sighs. Loud.

"It's not as bad as it looks. I can read Latin now! And look what I made!" I hold up the little leather pouch with pride. "An amulet!"

I'm pretty satisfied with this. I mean, I should've started with the amulet thing. You don't need to heat anything up, you don't need to distill any essential oils, and you don't need to make powders. All you really do is stuff the right kind of shit into a little leather pouch, wave your hand over it as you say some fancy words, and poof. You've got yourself an amulet.

"Nope." That's all he says.

"What do you mean, nope? What's nope about it? You didn't even look at it. It's good. I promise. I used the magical herb book to find something that wards off love spells."

Pell walks forward and I turn away, trying my best to ignore his swinging dick, and pretend to clean up a mess I made on the alchemy bench closest to me.

He comes right up next to me and picks the amulet up to study it. He's so close, his furry hip brushes against my arm. I pull away quickly, then scoot round to the other side of the counter.

Now that I'm safe from his huge dick, I watch as he sniffs the pouch and then opens it up and peers inside. "What did you use?"

"I used lily of the valley and blue lotus. I didn't have any pistachios, but I can pick them up at the market in town and just plop them in before I meet Russ at the restaurant."

Pell looks over at me, his eyes hooded. Maybe even narrowed.

"What?" I ask. Sometimes he looks at me like he wants to eat me. This is one of those times.

"You can't just pick up a bag of salted, processed pistachios at the local supermarket and plop them into your magical amulet, Pie. And an amulet?" He drops the leather pouch onto the bench. "What the hell? You had all day."

"What's wrong with an amulet?"

"They're weak. They're for non-magical people."

"Weak how? I did the spell. And I don't really need pistachios. There were only three herbs in the book that can break a love spell and the pistachio was one of them. But the lily and the lotus should be fine."

"Where's the book?"

I point to it on a nearby counter. He picks it up, thumbs through it, then drops it back on the counter with a thud. "It says you have to *eat* them, not put them in an amulet. Did you even look up the proper way to make this thing?"

"I did!"

He's shaking his head. "This isn't going to be enough. An eros is nothing to mess with. They're powerful. You already know that. He made you swoon."

"Swoon?" I huff. "I wasn't *swooning*."

"I'm sure you thought it was all natural. But it wasn't."

"So what do you suggest? If I don't show up tonight, he'll come out there. We've already talked about this."

He sighs and looks around. Then he walks over to the far wall, scans the jars, picks two, and comes back to the alchemy bench. "It's not going to be enough, but you've made a mess of this situation, so this is a last resort. You need to let him down easy." He points at me. "Don't piss him off. And then you need to get back here."

I nod. "OK. I can do that. What's that stuff for?"

He opens the jars, take one stone out of each, then closes them back up and returns the jars to the same place he got them. "Do you see what I did here?" He's throwing me a condescending look. "How I put them back where they belong?"

"I get it. I was messy today. But it's my first day. Jeez. Give me a break."

He walks back over to me, picks up the first stone and holds it up to the light. It's black—I'm talking super black—and so shiny, I can see my face in it. "Obsidian," he says. "It draws negative energy." He puts it into my amulet pouch and picks up the next one. "This is amethyst. It will protect you from psychic attack. Because that's what a love spell is." He drops that into the pouch as well. Then he does something weird. He puts his lips to the opening of the pouch and blows into it.

"What are you doing? I thought you said you can't do magic?"

"I said I *don't* do magic. Because it's boring. I have no interest in magic. That's why I have you. But I never said I *can't* do magic." Then he closes his eyes and whispers something in such a low voice, the vibrations kinda make the room shudder a little. It's that poem above the doors. *A hoof, a horn...* and the rest. He opens his eyes, pulls the leather drawstring on the pouch, and hands it to me. "Put it on and do not take it off."

"What did you just do?" I ask.

"It's the curse of Saint Mark's Sanctuary. You belong to this place so..." He shrugs, then sighs. "I put a claim on you."

My eyebrows go up. "A claim?"

"For the sanctuary. Not for me."

I take the pouch and dangle it in the air. It's a made from a very soft piece of lavender-colored leather. "Then why did you blow on it?"

"Because that's the claim."

I'm smirking. I can't help it. "Your breath is the sanctuary's claim?"

"Do you want me to forbid you from going?"

"No. I'm just—"

"Then mind your own business."

I have to turn to hide my smile. "OK. Thank you."

"It's just…" He holds up a finger, like he's about to make a list. "I have the door slamming." Another finger pops up. "I have the freezing." Another finger. "And I have breath." Then he mumbles something that I can't understand.

"What was that?"

"And a few other things. None of your business."

I surrender with both hands up. "Fine with me. And thank you."

He nods. Then he stares at me for a few moments. And I swear to God, this man—monster, whatever he is—he's so… unsettling. His eyes are this yellow-orange color that remind me of flowing lava. And they have this draw to them. Like you don't ever want to look away. You just want to stare back at him and get lost in those eyes. "What?" I ask. "Why are you staring at me like that?"

He changes the subject. "Did you look up satyr?"

"I did."

"And now you understand?"

"I guess."

His face is very expressive and sometimes he looks very human. Like, if he didn't have those horns, and he wasn't so tall, I'd just assume he was human because his lower half is almost entirely hidden by the alchemy bench.

"You guess?" he asks. "What part isn't clear?"

"No. I get it. You were made... lewd, and promiscuous, and highly sexualized. It's who you are."

"It's who I am."

"So..." I let out a long exhale. "I'm sorry. I won't ask you to wear pants again."

And again, he just stares at me.

"Why are you looking at me that way?"

"I'm trying to calculate how big of a mistake you're about to make. And if I should interfere and forbid you from going, or if I should just..." Now he sighs. "Let it go."

"And?"

"I'm letting it go. But this is bad. And things are going to come of it. I can feel it. That eros is going to be trouble."

"Maybe... *maybe*... I should just date him," I say. Pell growls. "I mean, for like two weeks. Let it run its course, then we break up, he's over me, we move on..." I shrug. "Telling him no might spark some kind of male competitive gene."

I can tell that Pell the monster hates this idea. But I'm not sure if it's because he doesn't want me dating, or if he's just truly concerned about me being around Russ Roth.

"I'm going to leave it up to you."

Now it's my turn to do the eyebrow raise. "You are?"

He nods. "Whatever you think is best. But here's the catch. If he comes here, I will kill him. I will pull his arms and legs off and feed them to…" But he pauses here. "Never mind who."

"Wait." I put up a hand. "Hold on. Is there another monster here who eats people? Because if so, I think I need to know that."

"There is not."

"It was a euphemism?"

"Consider it that."

"OK. Well, that wasn't weird. But I get it. If I fuck this up, he dies."

Pell points at me. "Exactly. And you? You will be punished. Because I don't like killing things. And if you make me do it, I will make sure that debt goes on your account." He taps the stone counter with his finger to illustrate how serious he is.

I swallow hard and nod. "Got it."

"And it will cost you dearly. My services don't come cheap."

"I said I get it."

"Good. Now state your plan back to me. Just so we're clear."

"I'm gonna have dinner with the sheriff. Be nice to him." I point at Pell. "I will not give up any secrets and I will not be too nice. I definitely won't send any of the wrong signals. I will steer him towards the friend zone, but if it feels like he's interested in more, we will fake-date while I simultaneously do a total *How to Lose a Guy in Ten Days* on him."

Pell says nothing.

"That means drive him away. It's a cultural reference—"

"I know what it means. I've seen the movie."

"You've watched *How to Lose a Guy in Ten Days?*"

He shrugs. "I'm a prisoner in a cursed sanctuary. Not a hermit."

"O-*kay*. Got it. You're hip and cool." I put the amulet around my neck. "And of course, it's all gonna be fine. Because now I'm under your breathy erection protection." I snort a little.

He *almost* smiles.

Damn. Tough room.

"I will prepare for the inevitable dismembering."

"That's not gonna happen," I counter. "I've got it covered." I take off my apron, throw it on the counter, and scoot towards the door. "I better get going so I can get ready." And then I dart out before he can say anything else or force me to look at his stupid dick.

CHAPTER THIRTEEN – PELL

I wait until she's all the way down the stairs, then start cleaning up the apothecary. I don't use this stuff, but I like things in their place. There is no possible way I can walk out and leave it looking like this. The apothecary is essential for what we do here. Which is curse-breaking. She needs to be mindful of our goals. If she ever leaves this place a mess like this again, I'll put it on her debt so she will think about her work flow.

Also, I need the distraction. This date is just pissing me off to no end.

Another *eros*. Living in the nearby town.

What are the chances of that?

And if there is one, there are more. An entire bloodline just miles down the road. How did I not know this? The only explanation is that they don't know what they are. This bloodline is some deeply hidden family secret. Because if the sheriff is an eros, and he had any inclination of what Saint Mark's was, then he would not have driven away with Pie. He would've come inside. He would've started a war.

One eros inside Saint Mark's is a caretaker.

Two is an invasion as far as I'm concerned.

They would've started a war. Because Pie is eros blood too.

Isn't she?

The eros belong to Saturn. *Did* belong to Saturn. Because Saturn is gone now. All the old gods are. And all their creations—all their *monsters*—were cursed.

Except for the fucking family of eros living down the road, apparently.

I'm not sure if this is a good thing or bad thing. On the one hand, the eros have broken their curse. That's... hopeful. For me, at least. But if they no longer even remember that they *were* cursed, let alone the power of the gods that they possess, then this curse-breaking happened a long, long time ago.

What have they been doing all this time?

And more importantly, did Grant know?

Eros are seductive. They emit pheromones that affect you in certain ways. They make you swoon with *longing*. Sometimes that longing is sexual. Sometimes it's a craving for a shared adventure. And sometimes it's just an overpowering compulsion to be near them. Forever. They cannot be out of your sight.

And every single eros caretaker who came into my sanctuary affected me in one of these three ways. At least for a while. I've had my share of swooning moments over the years. It can't be helped. But it's more of a casual swoon than a deep desire. It takes a while to wear off, but eventually, it does wear off.

Obviously the eros don't affect each other this way or they would be useless. Just a bunch of frolicking fools with no other ambition but to follow each other around.

So maybe Grant didn't know about the sheriff?

This leads me down another rabbit hole. The main tunnel, if you will.

Because everything about this new Pie phase in the curse is different. And I'm not talking different than the last fifty years, I'm talking different than the last two *thousand*. Aside from the sudden disappearance of Grant and the untimely appearance of an entire family of eros living in the closest town, never once in the history of Saint Mark's has a slave caretaker asked to get a *job* before.

Like… what the actual fuck is up with that?

And it's not even like I can complain about it, because she's trying to keep her debt down. Objecting just makes me look like a dick.

And none of them have ever dated before. At least, if they did, I didn't know about it. They were here for *me*. To pleasure me. That was their curse.

This one, she just throws it in my face. *I'm dating the sheriff.*

And she's the only one who ever showed up knowing no magic at all. All the other slave caretakers knew they were different. But Pie? No. She has a magic bird and she calls it her "personal hallucination".

This actually makes me smile as I gather up all the spilled herbs and put them back in their place on the shelf.

She's not boring, I will give her that.

And she has lit a fire inside Tomas.

Literally. Since he's locked himself in the dungeon.

I really need to keep an eye on him. He's always been dangerous, but dangerous in the way that we all are. I didn't see much when I was down there today, but I don't need to see things to understand that it's not going well for Tomas at the moment.

And who knows? Maybe this is normal? I haven't paid attention to the guy in a century, at least. Grant and I weren't even on speaking terms when he made his escape so he wasn't filling me in on Tomas's current mental state. But I never noticed anything off about Tomas when I saw him around the grounds.

Hmm. I pause here. Because Grant was a talented alchemist. Was he helping Tomas all this time? And now that he's gone, will Tomas struggle to maintain control? I want to say that is unlikely. Tomas liked Grant—Tomas likes everyone. But Grant didn't like him. No one likes Tomas back. His relationships are all very one-sided.

For good reason.

I will need to talk to Pie about this and tell her to stay away from Tomas.

She's not gonna take it well, and I don't blame her. She makes two friends—two men—and I've suddenly got a problem with both of them. If I were her, I'd think I was a jealous jerk. She will never believe me. This has always been my problem with humans. They never want to take anyone's word. They always have to see it for themselves. Always have to take the hard road. Always have to take the long way home.

And in the end, they have to admit that they should've listened.

Part of me wonders if maybe I should just butt out and leave the girl alone. What do I care if she gets involved with the local eros? It's not like she can run off with him. Her curse will only allow her to stay gone for so long. Then she will be sucked back in. She is mine as long as she is cursed and she's cursed as long as she wears the sanctuary ring.

And that ring will not come off her finger until someone of her bloodline shows up to take her place.

She didn't say this earlier, but I know she's holding out hope that the sheriff is her replacement.

His eros blood was enough to open the walking gate for an approaching Pie. That makes sense because Saturn is the one who turned the eros into his personal sanctuary keepers as Ostanes banished the gods. He sent them in here to get Ostanes's book. But Pie was the one who saw the flyer. She was the one who released Grant.

The sheriff of Granite Springs has been living in the closest town his entire life—if he was meant to be caretaker, wouldn't he have shown up at some point? Wouldn't he have seen that flyer first?

This is my main issue with the sheriff.

I think back, trying to recall everything I know about how we all ended up here in Saint Mark's Sanctuary.

It was a war, of course. It's always a war.

The God War that took place two thousand years ago happened for two reasons.

One. The alchemist Ostanes was making chimera for the gods, Saturn and Juno. Monsters. Like me. Like Tarq. Like Tomas. You take the blood of a pure monster—like the wood nymph, or the minotaur, or the satyr—and you mix it up to create a chimera.

But something went wrong. Overbreeding? Bad crossings? I don't know. I was a kid when that started happening. All I know is that with the exception of the eros, who had made an alliance with Saturn and were never used in the breeding program, all the pure monsters died out and only the chimera remained.

The second reason there needed to be a God War was because Juno and Saturn decided they were done with each other. And it was a messy breakup. As most breakups are. But when the two most powerful gods in all creation divorce, it takes on a whole other level of bad.

Ostanes worked for both of them. She could no more deny one request for more and more elaborate chimera breeding than she could the other. This is how the monsters got out of control.

This sanctuary was the last step in that war.

Ostanes had a very, very powerful spellbook. Both Saturn and Juno wanted this book so they could continue their monster breeding programs and be the most important god standing at the end of the separation. So there were desperate attempts to steal it.

Maybe Ostanes was prideful? Maybe creating the sanctuary and hiding her spells in here was just ego? That's entirely possible. If she didn't enjoy her power, she would not have been powerful. This is how power works. Only those who covet power get power.

But it's just as likely that the spells in that book simply do not belong in the hands of damaged gods.

At any rate, once the sanctuary was created Ostanes created tombs and locked all her chimera—except for me—inside them. She gave the book to the most formidable monster, Tarq.

Juno and Saturn responded with a fast and furious flurry of counterspells:

Saturn gave the eros the ability to enter the sanctuary as caretakers.

Juno countered by restricting the ability to enter the tombs to just one monster. Me, as it happens.

Saturn volleyed back and made the tomb doors invisible to me and only seen by the caretaker.

Juno returned fire and cursed the caretakers with the Book of Debt.

And... well, that's where I lost track of the story because I was already inside Saint Mark's.

Tomas was always here. I don't really know much of his story at all. And I certainly have no clue how he fits into the curse.

Or myself, actually.

I'm not here to guard the spellbook—that task was given to Tarq. And I don't have any useful powers. Slamming doors? Freezing people in place? A tiny breath of entitlement? It's all very stupid.

Well. There is that *other* power. Which I'm going to assume is some kind of desperate last-resort power. Because if I use it, Saturn wins.

And maybe it's not my place to choose who gets to be God, but as long as I have a say, it's not going to be *him*.

So. I dunno. I think I'm just a leftover from a long-ago age. I hadn't even been put to use before the God War. I was nothing more than a young chimera waiting for his purpose in the woods when this shitshow happened.

I am an unfinished project.

The only thing I've been focused on for the past two thousand years is how to get out of my curse.

And the only thing the caretakers have been focused on is how to get out of *their* curse.

And pleasing me. Because, for whatever reason, this is part of the deal. Maybe it's payment for my services?

But the caretakers have never really pleased me. All those tasks in the Book of Debt are intimate. Never mind the sexual things—which none of them ever did. The feet washing, the horn polishing, the bathing… it's all very personal. I never wanted any of them touching me.

Until now.

Until *Pie*.

Maybe I don't want her to stay forever, but it would be nice if I had a chance to get to know her without the interference of that stupid eros sheriff.

She's not going to like him.

She better not like him.

I'm not OK with this date.

By the time I'm done tidying up the apothecary it's evening. And even though I do not want to walk down to Pie's cottage and see her off on her date, I can't help myself.

I can hear her music when I cross over the top of the hill. It's blaring up from the house even though all the windows are closed. I knock, but she doesn't hear it. Inside, her music is deafening.

"Pie?" I call up the stairs. The upstairs of the cottage is really more of a loft. There are walls, but not four of them. There's a half-wall on one side and even from the bottom of the steps, I can see right into her bedroom. The top of the canopy, the valance of one window, the pale plaster of the far wall.

But no Pie.

"Pie?" I call again. Louder.

Nothing.

I go up. It's my duty. She could've slipped in the bathroom. She could be passed out right now.

Who am I kidding? I want to see her naked.

This actually makes me smirk. She's seen me naked. Fair is fair.

But when I get up there, she's not naked. She's dancing in the bathroom, twirling her hair around a hot iron as she sings to herself in the mirror.

This is a unique opportunity to watch her and I like what I see. She's cleaned up, all traces of potions gone wrong wiped away. Her long blonde hair is shiny and straight, except for the parts she's already curled. And she's wearing makeup. Not a lot, but her eyes are dark enough to make her look different. Less innocent. More… worldly. Maybe even magical and bad.

Well, she is one of Saturn's creatures, after all. That's how she got in here. An eros is always alluring.

But I'm not swooning over her. I'm not losing my mind with lust. So she's not like any other eros in the history of Saint Mark's. Because every time a new caretaker shows up, my stupid ass swoons all over the place. Sometimes I have to lock myself in my tomb until the magic settles.

Pie didn't evoke any of these urges when she showed up.

I was angry that night.

Pie is not dressed trashy, like the way she was when she arrived. But the cute velour pants and white t-shirt are not present either.

She is… *sexy*.

That's the only word for it.

Especially when she wiggles her ass as she does her little dance in front of the mirror.

She's wearing a very short black dress balanced out with opaque black tights. The dress has long sleeves that end in a bell shape at her wrists. The whole thing is very alluring, but at the same time, she is showing almost no skin.

Her eyes meet mine in the mirror and then she's whirling around. "Holy shit! Pell! What the fuck!"

Oops.

"Why are you here?" She walks over to her pocket phone, clicks the music off, and glares at me. "Well, what do you want?"

"I just…" But there is no good reason to be here. "I just wanted to tell you to be careful one more time."

She walks forward, places one hand on my chest, and pushes me backwards. "I get it. Now leave. I don't need a big brother watching me get ready for a date."

"Big *brother*?" I scowl at her. "And what the actual fuck yourself? You're not gonna let him down easy. You're going to date him for real."

She points her hot iron at me. "Get out."

"You like him, don't you?"

"He put a spell on me. Of course I like him."

"Speaking of," I snarl. "Where's your fucking amulet?"

She grabs at the counter behind her. Holds up the lavender leather pouch. "Right here."

"You're supposed to have it on. Never take it off."

She slips it over her head. "There. Satisfied?"

And… no. I'm not. I want to forbid her from going out. I want to lock her in this cottage. I want her to stay here, with me, and only think about *me*.

And in a few minutes, she will walk out of here. And maybe she thinks about me on that drive into town, but the moment the sheriff shows up, her mind will be wiped. She will swoon over him.

This is my last chance to stop it. Not by forbidding her from going, either. That will just make her like him more. I take four steps and close the distance between us. She looks startled for a moment and takes a step back. But there's nowhere to go in this little bathroom. She's trapped.

"What are you doing?"

I reach for the string of the amulet and then tug on the top of her dress to open it up. I dangle the amulet pouch over her cleavage—our eyes locked on each other—and then I drop it down inside.

She lets out a breath. "O-kaaay. What's this about?"

I don't take my eyes off her. But my hand comes up and my knuckles gently swipe down the side of her cheek. "You will be careful tonight."

She tries to swipe my hand away, but I grab her wrist.

"Do you hear me, Pie?"

"Yeah. I hear you. I said I would."

"You're not taking this seriously. You're up here, dancing around, doing your hair, putting on makeup like this is going to be *fun*."

"It could be fun."

I stare at her for a long moment, nodding. "It could. But it's unlikely, Pie." My hand slips down and I place my palm on the side of her neck, my thumb caressing the little dent of her throat. Then I slide my fingers around the back of her neck and squeeze just a little. She gasps. Her eyes are locked on mine. Like she's powerless. Like she's caught. And she is. The satyr blood coursing through my veins might not be good for much, but it is good for this. I can hold them captive with my sexuality. And I do that now.

I feel myself starting to become excited, so I close my eyes and will that desire back into submission, then open them again, completely in control when I lean down and touch my lips to hers. I do not kiss her. One breath. That's what we exchange. One breath of my essence slips into her mouth and she swallows. I feel the muscles of her throat move when she consumes my claim.

Then I pull back, release my hand, and back out of her room, only turning around once I reach the stairs. I go down, leave the cottage, and walk up the hill where I sit on the ruin of a stone tomb and watch as she leaves her cottage, walks through the gate, and goes into town for her *date*.

Then I walk back to her cottage and wait for her to come home.

Because I am going to make her tell me everything.

CHAPTER FOURTEEN – PIE

What did he just do to me?

It wasn't a kiss. Our lips barely touched. It was something else. He… I dunno. He gave me a breath. It's like the way he breathed into the amulet pouch earlier today. Magic. He filled me up with something. I could feel it enter me. He's inside me now.

For a moment I'm not sure if this is creepy or erotic. Then a familiar throbbing begins between my legs and that mystery is solved.

Wow. My life is seriously weird.

And the weirdest part isn't that I was given a breath of magic from a satyr chimera. The weirdest part is that I'm standing in a bathroom getting ready to go on a date with a cupid so I can distract him from the fact that I now live in a cursed cemetery filled with stone monsters and my master is now a guy called Pell who has horns and hooves.

No. That's not the weirdest part. The weirdest part is I might be OK with this.

Oh, sure. I'm putting up the good fight. I tell Pell that I'm gonna break that curse and move on.

But… is that really what I'm doing here?

I just stand there in the bathroom, looking at myself in the mirror for several minutes. Thinking about how I got to this moment in time. Because this is when I fully internalize that I might actually be insane.

Sure, I always kinda knew this. But it was a little bit cute, right? My quaint imaginary talking friend, the sparrow. It was like how some people embrace a stupid hairstyle or have a thing for ugly vintage clothes. Just a fun, quirky piece of me. Part of my character that made me unique.

But I dunno if I buy that anymore.

I let out a long breath, then turn and look at the room. It's so pretty. I like it. I like all this stuff, actually. I might even like that sheriff. I'm even starting to turn the corner on Pell. I'm not sure how he did it, but that breath-kiss didn't hurt his likeability score, that's for sure.

Maybe I'm still drunk?

Maybe I'm still passed out at the college?

Maybe this is all a dream?

Snap out of it, Pie. If Pia were here, that's what she would say. *Life is a mystery and you stumbled into something special.* That's what this is. It's special. *I'm* special.

And even though this line of thinking mostly starts out as an internal pep talk, I feel it. I do.

I like having Pia as my friend. And even though she's missing now, I will find her. I have no doubts at all that I will get her back. And sure, this place is a little bit creepy, not to mention it has some borderline evil symbology—but Tomas is super nice. And he was right about Pell. He's not *that* bad. If I have to be stuck in a curse, I could do a lot worse than those two.

And fuck it. If I really am crazy and this is all some kind of delusional hallucination or dream, then nothing can hurt me. So why not enjoy it?

Yeah. I'm going with this line of thinking.

I quickly finish curling my hair, take one last look at myself, and grab my purse.

The moment I walk out of the gate and take a fresh breath of lake air, my head clears, and most of my thoughts about insanity fade as I concentrate on how kinda cool this new life might be.

I conquered the sanctuary tonight. A part of me feels like it's trying to throw every possible inconvenience at me that it can. But it's not working. I've figured out that there's always a workaround.

Take my phone, for instance. I can't charge it at the sanctuary. But I can charge it in my car. And the twenty-minute ride to and from town is just enough. There is no internet, obviously, and I can't make calls or send texts, either. But the point is, the phone still works. It still plays music and it still takes pictures.

And even though I shouldn't be able to use the curling iron in the cottage, I can. Because I cut off the cord, stuck it inside the hot coal thingy that heats up the water, got it just hot enough, and boom. I had myself an old-fashioned curling iron. Then I put some coals on a plate, put the iron on the coals, took it upstairs, and that kept the iron hot enough to put some bounce in my hair in front of the mirror.

I feel like I took charge of things today. Maybe I didn't find my place just yet, but I definitely found my footing and I'm now convinced that I won't miss anything about modern technological conveniences. So I put aside my worries and get serious. If the sheriff is magical, I need to stay aware. Who knows how many curses there are out there? I could stumble into another one if I'm not careful.

And that's the last thing I need.

There aren't many places to park here in Granite Springs because it's a tiny town and most of it is built on the side of a hilly mountain. Main Street is narrow and paved with bricks, one of those old-timey roads that are common in some parts of PA. And there is probably some kind of historic rule that you can't disrupt said bricks for posterity reasons, so it has never been widened to accommodate cars and buses. This gives the downtown a bit of a claustrophobic feel and even though I've only been at the sanctuary for a few days, I find myself feeling uneasy in the presence of others.

I finally find a parking spot in back of the candle shop. And then I walk-jog down the hill to the steakhouse. It smells pretty good and my mouth is already watering when I open the door and practically smash into the hard, muscular chest of Sheriff Russ Roth.

"Oh, shit! Sorry!"

His wide grin is immediate and his eyes drink me in. "I didn't mean to run into you, Pie. But I saw you coming and wanted to be the first thing you laid eyes on when you opened these doors."

And… cue the cupid. My head is suddenly all flighty and butterflies flitter around in my stomach.

Pell was right. Russ makes me swoon.

Sheriff Roth takes both my hands, brings them up to his lips, and kisses each and every one of my knuckles and he gazes down into my eyes.

"Uhhh…" I'm at a loss for words. I want to pull my hands away, but he's not giving them up and I don't want this to become a fight. And… the longer he keeps a hold of them, the less I seem to care. "Hi!"

I finally manage. My grin is so big, my cheeks are stretching.

Russ's eyes slide down my body and this makes me tingle all over.

Fucking *hell*. Pell was right about the amulet too. It's not protecting me from shit!

Then again… I'm not sure I want it to.

Focus, Pie. Remember why you're here.

Why am I here again?

Russ's eyes track back up to meet mine and ho-lee crap. I want him to bend me over the nearest table and fuck me from behind right now.

No. No, no, no! *That is not how this ends, Pie. You cannot let the sheriff pork you tonight!*

Definitely not in the plan.

"I've got our booth ready over here, Pie." He says my name with that little western PA accent, which usually sounds a little too hick to be sexy, but not this time. And then he kisses my hands again before leading me into the dark dining room.

We pass a slew of other diners, most of whom greet the sheriff. He's not wearing his uniform tonight. He's got a crisp, white button-down shirt with a pair of tight gray slacks that hug his ass like a glove.

Mmm. Mmm. Mmm.

Shit. There's definitely something wrong with me. I don't think thoughts like this. I mean, I've had my share of dirty moments, but there is a time and a place for thoughts like that. And they usually come with copious amounts of alcohol and occur much, *much* later in the evening.

We're just getting started here and I'm already starting to feel out of control.

The sheriff bows and presents me with a little three-quarter circle booth near the back of the restaurant and kinda secluded between some strategically-placed potted trees.

Privacy.

Maybe he wants to get dirty in the corner with me? I go all hot just picturing it.

No. Stop it. Pull yourself together, Pie!

"This booth is so cute."

Russ Roth winks at me. "We call it the Lovers' Nest booth." Of course he does. "It's where everyone wants to bring their first date."

"So they can make out?" Why do I sound breathless?

Russ looks confused. "Well. Maybe. But that's not why I brought you here."

I slide into the booth and pat the seat next to me, looking up at him like I'm a siren calling him to the rocks. "It's OK. I get it. Privacy is good on the first date."

"Ye...ah." He nods his head, starts to look concerned. "Yes. I understand what you're thinking. But"—he places his hand over his heart—"I promise you, Miss Vita, I am a gentleman through and through. My mama would whoop my ass if I ever tried to make out with a woman in the Lover's Nest booth."

He slides in next to me and we are very close. Not squished, but comfortably... snug.

Wow. That's kind of a sexy word. *Snug.*

Am I losing control here? And why is it so hot?

"What are you thinking about?" Russ asks. "You've got a look on your face I'd pay a thousand dollars to understand."

"Oh. Sorry. I was distracted by our... snugginess."

"Snugginess." He laughs at the word.

OK. OK, OK, OK. Hold on, Pie. Maybe I'm reading too much into things? He's not sending me sexy vibes here. And if he's not sending them, then... who is? I look around, trying to find some other monster creature who might be interfering with my thought process. But no one is paying any attention to us.

"This is nice."

Before I can ask what he's talking about Russ's fingertips are brushing against my collarbone just above the neckline of my dress. I was careful to cover up as much skin as possible so he didn't get any fancy ideas about where this night was going. But there's enough skin there to feel the warmth of his fingers against my breastbone. And then he's pulling the lavender leather string up until my amulet appears in his hand. "Oh," he says, momentarily looking confused. Then he seems to get embarrassed, because he blushes. "I'm so sorry. I didn't realize it was something personal."

I am quiet through all of this. Not because I don't know what to say but because my lady bits are absolutely throbbing with... what's the word? Mmm. Let me think. Maybe let's just call it *burning desire*?

This is not going well and I've only been here thirty seconds.

I don't know what else to do, so I just tuck the little pouch back inside my dress and try to get my female urges under control.

"What's wrong?" He reaches for my face and before I can protest, or tell him I'm fine, his palm is flat against my cheek checking for *fever*. "Cheese and rice, Pie. You're burning up. Are you feeling OK?"

I'm not. I'm really not. Because in my head I am picturing myself *doing things* to this man. Things... so many things. Things I wouldn't normally do unless I've been with a man for a long time and since I have never been in a long-term relationship, these kind of things have *never* happened. Not even in my dreams.

I grab the drink menu and fan myself. "I'm fine, I swear. It's some kind of hot flash. I'll be OK."

Russ snaps his fingers at a passing waitress, but not in a nasty way. She stops, a look of concern on her face. "Everything OK here, Sheriff?"

"Stacy, Miss Vita here is feeling flush." He says these words discreetly and politely. "Could you bring us a bucket of ice so I can make her up a little cold pack?"

Stacy smiles at him, then me, then him again. "Sure thing, Sheriff." And she's off.

"It's really fine," I say. "I'm sure it will pass and that ice won't be necessary."

"Maybe so," Russ says. "But it can't hurt to be prepared." Then he shoots me another look of concern. "Are you not hungry anymore? I would completely understand if you'd just rather go home. And of course, you can't drive yourself. I'd be happy to take you."

Well, that won't do. I might be in some kind of swoon-induced fever at the moment, but I still remember my goal here. So my answer is, "No, I'm starving. Really. I'm *dying* for a steak."

Not exactly a lie. I do love my meat. But I can't let him take me home again. That defeats the whole purpose of the date. Which, despite the traitorous reactions in my body, was to make him *less* interested, not more.

But everything about this night is wrong. I'm the one who is infatuated with *him*, not the other way around. He's not looking at me like I'm a sexy piece of meat. In fact, he's looking at me like… "You think I'm weird, don't you?"

His smile never falters. "I like your brand of weird, Pie. I find it intriguing. I'm curious, though—"

But I don't hear the rest, because I'm so focused on his mouth—*hyper*-focused, like *tunnel-vision* focused on his perfect lips, on the way they might feel against mine—that the next thing I know I'm *kissing* him.

No. That's not what happens. That's not even close to accurate.

I have climbed into his lap, my fingertips mussing up his thick head of hair. My eyes trained on his. Searching for the passion I know is in there. Then I'm pressing my mouth to his and squirming my lady bits against his thickening dick underneath those tight pants. I'm panting, breathing so heavy, I might pass out. And then I pull the neckline of my dress down, exposing my bra, and I place his hand there, making him squeeze me. All the while I'm writhing in his lap, sticking my tongue down his throat, then pulling back to dirty talk. "I want to suck you. I want your fingers inside me." Squirming, and wiggling, and twisting, and quivering. Trying my very best to make myself come, right here in the—

"Pie?"

The delusion fades and I'm still sitting in the booth next to, not on top of, Mr. Sheriff here.

I blink.

He's just about to ask me if I'm insane when Stacy the waitress appears with one of those legit cold-pack thingies you only see in cartoons. The round kind, made of plastic, and they come with a cap. "Here you go, hon. Put this up to your head." Then she looks at the sheriff. "She can take that home, Sheriff."

Russ takes the cold pack and places it up against my forehead. "Thank you, Stacy."

It does help. But only the feverish part of my new... *disorder*.

What? No! I can't afford to have another disorder. I'm already afflicted with hallucinations, curses, and love spells. What more can this world throw at me?

There is a bell ringing somewhere.

I look around, but we're so secluded in the back, between these massive potted trees, that I can't get a clear view of anything.

"Are you sure you don't want me to take you home?"

I'm just about to answer him when that bell starts ringing again. And I don't know why I think this, but it feels like a summoning bell. The kind of bell you ring when you need service.

"Pie?"

"Do you hear a bell ringing?" I ask him.

He pauses to listen like a reasonable person, then presses his lips together and shakes his head. "Nope. Do... *you* hear a bell ringing?"

I sure can. But I'm not gonna tell him that now that I know that I'm imagining it. "Can you excuse me for a moment? I have to use the restroom."

"Sure." Even though I can scoot out of my side of the booth, Russ gets up with me like a trained gentleman.

I smile at him. He's really nice. And handsome. And his pants are so tight, I can see the entire outline of his dick.

I look away quickly and head towards a hallway that has a sign for the restrooms over it. I'm probably imagining his big dick. It's probably leftover delusions from Pell.

Oh, my God, Pie. Just stop. For all you know, this whole thing is a delusion. I mean... monsters? Horned gods with hooves? These things don't exist.

I'm just about to walk into the restroom when I spy a back door and head that way instead.

This date is over. I'm not sure what's real and what's not anymore and I can't sit in there and pretend to be sane. I end up in an alley behind the restaurant and when I look to my left, there are two police cruisers. I almost panic until I remember the station is next to the restaurant.

I turn in a circle, trying to get my bearings so I can figure out where I parked. Then I head in that direction. And with every step I feel just a little bit better.

Maybe Russ really is an eros? Maybe it was him, and not me? Because by the time I make it to the front of the candle shop, I'm almost feeling normal.

It was him.

It's not me.

I sigh out a long breath of relief and all I want to do is go home.

Home? I don't want to think about the sanctuary, but how can I not? It's not my home. I'm either insane and made the whole thing up, or I'm stuck in a curse.

Which one is worse?

I think I should just get in my Jeep and drive on out of here, never looking back. And if Pia is real, then she's with me. Always. Maybe I can't see her. But if I leave, Pia leaves. And if she doesn't come with me, she was never real to begin with.

Yes. This is what I need to do.

I'm convinced that I need to just get in my Jeep and drive to Toledo so I can beg Jacqueline to let me stay on her couch for a few nights.

This, at the very least, is some semblance of a plan. And plans always make me feel better. So I'm breathing normally and nearly calm when I round the corner of the candle shop.

And then I stop dead.

Because leaning against my Jeep is... "Grant?"

He smiles at me. "Hi, Pie." And he's young again.

I shake my head. "No. This isn't possible. I saw you leave. I saw you turn into an old man."

He pushes off my Jeep and shoves his hands into his pockets. He's *so* young. Much younger than me, I realize. His hair is blond and his body is lean and supple. No trace of the old man who got in that El Camino and drove away.

"You tricked me. And how are you young again? Pell and Tomas said you never paid your debts."

He shrugs. "I didn't trick you. I just didn't fill you in. And don't even try to tell me that you wouldn't do the same thing if another slave walked into the sanctuary. You'd take your chance, wouldn't you? And you know that with one hundred percent certainty even though you've only been there a few days."

I can't say he's wrong, so I don't.

"And here's a tip—that debt book is bullshit. You can wash his stupid fucking feet twenty-four seven and it won't erase your debts. It doesn't matter. And he knows it doesn't matter. I bet he lied to you, didn't he? I bet he told you you had to work it off by pleasing him, didn't he?"

I don't say anything, but that was the answer Grant was looking for. So instead of remaining silent, I change the subject back to my question. "How are you young again?"

"Do you think I'm stupid? I spent fifty years locked up in that place. Do you really think I didn't have an escape plan?"

"So what was it? You took the magic with you?"

"It's not just *the* magic. It's *my* magic. I made it. So yeah, I took it with me."

"So the books you left behind? They're bullshit, right?" I pull the amulet out from my dress. "This is a total waste, isn't it?"

He laughs, then walks towards me until he's close enough to take the amulet out of my hand. He slips the cord over my neck and opens the pouch up. Then he crinkles his nose and laughs again. "Oh, Pie. I'm sorry."

"And how do you know my name? I never told you my name."

He hands my useless amulet back and shrugs again. "I'm magic." Then he taps his temple. "I know things. And I can help you. If you want out. I can get you out. I know how to break the curse, but those monsters, Pie?" He shakes his head. "They can't get out. They were put there for a reason. And you've only met Pell. I've met them all. And I'll tell you what, you do not want to know them. Pell is bad, but there's worse out there in that cemetery. If they ever invite you inside, don't go."

"No shit, Sherlock. Do I look stupid? I'm not going inside no creepy tomb."

"And don't fall for Pell's sweet talk. He's a liar. Everything he says is a lie."

"That might be true, but why should I trust you?"

"I wanna help you. I just said. I want to put an end to this curse. And I can't do that as long as you're there. I need your help to break your curse—*our* curse," he amends quickly—"but not *theirs*. Those monsters need to stay at Saint Mark's. Invite me in, Pie. Get me back in and I'll make it all go away. I'll get you out. You can be on your way. Get your life back on track."

I don't trust him. I don't trust anything he just said. And it's not even the part about inviting him in that triggers this. It's all of it. That last bit, that's just the dead giveaway.

I put the amulet back on "No. I don't know who you are or what you're doing, but I will not be a part of this."

I reach for the door handle of the Jeep, but Grant blocks my way. "You don't really have a choice, Pie. You're not in charge here."

"I don't have a choice?" I kinda laugh at that. Because in my experience there are always choices. Sometimes you only have bad choices to choose from, so it's easy to assume you have none. But that's not true. You always have a choice. So I say, "What are you gonna do? Kill me, Grant? Kidnap me? Will the curse let you do that?"

But Grant isn't really listening to me. He's distracted by the ring on my finger. I absently play with it and realize… it's loose. I could take it off, if I wanted to. I could hand it over. I could let Grant take this problem of mine and make it his again. But everything about that feels wrong.

He's watching me play with the band of silver around my finger like he's mesmerized. I take it off, hold it between my fingers, then place it in my palm and offer it to him. "Take it. You want back in so bad, take it. We can trade places again."

He does not reach for the ring.

"What's wrong, Grant?" I'm baiting him, I realize. My tone is condescending, my invitation not even genuine. Even if he reached for the ring, I would pull back. I would not give it over. And I don't really understand these things right now, but I know one thing for sure. I need to go.

I slip the ring back on and reach for the door, but Grant says, "Hold on. Just wait."

"Why? So you can lie to me some more? I don't know what you're up to, but I do know I don't want anything to do with it. Or you."

He narrows his eyes at me. "So you like it there? You want to be stuck in a curse with those evil monsters forever?"

I shrug. "I'll figure it out."

"You will?" He guffaws. "You? Really? After thousands of years and dozens of caretakers, you will be the one to *figure it out*? That's… ambitious."

"So? What do you care? You're free. Go. Be free."

"I'm offering you the same. I'm trying to break the caretaker curse, Pie. That's my motive here. To get you *out* and keep them *in*."

"I don't believe you." But that's not entirely true. Some of what he's saying rings true. I can tell by the tone of his voice. The part about the caretaker curse. He does want to get rid of it. And maybe he even wants to keep the monsters inside. But there's more to it than that. I can feel this like it's a real thing in my hand.

Grant is still smiling. It comes off very fake. "What's not to believe?"

"You want back in, Grant. That's weird. Especially since I offered you the ring so you could do that, and you refused."

"I'm trying to break the curse, Pie. If I take the ring, I take the curse. And that defeats the purpose of getting out of the curse to begin with."

"You're talking in circles. Nothing you're saying makes sense."

"I'm offering you an out. What part of that doesn't make sense?"

"You want to hurt them."

"Oh." He guffaws again. "Oh. I get it. You've already become infatuated. Let me guess… Pell has given you a breath?"

"What?"

"The breath, Pie?" He must read something in my expression because he smiles wide. "I bet he told you he didn't do magic, either? But then he did magic, didn't he?"

I don't want to admit that, so I say nothing.

"Yeah. He did. Well." Grant shrugs and puts his hands in his pockets. "It'll wear off. And then you'll come to your senses and want what I'm offering you."

"What *are* you offering me?" I ask. "Exactly?"

He hesitates. But quickly recovers and begins speaking in a breathless rush. "I'm living a dream life, Pie. I started renting storage units on the outskirts of Pittsburgh four decades ago. I used the fake money to buy very expensive things. Watches, jewelry, art, cars. Collectibles. And then I sold it. I have made millions of dollars during my time at Saint Mark's. And not only did I get to keep it all when you answered my ad, I got my youth back too. The Book of Debt is bullshit. I have a spell that erased my debt and every moment I spent under the influence of the curse. If you invite me back in, I will give you that spell. You can stay, use the fake money to build your own fresh start, then leave when you're ready. I will catch you another caretaker."

Wow. I scoff at him. Because greed, right? It's sadly… predictable. Everything he just said goes back to greed. His amateur offer is a joke. "I'm not even remotely interested in using magic to find success. It kind of defeats the whole point of success, in my opinion. And I don't need you to catch me another caretaker, Grant. I already know where one is."

"What?" His word comes out sharp and fast.

"I'm not letting you in. You're… I don't know. Wrong, somehow. I don't want anything to do with you or your fake plan." I pull out my phone, press nine and one. "Now get out of my way or I will press that last digit and Eileen will answer, and I will tell her to send Sheriff Roth over to the candle shop parking lot. And then I will tell him you tried to attack me. And he will believe me, Grant. Because you're a sketchy-looking dude. I'm sure this town already knows there's something wrong with you. I bet you Sheriff Russ Roth would be more than happy to lock you up if I tell him what you did."

"You're a sneaky little liar, you know that? I'm just trying to help you."

I shake my head. "No. I'm not lying. I'm just jumping the gun a little. Because if I hang around you for much longer, I'm one hundred percent certain you *will* attack me. Now get out of my way."

"You're making a big mistake. I'm telling the truth. And you're gonna figure that out quick. But hey." He throws up his hands, palms out, like he's surrendering. He steps aside. "You're not even *real*. You're just a crazy girl with an imaginary bird for a best friend, so you're probably doing the whole world a favor by locking yourself in the loony bin with the monsters." Then he tips his imaginary hat to me and walks off.

I get in my Jeep and drive out of town towards the sanctuary.

I spend most of the drive trying not to think about what just happened, but it's inevitable.

He's stupid. I'm not real? That's insanity. I'm the only thing that *is* real. He's not real. None of this curse stuff is real. In fact, nothing after I woke up from the Halloween party is real. It's all a bad dream or… or…

Shit. I missed the turnoff into the forest where the road to the back entrance is. But instead of turning around, I stop outside the front gate of Saint Mark's and just look at it.

The moon is sizable enough. Don't know if it's growing or shrinking, but it's bright enough that I can see the building pretty clearly. From out here, it doesn't look like a cathedral. Not the way it does in the back.

It's all an illusion. And if I could just find a way to peel back the pretty paper over those imaginary walls, I'd see what's hiding underneath.

But I won't do that, will I?

I like the delusion, don't I?

That's why I keep Pia around, isn't it?

I flip a bitch, find the road into the forest, and then slowly make my way back to the lake and the gate, and the unreal life I'm living here at Saint Mark's.

I don't know what just happened back in town. I don't think I want to know what just happened back in town. I don't even want to know what's happening out here.

Something is wrong with Grant. That's why he wants back in.

Something is wrong with Tomas. That's why he's missing.

And something is wrong with Pell too. Fucking pleasure book or whatever.

It's all nuts.

I'm nuts.

This is the thought that lingers in my head.

Me. This isn't about them. They're the ones who aren't real.

This is about me and I'm *insane*.

Just like they all said when I was little.

Only now, I can't control it. My delusions have taken over my reality. That little hallucination with the sheriff tonight? That's proof.

He's not some weird love monster! I'm. *In. Sane.*

I turn the Jeep off and notice there's a light on in my cottage. I get out and just stand there in the parking lot for a moment, looking up at the bedroom window. Picturing myself up there with Pia that first day. Looking down here, where I'm standing now, and watching Old Man Grant get in his car, practically giddy with excitement.

And I guess he won, didn't he?

He got rich, didn't pay off any debts, didn't grow old, and he took his magic with him. That's quite an accomplishment. And I could do the same. All I have to do is invite him in.

"Ha!" I laugh out loud. "It's all fake. The whole thing is fake. And how pathetic am I? That I have to make up a cupid to find myself a love interest and a prison guard with a giant cock!" This time, when the laugh bursts out, I really start to feel crazy. I cover my mouth to stifle leftover giggles, push through the gate, walk around to the front of the cottage, open the door, and go inside.

And there is Pell. Sleeping on my little couch. His giant dick just lying there in wait like a lion in tall grass on the savannah.

I sigh as I look at him. He's a very nice delusion, actually. Sexy monsters are… well. Sexy. He's far, far too big for that particular piece of furniture, so only his upper body is actually on the cushions. From the hip down, he's dangling over the side of the armrest.

He's sleeping. Soundly, apparently. Since me walking in didn't wake him. His arms are crossed over his muscular chest and his head is propped up on a pillow. I study his horns. They are a deep chestnut brown with flicks of orange heat inside them. This heat glows and pulses, like there's a whole furnace of fire inside his body. The horns are interesting, I think. They do not go above his head like the mythological creatures in books. They kinda drape down over his shoulders, pressing against either side of the soft cushion that elevates his head. They are not the horns of a goat, or a bull, or a ram. Not a gazelle, either. Some other animal. His chest is almost hairless. In fact, his entire upper body is almost hairless. Even his head, which is only covered in a velvet of light stubble, just like his jaw.

I plop down into an overstuffed chair and clear my throat.

He awakens slowly, like he was somewhere else, his eyelashes fluttering a little. They're also blond, like his chin and head scruff. Then he draws in a deep breath as he opens his yellow-orange eyes and smiles at me.

"You're home." His voice is husky with leftover sleep. "How'd it go?"

I don't know what to say because there is only one way to describe what just happened to me. "It was a total disaster."

"What?" He sits up, his fucking package shifting around like a living thing. And that just reminds me of what happened back there in town with Russ.

Did it happen? Didn't it happen?

"At first," I say, my words very soft—so soft, Pell leans forward, like he's trying to hear me better—"at first I thought I was delusional. I made the whole thing up." A tear slides down my cheek.

"Pie?" Pell is confused. "What the fuck happened?"

I just shake my head.

"Did he hurt you?"

I can only shrug.

"What does that mean? He hurt you?"

"I don't know." My voice cracks. And I'm not sure what that is. Fear? Shame? I don't know.

Pell gets up, and with one stride, he's kneeling in front of me. "Why are you crying?"

I sniff and wipe a tear off my cheek. And then I whisper, "I don't know."

"What did he do?"

"I don't know."

"How could you not know?" His voice is loud.

So I get defensive. "I don't know what's real. I don't know if I really did those things in the restaurant. Did I climb in his lap? Did I pull my dress down and place his hand on me? Did I squirm like an animal? I don't know what's real anymore. I don't think any of this is real. I think you're fake. Or a hallucination, like Pia was. I think I'm dead. I think I died that night. On Halloween. I think I woke up a ghost and that's why that nun called me a whore of Babylon."

His eyes search mine, fast and hasty. "What the *fuck* are you talking about?"

"I'm insane, Pell. I'm fucking crazy. I've always been crazy. And this place…" I cry harder. I can't stop it. "This place is purgatory. It's punishment. Or I'm living in my mind. I'm in some coma somewhere, making this all up. Pretending to be real. But I'm not."

He sighs, and that's when I realize he's got a hold of my hand. His grip is tight. Not tight enough to crush my bones, but tight enough for me to know he's there. He's real.

I pull the amulet up out of my dress and then over my head. I drop it onto his knee, which is covered in shaggy, straw-colored fur. "It's all fake. Grant told me.

He took the real books with him. He made money out in the real world—"

"OK, stop." Pell breathes heavy for a moment. "Hold the fuck up. What did you just say?"

"I saw Grant. I had some kind of hallucination inside the restaurant—or maybe I really did climb into the sheriff's lap and grind on him—but either way, I ran out the back door and went back to my Jeep and Grant was there. Waiting for me. And he told me this is all bullshit." I point to the amulet. "All the books he left behind were bullshit. So I probably did climb in Russ's lap and stick my tongue down his throat. Because this amulet didn't fucking protect me!"

I throw it across the room.

Pell places his hands on my shoulders and my body immediately heats up, the same way it did in the restaurant. Like he's filling me up with magic too. "What else did he say?"

Or maybe he's filling me up with insanity. Ha. I've already got plenty of that.

"Pie!" he growls. "What else did Grant say?"

"Don't you get it? It doesn't matter. None of this is real!"

He sneers at me. That's the Pell I know. The sneering, snide, predator Pell. "Don't be fucking crazy. I'm real. You're real. This place is real."

"I'm so far past crazy, Pell, it's a done deal, OK? And now I would like to wallow in my insanity for while. So could you just please leave?"

He stands up and I think to myself, *Finally. Somebody gives a shit about what I want.*

But he doesn't leave.

He grabs my keys from my hand, picks me up and flips me over his shoulder, carries me outside, through the gate, into the parking lot, and then plops me down in the Jeep's passenger seat.

"What the hell are you doing?"

He slams my door, walks around to the driver's side, gets in, and starts the engine. His eyes blaze yellow-orange when he looks at me. "You're not insane, Pie Vita. And I'm gonna prove it to you."

CHAPTER FIFTEEN – PELL

Aside from moving the Jeep from the front to the back the other day, it's been a really long time since I drove anywhere. Grant hasn't been all that fun to hang around for the past few decades, and now that I know he really was working against me this whole time, my aversion to going places with him makes sense.

I guess I always knew, but before Pie told me that he snuck his books out, it was just a hunch.

Now it's real.

And that sucks.

But what sucks more—what really pissed me off—is he has no right to taint Pie's mind like this. She's already confused and even though I don't know a lot about her life, I get it. She's under the impression she's crazy because of that bird.

And maybe she is, I don't know. I never saw her talking bird. I've seen *a* bird. Just looks like a normal bird to me. But the sanctuary is real. This curse, as crazy as it sounds, is also real. And we're living in the real world at all times, even though there's a wall up that separates us from them.

That's why I'm taking her to the gas station.

Except… when I pull up to the crossroad where that gas station was the last time I came by here, it's just a shell. A rusted-out sign, no gas pumps, no phone booth, and the windows to the little store are all boarded up. So I just idle at the stop sign across the street.

"What are we doing?"

I look down the road to my left, then to my right. "This used to be open."

"Like fifty years ago, maybe. Do we need gas?"

I look down at the gauge. "It wouldn't hurt. But that's not why I brought you here."

"Why then?"

I put up a hand, asking her to be quiet. "Just let me think for a moment. I need to find another one."

She points to the left. "I think the highway is that way. There should be a gas station near the on ramp."

I look down the dark, lonely stretch of road. It's as dark as dark gets, even with the moon. Because the moon is almost always hidden by the tops of trees. This is what it means to live in this part of Pennsylvania. Thick, encroaching woods and no sky to speak of. That's what I miss most about the Old World. At least the part I lived in. There was always so much sky.

"Pell?"

"Hmm."

"Well, what are we doing?"

"OK. We'll go that way." I turn left and we drive for a while. There are houses, most of them with porch lights, but there are no street lamps out this way. So that feeling of being trapped in the trees never quite diminishes until, sure enough, the road opens to reveal a highway and just past the on ramp, there is a gas station.

"Do not pull in, Pell."

"Why the hell not?"

"You." She laughs a little. Well, maybe more of a scoff, really. But it's good to hear something other than panic. She was really upset back there in the cottage. Like losing her damn mind upset. I hate Grant. I never really liked him—he walked around in an aura of assholiness. And he did fuck me over pretty good. But that's not why I hate him. He has no right to confuse this girl the way he did. She's teetering on the edge. And I guess he knows that, doesn't he? That's why he's filling her head with this bullshit story about not being real.

"It's fine," I say. "I don't care if people see me. They won't believe their eyes anyway. People believe what they want to believe. And they want to believe there is no such thing as a satyr chimera. So I'm good." Pie ponders this as I make my way across the highway and pull into the gas station. But then I notice something. "Shit. They don't have a phone booth here?"

"Phone booth?" Pie looks at me like I'm the crazy one. "There are no phone booths anymore." Then she shuffles through her purse and pulls out one of those pocket phones. "We have cell phones now. Did you bring me here to make a call?" Then she giggles a little and some of the anger leaves me. "We could've done it back on the country road outside the sanctuary."

I pull up to the gas pumps. "Shit. I forgot. OK. Well, call your parents then."

"What?"

"I want to prove that this is all real. You're stuck in the sanctuary with me, and that's kinda like being in a different world. But this world, it's still here, Pie. You're not hallucinating. This isn't a dream, you're not dead, you're not in purgatory. We're just stuck in a stupid curse. But we still have access to this world. And I'm gonna prove it to you, because you're going to call your parents."

She frowns.

"Now what?"

"I don't have parents."

"What do you mean?"

"I never had a father. At least, I never knew him. And my mother dropped me off at CPS when I was nine because I refused to say that Pia wasn't real."

"I don't understand. Your mother abandoned you?"

She nods.

"Oh." This fucking night. Nothing seems to be going right. But all I can do is shake my head, look out the window, and mutter, "What a fucking bitch."

"Tell me about it." Pie sounds tired.

I look over at her and suddenly she's someone else. Someone who was walked out on. Someone alone in this world, like me. Like Tomas, too.

She interprets my staring as expectation. "I have her number, so I guess I *could* call her, but—"

"No. Fuck her. Someone else. Call someone else. A friend. Even if I wasn't trying to prove a point, you have to do this so they don't worry about you."

"Oh"—she laughs a little—"trust me. No one is staying up at night calling hospitals and wondering if I'm dead in a ditch anywhere."

"Well, why not? What the hell is wrong with them?"

"No. You don't understand. I don't have... *friends*. Just Pia."

"Well, you can't call her. I don't know much about the pocket phones, but I'm pretty sure your bird doesn't have one."

Her laugh is bigger this time. "No. She doesn't have a phone. She's never needed one. She was always just… there. And now she's not."

"You don't have anyone you can call to pull you back from the edge, Pie?"

"Umm." She looks a little panicked. Like this is a quiz question.

"Look, I'm not judging you. Hell, I don't have anyone either. But I need you to know that *I'm* real. And if you're sitting here with me and talking to someone out there at the same time, that's how I prove my existence."

She nods, looking at me solemnly. "OK. I have one person. I was on my way to see her when I got sidetracked by the caretaker job. Jacqueline. She was my foster sister in one of the homes I had to live in when I was a teenager."

"OK. Call her. I can get out so you can have some privacy."

I reach for the handle of the Jeep, but Pie puts her hand on my shoulder. "Don't be dumb. You can't go out there. Someone could pull up for gas. I will pump the gas and make the call."

I'm very focused on the way her hand feels on my bare shoulder, but before I can make sense of it, she pulls away and gets out of the Jeep. I watch her with a new interest as she walks into the store and interacts with the clerk inside. She comes back out, cell phone pressed to her ear, her mouth moving, her lips curving up into a small smile. And she comes over to the Jeep again, over to my side, and then starts pumping gas.

I can hear little bits and pieces of her conversation with her friend Jacqueline, but not enough to make sense of it. The gas pump clicks off, and Pie removes it from the tank as she makes a promise to go visit this friend one day soon. Then she looks down at the phone in her hand and I guess the call is over.

My eyes track her as she walks around the front of the Jeep and then she slides in next to me, sighing. "We got a full tank. I'm thirty dollars more in debt, and…" She pauses and her head slowly migrates my direction. "Thanks. She was actually so happy to hear from me. She said she thinks of me all the time and that I can come visit her any time I want. She just bought a house. She went to college, Pell. I never knew. She's doing so good. She even has a guest room."

Pie looks away, out the front window. Her shoulders drop. Relax. Like a whole world of tension was just lifted off of them. "I never knew, ya know?" She looks at me again. "I never knew I had someone. Not until this very moment." She blinks, her eyes a bit glassy with tears. "Thank you."

I nod at her, getting it. "No problem." I start the Jeep. "It's a crazy world so… yeah. It's easy to start thinking it's just you, when it's not. It's just… a crazy fucking world that never made much sense in the first place."

"Yeah," she agrees. "It sure is."

I'm really happy for her. I truly am. But it's hard not to compare our lives.

She has someone, I do not.

She could, theoretically, leave the sanctuary for good one day and never come back. The chances of that happening for me are pretty much zero. But even if my curse was broken, where the hell would I go? I'd be a satyr chimera in a modern world and then what?

And it's not like I even wanna be a human man. I don't.

I just want to be me.

I just want to be with my own people, in my own time, and live my own life.

That's never going to happen. Even if the curse is broken.

Pie and I drive in silence for a while. She messes with her phone. I'm not sure what those things actually do, but then she asks me, "Why do they call it Saint Mark's?"

"What do you mean why?" I shrug. "It's just the name."

"But Saint Mark was a real person. So says the internet." She holds up her phone. It's lit up bright with a lot of words. "He was a real saint, at any rate. And maybe you guys even lived around the same time. So I have to assume that he's part of this. The sanctuary is part of a church."

"A church?"

"One with saints?"

I actually guffaw. "No, Pie. We're not part of a church."

"Then why is it called Saint Mark's?" She shrugs, like this is obvious.

I let out a long breath, trying to search for an answer, but I just don't have one. "I guess... I don't know."

"You're sure the sanctuary isn't connected with a church?"

"Hundred percent."

"Well. Then it's a mystery, I guess. But a weird one."

"Yeah," I sigh, then concentrate on driving.

In fact, we're both silent after that. We say nothing all the way back to that abandoned gas station, and then Pie says, "I know what you're thinking. But you don't have to worry."

I smile a little as I turn right, heading back home. "What am I thinking?"

"You're thinking I'll leave you one day. That I'll go to Jacqueline's house and stay in her guest room. But don't worry. It's not gonna happen. This curse has been in place for two thousand years. I know I was all confident in the beginning, but I get it now, Pell. Reality check, right?" She sighs. "I just don't have what it takes to change anything here. That is painfully obvious."

I wasn't really thinking about her leaving. Not after her comment about the sanctuary's name, anyway. But it's hard not to think about it again now. It sucks that I'm stuck here. And I know I've been a jerk to all the other caretakers over the centuries, but that was all bitterness on my part. Maybe even jealousy. I don't have those feelings for Pie. I want to be supportive of her. I wouldn't want her to be stuck here with me. It's not fair. She didn't ask for this. She just wanted a place to settle and catch her breath and I totally get that. So I say, "You don't know that, Pie. I think your fresh perspective on things is exactly what this place needs. So don't sell yourself short. It could happen."

"No," she says without emotion. "It's not gonna happen. I mean, even if I did manage to figure out how to break the curse, Grant said the debt book is a trap.

He says you need a spell to get out of it. And I think he's right. I'm so in debt already, it's such a joke. And we'll never stop needing things. Even if it was keeping track and erasing debts, there will always be new ones. Like this gas."

"The Book of Debt isn't fake, Pie. It does keep track. And it's honest."

She does a half-hearted shrug. "It's not likely, Pell."

"You want me to prove that true too?"

"How?"

"Simple." I find myself grinning. "All you have to do is please me and watch your debt disappear in real time." I pull into the sanctuary's back lot, park the Jeep, and turn it off.

And when I look at her, I realize she's suspicious of me again, all my goodwill suddenly erased. "You want me to wash your feet, Pell? Like a fucking slave?"

"That's just one way."

"You want me to—"

I point at her. "Do not say 'blowjob.' I will stop talking to you forever. I'm not a bad guy. I didn't write that book. I didn't make up these rules. I didn't have anything to do with it. I'm stuck here, just like you."

She lets out a long breath. "Then how? If not feet, if not…" I caution her with my eyes. "If not that other thing, then how?"

"You could polish my horns. No one's done it in a very long time. They could use it."

She actually checks my horns for dullness and I have to cover my mouth with my fist to hide my amusement. Is she slow? Is she crazy? Is she naïve?

Or is she just cute?

"And this will knock a debt off?" Pie seems dubious.

"A nice chunk," I say. "I like the horn polish. A lot. It feels good. Like a back massage. And the debts are erased according to how much you please me."

"Why is it like that?"

"Why is it like what?"

"Why does this curse care about your... pleasure?"

"Huh." I think about that for a moment. I feel like I know the answer to this, but I can't quite conjure it up. "I dunno. I can't remember."

"Well, it feels like a plot device to me. It feels... fake."

"For fuck's sake. None of this is fake. You're wearing the ring. You're trapped here. The gray mist. The apothecary. Fucking Tomas! It's all real."

She exhales loudly, not looking at me, just focusing on something outside by the lake for a few moments. "Did Grant ever polish your horns?"

"Never. I didn't let him touch me. That's probably why he thinks it doesn't work. All he ever did was cook for me. And in the beginning, we used to go drinking. And he'd glamour me. He knows that worked. So all that shit he talked to you, that's all it was. Just shit. He's a fucking liar."

"I don't know. He seems to be in control of things."

"In control of what?"

She turns her head to look me in the eyes. Her eyes are a very pretty blue color. Like cornflowers. And somehow, maybe the moon is reflecting off the lake or something, but her eyes are lit up with a little glow. "He wasn't old, Pell. He was young when I saw him in town. He looked exactly the way he did when I first saw him. Before he took the ring off. He knows things. And he's in control of things."

"How?"

Pie, of course, has no answer for me.

"I mean… that's not possible. He had debts. He had so much debt, Pie. It would've taken centuries to wipe it away."

"It's an easy explanation," Pie says. "That book is bullshit."

"No." I'm shaking my head. "You saw him get old." I look at her for confirmation and she nods. "So it's not bullshit. The debt caught up. He got out of it. But how?"

"I think he really does do magic, Pell. Like…" She sucks in a breath and then blows it out with her words. "Like big, bad, *serious* magic. He said he had a spell. He offered it to me. He told me how to make money. He said I could stay for as long as I wanted, make money on the outside, and then he could call up a new caretaker with another flyer when I was ready to leave."

My mouth drops open. "What did you say?"

"I told him to shove it up his ass. Sorta. But I'm not interested in getting rich off this curse. That's such a bad idea. And I don't want to leave. Not yet. And anyway, we already know where another caretaker is. Russ Roth is my ticket out if I ever do want to go."

I knew Grant was powerful, of course. He's been very busy in that apothecary for decades. And the greenhouse is—I point at Pie. "At some point, sooner rather than later, remind me to show you the greenhouse. Maybe he fucked that all up too, but I doubt it. He didn't know when you would come. I mean, did he know you were coming?"

"No. He was surprised. And all the way across the sanctuary. He was so out of breath when he finally found me in that front hall, he could barely talk."

"Right. That's good. If he didn't know you were coming, then the greenhouse is safe."

"What's the big deal with the greenhouse? You got tomatoes out there or something?"

This girl. I swear. Is she slow? Is she crazy? Is she naïve?

She is just cute.

"The herbs. We need them to restock the apothecary. We'll have to go through it and get rid of all the plants he harvested. It's gonna be a mess, but it's gotta be done. The magic is important. We can look at that tomorrow. Tonight"—I point at her— "I'm gonna prove that the Book of Debt is real and you are in control of it."

Pie shrugs, flips the door handle, and gets out. "OK. Prove that I can work this debt off just by making you happy."

I get out too and wave her forward towards the gate, smiling to myself. Because this is gonna be fun, I think. We walk through and I head towards the path instead of turning towards the cottage. Pie balks, stopping in place. "What's wrong now?" I sigh.

She looks up the hill towards the cathedral, then back at me. "I don't want to walk past those tombs. Can't we do it down here?"

I nod in the other direction. "All the stuff is up there. The tombs can't hurt you."

She tsks her tongue and shakes her head. "I don't believe that for a second. There are monsters inside them. And I'm pretty sure that those statues outside are just a glimpse of what's waiting inside the tombs. I can't really see them in there, but I feel them moving around. They make shadows. And they could just slide out and take me as I'm walking."

"They can't, Pie. That door you see, it's not really there. It's just an illusion."

She is shaking her head now before I'm even done talking. "Oh, no, it's not. I can feel them." She gazes up the hill where the tombs pack the lawn shoulder to shoulder. "And there are so many of them." Pie looks up at me, eyes wide and questioning. "Why are there so many of them?"

"It's continuously being populated. Like the upstairs of the cathedral."

She looks around, trying this explanation on for size. "But where do they come from? I mean, if it's continuous, then where do these monsters start? Like… if this is their end, where is the beginning?"

"Huh. I guess I never thought about that."

"How could you not think about that?"

"In my defense, Pie, I've been here for a long fucking time. When I first got here, it was just me and Tarq. And Tomas, of course. He was already here though. And he doesn't live in a tomb, he's… never mind. My point is, these tombs all came later. Little bits at a time. One here, two there. And then, before I knew it, the place was full."

"And you never bothered to wonder where they were coming from?"

"Well." I let out a long exhale. "I just figured the curse was making the rounds."

"Making the rounds?"

"Yeah. Like… um. You know. There's a lot of fucking monsters out there, all over the earth, and it just takes time to find them all to pack them up in tombs." She actually stops walking to look at me. "What?" I ask.

She just shakes her head. "I don't know what I think about that."

"About what?"

"Are you clueless, ignorant, or just… Zen?"

I laugh, point at her. "Not sure what the Zen thing is, but I choose that one. The others are most certainly undesirable. Anyway," I add, before she can think up more questions about that line of thinking, "you can't get in the tomb, this is my point. Only I can enter the tombs. But here's the catch on my side, I can't see the doors."

"What?"

"Yeah. It's a paradox. I can enter, but can't see the doors. You can see the doors, but you can't enter. And none of them can come out. Trust me. I've been here two thousand years and not a single monster has found their way out of those tombs. So when you walk alongside me up this path, you can't even see the doors. No shadows at all."

She looks up the path again and her shoulders relax. "Oh. OK, then. But"—she turns back to me—"how do you get inside your tomb?"

"Well, that one's mine and I can see the opening."

"So I can't ever go into your tomb?"

"Why the hell would you want to go in there?"

"I dunno. To see where you live."

I spread my arms wide to encompass the entire sanctuary. "I live here. You can see all of it."

"So your tomb though." She is not letting this go. "It's like your bedroom? Your private chambers or whatever?"

"Sure. It's like my bedroom, I guess. But it's not a bedroom. It's the woods."

"What? How is that possible?"

"Can we talk about this tomorrow?"

"No. How is your tomb *the woods*?"

"It's like the cathedral. It's different on the inside than it is on the out."

"Like my cottage."

"No. Not really. That's like... I don't know. Personal design preferences or whatever. My tomb is more like the hallways up the staircases."

"What hallways? I need to hear all about this. Like... right this very moment."

"You'd rather hear about my tomb than know that the Book of Debt is real?"

She smirks up at me. "You just want me to polish your horns, don't you?"

"I mean..." I begin. She laughs. "I can lie and say no. But. Yeah. It feels good. It's been a long time since I had a horn polish."

And even in the dim moonlight filtered through the tops of trees, I can see her blush.

Is she slow? Stupid? Naïve?

No.

She is just cute.

I wave my hand towards the path. "Shall we?"

I take her back to the steam cave where we left the Book of Debt. I open it up to her page.

Pages. She's got quite a few of them already.

This makes her deflate a little, but I'm ready. "Look." I flip to the first page of the book and point to all the ways she can work off her debt. Of course, her eyes only see the sex. And she's about to start pointing that out when I smack her finger away and show her the only one that matters tonight. "Right there. 'Polish horns.'"

She leans down to get a better look at the elaborate calligraphy. "One thousand? Is that in dollars?"

"Dollars," I confirm.

"How come it's dollars? Shouldn't it be in... drachma or something?"

"You're definitely not stupid."

"What?" Her eyes narrow.

"You're close. The drachma? But that's Greek. In Rome we called them aurei or denarii. It's actually pretty complicated. But we're not in Rome, so we don't do things like the Romans. We're in PA, and we do dollars."

"Hmm. OK, then. I'll take a horn polish for one thousand, Alex."

"Who's Alex?"

She smiles, pats my chest like I'm simple. "It's not important. Let's do this."

And do I detect a little excitement in her voice?

I do believe I do.

I grab a wooden box off a nearby ledge and set it on a stone table just to the left of a configuration of rocks that allows me to sit and lean forward, resting my head on a smooth, flat stone to give her total access to my horns. I take out a pot of polish, remove the lid, and give it a smell.

"Mmm. That kind of smells good."

"Sandalwood oil," I say. "It's old. But the paste is infused with magic, so it's fine. One day though, you should learn to make your own batch of horn polish. It's better that way. It will leave your imprint on me." She goes still at this, maybe thinking too hard about that and what it might mean. So I change the subject. "Just dip your fingers in, get a little bit of paste, and then rub it into my horns."

She nods to herself, like she's having a whole internal conversation, then sucks in a deep breath and dips her fingers into the jar.

I lean forward on the stone, my chest pressing against the smooth rock, my face resting on my hands. And I close my eyes and almost moan when her gentle hands begin massaging the oil into my horns.

It's not as tame an act as I let on. My horns are twisted and hard like bone, but just picturing her hands as they slide around the curve of them turns me on a little.

It's a lot like a handjob, actually.

"They're hot," she whispers.

"Mmmm."

"How come they're hot?"

"I'm made of fire," I mumble.

"What?"

"Pie?"

"Hmm?"

"Can I enjoy it, at least?"

"Sorr-ree. Jeez."

I pick up my head and look her in the eye. "I know it's weird and you're uncomfortable, but I don't care. It feels good and I want to enjoy it. It's been a long time. And I've never had a woman in here with me. This is… quite nice."

She frowns a little, but nods. "OK. I'll shut up."

I feel a little bad for being so blunt. And now I can't enjoy it because I feel bad. "Fuck it. If you need to talk your way through it, then fine. Talk. It will still feel good."

"Never mind," she says. "We both want to get the maximum benefit out of this, right?"

I put my head back down without answering her and she resumes her massage.

Maybe this is just a transaction for her, but that's not how it is for me.

I am starting to enjoy Pie Vita and the debt is a reassurance to me.

I don't know how Grant got out of his debt and got his youthful body back, but Pie isn't anything like Grant.

There is no way she will break this curse and that means I could get stuck here with her forever.

I'm perfectly OK with that.

CHAPTER SIXTEEN – PIE

Polishing horns is very much, almost totally—
I mean, let's just be honest here, it's exactly like giving
a handjob.

I can only chuckle internally about this because…
yeah. He got me.

And he's enjoying the hell out of his "horn
massage." He's even groaning a little.

And reluctantly I admit, that sound he makes, it's
provocative. I can't deny it. It's like a rumble.
Something low, and deep, and threatening. Like a
growl, but quiet.

Anyway. I just polish away as he relaxes. And… I
might be studying the muscles on his back just a little.
They are hard and tense. He's got so many of them.
I'm not sure if this is normal, but his back is like a
topography of sexiness.

Holy shit. I think that fucking cupid charm is still
working or something.

The moment I think that, the evening comes
rushing back at me. And the whole shitshow with
Grant aside, I don't want to think about that
disastrous 'date' with Sheriff Russ Roth ever again.
Did I climb in his lap?

Stop it. Pack that up and put it away, Pie. Just… chill. And think about the glorious monster in your hands at the moment.

Fuck. I need to find an antidote for this stupid spell. Obviously, it's still working. Because glorious monster?

No.

A sharp pain shoots through my hands and I pull away, gasping. "What the hell was that?"

Pell sits up a little so he can look over his shoulder at me. His eyes are droopy and seductive.

See? There it is again! That stupid love spell!

"What's the problem?" Pell's voice is husky. Like he just woke up. Or just had sex.

"Your horns. They're so hot now, I can't touch them."

He frowns and looks put out about this. Then he nods his head to the little wooden box where he got the sandalwood oil from. "In that box there's another paste. Try that one." Then he drops his head down and just… assumes I will do that, I guess.

I find three containers inside the box. I lift the lid off of each one and smell them. They are not rancid. In fact, one of them smells like lilacs. I like that one. But there's another one that smells like eucalyptus and makes the tips of my fingers feel like ice, and I assume that's the one he was referring to. So I place that one on the stone table and start working it into his horns.

And sure enough, it does make the heat bearable. And even though the palms of my hands are bright red, they don't hurt. In fact, they begin to tingle and then I sort of start to get into what I'm doing just a little more.

His horns fall back over his shoulder blades in two twists. And my hands slide around these twists easily. The part where his horns meet the side of his head are very thick, and that girth continues until the first twist, then they taper around another twist until they come to a dull point at the end.

There are little chips in the bone or whatever. Like he hasn't been taking care of these horns. So I pay extra attention to those parts. And they glow a little. The way they did earlier when he was sleeping on my couch.

Fire inside him.

Literally, I guess.

This is what burns. He is made of bubbling brimstone.

A creature of Hell, no doubt. I looked up the satyrs in the books. They are lecherous monsters. Well, I think maybe monster is a strong word. They are more like… frat boys.

I snort a little thinking of frat boys. Because just a few days ago, that's who I was partying with on Halloween.

I mean, OK. No. Those boys from Mount Aloysius College weren't frat boys in the literal sense. No Greek scene at that place.

A muffled snore draws me back to my present situation.

"Are you fucking kidding me? You're falling asleep when I'm in the middle of giving you the best hornjob you've ever had?"

He doesn't wake up. Even when I laugh out loud.

I guess he really does like this. And when I look over my shoulder at the book, my page is glowing. A set of words is lit up in light purple. And then, right before my eyes, the entire line disappears.

I've erased a debt!

I keep going, putting more effort into the hornjob. But try as I might, no other debts are erased.

A sudden flash of economics class comes to mind. This must be a real-life example of diminishing returns. He has gotten all the satisfaction he's gonna get from my hornjob. So no matter how much longer I keep going, no more debt will be erased.

I guess it makes sense, but that means that I can't just give him hornjobs all the time. I have to mix it up. Probably he will still get pleasure the next time I do it, but it won't be anything like this time.

It seems that the Book of Debt's algorithms reward freshness.

I pause my massage, my eyes still drawn to the muscles of his back. And then I dip my fingers into the pot of soothing paste, and begin working it into them.

Pell stirs at this change and sleepily looks over his shoulder at me. "What are you doing?"

"The hornjob is over. The Book of Debt said so. But I figured you could use a back massage too. You're kinda tense."

He just stares at me.

"Should I not?"

Then he puts his head back down and mumbles something that I assume is permission.

I hold my breath, waiting for his reaction as my fingers resume their workings. I push into the tight muscles and he groans. But not with the satisfaction of the hornjob. It's more of a painful reaction.

"Am I hurting you?" He shakes his head, so I keep going. I press my fingertips into the long muscles that line either side of his spine, sliding them up and down.

He groans again.

"Are you sure I'm not hurting you?"

"Pie."

"What?"

"Look at the book. Then you tell me if it hurts."

I glance over at the book and there are three lines of debt lit up purple. I can't hide the chuckle. "I guess it feels good then."

"So fucking good," he whispers.

It's such a small thing, too. A back massage. I mean, this is something couples do on the regular in the real world, right? But he's been here for two thousand years with no woman. And assuming he's not into men and didn't have affairs or get hornjobs and back massages from any of his other caretakers, that… sucks.

This makes me want to do a good job. I'm not any kind of expert on massages, but it's not that hard to find the tight muscles. And he's got so many of them, by the time I've gone over every square inch of his back, my hands are actually cramping.

I stop to shake them out and then, exhausted, I sit down on the extra length of stone bench behind him.

He lazily turns to the side and peeps at me from under his hooded eyelids. "Tired?"

I nod and laugh a little as I shake out my hands. "I've got a cramp."

He sits up, turns, and suddenly he's straddling the stone bench, facing me.

I'm so surprised when he reaches for my hands, I pull them away. "What are you doing?"

He grabs one back and start pushing on my palms as one corner of his mouth lifts up in a half smile. "You ask way too many questions."

"Oh." It comes out with my breath. And then I don't know what to do. Let him massage my cramped hands? Or stop this before it turns into something too much?

I let him keep going and I'm almost immediately sorry when he just… stares at me, looking straight into my eyes like he's some sort of charmer and this is his superpower. Because his intense yellow-orange gaze renders me speechless and paralyzed.

"You don't like it?" The other side of his mouth lifts up now. And he's wearing a full-on smile.

"I like it." I barely manage to get those words out because my whole body is suddenly on fire. Almost the same way it was back in the restaurant with Russ.

"Wait." I pull my hand away. "Just…" I have to take a deep breath. "Just hold on. I have to tell you something."

"You really are magic and you're gonna take on Grant and save me and the sanctuary?"

"What?" A laugh bursts out of my mouth before I can stop it. "No. Definitely not."

He shrugs. "A guy can dream, right?"

I narrow my eyes at him. "I just gave you the best hornjob you've ever had and you're thinking about the stupid curse?"

"First of all"—he points at me—"I love that word." He licks his lips like he wants to taste me. "Hornjob is the very best thing about this day. And second, I'm always thinking about that stupid curse."

I open my mouth to say something back, but he presses his flat palm towards me. "You can't hold that against me. I've been here for two thousand years."

"OK. Then I won't."

"Good. Now seriously, what were you gonna say?"

"Well." Where to start? "When I was with Russ, I got all heated up and hot. Like, he was checking me for fever and everything." Pell's face changes instantly. So I hurry past this and get to the point. "I got all hot then, and now I'm getting all hot again, so I'm thinking… this… what I'm feeling right now, it's part of the spell I put on myself."

Now he looks confused. "And you think this why?"

"Grant fucked up the books, remember? I think I put a love spell on myself."

"No. I mean… why are you thinking about this now?"

"Oh." Shit. "Well. You're making me hot, and he was making me hot, so it's… the love spell."

"Are you *sure* it's the love spell?"

"What else could it be?"

He's all smirk when he chuckles, points at me, and says, "Definitely cute."

"What's that mean?"

"Never mind. If this is bothering you, Pie, I will stop. How's that?"

"Well." I look down at my hands. It does feel pretty good. But I need to be practical about this. "I just don't want us to get caught up in a love spell."

"Oh." He nods. Pretends to look serious. "Well, then we should wait."

"Wait?" For some reason, this conversation suddenly has sexual undertones and I'm not sure how that happened. "I'm literally just talking about a hand massage."

"A handjob?" He laughs out loud.

"No." And I laugh too. "Not a handjob. My God. See? This is what I mean. This is getting all mixed up when it shouldn't."

"Shouldn't it?"

I sigh. "You know what I'm talking about. You're just trying to be difficult."

"Fine." He stands up and stretches his back. His arms go up towards the cave ceiling and he closes his eyes as he yawns. His fangs are long and sharp and he looks every bit like a beast in this moment. A lazy, content, I-am-the-king-of-this-jungle beast.

And I'm suddenly on fire. So I get up too, then start fanning myself, like I was in the restaurant. "Yep. This is definitely the love spell working right now."

Pell just grins at me. "If you say so, Pie. I'm going to bed, I guess. Want me to walk you home so the monsters don't get you?"

"No. I think I'll sleep on the apothecary couch."

He frowns. "Why?"

"The cottage is too far away. I don't like being so far away."

He looks around. Like he's thinking. When he looks back at me, I know what he's gonna say. "Want me to stay with you?"

"I don't want to impose."

We both laugh out loud. Then he grabs my hand and starts pulling me out of the cave. "We'll figure something out tomorrow. But you're not sleeping in the apothecary. That was Grant's realm. It's far safer for you in that distant cottage than it is in there."

"Fuck. That's true."

"I'll stay with you tonight."

I expect him to let go of my hand when we get to the stairs, but he doesn't. He keeps it. Holds it firmly all the way down the path to the cottage. And everything about this walk home is awkward. But when we get inside and I look upstairs, and he looks upstairs, it's more than awkward. It's embarrassing.

We both say, "I'll take the couch," at the same time.

Then, again, together, we say, "No, you take the bed."

Then we both laugh.

"Pell." I place a hand on his chest, acutely aware that he's still got a hold of my other one. "You're like seven feet tall. You cannot sleep on that couch. Take the bedroom."

But he's already shaking his head. "I'm not letting you sleep down here alone. It kinda defeats the purpose of staying over to make you feel safe."

And yep. There's only one way this goes after that.

"Well. That bed should be big enough for both of us."

And there it is.

It's out there.

He nods and starts up the stairs. And because we are attached at the hand, I go with him.

I am going to bed with the monster of Saint Mark's.

CHAPTER SEVENTEEN – PELL

One thing is abundantly clear when we reach the top of the stairs and stand in front of her bed. It's definitely not big enough for the two of us. It's barely big enough for me.

"I'll sleep on the couch," I say.

"No. Don't be dumb. It's my fault you're staying over in the first place."

I don't mean to sneer down at her, but I do. "I'm not kicking you out of your own bed."

She shrugs. "Then I guess we're sleeping together." She points at me. "You know the good part about walking around naked all the time?"

I grin.

"You don't have to change clothes at bedtime. But I do. BRB."

She grabs some clothes from her closet and disappears into the bathroom while I circle the bed trying to imagine how this will go. It's a nice bed, for sure. A cool canopy. Very elegant and old-fashioned. It's a mess of covers, so she doesn't make her bed up when she wakes, which I sorta love. There's nothing worse than an uptight bedmaker. We will fit. Obviously. But there will be no way to avoid contact with each other.

I'm still standing there when she comes out of the bathroom wearing a pair of tight black shorts and an equally tight black top. And her breasts are... yeah.

"What are you doing?" Her voice snaps me out of the image I'm forming of her breasts.

"I wasn't looking." It comes out defensive and this makes her laugh.

"Oh, my God. Is the monster blushing? Is he shy? Is he"—she pauses to smile—"a *gentleman?*"

I snort. "Get in the bed, woman."

"Oh, he's a caveman." She sends me a sly smile as she slides between the sheets. I walk over to the gas lamp and turn it off. And it's immediately dark. So dark I have to feel my way along the bed before getting in next to her.

I sigh. Because I'm fucking huge and this bed—

"Just relax, Pell. Think about how nice it was to get a hornjob."

I almost guffaw. "Trust me. That's not the answer."

She turns on her side, which gives me more room, and I settle on my side as well, so we're facing each other in the dark.

"So this is real, huh?"

"Obviously, it's not ideal. I get that. But Saint Mark's isn't that bad."

"Says the monster who was lecturing me two days ago about how my entire job here involves breaking your curse."

"I did say that." I wish there was more moonlight because I'd like to see her face once more before this night ends. This whole day definitely took a strange turn.

"What are you thinking about?"

"You."

"Good? Bad? Or ugly?"

"Cute," I say.

"What?"

"I was wondering earlier if you were slow, stupid, or naïve. And then I just decided on cute."

"Cute." She says it like she's mulling it over. "I don't think anyone has ever called me cute."

"Then they don't know what the fuck they're talking about."

She shifts position and her bare leg brushes up against mine. Then she hums out a, "Hmm."

"Should I ask what that hmm means?"

"Your legs are soft." She illustrates this by rubbing her thigh against mine.

"Are you trying to pet me?"

A giggle in the dark. "No. Maybe tomorrow though. Tonight…" She yawns. "Tonight, I think I'll just go to sleep."

We lie there in the dark. Silent.

Then she says, "Good night, monster."

And I whisper back, "Good night, Pie."

She hums a little, then turns over. Pushing her ass right up against me.

And even though I want to flip her over and ravish her like a sex slave—I don't.

Because I want to take her somewhere tomorrow.

I want to show her that being stuck here with me isn't all about the curse.

It can be a fun place.

She could be happy here.

CHAPTER EIGHTEEN – PIE

Three things go through my mind simultaneously when I wake in the morning.

One. He's still here. He's still in my bed.

Two. He's got his arms around me. Like, we are full-on spooning. And that means his morning wood is pressing right up against my ass.

Three. None of this is terrible.

I mean, he's half monster. There's no getting around that. But his monster bits aren't as scary today as they were earlier in the week. Seeing him come at me that first day—that was like seeing a demon out of Hell. He was terrifying on a level that I wasn't able to comprehend.

And yes, he was kind of a dick the first couple days. But yesterday he was... well. On a micro-level, he was my hero. He pulled me back from the edge. And OK, I wasn't in danger of actually jumping, but I was in the middle of a serious struggle and he put me in the Jeep so he could refocus me.

Talking to Jacqueline was the reality check I needed. I hadn't realized how much I missed her until I heard her voice on the other end of the phone last night. She is my tether to the outside. That's what Pell did for me last night.

He gave me a tether. He was my hero.

Sure, I'm still stuck in the curse, but we're stuck here together. It could be worse.

He stirs behind me, but doesn't wake.

I gently move his arms so I can slip out of the bed, then go downstairs and throw some more wood into the water heater thing. He's still sleeping when I get back upstairs, so I use the bathroom. When I'm done, I check myself in the mirror as I brush my teeth. My hair is a little wild, but in a sexy way. I splash cold water on my cheeks, apply some of the fancy lip balm I bought in the spa boutique during the shopping spree that cost me my eternal soul, then take a deep breath and step back into the bedroom.

He's awake, sitting up in bed with his lower half hidden under the covers, and even though the horns kinda ruin the illusion that he is just another man and not really a monster, there is no way to deny that Pell is sexy as fuck. And he's grinning at me.

I walk over to the closet and pull a light satin robe off the hanger. I bite the tags off with my teeth, then slip it on, suddenly feeling very self-conscious. "Why are you smiling at me like that?"

He grins bigger. But all he says is, "Cute."

"Right." I point at him. "Is she slow, stupid, or just naïve?"

"Cute," he repeats.

And now it's getting awkward. "So. I guess it's time to feed you. What do you want for breakfast?"

He doesn't say it, but I hear it anyway. *You.*

I bite my lip, unsure what to do. Maybe letting him sleep in my bed was a huge mistake? Does he think we're like… a couple now? Because we're not. He's got a very nice upper body and no lie, that dick of his would definitely be a pleaser. But he's still a monster. I'm pretty sure there are rules against falling in love with a monster.

He pushes the covers away, swings his legs out of bed, then bends over with his face in his hands, like he's a slow waker and needs a moment.

But that's not what he's doing. He's thinking or something. I'm just about to leave and go make breakfast when he slowly turns his head towards me. "I know what you're thinking."

"Me?" I point to my chest. "What am I thinking? I'm not thinking anything."

"You're thinking, *He's a beast. He's half animal. He and I aren't going anywhere.* And I get it." He pauses here to stare into my eyes, checking to see if I'm listening. Checking to see if I'm taking him seriously. "I get it. You're a very pretty human. And you're stuck here with me. Tomas and I are the only people you will ever get to be yourself with. And that can lead to things, or feelings—"

"Pell. Look. We slept next to each other for one night. It's no big deal. You were being... heroic last night. Saving me from my fear of living all the way down here in the cottage. That's all it was." I smile broadly at him, trying to make myself believe that line of bullshit I just spewed. But my heart is beating wildly because everything is different right now. Nothing is the same between us. And it's not about the hornjob or sleeping next to each other last night.

There is something different about *us*.

"That's all it was?" he asks.

I nod. "Yep. And thank you, by the way. For coming down here with me. But you won't have to do it again."

He stands up. No pants. And I have to remind myself that his kind don't wear pants. "You're not afraid of the monsters anymore?"

"I am." I keep my eyes stoically trained on his. I will not look down. I will not. "But I'm not gonna stay down here in the cottage." I look around at the bedroom and then my eyes wander to the loft and get caught on the shutters of the tall windows down below. "It's weird. There's something wrong with it."

Pell looks around too. "Looks pretty nice to me."

"That's just it." I look back at him and shrug. "When I first applied for the job and Grant mentioned the caretaker's cottage, my mind conjured up this image, ya know? A cottage. Quaint, cozy, fireplace, and kinda French countryside." I point to the open half wall. "The shutters on the windows. And on the outside, it doesn't look anything like the cottage I imagined. It's really just another stone building with some cool symmetrical windows. But in here it was everything I pictured. Right down to the shutters, Pell."

He's got a stupid grin on his face. And then he sighs and shakes his head a little. "This is what's worrying you? The décor is yours and doesn't go with the outside?"

"What? It's creepy, don't you think?"

"Pie." He walks over to me. I will not look down. I will not do it. He puts his massive hands on my shoulders and looks down at me with a pretty serious face. I have to tilt my head way up to meet his gaze, that's how big he is. "It's magic. Don't you get it?"

He lets go of my shoulders, but grabs my hand and leads me downstairs and out into the cool morning air. He points up the hill at the top half of the cathedral that's visible from down here. "That's the same way. On the outside it's one thing. It's a church, it's a cathedral, it's a sanctuary. But what is it on the inside?"

I huff out some air as I pull my skimpy robe tighter around me. "I've noticed. It makes no sense."

"It's the same thing here. All the buildings here are like that. Even the tombs. The inside is magic, Pie. And these buildings will adapt and change. The caretaker cottage adapted to your expectations that first day. And I think it's kinda cool."

"How do you figure?"

"It recognized you."

"I don't think I like the sound of that."

"Why not?"

"Because then… then this whole thing becomes something inevitable. Like… fate. Like I never had a choice in it." I look up at him. "How did you get like this? Were you born this way? Are monsters just real and you're one of them? Or were you a man once?"

His smile falls immediately. "Oh. I get it."

"Get what?"

"This is about the hooves, right? The horns, the fur. This is where you try to reconcile the two parts of me. Because you need me to be one or the other."

"I'm not judging you, if that's what you're getting at."

"You absolutely are judging me, but that's not what I'm getting at. You can't cope with the idea that I'm just… *both*. Man and monster."

I turn away from him and go back inside.

He follows me. "I get it. I've lived in this body my entire life, so there's part of the answer to your question. I am a satyr chimera. I was born a satyr chimera. But I am still very much a man. I was born a man too."

I check the water heater fire, throw some more wood just to make it flare up, and then go back upstairs and start the tub for a bath. Again, he follows me. So I guess I have to say something about his last comment. "I'm not insulting your manhood, Pell. I'm just curious."

He leans against the doorjamb as I sit on the edge of the tub, waiting for the water to get hot. "You're not hearing me. I'm not insulted. I'm just frustrated that you fucking humans can't cope with things like me. I have to be myth. I have to be cursed—"

I throw up my hands. "Dude. You're completely cursed!"

"I am cursed to stay here as the monster of Saint Mark's. But I wasn't cursed into this body. I was made this way. Just like you were made that way."

I try to rewind the conversation to see how we got here. Because just a few minutes ago we had this weird, but nice, morning glow going on and now we're suddenly in some kind of identity fight. "Look, I appreciate what you did for me last night. My only point is, you won't need to stay down here with me anymore because I don't want to stay here."

"Where will you sleep then?"

"I dunno. I'm sure there's a room in that giant fucking cathedral with a bed."

"OK. Do you know how the rooms work up there?" He nods his head to the cathedral.

"What do you mean, work? They're *rooms*."

"They're variable. The inside of that place changes all the time. Just like the inside of this cottage. The only rooms that stay the same are the rooms on either side of the entrance halls and that main staircase. Upstairs it's all magic, all the time."

The water is finally hot so I plug up the tub, get up, push past him, and go back out into the bedroom to grab some clothes. "What kind of magic?"

"It's a…" Pell pauses like he's thinking. "They're like… I don't know how to explain it. It's like a record of all the days."

"Oh, yeah. Tomas mentioned this. OK. I'm following. Go on."

"It's just magic. Naturally magic. And magic isn't good or bad, it just is."

"Well, that's not true. This is a curse, remember? That's obviously bad."

"You're assigning feelings to a force, Pie. Is wind bad? Is rain bad? Is fire bad?"

"It can be."

"Yep, it can be. But the wind blows sails, and the rain grows crops, and the flame lights your way home. None of that is inherently bad. And neither am I."

"Whoa. That came out of nowhere."

He sneers at me. "No, it didn't. You think I'm evil because I have horns. You think I'm a monster out of Hell because I have hooves. This is the whole point of what I'm trying to say. I'm not good, I'm not bad, I'm just a flame in the dark."

"OK. I completely follow that logic. But what I'm also hearing is that you're both. You can destroy and save."

He spreads his arms wide, an all-encompassing gesture. "Aren't we all?" But he's no longer sneering at me, so I feel like we've arrived at some kind of common ground.

"I guess," I admit. "But I don't have a monster side. I'm just cute, remember?"

His wide grin is back and this tells me that while we have not really settled this, he's comfortable ending the convo here. "Take your bath, wear comfortable shoes, and meet me in the cemetery when you're done. We're taking a trip today."

"A trip? Not to Granite Springs, I hope."

He growls. "No. And don't bring that fucking sheriff up again. The more I think about what happened to you last night, the angrier I get."

"I didn't bring up the sheriff. That was you."

"Well, don't do it again."

I push him out of the bedroom. "Go away. Your man side is showing."

I take my bath and put on a really cute light-blue sweater dress with some knee-high brown boots with a short heel and pull my hair up in a simple ponytail. These clothes are nice, but if I had known that I'd have to work off the price by giving a monster a hornjob, I might've thought twice before buying them.

But then again… I twirl in front of a gorgeous gilded full-length mirror that was not even here when I woke up this morning and decide, *Nah. I'd have bought it anyway.* These clothes might be expensive, but they are clearly quality and I feel like my status in life went up several levels just by putting them on.

Pell is sitting on a tomb at the top of the hill. He's backlit by the sun, and the silhouette of his horns looks a little ominous. In fact, for a moment I think he's someone else. But he stands up as I get closer and that mirage fades. He meets me on the pea-pebbled path with a scowl.

"Why are you looking at me like that?"

He looks down at my boots. "I said *comfortable* shoes."

"These are comfortable."

"Could you walk a thousand years in those shoes?"

"What?"

"Because that's what we're about to do." Then he takes my hand and pulls me towards the cathedral.

A thousand years.

I let that sink in.

"We're going back in time? Tomas said we could do this. Hey, where is Tomas? Should we be worried about him? It's been two days now."

"No. Don't worry about Tomas. He's got his own issues going on. But trust me, he's not going anywhere."

"Huh. You know, Grant said that same thing to me when I asked about Tomas the first day."

"He said what?"

"That Tomas wasn't going anywhere. He's not like you. And he's not stuck in the tombs—by the way, was that big black one there yesterday?" I look over my shoulder at the new mausoleum.

"No. New tombs pop up all the time. That's why the cemetery is so crowded."

This makes me shudder. I don't like the tombs. I don't like the statues in front of them, I don't like the doorways—which, by the way, are no longer there. So Pell was telling the truth. I can't see them when we're together. But everything about the cemetery is *monster*.

And I have a feeling that Pell is the exception to the rule about monster behavior. Some of those statues are terrifying.

These thoughts distract me as we enter the cathedral and then we are standing in the center of the lower great hall, looking up at the staircases.

"Tomas said they have lots of rooms up there."

"They do. But they're not really rooms in the general sense. They are points in time."

He's still holding my hand. Like we're a team. And this feels real. I just have a sense that this is what the curse is about. Me and him. Monster and caretaker. Fighting our way through life together.

That might be overly dramatic, but at the very least, I'm here to support him.

But what is he doing?

"Why are you here, Pell?"

"Hmm?" He's not really paying attention to me. He's looking intently up one of the stairwells. His gaze falls down to me. "What?"

"OK. So I'm here to take care of you."

"Right."

"Why are you here?"

"I was cursed."

"By who?"

He nods up. "I can show you, if you want. I can't guarantee we'll find it today. It could take hours, or weeks, or years to find what you're looking for up there. But we'll find something interesting, that's for sure."

I look up at the stairwell and take a moment to reflect on what he just said. "We're going back in time?"

"Kind of. It's not real, Pie. It's *magic*. Sometimes you're almost real, ya know? You can eat the food, talk a little with the people, participate. But other times you're like a ghost. Just floating through."

"Wow. That's… kinda creepy."

"There is no creepy. There is just misunderstood."

I don't really agree. Because I feel like that brand-new black tomb is watching me. But whatever. I don't think anything can hurt me when Pell is around. And even though I don't think I will be sleeping down in that cottage anymore, I appreciate the fact that he stayed to protect me last night.

"You ready?"

"I'm a little nervous, to be honest. What will we find up there?"

Pell shrugs. "You never can know. We don't have to go. But we could stumble into something amazing if we do. What else do you have to do today?"

I point at him. "Well, since I didn't get a chance to please you with breakfast, I'm pretty sure there's a hornjob in my future."

He squeezes my hand a little too tight. "Stop saying that word. It was kinda funny at first, but now it's just fucking stupid." But he's smiling, so I'm not gonna stop teasing him about my job here. "Besides," he continues, "you'll have plenty of chances to please me up there."

"Oh, I feel a challenge coming on. I'm in. Let's go."

We walk up the steps slowly. Almost reverently. And this makes my heart jump with uneasy expectations. What kind of things will I see today?

Like the other staircases, the steps are shallow and short. It's barely a step and you just want to extend your legs and take many at a time. Pell could take ten of them at once if he stretched, but he doesn't because I can only manage to climb three at a time. And when we get to the top we pause. It's a long, endless hallway with hundreds of doors lining either side.

And if I had any doubts that this place is made up of magic, they're all gone now.

"OK." I don't know why I'm whispering. "I'm suddenly nervous. And how do we know which door goes where?"

"We don't," Pell says. "That's kind of the fun of it."

"But—we could end up somewhere terrible. Like in the middle of a battlefield."

He sighs. It's sort of a wistful sigh. "One could hope."

"You want to be in a war?"

"Not any of the modern ones, no. But I would not mind going back to my real life. I would not mind getting another chance to see it from another perspective."

"You were a… what? Like a gladiator?"

"No, not really. I was someone's property. Someone important. But I was a child back then so I did childish things."

"Like what?"

"Maybe you'll see?" Perhaps sensing I'm about to chicken out of this little adventure, he pulls me down the hallway. "Relax. It's not real, remember."

And then, before I can respond with any more objections, we're standing in front of a set of double doors that look exactly like the ones I came through that first day.

I panic. And I'm about to pull my hand away and just go back downstairs to the world I somewhat understand when he pushes the doors open and we find ourselves staring into the banquet room of a medieval castle. There are hundreds of people here all dressed up like actors on the set of *Game of Thrones*. And when I look down, I'm dressed that way too.

Gone is my light-blue sweater dress and knee-high boots. Now I'm wearing a dusty-pink velvet gown with an empire waist and a corset that is trying its best to suffocate me.

And when I look over at Pell, I gasp aloud. "Your legs!" Then I look up at his head. "No horns! And your hair!" He's not a monster anymore. He's a man. Just a man. But wow. He's way more than just any ordinary man. He's like a very fucking sexy Viking warrior. And his clothes. The pants are black leather, worn and well used like his black boots. And his upper body is covered in a leather coat that fits tight to the waist, then opens up in a V for ease of movement.

He grins. "Pants. I knew you'd like that part."

I feel a little guilty about this. So I tsk my tongue. "I'm over it now, Pell."

"When in Rome…" He shrugs. "Anyway, I don't know where we are, but this is what they wear here."

And he's right. Everyone is dressed like us. Or we are dressed like them. Women are all floating around the middle of the room in their elaborate gowns and all the men look like they are about to fight in a fancy war.

Pell leans down and whispers, "I think it's a wedding." He's still very tall, much taller than me. But he's not nearly as towering as he is in real life.

I study the room. The middle is filled with dancers, the edges with happy people, drinking and eating. Servers flit in and out of the crowd carrying trays. And at the top of the room is a long table of men and women wearing clothing that clearly indicates they are the hosts here. The young couple in the middle must be the bride and groom. He looks drunk, she is blushing profusely, but also looks like she's having some wedding-night jitters.

Pell squeezes my hand. "Ready?"

"Ready for what?"

"To join them, of course."

"Uh… no," I say. He laughs at me. "I mean, we don't even know these people. Won't they get mad?"

"They don't see us. We have to participate to make them see us."

"And what do I say when they ask if I'm with the groom or the bride?"

"They won't. Trust me. I've crashed thousands of parties like this. Besides, I've got man legs, Pie. Tell me that doesn't delight you."

I look him up and down. His blond beard is longer than the scruff he wears in real life. But it's neatly trimmed. And his hair is long and thick. He really does look like a fucking Viking.

He grins down at me, waiting to see what I will say next.

"I am… delighted," I say. He huffs at my word choice. "But I don't know how to dance like that." I point to the people in the center of the room. It's a very coordinated dance with lots of turning, and changing partners, and all kinds of moves I do not have.

"Should I teach you?"

"*You* know that dance?" I snort.

He leans down again, so far down, his mouth is right up next to my ear. His whisper is loud and the hum, in combination with the light breath of air, makes my stomach go all soft and fluttery. "What part of 'I'm two thousand years old' aren't you getting?"

He's teasing me. I can hear it in his tone. But he's serious too. Because I'm really *not* getting it. And he's probably starting to change his mind about that whole cute thing. Pretty soon he's going to be pointing at me, saying, "Slow."

"Trust you." That's what I say back.

And at this, he nods. "It wouldn't hurt."

I shrug. "OK, monster. School me in the ways of medieval wedding dances."

He steps in front of me, bows a little, but his eyes never leave mine, and then he extends his hand, inviting me into this magical dream with him.

I take that hand and when we walk forward, we're walking down steps. A very grand entrance. And when I look over my shoulder, I have a little wave of panic that someone will close the door and we'll get stuck here, lost forever in a dream-world filled with well-dressed Vikings.

"It's not going anywhere," Pell says. "They can't see the door, they can't close the door, and even if we lose sight of it, that door will never lose sight of us."

I'm not sure what that last part means, I just know it's more than I understand right now.

We pause at the edge of the dancers and Pell leans down to once again whisper in my ear. "Stop thinking,

Pie. Just be here. That's the only thing this place is good for. It's just a moment and we get to crash it. There is nothing to fear here. It's nothing more than magic. It would be a sin not to enjoy it."

And he's right, I think. To be in the moment and not live in it is a sin.

So I let him lead me into a dance I do not know, shoulder to shoulder with people who do not exist, and it doesn't matter. I don't know what's happening to me. I don't know how long I'll be here, or stuck in the sanctuary, or hell, if I'm being honest, stuck in this life.

Moments count.

Especially moments like this.

I had nothing going on before Saint Mark's.

There is nothing in that old life that can compete with this monster man and his magic room.

CHAPTER NINETEEN – PELL

We have no idea what we're doing. But it doesn't matter and even though Pie looked nervous as hell when I pulled us into the dance, she got over it as soon as she realized these people truly cannot see us. We are free to be foolish and just have fun with it.

I'm not used to having human feet and legs, but I've spent my share of time in these rooms, so it's like riding a bike.

Pie's face is flushed and red just a few minutes in, but we keep going, trying our best to keep up with our neighbors, which is impossible, because they just keep switching partners and twirling around in a line, then a circle, then... whatever.

Sometimes the people do see us. But you have to stay a while and really get invested in the moment for that to happen, and about an hour into this, we're sweaty and laughing too hard from tripping all over ourselves to give any fucks at all about fitting in.

When the current dance ends, we clap, and then I take Pie's hand and lead her over to the other side of the room where a new door has appeared.

She is confused for a moment, looking at the door we came through first, across the great hall, then the new one. "What's this?" She's breathing hard, but her smile is bright and her blue eyes shine in the low-level torch lighting. Subdued shadows flicker across her face as she stares up at me.

"It's just an option," I tell her. "That's all."

"But where did it come from?"

I look over at the door. It's exactly like the one we came through to get here. Which is exactly like the one that leads to Saint Mark's from the front. "Does it matter?"

She shrugs. "I'm just having a hard time accepting the idea that this magical world lives side by side with the normal one."

"Says the girl with the talking bird. You know what though?"

"What?"

"I've never seen that bird talk."

She narrows her eyes at me. "You don't believe me."

I chuckle. "Why the hell wouldn't I believe you?"

"No one believes me."

"How many people have you told?"

"None. Not in a long time. But trust me, the ones I did tell all thought I was crazy. My mother took me to doctors for years, desperate for a diagnosis. Pia has always been there. And when I was very little, there was no way I could know she wasn't real. So I just talked about her like any kid would a friend. And everyone was OK with it. For a while. But then, when I went to school, I would talk to Pia during class and sometimes she would give me answers. I was a late reader. The letters just didn't make sense. But Pia would listen to other kids as they read aloud—she couldn't read either, still can't—but she would dictate the story to me. Anyway, it was all very confusing for my teachers and my mother." She pauses to let out a heavy sigh. "That's when the doctors took over. I told them all about Pia, and they said that I had to admit she was fake. Just my imaginary friend. And I resisted, so they diagnosed me with schizophrenia when I was six."

"Well… fuck. I'm sorry that happened, Pie. But you're not crazy."

"I know. I mean…" She looks down, trying to pull off a laugh. "I get it. There's something more to this world and for whatever reason, I've been given a glimpse of it." She looks back up at me. "But it's not easy living in the wrong world, ya know?"

I think about that for a moment. The wrong world. Is that what it is? Could it be that simple? We're just in the wrong world?

I keep eye contact with Pie as I nod my head at the new door. "So. How about we go find the right one?"

She studies the new door, then looks over her shoulder at the old one before meeting my gaze again. "Will we get lost?"

"We can't get lost. Trust me, I've tried. There are some pretty cool places in these hallways. I've found a few that I wouldn't mind staying in. Like, forever. But, unfortunately, the rooms move on. They are always moving. And you don't go with them. If you don't find your own way back, the hallways just rearrange themselves until eventually, there you are. Standing at the top of the stairwell, looking down at the sanctuary through the tall stained-glass windows."

"How long can you be lost?"

"I don't know. No one ever knew I was gone. Hell, I was gone the other day for a while. I had to find pants."

This makes her guffaw. "This is how you found pants?"

"Yep. There's a cool closet room hidden up here. And sometimes, when you come up the stairs with a certain thing in mind, the hallway gods will take pity on you and give you what you're asking for. And the hallways were on your side that day, Pie Vita. Because I came back with pants, didn't I?" There is no way she can stop her eyes from migrating down to my package underneath my leather pants. "Looks good in this, doesn't it?"

She pretends to slap my chest. But it's playful.

"So, do you want to try to go back? Or forward?"

A small bit of panic flashes across her face. "What do you mean *try* to go back?"

"It's never straightforward. If you go back through the door you came in, you'll be closer to where you started than if you leave through the one going forward. But it usually takes a few rooms to get home."

"You're sure we can't get lost?"

"I'm still here, aren't I?"

She lets out a breath. "All right. Then let's go forward."

I hold up a hand. "One word of caution. The places we go... they're not... they're not, um... how do I put this?" She has no idea what I'm trying to say, so she offers up no help. "They're not family-friendly." This is when she looks around and realizes that there are people fucking in dark corners. "This room is tame. There are some that... well. Sex parties were a thing in my time. And I always end up back in my time eventually."

"The hallway gods send you what you need, do they?" She blushes immediately after saying this.

"I'm just warning you. They don't all look like this. In fact, most of them have no people in them. It's just a place. Like you have arrived at the wrong time. In between parties."

"Are they all parties, then? The ones with people?"

"Hmm. I've never thought about it. But yeah, I guess they are."

"OK, I'm all for going forward. But one more question."

"Shoot."

"Do you always look like a human in here?"

"No. Not always."

She narrows her eyes at me. Like she can almost hear the words I'm not saying. "*Buuuut*… There's a but after that. So spill it. What's the but?"

I just want her to be prepared. I'm not a human and these human legs aren't doing me any favors for making that case. And she's used to them now. Used to me being like this. So. I just want her to be prepared when I revert back to what I really am. A monster. "Most of the time," I say. "I do look like a human. But if I don't, we'll be in the forest and I was the object of a minor cult in my Roman days."

"OK. I don't like the sound of this. A cult?"

"That's just what we call the followers."

"You had followers?" Her look is one of doubt.

"You don't believe me?"

"I was just asking."

"It wasn't a big cult. And my involvement in it has been lost to obscurity—"

"Can you just—I mean, I don't want to be rude here, but can you just tell me what this means? You're killing my happy buzz, Pell."

"It doesn't really mean anything." I smile at her. Because this is starting to make her nervous. "There could be virgins, Pie Vita. That's all I'm saying."

She guffaws so loud, some of the people actually hear her and turn in our direction, looking confused. "Virgins?"

"You know." I shrug. "Offerings and shit?"

"For you to… what? Kill?"

"*No.*" I make a face at her and guffaw. "To *fuck*. What the hell, Pie?"

She laughs again, and this time I'm certain that we're visible to the drunk Viking wedding party. Our laughter is too loud, our presence here palpable. "OK," she says, once she's calmed down. "So I am supposed to… what? Watch?"

My eyes narrow down. "Do you want to watch?"

"Not especially. But"—she smirks at me—"you put me in a costume and there's no telling what I'll be up for. Halloween night, exhibit A."

I picture her in that outfit she showed up in, then grab her and pull her towards the new door. "I think we're gonna be fine. And let's get out of here before that big guy with the ax decides he wants to fight me."

Even after two thousand years, there is always a sense of apprehension and excitement when I approach a door. It never gets old. The wonder of what you might find on the other side of that door never disappears. Even when I've come up here raging drunk and out of my mind with anger, my heart pauses mid-beat when I step through.

But this time, it's more than that. It's a held breath. It's a weird feeling in my stomach. And when Pie and I come out on the other side, we're in a gloomy, empty room dressed in plain clothes.

"It's an attic," Pie says. And she's right. The windows are small and circular. Only two of them, one on each endcap of a pitched roof. Outside gray clouds are rolling and when I walk over to the window, I know when we are.

"World War I," I mutter. Then I grab her hand again. "We're not gonna to stop here. There's no point." She doesn't argue, but it takes a moment for the magic to catch up and produce a new door.

This time when we walk though, we come out into a stifling heat and when I look down and find myself in the long, white toga of a Roman citizen, I can't stop the smile.

Pie is looking down at her clothes as well. She is wearing a stola, but a short one that barely comes to her knees. No shoes. This means she is not a citizen, not a wife in this room, but some kind of slave. The stola has a fine embroidered edge though, which means she belongs to someone wealthy.

Me.

"Well." She huffs. "That's fucking special. I'm no expert in ancient fashion, but it's pretty clear who I am in this scenario." She leans up on her tiptoes and whispers, "I'm not even wearing underwear!"

I wink at her. "Neither am I."

She blushes, then turns away so I can't see it. "So where are we?"

I look around. I would not call this place familiar in the sense that I've ever been here, but this long room flanked on both sides with traditional Doric columns and marble floors is something I recognize. "Party room in a palace, from the looks of it."

"It's a pretty boring party, since we're the only ones here."

A new door appears on the other end of the room and I nod my head in that direction. "Do you want to move on? There are endless places to discover. We don't have to stay."

"There's food over there. Do you think it's good?"

"It's not real food, so it doesn't matter. You can eat all you want in here. It even tastes good. But it's magic. It's not food. So you will be very hungry when we get back."

She lets go of my hand and walks over to the spread of meats, and cheeses, and fruit. "I don't recognize anything."

I join her at the table, grab a flask, and pour us both cups of wine. "Might as well start with the alcohol."

She smiles again and I find that I'm looking for it now. I'm trying to make her smile. I would not call Pie a stunning girl. Cute is actually a very good word for her. She's got very pretty long, blonde hair. And it's a true blonde, not a light brown. And her eyes are blue and wide, and this looks good on her. But her face… her face is just a young face. Symmetrical, unblemished, with a perky nose and somewhat round cheeks. No harsh edges to this girl. It's all very soft. All very cute.

And I like it. I don't mind looking at her. In fact, she almost seems like a… reward. After all these centuries being stuck with men, some not very attractive at all—and Tomas, of course, who is attractive, but his good looks are more than just deceiving, they are lies—Pie is a present wrapped up in a bow, because she's more than just her beauty. Her personality is quite fun.

Pie takes her cup and sips. "Mm. It's good. I don't know what I was expecting, but it's a little sweet."

I sniff it and the scent conjures up barely-there memories of long-ago days when sipping wine for breakfast was just how it was done.

"You're smiling," Pie says.

"Mm. This wine is familiar. All of this is kind of familiar."

"So you've been here?"

"No. And it's not my era. Maybe a hundred years off, but it's close enough."

Pie picks up a red grape and studies it, then pops it into her mouth. "I think I get it. It would be like me being thrust into a far future where nothing is like it is now. I mean, holy shit. The wheel was a newfangled thing back in your day."

I laugh loudly. "That's so not accurate. We were engineers. We built the greatest cities this planet has ever seen. We had running water, and bathrooms, and the gods, of course. They were here, back then."

She points at me with her cup. "You were one of them."

"No," I admit. "A wood spirit, and not much more. But like I said, I had my own small cult. So men would pray to me on the hunt."

"And would you give them a deer, or whatever?"

I shrug. "Sometimes. But there was a deer spirit too, and he wasn't inclined to make deals with me unless he got something in return."

"What did the deer spirit want?"

"Girls."

Pie laughs out loud. "OK. I should've seen that coming."

"And wood nymphs"—I shake my head—"they are not stupid. The deer spirit, he wasn't well liked. So I had to charm them… and it was just a lot of work to deliver on a hunt prayer. So. Whatever. I was usually just drunk. And the girls were amicable if you weren't trying to sell them into slavery, so they liked me better when I let the hunters go hungry."

"Ah. Now I understand your fascination with wood nymphs."

I nod. Can't stop the grin. "That would be why."

"Well, I've been told that I'm not a wood nymph."

"Not even close," I mutter. "That's not a bad thing, by the way. They're very treacherous to navigate around."

She huffs. "I feel like you're not appreciating my bad-girl side. I'm a rebel too."

"Sure you are."

"You don't believe me?"

"Not even a little bit."

She eats another grape, drinks her wine, looks around, chewing and swallowing. "What do you think is on the other side of that door?"

She's pointing to a regular door belonging to this time, and not a portal door. "This is a palace, so… the usual. Debauchery, decadence, depravity. Just a bunch of wickedness."

"So are we waiting for the party to come to us? Or what's the deal? Are we going to the orgy or what? I want to explore. Are you coming?"

She's kidding. I can tell. Her words are filled with laughter. But hey, if she wants to see a Roman orgy, I'm not turning that down. "I'm in. Let's go."

I start heading in the direction of the interior palace door, but she pulls on me. "Wait. Can we get lost if we go exploring? Do we have to backtrack to this room? How does that work?"

I pause and smile at her. "You didn't think I'd say yes to your orgy plan, did you?"

She straightens. I called her bluff and now she's nervous. But she's too proud to admit she's nervous, so now she's gotta go with it. "There are no orgies. Just another lie."

"Ohhh." I guffaw at that and cross my heart with a fingertip. "I swear. Orgies all day, every day. This is what the emperor does. And depending on who is emperor right now, it could get really sketchy. If this is Caligula's Rome, there's no telling what's going on in this palace."

She squints her eyes at me. "You're afraid."

"That's it." I drag her to the door, and before she can object any further, I open it and pull her through with me.

"It's empty." She sounds disappointed.

"It's a hallway, Pie."

"Hallway?" She looks up and around at the massive room.

"Just a way to get to the other rooms. Pick one."

She heads for the first one, pulling me with her, and sends me a smirk over her shoulder. "I'm not a good girl. You've got me all wrong."

"You think because I'm wearing the legs of a man, I'm safe, don't you?"

"On the contrary, Mr. Hornjob. I'm dying to get to the woods and see you in your element. But first, I want to check out the historical shit. This place is like a living museum. I'm not gonna miss out on this educational opportunity."

"Educational opportunity." I can only shake my head. "That's one way to put it. You're about to see things that will make even me blush."

She cocks her head. And everything about her expression is crooked. "I don't know where you got the idea that I'm a good girl, but I'll have you know that I was called a Babylonian whore by a nun two hours before I met you. Halloween night was…" She frowns. "Well, I don't remember most of it. But let me tell you—those Catholic boys? Party central."

I laugh so loud she startles. Then I laugh again.

"What? They had their moments."

"Well. I'm glad you're a properly seasoned Catholic college boy-toy, Pie Vita. Because you'll feel right at home here in ancient Rome."

Then I open the door to the closest room.

CHAPTER TWENTY – PIE

I'm still on the other side of the threshold when my senses are assaulted. The room before me is packed with people. And even though there was no sound—no hint that this party was happened before Pell opened the door—the noise level is almost deafening, a cacophony of commotion. Singing, laughing, yelling, moaning, screaming. Birds are flying in the high dome ceiling, which is painted to look like a blue sky with lazy clouds passing overhead. Monkeys cling to branches of real trees in the four corners of the long, rectangular space and vines climb up the many columns that line the room. They creep across the floor too, winding between the stone-paved pathways. There is a circular fountain in the center of the indoor garden and many people are stomping around in the water, laughing and falling down like children.

But they are not children.

This is definitely a not-safe-for-kids space. Naked men are everywhere. Young, taut, beautiful naked men, their hair tousled like they just got out of bed, and maybe they did. Most are carrying trays of drinks and food, but there are plenty of them paying special attention to men and women of status at the party.

There are several seating areas consisting of three slightly curved couches that almost make up a circle. Each of these seating areas holds at least a dozen people. Women with their legs open, the nubile young men between them. Men with whores on their laps.

Pell leans down and whispers in my ear. "Which one?"

I look up at him, confused. "Which one what?"

He grins. "Which one will you admonish first? For having no pants on?"

I slap his chest. "Shut up. But at least I know where you get it from now. This is some party."

Pell looks around. "It looks like it's barely getting started. Just wait until people are really drunk and *all* the whores and slaves are naked. It's one giant fuck fest."

I look around, trying to take it all in. But there is just too much to see and it's immediately overwhelming. There is a long table with a stuffed hare in the center, legs stretched out, like maybe it's running for its life. Or maybe it's flying. Because the chef has attached goose wings to it. They are large, and gray, and outstretched. Surrounding it are all sorts of equally fantastical dishes, most of which I barely recognize. Crabs cradled in grape leaves. Hens stuffed with plums and pomegranate seeds. Honey cakes, and honey bread, and honey wine. There is a lot of honey and most of it isn't on the table.

The beautiful men are holding honey dippers over the exposed thighs of the important men on the couches while the whores lick it off. But it isn't just the men. Women I presume to be wives, due to their higher-status clothing, are also being drizzled with honey. Down their breasts, down their legs, between their toes. And tongues. Everywhere a tongue can be, a tongue *is*.

But not all of it is erotic. Some of it is just plain ridiculous. Acrobats spin along lengths of brightly colored silks attached to the ceiling, twisting and turning above our heads. The aerial dance isn't the absurdity. It's that they are singing as they do it. And the singing is not good. In fact, lots of people are singing and none of it is good. It's almost as if all the singers are trying to outdo each other with their off-key crooning.

There is a camel, there are too many goats to count, and there are at least three horses. I wince as I look up at Pell. He's smiling down at me, enjoying my shock. I begin, "The animals—"

He quickly puts up a hand. "Don't ask."

"OK, then. What are we gonna do here? Hmm? Eat weird food? Sing badly? Frolic in the fountain? Slather each other in honey and lick it off?" He raises his eyebrows at my last offer. And I can't help it, I blush. "Kidding," I add quickly.

He looks around for a moment, then tugs me along to the other side of the large space until we come up to a long bench where men are sitting down, their robes open, exposing themselves to the slaves at their feet. But they're not getting blowjobs. They're getting a foot wash.

I stop in my tracks, making Pell stop too, since he's holding my hand. "Oh, hell no. I did not come to the fantasy hallway rooms to give you a foot-washing."

"Relax," he says. "And sit."

"Sit where?"

He points to an empty space on the bench. "There."

"Why would I sit there?"

Even though Pell looks like every other beautiful man in this room, I don't really see Pell the man. I see Pell the monster. But not in a bad way. In fact, I don't like this version of him. Sure, he's handsome—he has human legs and no horns or hooves—but... it's not really him, is it?

Until he grins at me. Until the illusion falters and those wild, straw-colored eyes of his light up with amusement. And then there he is. "Because," he says, "I'm gonna wash your feet, Pie."

"You? You're gonna wash *my* feet?" There is no way to stop my laugh.

Pell just pushes me over to the bench. "Sit. I'll show you how it's done. And then"—he leans down into my ear again, whispering—"you'll see."

I sit. But I'm grinning up at him. Blushing too. "I'll see what?"

He kneels down in front of me and takes my foot in his hands, caressing it softly, the pads of his thumbs pressing into the fleshy middle. "At no point during this foot-washing will I ever feel like a slave, Pie Vita. That's what I want you to see."

"Oh." I'm... well. A little speechless. Because did he just insinuate that I will enjoy washing his feet after this is over because he's going to show me how good it feels?

I try to quickly think up a sassy comeback, but he gets up and walks off, heading towards the corner of the room where there is yet another, smaller fountain, while I remain where he left me, tongue-tied.

Even if I tried, there would be no way to take my eyes off Pell as he procures a large shallow dish and fills it with water so hot, there is steam coming off it, even though this room is already the temperature of Rome in August. He grabs a cloth off a tray being held up by a gorgeous young woman with one shoulder of her toga thing pulled down to reveal one large breast.

And when I look around, I realize all the women with clothes on all have at least one breast exposed. And even though there are many, *many* naked people in this room, the single-breast thing is provocative for some reason.

When he arrives back at my feet he bends down, placing the bowl on the floor. Then he carefully lifts up one foot, slides the bowl underneath it, then picks up my other foot and rearranges the bowl so both of my feet are immersed in the hot water. He does all this with a surprising amount of gentleness. And he keeps grinning at me. Like he's got something up his sleeve. "You're gonna like this. Trust me."

I don't need to trust him. There is no possible way in hell I'm not going to enjoy this foot-washing thing. My entire body is buzzing with anticipation as well as... other sensations. And he hasn't even started yet.

A young man bends down to the slave washing feet to my left, offering him pots of things. Pell takes two pots and one of them has a honey dipper.

He's looking straight at me when he places both the pots on the floor next to the bowl. I don't know how he manages to keep a straight face, but he does. Meanwhile, I'm ready to burst out laughing. Not because this is funny, but because I'm embarrassed. I don't know how to feel about any of it.

"You're blushing, Pie. And I haven't even started yet."

"I know," I breathe. And then I laugh. "But I can't help it. There's something—"

But I can't even finish my sentence because he takes my foot in his hand and begins massaging his fingers up my calf, pressing on and kneading the muscles. I let out an involuntary moan and have to bite my lip to stop these unexpected noises from falling out of my mouth.

It should not feel this way. He doesn't have his fingers between my legs. He's not kissing me, not whispering things into my ear. He's not doing much of anything and yet it feels like he's in total command of me in this moment and I'm ready to beg for more.

Like what the hell?

And then I let out a squeak.

"Everything OK, Pie?" He knows what he's doing. Of course he does. He's two thousand years old. He's done this many times, to many women—or men. He understands perfectly well how good it feels. And he wants me to understand it too. So that when we get back home, and I do this for him, I will remember this feeling and I will picture him enjoying my attention the way I enjoyed his.

I point at him. "You're sneaky." But my words are already breathless. Already heavy with lust and dripping with longing.

Pell says nothing. Just continues to massage my feet and legs.

The man next to me is moaning. His slave is working the cream from the pot all the way up his thighs. I look away. Look across the room instead. But there's a woman over there, an important woman with one breast exposed, her hand to her sweaty forehead, her eyes closed, her legs open and one of the beautiful slave men between them, licking her.

Shit.

I find someone else to concentrate on. But everywhere, there is nothing but naked bodies, and singing, and dancing, and wine. So much wine. And the scent of honey mixed in with sex.

"If it's overwhelming, just close your eyes," Pell says.

I take his advice.

"Or"—Pell pauses his massage—"we could stop. Move on to another room."

I can't open my eyes. I can't look at him. If I look at him, I will blush. I will get embarrassed. And I don't want to do either of those things. I really do just want to enjoy this because in my twenty-five years of life, I've never, ever felt this consumed with… whatever this is.

And it's not this stupid sex party, either.

It's his touch. It's *him*. Not Pell the man dressed up like a Roman citizen. Pell the *monster.*

Because that's who I'm picturing doing these things to me.

And I don't want to spoil it by looking too closely or thinking too much.

I relax and Pell lets out a breath. "That's it," he encourages. "Just enjoy. That's all it is. Just joy."

He pauses his massage and then something cold is drizzled down the inside of my thigh. I shudder and hiss a little, because I know it's honey and I know what he's going to do next. But I do not open my eyes. I let the sounds and smells of the party overtake me and drift into a state of sedated acceptance.

And when his lips touch the soft, soft skin and kiss it, I let out a small moan of ecstasy.

He bites me. Not hard, but it has the same effect. My back bucks, my eyes still tightly closed. And I hiss and twist a little as he begins to lick off the honey. His hands never stop massaging my foot, pressing even harder now on the soft, tender flesh of my sole. And this combination of his attention is too much.

That's what surprises me most.

I am more turned on by this monster's subtle ministrations than I ever have been having actual sex with a man.

Then one hand is on my knee, pressing it open just a little bit, and I almost come apart. Not in a bad way. But my fist comes up to my mouth and I bite the side of my thumb.

"Everything still OK, Pie?"

How did he get so close? His soft words pour into my ear and my entire body shivers.

"Pie?"

Yes. Yes. "Yes." I finally say it out loud. "I'm fine. I swear. It's just…"

"Good?" I can hear the snicker in his voice.

"Yeah." I sigh.

"Want me to stop?"

"No."

"Will you open your eyes, at least?"

"Why?"

He presses a fingertip up to my lips and I don't know what comes over me, but… I open my mouth and suck on it.

He tastes like honey.

"Fuck," he mutters. "I really hope you let me keep going. Because you're driving me crazy."

I do not open my eyes. If I open my eyes, it's over. I will pull him towards me and kiss him, and then… I will let him have his way with me.

Hell, who am I kidding? I will have my way with him.

"Is that a yes or a no? I can't tell." And he pauses. Everything. It all suddenly stops. His hands are still on me, one still pressing my knee open, the other still holding my foot, and he's still very close. I feel his breathing. It's not slow, but not fast either. Like he's on the cusp of letting go. But this pause tells me he's not going to until I participate.

I open my eyes. Then I reach down, take his hand off my knee, and pull it up to my mouth. He grins. And he's a very handsome human man. Like... I'm talking young Brad Pitt hot, but not that young. He's got age to him. No wrinkles or anything that obvious. But I can see it. I can see all those years he's lived in his eyes. I smile at him and slowly bring his fingers up to my lips, never breaking eye contact with him. I kiss the tips of them. Each one gets attention.

And then he's kissing me. Hard, punishing kisses. Pressing his tongue inside me. His knees straddling my lap, his chest pushing up against my breasts.

The next thing I know, he's lifting me up and carrying me across the room. When he places me on a couch, I take another long look at him. His Roman robe is open, his eyes hungry for more when he lowers his upper body down on top of me.

His kisses are softer now, his words nothing more than a whisper. "If this isn't what you want, tell me no right now. Or I'll just keep going."

There isn't a single moment of hesitation before I say, "Keep going."

CHAPTER TWENTY-ONE – PELL

I want to do things to this girl.

So many things.

But not like this. Not in ancient Rome. Not as a man, either. Because while I don't mind being this guy, this isn't me.

If I were stronger, I'd make her wait. I'd pull her into another room, take my chances, and make her wait for a better—more real—version of who I am.

But I'm not feeling particularly strong in this moment. In fact, my desire for her body far outweighs my desire for her to want the real me instead of this poor substitute.

I don't want to be in this room either. I don't want to be at this party. It's affecting her. Of course it's affecting her. How could it not? I knew what would happen the moment we stepped through the door. That's the whole purpose of these parties. If you're here, you participate. You *do* things. Things you normally wouldn't. This is why the ancient Roman men allowed their wives to attend. It was a win-win all the way around.

But Pie isn't my wife. And our relationship is already lopsided enough. She doesn't need this kind of added pressure.

I should be strong. I should be the one saying no.

But she's already said yes, so even this small bit of hesitation on my part is dangerous. She's starting to think... *Did he change his mind? Will he tell me no? Should I have been the one to tell* him *no?*

And that's not good for anyone. Because that line of thinking comes with shame.

She's just about to ask me what's wrong, but I don't give her the chance. I wipe all her doubts away when I reach down with one hand and open up her legs.

She moans into my mouth as I kiss her, becoming soft and pliant, willing and eager.

I pull back from the kiss but immediately lean down into her ear and whisper, "We're not here."

She giggles a little. "We're not?"

"No. We're not here. We're somewhere else."

"Where are we then?"

"In a wood. In a summer wood. With water nearby. We know this, Pie, because we can hear the slow stream trickling over the rocks." I pause here to let her use the sound of the fountains as her trigger to another world. "There is no bad singing in this wood. No off-key music. No smelly animals and no sticky honey."

"Mmm. I kinda like the honey."

"No honey. It's just you, and me, and the forest. Because that's where I belong. And this is where I want us to be right now."

She lets out a breath. Not a sigh, though. Not something tired or exasperated. It's a breath of... *OK.* It's a breath of giving in. And in that same moment, I push inside her. She gasps and I know it hurts. But I don't say anything. She could tell me to stop if she wanted, and she doesn't. And anyway, I go slow for her. It's not rushed and hurried, like the sex going on all around us in the palace room. It's not primal and hedonistic, either.

It's easy.

So easy, and gentle, and quiet. Just the sound of the birds. Not the screaming ones from the party. Not the frantic song of caged things. But the lazy, content chirping of freedom.

Her hips rise up to meet mine, letting me know she's good now and I can continue. I keep it slow, gently pulling back and pushing inside her again. She bites my shoulder and I love that. I fucking love that. Because biting is something I like to do as well.

I continue the slow pace for a little bit longer, but it doesn't take much long for her to catch on and begin to subtly ask me to go faster with her body language. She moves her hips with mine. Bucks her back. Digs her nails into my shoulders and back. And when we kiss, it's not frantic—because that would ruin the illusion—but it's definitely more passionate than erotic.

I push her knees up higher, gaining a little more access, and when I ease myself fully inside her, she gasps and goes still.

"You OK?" I want her to enjoy this. I don't want to hurt her.

"Yeah." Her single word is a soft moan. "Better than OK."

We both relax and our rhythm smooths out and becomes more natural. And as this new intimacy builds, so does my desire. The slow, even pace becomes something more than sex and I realize that I've missed this feeling. I've been missing this connection for thousands of years.

I picture her with me forever. I could make it happen. It would not even be hard. She's stuck with me. I could keep her forever.

"Pell," she moans, her hips urging me to go faster.

But I don't. I won't.

I slow down, choosing to turn her on with the closeness of us. The passion in our kisses. The way I softly caress her breast and the depth of penetration.

She gets it too. Because even though I'm going slow, everything about her begins to pick up pace. Her breathing. Her heartbeat. The way she rubs her thighs up and over my hips and the pressure of her fingernails digging into the hard muscles of my shoulders.

Then she's there.

We're both there.

It creeps up on us. And I like that. I like the surprise when we both realize that this joining is perfection and our progression to climax was easy and natural.

Our release isn't an explosion. There is no epiphany, no song of angels and trumpets.

But it's better than all those things combined.

It's like an out-of-body experience. It's like we become one.

Two souls merged. A couple connected.

In the middle of this climax I open my eyes and find us—not in the Roman party room, but truly in that forest of trees. The woods. *My* woods.

Her nails dig deeper into my flesh as she squeezes her pussy around my cock. Gushing her release as I fill her up with mine.

I close my eyes to groan with pleasure, and when I open them again, we're back. In the middle of the

278

palace orgy, surrounded by hedonists and their extravagant sexual exploits.

And even though it was easy, I find that I am spent. So I lower myself down, then roll to the side of her, pulling her close to me the way I wanted to when I was in her bed last night, but didn't.

Here, we can do what we want.

Here, we can be what we want.

And maybe, one day, out there we can do that too.

She's breathing hard and when I press my chest up against her back, I can feel her heart racing. A quick, staccato, pounding beat. We lie there silent for a little bit as the party continues on without us. But eventually, we both know this is over.

"Regrets?" I ask.

She sits up a little so she can look at me. Her hair is a mess of blonde waves, some of it sweaty. Her cheeks are flushed and her eyes and mouth give off a tired, but satiated look. Then she opens her eyes wider and straightens her back. "Shit, you're already having regrets?"

"No, not me." So innocent. So naïve. So damn cute. "*You*, silly."

She points to herself. "Me?" Her blush increases. "No. Why do you say that?"

"Just making sure."

She sits up a little more, leaning back against the cushions, her fingers absently twining around in my hair. It's longer here. I shave it regularly back home because it's bothersome. But I like the way this feels and so I close my eyes and enjoy it.

"Are you ready to go back?"

"Are you?"

She thinks about this. "No. This place was OK. But the best thing about it is you."

I smile at that. "What is it you're looking for, Pie Vita?"

I can feel her shrug. "I dunno. Does the hallway take requests?"

I chuckle, eyes still closed, the memory of being inside her still very real. "Not really," I finally say.

"I'm willing to take my chances."

"If you had a request, where would you want to go?"

"Well." She pauses. "Not here. You said you lived here—"

"I did."

"OK. But you're a *man* here."

I open one eye. "And?"

"And there are places where you're not a man, obviously. I want to see those places."

"I won't look like this in those places."

She nods. "I know."

Now I sit up. "You like me the way I am. When we're not here, I mean."

It's not a question, it's a statement. And it makes her smile, then laugh. "What's not to like? I mean... horns, Pell. Horns come with hornjobs—"

"You're just being silly now."

"No, really. This is OK. I mean, don't get me wrong, you're a *hot* man. But it's not you. Unless I'm wrong and this *is* you?"

"No. It's not me."

"You've never been a man, have you?"

I scoff. "I've always been a *man*, Pie. The word you're looking for, the word everyone is always looking for when they ask this question, is *human*. I've never been a *human*. But I have always been a man."

She stares into my eyes for a prolonged moment. Then she nods. "OK. I get it."

"I doubt that." But I drop it and move on to something else because this topic bothers me and I don't want to get into it now. "Should we keep going then?"

She side-eyes me and shrugs with one shoulder. "Do we have a choice?"

"Not really. I mean, we can stay here or we can leave. Those are our choices."

She looks around. The party is even wilder than it was before. Almost everyone is fucking. Dancing, singing, naked, fucking. "I'm bored with this place."

I laugh out loud. "Bored?"

She nods. "It's way too much."

"Completely over the top."

"I want something… slower. Do you think we can find somewhere slower?"

"Probably." I reluctantly get up, wishing we were already home so I could take her into the steam cave for a dip, then take her to bed in her cottage. But who knows how long it might take us to get back to the hallway?

Then I pull her to her feet and we both look around for the door.

"There," I say, pointing to a door that was not there earlier.

We walk towards it and I'm just about to tug her through when she balks and plants her feet. "Wait."

"What?"

She looks around at the lewd and lecherous Romans, and then nods her head and sighs. "I will never think of Rome the same way again." Then she turns to me, rises up on her tiptoes, and kisses me on the mouth.

It's a nice, long, slow kiss too. Something to be remembered. Because when we pull out of it, I'm still thinking about the way she tastes. I'm still thinking about the pressure of her lips. I'm still thinking about where exactly her hands are. How her one knee is between my legs. How her fingertips are curled into the fabric of my clothes.

She is giggling and breathless when I pull her through the next door and we find ourselves in the woods.

I am finally myself again, all the trappings of ancient Rome gone now. But I'm still lost in the memory of the palace kiss and the way I felt inside her.

"Birds," Pie says.

And at the same time, I say, "Nymphs."

"What?" She's smiling when she turns to me, not understanding the danger.

"I can smell them." Then I turn to her and take a step back.

"What's wrong?"

"Pie… look down."

She does and she takes her own step back too. But it does no good. The shocking thing isn't a bug on the ground or a snake slithering too close. It's… *her.*

"What the *fuck*?" She takes another step back. But the legs are too long, too gangly. She's not used to being half deer, so she tumbles backwards onto her ass. And then she is crab-walking into a mud puddle, trying to get away from herself. "Holy shit! Holy shit!"

I kneel and take her hand. "Calm down. It's fine."

"Fine? Nothing about this is fine!"

I pull her up out of the mud and place both my hands on her shoulders so I can look her in the eye. Which is nice—being nearly eye level with her, that is. Because in normal life she is much shorter than me. "It's no different than me having human legs in the other rooms. That's all this is."

She looks down at herself. "I don't have pants on!"

There is no way to stop the laugh. "Feels good, doesn't it?"

She's breathless again, but for wholly other reasons than sex. Her hand is over her heart. And that's when she realizes she has no shirt on either. "Shit! I'm totally fucking naked!"

Her blonde hair is longer here. So long that it covers her breasts entirely. A few pieces are pulled back from her face with an intricate braid with flowers woven in. And every time she moves, there comes the familiar tiny jingle of spirit bells. She's wearing a length of them wound around each wrist, and a longer strand, the bells alternating with small pink opals, around her neck.

She is the nymph I smelled upon arrival, so I relax.

But in that same moment I become immediately excited.

Because she's not just *any* nymph. She is spectacular. Like someone has been breeding wood nymph chimeras for several eternities to get this one perfect specimen.

And this realization is what renders me speechless.

Pie is so stunned, taking in her new body, she just stands there, silent. Looking down at herself.

"You're so… *pretty*." I break the stillness. "I'm not just saying that. You might be the prettiest nymph I've ever seen, Pie Vita."

"Nymph!" She exclaims this as she looks up at me.

It's only then that I notice she has the eyes of a water-god. A dreamy blue that reminds me of clouds slowly floating by on a mid-summer day.

While I'm thinking this, her fingertips have suddenly found her horns. Pie gasps as she probes the gazelle-like spikes jutting out from the top of her head. "What the fuck is this? Holy shit!"

"It's just the rooms," I remind her. "You didn't freak out when you were dressed like a prostitute in ancient Rome."

"I didn't have horns, Pell! I was still human in ancient Rome!"

I get it. She has every right to be shocked. But this is fake. It has to be fake because if it's not fake, then… well. I don't know. I need it to be fake just as much as she does, so I say, "Don't you think you're kind of overreacting?"

And of course, this is the wrong thing to say.

Her eyebrows knit together. "Over. *Reacting?*" It comes out as two words, letting me know that I'm not reacting nearly enough. "I'm like…" She looks down. "I'm like a fucking pagan goddess or something!" And then she looks back up at me with super-wide eyes.

"Are you holding a grudge against the pagans?"

She breathes deeply for a few moments and when she actually considers my question, I find myself saying *Cute* in my head again. "I guess not," she finally admits.

"OK. So…?"

"Sorry. It's just shocking." Now she's staring at her feet. Rather, her hooves. They are a light caramel color, like the fur on her legs, which is just a shade or two darker than the fur on my legs. "I look like you!"

I keep my tone playful. "Should I assume that's a bad thing?"

Now she's irritated with me. But that's better than her being outraged about her new look. "Don't tell me that the first time you walked into a room with human legs and feet, sans *horns*"—she points to her own set—"that you weren't shocked! Because you'd be a liar!"

I rub my chin, trying not to smile. "That's probably true, but it's been so long, I could say it never happened and have a fifty-fifty chance of telling the truth."

"You think this is funny."

"I think this is… *fun*." I shoot her a crooked smile. "I mean come on. It's cool, right? Try walking. It's so different when you have hind legs and hooves."

She takes a few steps, makes one of those frowny expressions one does when they have to reluctantly admit something, then lets out a long breath. "It is kinda weird."

"A good weird," I say, looking her up and down. Because she's so fucking stunning. Wood nymphs are known for their beauty. The face of a wood nymph is like the song of a siren. Meant to lure men into questionable places, prod them into doing dubious things.

So they always have pretty faces. They are always sexy and alluring. But Pie is more than that. She is the pinnacle of wood nymph magnificence. Very, *very* beautiful. But not in a I-might-lure-you-to-hell kind of way. She also has an innocence to her and I like that a lot.

"Why are you looking at me?" She's arranging her hair self-consciously, making sure I can't see her nipples.

I only sigh. "I'm not looking at your tits, Pie. Come on."

"Then why are you staring at me that way?"

"Well, I hate to be the bearer of bad news, but it's pretty hard not to look at you. You're quite... stunning."

"Hmm." She looks down at her legs again and runs her fingertips through the shaggy fur on her upper thigh. "I like the color."

I nod. Because I like it too. I would like to open up her legs and press my face against the velvety hide that covers her inner thighs.

"And my hooves," she continues, oblivious to my daydream happening between her legs. "They're not striped, like yours." She looks up at me with those wood-nymph blue eyes. "But they are multicolored."

"That's banding," I tell her, trying to take my mind off what it would be like to take her in this body. To do everything we just did, and more, with this version of her. "It's kind of a special thing. At least in the world of satyr chimera. But you're not a satyr, because they're only male."

"Hmm. That's interesting."

I raise my eyebrows at her. "So... you like it?"

She takes one more look at her body while both hands go up to touch her horns in a way that reminds me of a human woman checking her hair. "I mean... I would not want to be like this forever. But when in Rome..."

I grin at her. "Do as the Romans tell you."

"That's not how it goes."

"No? How does it go?"

"Do as the Romans do. Not as they *tell* you."

"Funny." I point at her. And then we stare at each other for a moment. And it's only now, in this moment, that I realize what a gift this is. Because I have not been with a woman like this—in this form— in two thousand years. "You know what's weird?"

"What?"

"All this time I've been coming up here to these rooms and never once has the hallway showed me a forest like this."

"Like *this*… what do you mean?"

"A wood with a girl like you. With a nymph."

She looks around. "You've never met a nymph up here?"

"Nope."

"What about the virgins?"

"I was fucking with you."

I earn a side-eye for that remark. Like she's not sure if I'm for real or not. "So." She looks confused. "Who have you been… you know."

"Who have I been fucking?"

She blushes a little. "Yeah. You haven't had any women?"

"Of course I have." I think that disappoints her, but whatever. It's the truth and I'm just not much of a liar. "In the old days, I just went out as myself with my slave caretaker. People were different back then."

"They didn't notice you were only half…" And she's about to say 'man.' I know she is. But she stops herself and thinks. "They didn't notice that you weren't *human*?"

"They did. They didn't care. It was kind of a big deal to fuck around with a guy like me back then."

She holds in a laugh. "Is that so?"

"And then, you know. People changed. We came to the New World. The natives here, let's just say they weren't fooled by any of my charms. They thought I was a demon. So then I had the caretakers work on spells that could glamour me."

"So you could have sex."

"Hey, you asked."

"That I did." She turns away from me and I get lost in her curves. Her tiny waist, her hips, the shape of her ass. And I have an urge to walk forward, press my chest against her back, lean in to her neck, and kiss her. It actually takes a lot of self-control to not do this. Pie turns back. "So. You have not been with a wood nymph for thousands of years?"

"That is correct."

She turns the side and shoots me a coy look. "I would be the first."

I say these words back in my head. Let them echo for a few moments before I allow myself to picture this. To imagine what it would be like to just… be me. And to have someone like me as a partner. Someone I was *meant* to be with. Someone who wasn't thinking I was a freak in every awkward silence.

Because believe me, I have dreamed of fucking women in my natural state, but it comes with so many hesitations, it's just not worth it.

If those women I've been with over the years ever knew what I was they would see me as a demon, just like the natives did. Or worse, an animal.

Pie clicks her tongue. "Holy hell. That was like… a lead-in, Pell. I was practically inviting you to ravish me. What the heck is going through your head right now?"

"Sorry. I was just… picturing it. Ya know?"

"You and me?" She wiggles a little, shaking her tits and hips.

"Yeah. I mean, no. Not you and me specifically. But me as me and you as… *that*."

"Hmm." Her eyes are dancing and her tone is still light. "Me as… *what*?"

"These hallways, they're fucking with me or something."

"I don't get it."

"Because, like I said, I've been up here so many times and they've never shown me someone like you. Like *this*." I pan my hand down her gorgeous body. "And now, all of a sudden, everything is changing. You are the first female caretaker in two thousand years. And not only that, you're… *this*."

"OK. Let me stop you." She looks confused and maybe a little hurt. "This is good or bad? I don't understand."

"Good." I laugh. "Fucking fantastic. I'm…" I sigh. "So in awe of this moment."

She points to me. "This isn't awe, Pell. It's… well, I don't know what it is. But what the hell is going on?"

I cross the distance between, take her face in my hands, and look her in the eyes. "It *is* awe. With caution. Because if I get a taste of us like this, nothing will ever be able to compete with it."

Her eyes search mine. And her response is low and soft. "It's that good, is it? The way I look to you right now?"

I nod, smiling. "For me. You can't understand. You can't know what it's been like to be stranded in another world where I don't belong, but as myself."

She reaches up and places her hand flat on my face. And then she just leans in and kisses me.

I kiss her back. Of course I do. Her tongue darts to my canine teeth, pressing against their sharpness, and I don't know why that turns me on, but it does. It really does.

And now there is an ache building inside me. There is a longing for more.

We're still kissing and all I can think about is how, eventually, this will end. And I never want it to end. And even though I have lived through so much, and it never ends, I just know that this moment is a finish line. And nothing will ever be the same again.

"Stop it." Pie whispers these words into my mouth as we kiss. "Stop thinking. Just enjoy it."

I want to. The fucking gods above know, I truly want to. And I will. I'm not going to let this one chance slip away.

But my heart is already starting to hurt when I walk her backwards, press her up against a tree, and slip my fingers between her legs.

The fur there isn't fur. It's skin, with just a shimmer of velvet covering. It's as smooth as bare human skin, but better.

She moans when my fingers slip inside her. And then I return that moan with a growl of dominance when I lift her leg up and enter her as my true self. Her back arches against the tree as I reach down, hook my hands under her ass, and lift her up, pressing my body as close to hers as I can possibly get.

She grips my upper arms, digging her long, claw-like nails into my flesh as we fuck. And this time it is a *fuck*.

It's not slow. It's not easy.

It's the kind of fucking you do when you can't get enough of someone.

I grit my teeth, but it's not pain I'm feeling. It just makes me want her more. Makes me thrust my hips forward with more force, pushing myself deep inside her. Her head dips down and she bites me on the shoulder and at the same time, I grab her hair, pushing it out of the way so I can push her tits up to my mouth and take her nipple between my teeth.

She lets out a moan when I bite back. But she doesn't complain and she doesn't ask me to stop.

And maybe that's my problem?

Maybe that's why the ache is there?

I have been trying to hold on to my humanity when I was never human to begin with.

We are fucking like gods and goddesses, because that's what we are.

Damaged versions, yes. But does it matter?

And that's when reality just... *slips*.

CHAPTER TWENTY- TWO – PIE

There is suddenly a lot of laughter in the air. And the jingle of those tiny bells I'm wearing as jewelry. And we're running.

I look over at Pell and smile. "Pell! You're… little!"

That's when I realize it's me giggling. Because I'm not a grown-up—well, have I ever technically been a grown-up? Debatable. But the point is, I'm a kid again. Only I'm nothing like the kid I remember. I'm still a wood nymph chimera. And Pell is still a satyr chimera. But we can't be more than twelve. Definitely not teenagers.

Pell looks super confused for a moment as we continue to run through an amazing field of tall grass and wild flowers. Blues, and yellows, and purples, and oranges. So many colors just bursting out all over the place. And the field is surrounded by a thick wood. But not a foreboding one. The trees aren't dark and twisted. The leaves are the most spectacular shade of gold and the trunks are covered in smooth, white bark.

It's incredibly spectacular. Some CGI right out of a blockbuster movie.

Pell's confusion melts away as I continue to giggle at him. Then he's laughing too.

I feel like we're maybe a little bit high, that's how surreal this is.

But we're just kids. So I don't think we are.

I think… I think we're just happy.

Pell laughs. And we're still running. My new legs feel natural now. I can jump things like a deer. Single leaps and I'm over things. I can bounce, and vault, and trot. I feel like a horse, but better.

I feel… like a wood nymph and the moment that thought manifests, I suddenly have this overwhelming sense of *belonging*.

My hooves are better than feet. The cloven halves can grip. There is no possible way I will slip, even when we run through mud. I am sure-footed, and nimble, and I love it. Like this is what it means to be me.

I laugh as we run. And Pell looks back at me, grinning. He's faster, but he waits. And I am a hundred percent sure he will never leave me behind.

Soon we're at the edge of the flower meadow and then we slip under the shady canopy of golden leaves and enter a world of white tree trunks. There's a path in the woods. It's dirt, and smooth, like you could be a human running barefoot on it and never step on a stray twig or pebble.

Then I giggle again, because I *am* barefoot. I just have hooves.

My body is similar to the one I was wearing in the last room. Surely that's what's happened here. We went to another room and now we get to be kids.

I'm maybe, kinda, sorta pissed that Pell and I didn't get to finish that sex we were in the middle of having, but not really.

I'd rather be a kid. Not the kid I was, because she sucked. Her life was shit. No one was ever running beside her in a wood or slowing their pace so she wouldn't get left behind. That life was nothing but being left behind. But a kid like this? I could be this kid forever.

Pell lets go of my hand and takes off in front of me. "Race you!" he calls.

And we do race. I'm good with these legs now. My running is natural and I'm so fast. I bounce from step to step and leap fallen trees like they are nothing.

This is what freedom feels like.

The race becomes a chase. And it feels never-ending. And that's OK with me. This is all I want to do. I just want to run in these woods with Pell forever and ever.

But eventually we come out on the other side of the wood and I'm just about to pass Pell up and enter a new flower meadow when he grabs my hand and we stop. Just on the edge of the new space. Right there under the canopy of golden leaves.

Something is different about this place.

"We should go back," little Pell says. He's panting from the effort of the run. "We're not supposed to be out here."

"But it's so close," I hear myself say. "If you squint your eyes, and look through the trees, you can see. Can't you see it, Pell?"

He's quiet for a moment. Then he nods. "I can. But we should stay here." He's looking at me now, his eyes filled with hesitation.

"Don't you want to peek?" I don't even know what I'm talking about. But I don't care, either. I stop trying to understand it and just give in to the wood nymph life with Pell.

"Of course I do. But if we're caught—"

"We won't get caught. We're *so* fast. We're like the wind."

Pell isn't buying it. "He doesn't need to chase us to catch us."

I look across the flower meadow and sigh. Things are different here. The tree leaves on the other side are a burnt orange color. Like fire. They remind me of the burning glow of embers inside Pell's horns. And the flowers are mostly yellow. And both orange and yellow are pretty, but these flowers and trees use the color as a warning. Like a poisonous frog.

I hold out my hand. It's balled up tightly into a fist. Pell looks down at it, then back up at me. His yellow eyes are the color of sunshine on a summer day. He knows what the fist means, even if I haven't quite caught up to myself yet, so he just nods his approval.

I take a deep breath, then close my eyes and picture what I want to see. Then I open them and my fist at the same time and an army of fluttering moths bursts up out of my palm.

The beautiful wood nymph moths are a flurry of orange and brown and yellow spots as they take off across the meadow. They hold a swarm formation until they reach the burnt orange leaves of the trees. Then they drift apart and flutter off and when I close my eyes again, I can see *through* them. As them. Hundreds of eyes see millions of things as we make our way through the wood, our wings brushing against leaves.

Some of us are eaten by perching lizards or waiting frogs. But most of us just keep going.

"What do you see?" Pell's voice is low. Like he's afraid. I don't blame him. This wasn't his idea. It was all me. I'm the one who wants to break the rules. I'm the one who wants to see their secrets.

He's here so I don't have to be alone.

I'm never alone. I love that about him.

"There's a temple," I say, telling him what my million eyes are seeing.

"What's it look like, Pia?" Now he's excited. He wants to know just as much as I do.

"It's stone," I say. "Dark stone like the kind you see in a river. And there's an archway—"

Then… I don't know what happens. I shift. My current consciousness collides with the fantasy and the little chimera me says, "It's the freaking sanctuary. And did you just call me Pia?"

But it's my grown-up voice, not my kid one.

Pell says, "You feel so fucking good." But his voice is different too. And when I stop looking through the eyes of the beautiful wood nymph moths and see through my own eyes instead, he's regular Pell again. Tall, muscular, monster Pell.

And when I look down, I'm grown-up Pie. Wood nymph Pie. Sitting in his lap, gripping his shoulders as we move in a rhythm. We're still in the woods. But the dream world of chimera children is gone. Now we are just heavy breathing and sweat. Pell is looking at me with lust. We're on the ground now, his back pushed up against the smooth white bark of the tree trunk, and he's twisting his fingers into my long, blonde hair as we go searching for the climax.

I close my eyes, and for a moment my vision flickers between the two places. Those moths are still on their mission. Circling the temple in the burnt-orange woods. And I can still see through their eyes.

"What do you see?" It's little Pell again.

"Gods," I say. "Fighting."

"Who? Which ones?"

"Juno," I whisper. "And Saturn. Ostanes is there as well."

"What is he doing to her?" Little Pell's voice is no longer calm. He sounds worried. In fact, he doesn't sound like Pell at all.

"They're just shouting."

"He's going to hurt her, Pia. He's going to hurt her until she tells him where she put it."

I shake my head, eyes still closed. "She's going to hide us. She told me."

"What?" Pell's voice is deep again, but his question is just an instinct. Like the running. He and I are moving fast. Frantic to reach the end and get relief. And when I open my eyes the view of the temple is gone and there is nothing left but us.

Grown-up us.

Cursed us.

We come at the same time. He pulls my hair when I bite his shoulder, hugging each other tight, like we never want this moment to end. And then I collapse against his chest and we slowly lean over and curl up together on the soft mound of cool grass under a canopy of gold leaves, surrounded by white trunks.

We sleep.

When I wake, the moths are back. They walk across my face, and my shoulders, and my legs. Some of them flutter above me, like they are waiting for orders.

I look over at Pell so see if he's watching, but he's still asleep.

He's not small though. And neither am I. We're ourselves again. Well, he's himself and I'm the new wood nymph chimera me.

I don't know what that means. The dream—if that's what it was—is still very fresh in my mind. I can see that forest of trees. I can see through the eyes of the moths as they traveled through the woods. I can see the temple—that was one hundred percent our sanctuary, even though it seems very out of place in time and architectural style. And I can see the god. What did I call him?

Saturn.

And the women? Ostanes. The alchemist. I don't know how I know that, but I do. And Juno, of course.

Wait. How do I know that?

But in the same moment that I'm thinking those words, my palm is opening and then all the moths begin to flutter their way into the center of it. One by one by one they tap their little feet to my skin and then disappear. Like they're falling into a hole.

Did I know that would happen?

Yes.

Do I know why it's happening?

No fucking clue.

Moths. I make a face. I mean, they really are pretty. They're not called the beautiful wood nymph because they're ugly. But they are still moths. I'm just not sure how to feel about playing host to a bazillion insects and being able to send them out like a swarm of drones to spy on ancient gods and their alchemists. Even if none of this is real, just the product of a magic hallway, it's disconcerting to control moths.

"What the fuck is that?"

I turn and see Pell looking at my hand. The moths are still piling into my open palm. Disappearing one, by one, by one.

Out of instinct I close my palm and all the moths just disappear. Even the ones who hadn't made it back inside me yet. I spend a brief moment wondering if that will affect me in some way. But when I open my palm back up, they don't reappear. "Oh, well… that's just my little magic moths coming home from a recon mission." I laugh and look over at Pell.

He's not laughing. "What?" And his one word comes out with so much annoyance, I kinda lean back a little to put distance between us.

"Wow. For a guy who just got fucked into unconsciousness, you're in a bad mood."

His eyes narrow down and the yellow sunshine turns into a hellfire. "What the hell were you doing with those moths?"

I look at my palm again. "Putting them away, I think."

"Explain that."

I sit up and scoot back from him. I'm still in my wood nymph chimera body, and I'm nothing like the little girl who was running through the woods. I'm not used to these long, gangly limbs, so my hoof kicks against Pell's leg. He winces and pulls away. And now we are twice as far apart as we were when we woke up from the hot sex.

"Sorry," I say, pulling my too-long legs up to my body and tucking them underneath my hindquarters. Wow. I have to pause on those words in my thoughts. I have *hindquarters*.

"What. The fuck. Were you doing with those moths, Pie?"

"Are you mad at me?"

"I want to know what that was."

"I don't know. I'm not in charge here. I was in a dream. You were there. And we were kids. Kids like this." I pan my hand down my body. "And we were running—"

"The moths, Pie! I want to know about the fucking moths!" He gets to his feet so he's towering over me. Pointing at me.

I scramble to my own feet, because I'm not getting stuck in that submissive position while he goes on a rampage over some fucking bugs. I smack his hand away. "Don't point at me. It's rude. And I don't know what the hell your problem is, but you're not allowed to talk to me that way."

"What way?" He sneers the words.

"All rude and shit. Like you're my boss."

"I am literally your boss." He lets out a long breath and rubs his hand over his head, scrubbing at the stubble on there. He had longer hair as a kid. It was rippled and blond and it fell over his shoulders in tangled waves. "Pie?" His voice is softer now. Sweeter. But it's fake.

"Pell?"

"What were you doing with the moths?"

"I was… well. Do you remember the dream? Where we were during our romp?"

"What *dream*?"

Clearly, he does not. "That's the only way I know how to explain it. We were running in a meadow. There were flowers and trees with gold leaves and white trunks." His face. I don't know what to make of his face. "Pell? Are you OK?"

"What are you talking about?"

"The dream? While we were having sex? I was running in the woods with you. But we were kids. And we were spying on a temple. No. On the sanctuary! And there were gods there, Pell. Juno and Saturn. And some alchemist called—"

"Ostanes."

"Yeah. Her. Well." I shake my head. "I only saw them through the eyes of the moths. They came out of my palm and flew into the forest and I could see through them."

"No, Pie. You weren't there. I was with Tarq that day. There was no Pie. It was me and it was Tarq."

"Well, in the dream it was me. I saw it. I let my moths loose to spy. I wasn't this other guy called Tarq."

"Trust me, Pie. You were not there. I was there. Tarq was there. Tomas was there... *somewhere*. You?" He points at me. "Not there."

I want to fight about this for some reason. I'm not even sure it's worth fighting over, but I have a sudden urge to volley back a counterpoint. And that's dumb. So I force myself to act rational. "OK. I mean, what am I gonna say? I saw it."

"It must just be the hallways messing with us. Showing you things from my past."

I want to object to that too, but it feels wrong to do so. Like I just want to keep the argument going. Because I don't know for sure. It was, maybe, after all, just a stinking dream. I blow out a long breath. "Sure. Yeah. That's probably it."

We pause the fight. Stare at each other intently for a few moments. Breathing hard and both of us unsettled.

"Helloooo!" a voice calls out through the woods.

"What the hell is that?" I ask.

But Pell is smiling. Big. "Helloooo!" he calls back. "Over here."

And then I forget about everything we've been talking about because who comes strutting down the smooth dirt path before us but Tomas?

And he's not just a hot guy anymore.

He's a hot dragon chimera.

CHAPTER TWENTY-THREE – PELL

Tomas struts down the path like this is all no big deal, his grin as wide as ever, his eyes bright with mischief.

"Holy shit!" Pie trots over to him. "Where did you come from?" Then she looks him up and down. "Nice look. I love it!"

She would. Because she *loves* Tomas. Literally everyone else in the world who meets Tomas hates him. But not Pie. And he's just flaunting himself showing up as a dragon chimera. I huff.

His legs are covered in silver-gray ammolite scales that flicker an iridescent red-orange when he moves. His hair is slicked back, but it curls up in front of his ears, giving him a charming, devilish look that even I can't pull off. His chest is his normal skin color, but it glows much the way my horns do. I mean, everything about him says 'I'm not human' and yet Pie is... enthralled. She is looking at Tomas like she wants to lick him from head to toe.

"You're not going to tell him to go put on pants?" I don't mean to sneer those words, but I do. And I already know what she's gonna say, so I should just shut up about it.

305

"His package isn't hanging out like a lecherous satyr's."

"That's because he's a fucking *blood dragon*."

"And all dragons can read a room. We have limits." Tomas winks at Pie and she goes all melty and stupid over it, giggling and laughing. "Our packages are always tucked neatly away while not in use."

I turn my back to them and roll my eyes.

"How did you even find us?" Pie asks him. "I wouldn't even know where to start looking for you if I was the one left behind. And where were you for the past few days? I've missed you, Tomas."

I turn to face them again, but my eyes are still rolling back into my head with annoyance. "You barely know him. How can you miss him?"

Pie makes a face at me. It's not communicating nice things. "When there's only you, me, and him in the entire place, it's not hard, Pell. If you went missing for days, I'd be happy when you came back too. There's no need to be jealous."

I glance at Tomas, waiting to see what he has to say about this. But he's smart. He knows when to shut up. Pie is loving everything about him right now. He gets to show up looking like a cool dragon and not even have to explain it. Because Pie thinks this is a dream world or whatever. She's clueless.

I want to out him. I want to tell her exactly who he is and why he's here. But I get the feeling that Pie wouldn't even care. Not in this moment, anyway. She's trying to convince herself that I'm wrong. That I don't know what I'm talking about. That her dream, or whatever, of us being children together is what's real and my actual fucking knowledge and memories of what I know to be *true* is just bullshit.

So I shut up.

"Hey, do you know how to get out of here?" Pie is talking to Tomas, not me. "I'm ready to go."

"I just got here," Tomas complains. "I've been locked up in that fucking dungeon for days and now I'm finally free. We can't just leave."

"What dungeon?"

I expect Tomas to shy away from this question. In fact, I didn't expect him to even admit to where he was. But he doesn't. This chimera form must make him confident. "I'll tell you later. I'm over it now. Let's do something fun."

"We already did," I deadpan back.

Pie shoots me one of those looks. "He's not talking about sex, Pell."

"You two had sex?"

"Yep." I'm bragging. And it's not a good look. I get that. But I don't care. "Twice."

"Pell!" Pie is no longer annoyed. She's angry. "Why are you being such an ass?"

"Twice?" Tomas's tone doesn't come off jealous or angry. It comes off... wistful.

And now I feel like a dick. So I actually apologize. "Sorry. I am being an ass. But Tomas, shit just happened, man. You missed it."

"I know. I always miss the sex when we come up here. Why do I even bother?"

"No. Not the sex. Fuck the sex!"

"You have complaints with the sex?" Pie is shooting me a look of are-you-fucking-kidding-me?

"No. That's not what I meant. I mean"—I nod my head to Tomas—"he... never mind. Tomas, I found a lost memory."

"Oh, that. Yep. Pell and I were childhood friends, Tomas. Can you believe it?"

Tomas looks at me with one raised eyebrow.

I wave my hand in the air, trying to erase Pie's statement. "Ignore her. She has no idea what she's talking about."

"And now we're back to this? I'm the stupid one. I'm the clueless one. I have no idea what I'm talking about?"

Tomas puts up his hands. "Hey. Can we not? Like… just for a little bit? I just came off three dungeon days and we're here in a magical forest—"

"Told you it was magical," Pie says.

"It's not magical. It's a fucking memory. Tell her, Tomas."

Tomas just looks between us and then says, "How about we move on? Hmm?"

"Do you know the way out?" Pie asks. "I would like to move on too."

Tomas bows low, waving a hand down the pathway. "This way, my lady."

I mumble, "Fuck's sake," under my breath as we all tread the path. I'm ready to get out of here too—it feels like a very long trip.

Pie and I were not children together. That never happened. That's not what I saw in the forest room. Anything is possible, but Pie is of the bloodline. So she has to be an eros. And sure, there were a lot of different combinations of monsters back in the day— pretty much every combination possible. With the exception of one. The eros. They were the only pure bloodline left. They were never crossed with anything.

And anyway, I spent my childhood with Tarq. He's the kid I ran with in the forest, not her.

Tomas and Pie are walking hand in hand. They lean in to each other, like they are gossiping. And who could they be gossiping about? I'm the only person they have in common, so not a hard deduction.

I let that go. Mostly because I have a nice view and I'm a little fixated on Pie's shape. If she was in human form, I'd be checking out her ass. But as a chimera, her ass is furry. Not shaggy furry, but velvet smooth, the way it is between her legs. I don't think she realizes that yet, because it's a lot like a human butt, but it's got the very light velvety fur over it. It's cute as fuck, don't get me wrong. But wood nymph chimera girls are all about the legs and the horns.

And Pie's are striking on both accounts.

Her horns are gazelle-like. They curve up and twist back, alternating between a light tan and a deep brown. They are more delicate than mine—sharper on the ends and not as thick. And of course, they don't glow with the heat of hellfire, like mine can under the right circumstances. But they fit her. Perfectly. Because her body is thin and lithe, just like her horns.

Her legs are so damn long, I'm amazed she learned to walk in them so quickly. She bounces with every step, like at any moment she might just spring up and disappear into the canopy of leaves. The fur on her legs is not as shaggy as my own, but it's very soft and fine. I know. I touched it.

It's weird that there is all this animosity between us right now when just a little while ago we were in the throes of passion. I was inside her. She was biting my shoulder and moaning into my ear with pleasure.

And now she's hanging onto Tomas.

I am not jealous of Tomas. I feel sorry for Tomas. If she wants to shower him with personal attention,

I'm OK with that. He's had a rough time and I would be a huge asshole if I was jealous of this little bit of affection she's showing him.

Because once she finds out what he really is, she won't be acting like this, that's for sure.

Pie seems like a nice girl. She is, at the very least, considerate of people. So she would not shun Tomas on purpose. But it's inevitable. She won't be able to help it.

"Finally!" Pie squeals and bounds off towards the door that has appeared in the trunk of an unnaturally large white-bark tree. She doesn't open it. She waits. She's had fun in here, that's obvious. But she's still not sure how it all works, so this waiting is her being careful.

I like careful Pie.

I don't think she's very careful in her real life or she wouldn't have ended up as the slave caretaker of a cursed monster. So this is a good sign that she's taking things seriously now.

Tomas pauses at the door too, both of them waiting for me to catch up.

"Ready?" I ask. They both nod, Pie's being more enthusiastic than Tomas's. This makes me wonder if she's enjoyed herself here in the hallway rooms. Rather, did she enjoy herself with me?

I certainly had fun, and I would hate for it to be one-sided.

But this is not the time for that conversation, so I grab the door handle and pull it open.

Pie is pressing up against my back, almost using me as a shield as she peeks around my shoulder to get a look.

"Hmm." Tomas and I both say this at the same time.

"What?" Pie asks. "What's the problem?"

"Typically, dark hallways are a sign," I say.

"A sign of what?"

"Fuckery," Tomas responds.

Pie steps out from behind me and then all three of us are shoulder to shoulder. "What fuckery? I'm gonna need details. Is it bad? I don't get it."

"It's not bad," I say.

"It's just... fuckery," Tomas repeats.

"It means the hallway gods are playing with us."

Pie steps forward, peering into the darkness. "Well, how do you know? I can't see any fuckery."

"Exactly," Tomas huffs. "It's gonna be like a little maze in there. You go around a few hallways, and come out into a room. And then bam. You're inside the fuckery."

"But what kind?" Pie is starting to lose patience with this explanation, but what Tomas said was accurate. "Are people gonna chase us? Kill us? What's gonna happen?"

"None of that." I chuckle. "It's just..." She shoots me a look that says, *If you people say 'fuckery' one more time I will lose it,* so I just spit it out. "It's gonna want something from us."

"And there will be no way out," Tomas adds. "Not until you give in and do what the hallway gods want."

"What will they want?"

Both Tomas and I shrug. Then I say, "We won't know until we get in there."

"So you two are saying we should not go in?"

"We have to go in. It's the door," Tomas explains. "There won't be another one. It's move forward and find our way out, or stay here and hope the powers that be get bored with us."

"Hm." Pie is thinking. Then she shrugs. "To hell with it. Bring on the fuckery." And she passes through the door.

Tomas and I both shoot each other a look. He and I have not been in the hallways together in... hell, over a thousand years, at least. And if there was ever a time when we were stuck inside a fuckery room together, I certainly don't remember it.

He follows Pie in without comment and I follow him.

The door behind me disappears the moment I step through it. And then the hallway I'm in brightens a little, just enough to see where I'm going. Tomas is not that far in front of me. I catch a glimpse of Pie just as she rounds a corner, then disappears.

She calls out, "Holy shit. What is this?"

Tomas and I catch up with Pie and stare down at the contraption in the middle of the room we end up in. It's not a large room. Maybe twenty feet by twenty. There's a large window with billowing sheer curtains on one end, but no door. And the minute I step out, the hallway behind me disappears.

"That's a hookah," Tomas says, pointing at the contraption. And he's smiling. "I've seen these before. This is gonna be fun, I think."

Pie looks confused as she stares down at it. "What do we do? Smoke? Then what?"

The hookah is massive. Almost as tall as Pie. It's made of glass and ceramic painted in traditional designs. There are three hoses spaced equidistant around the central bowl, one mouthtip for each of us.

"Fuck, yeah." Tomas is smiling big as he plops down on one of the three massive velvet pillows positioned in front of each hose. "I'm gonna smoke the fuck out of this thing. Give it a light, Pie."

Pie looks at him like he's already high. "Light it with what?"

"I dunno." Tomas is already inspecting his hose. "Look around."

Pie begins searching for matches, but I walk over to the window and throw the curtains aside. "Well, I wasn't expecting that."

"Why? Where are we?" Tomas is only half interested.

"Looks like Morocco."

Tomas chuckles. "I love hallway Morocco."

"Have you ever been here?" I ask Tomas.

"Nope."

Pie has found a box of wooden matches. She lights one and stands over the hookah bowl, touching it to whatever's inside it.

Tomas is already pulling in smoke.

I'm appalled. "You don't even know what that is in there. It could be anything."

Tomas coughs as he blows out smoke. "Who cares what it is?" Then he takes another pull on the hose.

Pie is still standing in the middle of the room. But she's not looking at me, or Tomas, or even the hookah. She's looking at the floor.

I look down too. There's a pretty intricate design made out of inlaid wood.

"What does it mean?" Pie asks.

It's a circle. And it's partitioned off into twelve parts. Like a zodiac wheel. But there are no zodiac signs inside. Instead, there are letters in an unfamiliar language. I don't answer her because I don't know. But the pictures are easy to read.

"Look." Pie points to the section Tomas is sitting in. "He's on that pillow, and in that section there's a dragon." She considers this. "House. It's a house. Like the zodiac. So that's the House of Dragons."

Tomas and I both look up at her at the same time. "What?"

"Dragons." She bends down and traces her finger along the line of markings. "This says 'House of Dragons.'" Her eyes dart to the next pillow, which is three sections to Tomas's right. "And that one is the House of Bucks." I walk around the hookah and bend down next to Pie. "This is where you sit, Pell."

"How do you figure?"

She shrugs. "You're Bucks and this is your seat." She scoots over, making me step aside, and then stops at the third pillow. "Because this one says 'House of Moths.' And that's definitely me." She makes a face when she looks up at me. "Moths are gross. Why do I have to be a moth?"

"Beautiful wood nymph." Tomas is still choking on his smoke. The entire room now smells like a mossy wood. Kinda like the place we just left. Damp, and earthy, and humid.

"What?" She's annoyed with him.

"That's you." He points at her. "The beautiful wood nymph is a kind of moth. They're pretty."

This makes her even more annoyed with him. "I know that. They were coming out of my hand in that last room."

314

"Pie, we didn't grow up together," I say. "I don't know what you saw in that dream or whatever it was, but that's all it was. A dream."

She crawls on top of her pillow and grabs her hose, then draws in smoke without answering me.

Whatever.

I sit down on my pillow and take my hose too. I'm not much of a smoker. I drink a little if there's a reason—like this day in the hallways—but after two thousand years, partying mostly bores me. So I'm not expecting much when I inhale.

But holy shit. I am so wrong. The smoke I inhale is sweet. Not earthy, like the stuff that comes out after. And when I blow it out, my head swims. But not in a dizzying way. It's more like… clouds. Like wandering through a mist. But not a dark foreboding mist, like the one outside the sanctuary if you try to leave without permission. More like a rainbow.

Tomas is laughing at Pie as she chokes on her smoke and I'm already taking another hit.

I'm not a hundred percent sure what happens next, but all I hear is laughter. Time has passed. I know this because the room is darker now. There are torches on the wall. Lit torches. But none of us did the lighting.

"Oh, my God," Pie says, getting up from her pillow and crossing the room. Have we been sitting here all day? I can't remember. "Oh, my *God*," Pie says again. She's peering over her shoulder at us. "Look! It's a truth or dare machine!" She bends over to pick it up.

Tomas falls over sideways, laughing.

"A what?" There's smoke in my mouth and it comes out with my words. Then I'm laughing too.

Pie takes her place back on her pillow, holding the heavy cast-iron contraption in her lap and staring down at it fondly. Her eyes are bright with mischief when she looks at me. "They had these at every table at the Penny Arcade Brewery in York. Right after I turned eighteen, I was homeless. I was pretending to be a student at York College that year." She pauses to smile. "That was fun. I lasted almost four months in the dorm before the RA finally figured out I was living in a top-floor attic everyone had forgotten about. And I sorta dated this guy." She actually sighs. "For a night." Then she and Tomas are laughing again.

"Anyway," I say, annoyed by her college story. "The *machine*?"

She looks down it in surprise, like she forgot it was in her lap. "Right. Truth or dare! Best. Game. Ever. And that's not the hookah speaking. It's just as fun with shots."

Tomas is still sideways on the ground clutching his stomach as he cackles.

I kick him with my hoof. "Dude. Nothing is that funny."

But this is when I realize that both he and Pie are still in their chimera forms.

I should've been paying attention to this. Because Pie is still topless. Her long hair is pretty much covering all the good bits up top, but now that I watch her, I don't think she understands she has no pants on. And no fur down there.

Suddenly I'm laughing too. Guffawing like an idiot. Because this is why Tomas thinks everything is so funny. He's got a perfect view between her legs. And Pie is not being ladylike as she sits. Her gangly legs are all over the place.

"For fuck's sake. You two are like children. Play the game with me!" Then she pulls her knees up and balances the iron machine on top of them so she can play with the knobs.

Tomas loses it again.

"Pie."

She glances at me, annoyed. "What?"

I point down. "You do realize that you have no *pants* on."

She rolls her eyes at me. "I'm wearing *fur*."

"Yeah, but…" I grin at her, all teeth. "Not down *there* you're not."

She looks down, realizes she's been giving Tomas pussy shots all day and that's why he's so happy, and then blushes so bright, it turns me on.

"Ooops!" She rearranges her legs so she's sitting on her butt, knees together. Then she casually arranges her long hair over her breasts, and looks at me. "Truth or dare?"

"I don't get it."

She squints at me. "You've never played?"

"No. How's it go?"

She rubs her hands together. "Oh, this is gonna be fun. You have to choose truth or dare. Do you want to answer a question that we ask? Truthfully." She holds up a finger, like this is a sticking point. "Or do you want to do a dare?"

"A dare?"

"Yeah. Like… I dare you to… go over to the window and yell, 'I have a small penis!' to the people down below."

Tomas loses it again.

I also chuckle. "Pie." I point to my package. "It's not small. You know this. It's been inside you."

Pie gasps, but Tomas sits up. "Fuck. I forgot about that!" He falls back onto his pillow. "Aww, man. I miss out on everything."

I reach over and pat his dragon-scale leg. "Sorry, friend. You snooze, you lose."

"The point is," Pie seethes, "it's a dare, you jerk. And if you choose dare, then you have to do it. Even if you don't want to. And stop talking about our sex life. It's rude."

"I have to say things like that? Even if it's a lie?"

She nods. Smugly. "Not just say things. I could make you…" She shrugs a little, blushes a little too. "Kiss my toes, for instance."

Tomas is paying attention again. "Can I dare you to kiss my toes?"

We all look down at Tomas's toes. Which are nothing close to toes, they are claws. "In my defense," he says, "you two have hooves. So fuck you."

Pie and I both laugh. "Forget the toe thing. Dare is just a dare. And new rule." She side-eyes Tomas. "Since you're gonna use the dare to please yourself."

Now I laugh and take another smoke. This is getting fun. And that hazy high feeling has settled into something else. Happiness, I think. Though it's been so long since I've had a day like this, I'm not sure I trust my recollection.

"New rule is… you cannot dare someone to do something *to* you or *for* you. Agreed?"

Tomas and I both agree.

"OK, here's how it works. You pull this lever"— she demonstrates on the iron machine in her lap— "and then that dial thingy spins and lands on truth or dare. If it's truth, the person who just went gets to ask you a question. If it's dare, then the person who goes next gets to make up a dare. Who wants to go first?"

Tomas scrambles around the hookah, grabs the little machine, and is back on his pillow before Pie or I can say anything.

She looks over at me and laughs.

I like her laugh.

I like *her*, actually.

And today was pretty fun. It's not even the sex, either. It's that wood nymph body she's wearing. I'm not mad at her. I'm not even frustrated with her that she's not understanding things right. I wish we *were* kids together. I bet she would make a really great best friend.

Her smile is still bright. And she winks, then looks at Tomas. "You do realize that going first means you're in the hot seat?"

"Huh?" Tomas is smashed out of his mind. "I go first. That means I'm in charge!"

"No." Pie laughs. "You spin the dial, then one of us gets to truth-or-dare you."

Tomas looks down at the game. "Fuck. I read that wrong."

"Oh, my God." Pie fakes exasperation. "You're so stupid, Tomas!"

She likes Tomas. I know she likes Tomas. And he likes her too. A lot. I want to like Tomas. I've literally known him forever. It's just… he's a dangerous guy. At least out there he is. In here, he's different. Fun and easygoing. Happy and carefree.

But when he's his true self, you can't trust him. Not even a little bit. That's the mistake people always make with his kind. Well, what used to be his kind. He's the last. But when they are in their base form, they are not anything close to human. They don't recognize faces or scents. They will kill you and not think twice about it until they change back into another form and realize what they've done.

Tomas, not me, is the true monster of Saint Mark's.

Hell, he might be the whole reason this cursed sanctuary exists.

Fine. Probably not. I pause my introspection to chuckle. But he's definitely part of it.

"I got a truth." Tomas turns the machine around so Pie and I can see it.

"OK, that's you, Pell."

"Wait." I point at myself. "What's me?"

"You have to ask him a question. You always pass to the right, so I go next. Which means you have to ask the truth question for Tomas."

I spend a moment trying to sort those words out into something that makes sense, but then I just give up. I actually do have a question for Tomas. I would not *say* I've been wondering this, but I've been wondering this. "Have you ever had a woman, Tomas?"

"What?" That's Pie. "Pell, what the hell is wrong with you?"

"What? It's a question I have. I've never seen him with a woman. Or a man, if that's what you're into."

"I'm not into men," Tomas huffs. "And it's hard to meet a woman when you've been stuck in a cursed dungeon for two thousand years."

Pie looks at him. "You've never—"

"It's not a big deal," Tomas says. "I'm fine." Pie is about to object, but he puts a hand up. "I'm not even human. And if you think this is me?" He points down at his dragon chimera body. "It's not."

"O. Kaaay." Then Pie glares at me.

"Why are you looking at me like that? It was a legit question. I am curious."

She shakes her head, takes the machine from Tomas, pulls the level to spin the dial. "Oh, great." Her shoulders slump. "Dare." Then she side-eyes me. No, glares at me. "You better not make me do anything stupid."

"Wait, now I have to dare you something? How come I have to do all the work in this game? Am I the only one playing? What is happening?"

The rules come spilling out of her mouth again. "If it's truth, the person who went before you gets to ask you a question. If it's dare, then the person who goes next gets to make up a dare."

"Fine. Whatever. Give me a minute." Honestly, I'm really not in any condition to think and this makes me laugh.

"If you're plotting something evil, I swear to God, Pell, I will—"

"Calm down. I'm not capable of plotting anything right now, let alone something evil." But just as those words come out of my mouth… I get an evil idea.

And then, because I have no filter at the moment, I actually say it out loud. "Pie Vita—*Pie is Life*—" Tomas and I both fall over laughing.

"I'm going to let Tomas do your job if you don't stop it right now!"

"She's cute when she's mad, huh, Tomas?"

Tomas is lying down on his side, clutching his stomach again. "She's so fucking cute."

"What is *the dare*!" She screams it.

"Fine! I dare you to give Tomas his first kiss."

"What?" She blinks at me.

"What?" Tomas sits up, suddenly keenly interested in the game. He cocks his head at me. "Why?"

"Why what?"

"Why are you telling her to kiss me?"

"Because you've been stuck in a cursed dungeon for two thousand years, she's pretty, she's funny, and she's mine to command at the moment. And I would like to dare her to kiss you."

"Whoa!" Pie puts up a hand. "I'm so not yours to command."

My tone is deadpan. "You *literally* are. How many times do I have to remind you? Forget never being fucked, he's never even been *kissed*, Pie. Kiss the man. Make it good, too. It might be the only one he ever gets."

CHAPTER TWENTY-FOUR – PIE

It's not the dare that has me thinking. I will gladly kiss Tomas. I'm a little bit attracted to him. Have been since I first saw him on that second-story balcony the day I arrived here.

That's not it.

It's not that in Pell's mind, this request falls more along the lines of a my-wish-is-your-command kind of thing instead of a dare in a game.

It's not even the surprise of learning that Tomas has never been with a woman. Certainly, never been kissed is a little bit of a shock, since he's so very handsome. But he's cursed. It's really hard to meet people when you're not allowed to leave your monster sanctuary.

None of that is what makes me pause. It's just Tomas himself.

He looks… scared. Which makes zero sense because it's *me*. But before the words are even out of Pell's mouth, Tomas is shaking his head and waving his hands and saying, "No. No. It's not necessary."

And Pell is saying, "This has nothing to do with necessary, Tomas. We all know you're infatuated with my slave."

My head swings over to Pell to shoot him a disapproving look regarding the slave comment, but we're all kind of high on this hookah shit and I'm way too stoned to put any kind of effort into correcting him, so I'm willing to write this comment off as an in-the-moment faux pas instead of malicious ignorance.

"Pie," Tomas says. I look back over. "It's not you. I swear. I think you're hot. I'd... you know. But I don't want to do it like this." But here is where it gets interesting. He looks over at Pell then. And it's a weird look.

"Wait." I feel like I'm a little bit behind here, but now I'm finally catching up. "Why are you looking at Pell like that?"

Tomas puts on that smile. I might be new here, but I recognize that smile. He's a good-natured guy. He's not moody and difficult like Pell, even though out in the real world, that's the kind of guy Tomas probably *would* be. He's far too attractive—like, *supernaturally* attractive—to be one of those aw-shucks guys.

Tomas has a darkness in him. Though he hides it well. Because I'm only just now noticing it.

"What?" And now Tomas is showing off his innocent smile. "What look?"

I point at him. "You're hiding something. And if I wasn't so shit-faced high, I'd figure out what it was."

Pell groans. "Just kiss the man. I'm dying for my turn."

I can't help it, I laugh at Pell. At some point while I was not paying attention he changed position so he's lying down on the floor, on his back, with his head on the pillow. But he's backwards. So his legs are pointing out of the circle instead of inward. And his hooves are kicked up on the seat of a red velvet chair.

He's not even looking at us. In fact, I'm pretty sure his eyes are closed.

This annoys me. "You're not even gonna watch?"

Pell snorts. Like actually snorts. Then he turns over and sighs, resting his head sideways on his hands, one eye open and looking at me. "Do you want me to watch?"

"This was your idea."

"Guys," Tomas says. "There will be no kiss."

"It's my dare. I can't not do it."

Pell opens his other eye. "Are there penalties?"

"Of course! If you refuse, you are a loser. I'm not a loser."

Tomas raises his hand. "I'll be the loser."

I look over at him. "Why don't you want me to kiss you?"

And finally, his smile falls. His whole face changes. He's still hot as fuck. Especially in that dragon chimera body. I'm not totally on board with the claws instead of feet—they look pretty sharp. But overall, I kinda love this look.

"What?" I ask him. "Just tell me what the problem is. Am I not good enough for you?"

He laughs. "No. That's not it."

"Then why don't you want me to kiss you?"

"Because he likes you," Pell says. "Wake me up when we're ready to move on." Then he yawns. A huge, cavernous yawn that shows all his sharp teeth. "I'm bored with this game and at the rate we're going that door will never appear. All because Tomas is too scared to be kissed by a pretty girl."

I smile, because he called me pretty, but then frown. "Wait. We have to play the game to make the door appear?" Did I know this? Maybe. I can't remember. But when I look around, sure enough, there is no door. And this room is not big the way the others were. If we didn't see the door right away, there were hallways or forest paths to follow and eventually it would be there. But there is nowhere to go in here. It's just this room and that's it.

"You better get comfortable, Pie is Life." Pell chuckles. He likes that stupid joke. "We'll be here for months the way this is going."

I look back at Tomas. "You really don't want me to kiss you? Because if you really feel that way, then I'll be the loser."

"Tomas is the loser here. He's just afraid you'll figure out what he is."

Tomas growls. "Shut up, Pell."

"What he is? A kiss can tell me that?"

"No." Tomas huffs. "The kiss isn't gonna tell you anything. It's not the kiss. I would love to kiss you, Pie. But…"

"But?"

"But it's not fair. And Pell knows this. He's setting us up."

Pell laughs. "Like I care."

"That's the problem," Tomas snaps. "You don't care. But I do. I'm not going to kiss her. And I'm not going to let her kiss me. Not like *this*." And then he points to himself.

"Not like… what?" I ask. Then it hits me. "Not in this body? What's wrong with that body? I like it, Tomas. I think you're super sexy."

Pell guffaws.

"What?" I look at Pell, then Tomas, then back at Pell.

Tomas finally sighs. "There's nothing wrong with this body."

"I mean, you are kind of a dragon," I say. "So there's that. But all in all, it's a good look for you."

Pell is laughing again. But Tomas looks crushed.

I crawl over to him, realizing that I'm giving Pell a pussy shot when I do this. I quickly push that thought out of my head and sit down next to Tomas. "What did I say? I don't understand. Did I hurt your feelings? Tell me."

Tomas stares straight ahead, looking at the window. The curtains are still billowing, but there's no light passing through them, so it must be night time wherever we are. "You know what," he finally says. "Fuck it." Then he looks straight at me. "Fuck it. I'll just tell you."

"Fuck it. Yeah. Tell me what's going on."

He sucks in a deep breath and holds for a moment, then lets it out. "I'm not human."

"Mmhmm. OK. I mean, hello? I think I knew that."

"No." He's shaking his head. "You don't understand. I mean… I'm not *human*."

I don't want to look at Pell for clarification, but I can't stop myself. He's sitting up again, but he puts both hands in the air. "Don't look at me." Then he points at Tomas. "And don't you look at me either. I was trying to do you a favor, friend. And"—he shrugs—"fine. I thought watching you two kiss would be hot. I swear, it wasn't a setup. I just wanted to see her kiss you."

"Wait." Did I hear that right? I think I did because this entire conversation is a total buzzkill.

"You wanted to watch us kiss? So you could… what? Jerk off?"

Pell's eyes are dancing. "Do you want me to jerk off while I watch you kiss him? Because that might be hot."

This makes Tomas laugh. And when I look back at him, his frown is gone. "You're a sick freak, Pell."

"Just let her kiss you, Tomas."

"No." Tomas looks at me. "It's not fair, Pie. You think I'm this hot human-dragon chimera. And I'm not."

"Well, what are you?" I ask.

He sighs. "Haven't you guessed yet? I mean, look at me."

I look at him. "Yeaaaah. OK. I don't get it."

"This isn't me. That guy I look like downstairs isn't me either. I'm a *dragon*, Pie."

"A big, scaly, red, *smelly*, blood dragon," Pell adds. "And in case you're not all up on the different kinds of dragons, the blood dragon is the worst. They are—"

"Fuckin' A, man," Tomas protests. "You will never be my wingman again."

"You're *my* wingman." Pell laughs. "And let's just get it all out there because I'm tired of this conversation. It's not a big deal. He lives in the dungeon. This"—Pell waves a hand at Tomas—"this body—all the bodies he's in—they're just shells he walks around in every now and then. Didn't you notice he was missing for days? That's because he used up all his magic and had to revert back to the blood dragon in the dungeon to rest so he could make another shell. That's why he's never been kissed. He's not even real. He's an *animal*."

Tomas says nothing. And when I look at him, he's just looking down at his hands in his lap. His fingers are playing with a misdirected scale over his knee. And this distracts me, so for a while I just say nothing.

"See," Tomas finally says. "That's why I don't want you to kiss me. It's exactly like he says. I'm not real. This is a shell. I'm a stinking, filthy fucking dragon who has been chained in the dungeon of Saint Mark's Sanctuary for over two thousand years. They didn't make this place to hold Pell and his ilk. They made it to hold me. All the other monsters just ended up here because the prison was already made." His head lifts up and his eyes find mine. "So. Now you know. And I'm the loser, not you."

I lean over, place one hand on his handsome face, and bring my lips up to his. He sucks in a breath just before we make contact. Like he's truly afraid of what comes next. But I whisper, "I don't care what you look like, Tomas. We're friends now. Looks have nothing to do with that. And this kiss has nothing to do with Pell, or this game, or the smoke, or the magic. This kiss is just me and you."

He's looking down when I say all this. But at the end, when I get to the part about us, his gaze meets mine. "You say that now—"

But he doesn't get a chance to finish. Because I kiss him.

He's stiff for a moment, his lips unresponsive. But then they soften and mold against mine. His mouth opens first and his hand slips up to my head, his fingers twisting around my hair. He pulls it into his fist as our tongues tumble into each other.

Then there is a pause. A moment when we're deep into it, but also thinking about the consequences.

About Pell sitting a few feet away, watching. About who he is, and who I am, and how we fit together.

We don't know.

So the kiss ends. But it ends slow, the way it started.

We're looking at each other when I draw away out of his personal space and back into mine. Then we sigh.

"So," Pell says. "Was it everything you thought it would be?"

I look for malice in those words. I look for jealousy and anger. But there's nothing to find there. The question is genuine.

Tomas must think so as well, because so is his answer. And it comes with a smile as he plops backwards onto his velvet cushion. "It was better."

I blush a little, unsure what to do now. Unsure who I belong to. Which is a stupid thought because obviously, I belong to no one. But we all say that, right? It's something we say. We are our own person.

And we mean it, but…

But. Don't we all want to belong to someone?

And I want to belong to Pell.

Maybe I didn't know that before today, but I sure do now. He doesn't believe in us, but I saw it. So whatever his memories are, they're wrong. I didn't make that stuff up.

"Helloooooooo!"

The call is both distant and surprising. It comes from somewhere deep inside the cathedral.

"What the fuck was that?" That's what I'm thinking, but it comes out of Pell's mouth.

Tomas jumps to his feet. "There's the door!" He laughs. "My kiss gave us a door!"

"Shut up, monster." Pell gets to his feet and then he does something unexpected. He crosses the small distance between us and extends his hand to me.

I look up at him and he gives me a little shrug. That shrug says a thousand things. *It's my fault. I'm sorry I made the dare. Did you like it? Do you like him? Do you like me? What have I done?*

And I answer every single one of those questions simply by taking his hand and allowing him to pull me to my feet.

I am his and he is mine.

The kiss between Tomas and me was… something else.

"Hellooooo! Is anyone here?"

"Who the fuck *is* that?" Tomas is enraged. "Who the hell is inside our home?"

And then he is through the door. Pell takes my hand and we follow. But when I come out the other side and find myself in the upper hallway, just a few feet from the stairs that lead down to the lower great hall, I am *me* again.

My horns are gone. My fur, my hooves, my cool hind legs—all gone. I'm wearing my classy blue sweater dress and knee-high boots. And despite my earlier claim that they were comfortable, and the fact I wasn't even wearing them for this whole time, my feet are so achy. I think I have blisters.

Interestingly, Tomas stays the way he was. A dragon chimera. Of course, Pell doesn't change. He's just himself.

"Helloooo! Pie? Are you here?"

"Ho-lee fuck," I gasp. "It's the fucking sheriff."

"How did he get in?" Pell asks.

"How should I know? But I told you! I freaking told you the other day that he walked through the gate."

"He's bloodline," Tomas whispers. "He has to be. That's the only explanation."

And just as that last word leaves his mouth, my ring—the very thing tying me to this place and this curse—slips off my finger and falls to the floor with a sharp *clink*.

"Pie?" Russ Roth calls. "Is that you?"

How did he hear that? There is no way he could've heard that.

I quickly pick up the ring, but don't put it back on. "Russ!" I call down. "I'll be right there."

When I turn to look at Pell and Tomas, they are both pale. And they are both looking at the ring in my hand. Slowly their eyes migrate up to meet mine and neither of them needs to speak for me to hear their questions.

Now what? Will you leave? Stay? What will you do with this choice you've been given?

I don't know, so I don't answer. I just turn away and start down the stairs.

Pell whispers, "Go after her," to Tomas.

"Like this?" Tomas whispers back.

"*Change.*" Pell's words are both a growl and a command.

But that's all I hear, because I'm practically jumping down the stairwell and then there he is. Sheriff Russ Roth in the flesh. Standing in my lower hall like he's allowed to be here. Hat in hand, smile on his face, looking super fucking hot and emitting those damn cupid pheromones. I can sense them from all the way across the room.

It's *not* me. It is *him* making those attraction smells.

"Sheriff," I say brightly. "What brings you out this way?"

He cocks his head at me, still smiling, but it's a look I recognize. His look says, *Are you fucking kidding me?* But his mouth says, "You... kinda left our date in a sudden and unexpected way. I was worried."

"I'm fine. As you can see."

He smiles. Nods. Calls me a liar in his head. "I can see that. And I'm not trying to make a big deal about this." He puts up a hand. "If I'm not your type, that's totally fine. But... Pie. Come on now. Your exit was unconventional and, maybe this is just the lawman in me, but it was also suspicious."

I point at myself. "You're suspicious of me?"

"Not you." He looks up and around, his eyes landing on the left stairwell, then the right. He sees it. He understands it instinctually. They don't belong here. "This place," he finishes. "There's something..." He taps his head with his hat like that's his thinking gesture. "Something not right here."

I don't want to get too close to him. I don't understand what he is or what his weird power is doing. I don't even know for sure that he's aware of the way he affects me. But I don't need to understand any of that stuff to know I can't be near this man. And he needs to go. Like... now.

So when I reach the bottom of the stairs, I simply turn to the center stairwell and begin climbing back up.

"Where are you going?"

"I'm working, Sheriff. I have things to do and they are all up this way."

I don't look back to see if he's following me, but what else can he do? Just stay down there by himself?

He follows. And he comes up those stairs fast, taking them several at a time. So fast that I have to stretch my legs and hoof it to keep the space between us at a reasonable distance so those sex pheromones he's shooting at me can't catch up.

When I get to the top I head straight to the front door. I know he's not going to leave without some kind of explanation, but the closer I can get him to that exit, the easier it will be to push him out.

"Miss Vita," Russ calls. "Are you running away from me?"

"Nope." But I am, and we both know it.

The door is open and even halfway across the room I can see through it. I can see the outside. I don't have the ring on, but I can see the wall, and the gate, and the Granite County Sheriff's Department SUV parked out front.

This is when it hits me—I can *leave*.

I can drop my ring on the floor, walk out that door, and then...

And then what?

What the hell am I going to do? Steal his car?

This is why Grant needed to take me down to the caretaker's cottage that first day. He couldn't leave by the front door either. His car was on the other side of the sanctuary. And I'm not all up on the magic surrounding the lake and the forest down the hill, but if Pell's remarks the other day were true, then they are hidden from outsiders. And I probably wouldn't be able to find my Jeep again. I'd have to walk out of here with nothing.

I'd have to walk out of here without Pia too.

What would that life look like?

I don't care about the Jeep. I don't care about being so poor, I can't even feed myself. I am a survivor. I can find a way. I *always* find a way.

But a life without Pia—or, rather, a life without *magic*—what would *that* be like?

What would it be like to be *normal?*

To not be the crazy girl who talks to herself?

To not have a real imaginary friend sitting on my shoulder or hiding in my pocket?

I slip the ring back on and turn to face the sheriff. "What exactly do you want from me, Sheriff?"

He stops in the middle of the great hall. The day is nearly gone. I couldn't even begin to guess how much time we spent up there in the hallway rooms. But there's sunlight coming through all those magnificent stained-glass windows and it's backlighting Russ Roth, making him appear as a black shadow.

He's still got his hat in his hands. He's still smiling. "I would like you to tell me exactly what the heck is going on here."

"Or what?"

"Or—" He pauses. His smile drops. His eyes narrow. "Or… I'm gonna start taking a special interest in Saint Mark's. Because you know what?"

"I couldn't even begin to guess."

"I just remembered something about this place. And that's interesting, you know? That I would forget something like this, and then all of a sudden it pops back into my head."

We both pause. The silence hangs there, making the air around us feel heavy and thick.

"Well, you gonna let me in on it? Or you gonna make me guess?"

"I remember my granddaddy telling me a story about this place. This was a long time ago. I was maybe… eight, nine. And he said, 'You stay away from that place, Russ. You stay clear of it. Or those monsters up there? They'll come getcha.' Of course, being eight or nine, I wasn't about to stay clear of this place. Me and all the boys from town came up one day. Hiked through the woods for hours following the train tracks. And we came out by a lake. Which is very strange, now that I can remember this. Because there aren't any lakes up here, Pie Vita. Not a one."

"Is that so?" My voice is trembling. I think I know what happened. Grant put a spell on him. Maybe the entire town. And now that Grant is gone, that spell is wearing off.

That's part of it, at least.

How he got in here? I don't know. But Tomas is probably right. He is bloodline.

He is *my* bloodline?

Am I part cupid?

"That is so. I was never able to find it again." He puts up one hand. "Hold up. Let me correct myself here just so we're all understanding. I never *looked* for it again because I forgot about that trip up here. And do you know why me and all the boys forgot we found a lake up here at Saint Mark's all those years back?"

I say nothing.

"Because a young man named Grant—"

Here it comes.

"—he put a spell on us, Pie. That's what's going on here, isn't it? Magic."

I force a laugh. "Sheriff—"

"*Don't.*" He growls his word. His smile is long gone. His amicable, aw-shucks demeanor never existed. He is hard, and he is serious. He is the law of this land, and he knows this. "Do not tell me I'm crazy, girl. Don't even try it. I don't know why those memories just came back to me the other day."

The other day! He set me up. He asked me out on that date as a setup.

"But," he continues, "they are back. I know what this place is because my granddaddy told me. The monsters live here. The monsters of Saint Mark's. And you, dear girl, are the new caretaker. Tell me I'm wrong."

I… am… speechless.

"Hey! Sheriff!" We both turn to find Tomas— regular, old, hot-as-fuck Tomas—just coming up the stairs. "Long time, brother."

The sheriff takes a step back. Which is actually a step towards me. And then he draws his gun. It's not some little pistol, either. It's not some six-shooter like you'd imagine a sheriff would carry. It's not even one of those compact modern types. It's fucking huge. Even I can tell this is no ordinary gun and everything I know about guns, I learned from old-ass TV shows. "Stay the fuck back, monster. I don't know who or what you are, but you had better stay the fuck back or I will blow a hole in you so big, we'll all be able to see out the other side!"

I don't think this is an empty threat, either. I think that gun of his has many hidden talents and blowing big holes in people is one of them.

"Sheriff!" I yell it.

And then Russ Roth turns towards me, aiming that big gun at my face. And I don't really know what happens next. Tomas is moving towards us and a bird comes swooping down from the ceiling. Pia! She passes over the top of my head, straight towards the sheriff and then... *BOOM!* My hands fly up to my face, trying to shield myself from the incoming bullet.

But everything is suddenly slow motion and swarms of beautiful wood nymph moths are fluttering up out of my palms. Exactly the way they did in the hallway forest dream.

They circle around the sheriff like a gorgeous twister of destruction out on the plains. Spiraling around his body until I can't even see him anymore. There's a sharp twang on the floor at my feet, and when I look down, there is a slug. The remnants of the bullet that never hit me.

I look back up. The sheriff is stumbling backwards, towards me, past me.

And there is fire.

Everywhere.

Shooting out of Tomas like a flamethrower.

Russ runs. He's through the door, outside, and it slams closed in his face with such force, the entire building shakes. I look over my shoulder to find Pell, palms up, one of his limited magic talents in progress. The door is closed and locked. But we can hear the sheriff pounding on it. Demanding to be let in.

In that same moment, Tomas disappears and my moths fall to the floor at the threshold of the door, dead.

And then I drop to the floor too.

Unsure if *I'm* dead.

CHAPTER TWENTY-FIVE – PELL

I see it all from across the upper hall—the gun, the moths, the man, the girl, the dragon boy, my hands coming up to slam the door closed with a finality of an eternal curse—and I don't understand a single second of it.

But Pie is unconscious.

I rush over to her, not wanting to step on the lifeless bodies of the beautiful wood nymph moths, but unable to help myself.

A groan from deep below the sanctuary reverberates up from the floor and I know that is Tomas. Spent. Hurting from his fire display. He will need time to recover from this. Lots of time.

But Pie also did magic, and she is spent too.

Tomas—I can't do anything for him. I can't even get close to him. He is not himself down there. But I can help Pie.

I pick her up in my arms and carefully carry her down the hallway near the stairs to the steam cave. Once inside, I remove her clothes, then step into the water with her in my arms and hold her as the mineral water brings her back to life.

She is not dead. It doesn't literally bring her back to life. But this spring is special, and soon she is squirming in my arms.

"What happened?" Her voice is weak and shaky.

"Magic," I say. It's the only answer I have.

She sighs, turning her body in to me. And I settle on a rock ledge, leaning back and letting the moment just exist.

She's still and quiet for a little bit. But then, slowly, she comes awake again. "Pell. Where's Tomas?"

"Don't worry about him. He'll be OK. It'll take a few days, maybe. But he'll be OK."

"What will happen to us? Will the sheriff come back? Will he bring others? He can let them all in!"

"Shhh," I tell her. "Don't worry about it. I think your spell and my door lock will hold for a little bit."

"What *spell*?" She struggles to sit up. And even though I don't want to allow this, she doesn't give me a choice. She sits in my lap with her head on my shoulder. "I didn't do a spell."

"Oh, you did. You most certainly did. Don't you remember all those moths?"

"Yeah, but I didn't do that. They just appeared from my hands. I wasn't in control—"

"Pie, you need to face facts. You're… well, I don't know what you are, but you're not human. Not completely, anyway. You did do a spell. I have a feeling it was a warding. To keep him out. And it seems to have worked. At least with all three of us participating. You bound him up, Tomas pushed him back, and I closed him out. It should hold. For a little bit. But we're gonna have to come up with something better than that. Grant's wards were strong. Very strong. But they're obviously wearing off. We need to do them again."

"How?"

340

"That's a talk for tomorrow. You need to rest. And eat. We all need to rest after that. We were stuck in the magic all day. Hell, maybe longer than a day. That's enough to give us a hangover. But getting rid of the sheriff will have pushed us to our limits. We need to recover first."

I can tell she wants to fight me on this, but she's too weak. So she can't. She knows I'm right.

We stay there for a while, just leaning on each other. Every once in a while, I can hear Tomas's groans from below. He breathed fire. I have never seen him do that before and I don't think it's good for him. In fact, I think his dragon magic is a very, *very* bad thing for all of us.

Eventually, Pie is awake enough to get out and put her clothes back on. I want to carry her back down to the cottage, but she insists on walking. She does lean heavily on me as we make our way down the hill.

Once inside, I make a fire while she rests on the couch, then go through all the food we have and come up with cans of soup that can be easily warmed up on the wood stove. We don't sit at the table. We just hold our bowls in our hands and eat on the couch.

"I would give anything to be able to go out to eat right now," Pie says.

"You can." I blow on my soup and then take a bite. "You don't need to worry about me. Regardless of how I came off that first day, I can take care of myself."

"I don't want to go alone. And before you take that the wrong way, I didn't go out to eat before I came here, either. Pia and I would just get something from a drive-through. Eat it in the car. But it would be nice to sit down at a restaurant and have someone

341

serve me, ya know?" She blows on her soup too, then slurps it down.

I think about her statement. How nice it feels to be taken care of. I don't disagree. I like being fed. I liked the horn massage she did. And when she took it to my back, fuck. I wanted to die, it felt so good.

"One day," Pie says, "I'm gonna take you out to eat."

"Shouldn't it be the other way around?"

"OK. You can take me."

"We will have to wait a whole year for that. Next Halloween. When people might accept the idea that a satyr chimera is eating in the booth next to them."

"Or I can just learn that spell. You know, the one to make you look human. The way Grant did."

I don't say anything to that. I can't blame her for wanting me to be a certain way. It's not her fault.

I mean, I want her a certain way as well.

I want her to be my wood nymph. I want to take her back upstairs and get lost in that forest with her forever. I want her to have horns, and hooves, and fur.

I want her to be like me, the same way she wants me to be like her.

"What are you thinking about?" she asks.

When I glance over at her, she's smiling. Big. Happy. Rejuvenated, I think. Maybe it was the hot spring? Maybe it was the soup? "Our day." The words come out as a sigh.

"It was definitely one for the books. And I'm super worried that the sheriff will come back tonight. Isn't there anything we can do?"

"Not the sheriff. I don't care much about the sheriff. I'm talking about earlier."

"Should I apologize for kissing Tomas? You did dare me."

"Not that, Pie. I'm not talking about that. I don't care about the kiss."

"Was it hot?" She waggles her eyebrows at me. "Did you like watching?"

I smile. Can't help it. But I'm getting frustrated. "No. I mean, yes. I did like it. It was hot. I'm sure Tomas will never forget that kiss. But that's not what I'm talking about, Pie. I'm talking about us."

She nods solemnly.

I can tell this isn't the time for this talk. I can read a room. I just usually end up not caring. But I can't let this go. I can't stop thinking about it. "Why didn't you just leave?"

"Leave?"

"You had that sheriff right where you needed him. All you had to do was drop the ring and walk out. And it would be over for you."

"Yeah." She sighs. "Yeah, I know."

"So. Why didn't you?"

She shakes her head at me. "I have nowhere to go, Pell. And I'm not just saying that. I don't have anywhere to go. I don't have a single relative—"

"Well, that's debatable," I cut her off. "Since the good sheriff of Granite Springs seems to be your kin, as they say around these parts."

"Maybe." And now she is really sending me I-do-not-want-to-talk-about-this signals.

"There's no maybe. If he can come through the door, he is bloodline. And we already know you're bloodline. So." I shrug. "There it is. He, and whoever he has in that town, those are your people. But all that bloodline stuff aside, do you have an answer for me?"

"About why I stayed?"

I nod.

She looks away from me. "I mean, I think I already said it. I don't know what you're looking for here, Pell. I don't have anywhere to go. My bird, my Pia—she's still here. I can't just walk out and forget she ever existed." She must read the disappointment on my face, because she continues. "It's nothing against you. You know that, right? I like you. A lot. You're not a bad boss."

Boss? Did she just call me her *boss*?

"And yes, I'm staying because of you. And Tomas. This whole place, really. I feel like I belong here. With *you*, of course."

"And Tomas," I add.

"And Tomas. Yes."

I don't know what I expected her to admit to after one romp in the hallways. Well, to be fair to myself, it was two romps. But. Whatever. I just expected… more.

And for whatever reason, she's not going to give me what I want. Not tonight, at least. So I decide to drop it. "Do you want to know what we'll need to do in order to ward this place again?"

"For sure. We need to do something to keep the villagers from pitchforking us."

"There's a book inside a tomb up there. It's a powerful one."

"How do you know?"

"It's inside my friend's tomb. Tarq is his name. It's not his book. He's a monster like me. But I know it's in there and I know who it belongs to, and I know it's what we need."

"OK."

I chance a side-eye glance at her. She's not even looking at me. She's looking out the window at the tombs up the hill. "So you're the only one who can go in there and get it. You're the only one who can see the doors."

"Oh, man." Her voice is whiny and kinda cute. "I hate those tombs. They're so creepy."

"Yeah, but this is just Tarq. He's not a bad guy. He'll probably love the company. And you will have me in common with him. You could bring me news back. Of him. I talk to him all the time. I'm dying to know if he can hear me."

Her sigh tells me she's not convinced, but I don't dwell on this. It's Tarq. She will be fine. "I would not send you in there if I thought you were in danger, Pie."

"I'm not thinking that."

"Then what are you sighing about?"

"I just think those tombs are creepy."

"That book is important. You don't need to stay in there long. Just fill Tarq in, ask him nicely for the book—tell him it's a favor to me—and then leave."

"What if he wants something in return? Like… what if he wants me to get him out of the tomb?"

I shrug. "Tell him yeah."

"Will I be lying?"

"You got a problem with freeing Tarq?"

"I don't know Tarq."

"He's a pretty cool guy."

"Monster."

"Right. Same thing."

She sighs again.

"What?"

"It's just… I'm already outnumbered, ya know? Adding another monster is—"

"Hey." I laugh. "If you want to go find another magic girl for us, I won't complain."

"Oh, really?"

"What's that look for?"

"You know what? I'm tired. I'm going to bed. You can sleep on the couch if you want, but you can leave if you'd prefer to go home." She shrugs. "It's up to you, I guess."

"What did I say?"

"Go get another girl?"

"It was a joke, Pie. There are no other girls out there. You know this."

"So that's the only reason? Because there aren't any available? Otherwise, you'd be all for me grabbing another one to satisfy your pleasure needs? And that's not even true. If Russ Roth is kin then there's more of them, right? And that means there's more girls out there for you."

"What?" I actually laugh. That's how funny that is.

She gets up, ready to storm up the stairs, but I grab her wrist and pull her into my lap. She struggles against me, but I'm far too strong for her to win that battle. Finally, when she is straddling me, facing me, I place my hands on her cheeks and make her look at me. "It was a joke. I'm not looking for a harem, Pie Vita. I'm just fine with the way things are. So if you don't want another monster around, then lie to Tarq if that's what he asks for. Get what we need, and none of us will ever say another word about it again. It's me. And you. And Tomas." I shrug. "We can't get rid of him. He's kind of the landlord."

"I don't really understand that."

"I know. But soon enough, you will. I'm tired. You have to be tired. There's nothing more we can do tonight, so we're going to bed. And I'm not leaving you here alone. I'm sleeping with you."

"Are you?"

I can't tell if that's a serious question or just a complicated challenge. "Yes. I'm staying. And we're sleeping in the same bed. I'll stay on my side." This remark makes her frown. "Tomorrow, Pie. Save all that for tomorrow."

I watch her give in and it's satisfying. Not the actual giving in, but the trust. And the upcoming obedience. It's a hesitant trust and the obedience will come with conditions, I'm sure. But I'll take it.

She sighs heavily, then shrugs. I'm still holding her face. But she backs out of it now and starts for the stairs.

I follow her up and she excuses herself to the bathroom with a small pile of bed clothes in her hands. I am my usual naked self, so I just pull the covers back and get in on the same side I settled on last night. I have a side, I realize. We have sides.

There is no way for me to hide the grin that emerges. And when Pie comes out of the bathroom, that grin is still there.

She lowers the lamp light until the tiny flame is gone, then walks over to the bed like an apparition in a short white nightgown and when she slips under the covers next to me, I don't wait for her to settle or grant me permission, I just tug her close and hold her tight.

She wriggles against my embrace immediately, but I keep hold. "Pell," she complains. "Let go."

"No. Not yet."

I wait for the battle, but my effort pays off. Or maybe I've just worn her down. Because she gives in with a long yawn. And then, without another word, she just drifts off to another place.

A place without me. Perhaps that dream world she claims she saw?

It's weird how she could describe the woods around the forest temple in detail. Right down to the color of the leaves and the tree trunks.

Was she there?

I mean, that's a dumb question. We were in the hallway fantasy rooms. That's all it was, just another room.

But it didn't act like another room. I didn't go with her, for one. And it was in the middle of us having sex. All of that is confusing enough. But there's more.

Much more.

Things I haven't told anyone.

Things I haven't even thought about since... well, since I was a child. Since Tarq and I used to run in those forests. Things like what Ostanes did to me. How she made me.

What she turned me into.

I think about this for hours. Because I know there's something there. And not only that, something has changed around here since Pie came.

Of course, I felt this change immediately. And at first I thought, *Well, Grant's gone. That's what's different.* But that's not it.

It's Pie.

I didn't lose something, I gained.

I just haven't figured out what it means yet. That's why I need that book in Tarq's tomb. I know it's in there. It has to be in there. He was Saturn's chimera. Who else could have it but him?

It has to be there. And Pie will be fine inside his tomb.

If it were anyone else, I wouldn't let her go.

I would forbid it.

Wouldn't I?

CHAPTER TWENTY-SIX – PIE

When I wake up the next morning, Pell is standing in front of the window with his back to me.

"Hey." I try to rouse myself but I'm still pretty exhausted from the previous day. "What are you looking at?"

He doesn't turn to face me. But he does answer. "The lake. I was thinking… we should go out there."

"Out there… for?"

Now he turns and I can't stop myself from studying his chest. His face. The curve of his shoulders. His horns.

We had *sex* yesterday.

I had sex with a monster.

I hate that thought. I do. I hate it. He's not just a monster. In fact, he's not a monster. He's just… something else.

"Just to see it," he says. "Walk around it. There are birds out there. I've seen ducks on that lake. And deer in the woods." He shrugs. "It's been a while, that's all."

"Oh." I shove the covers off me and swing my feet out. His eyes track down my legs, then back up. But he's studying me too. Just like I was studying him. And I wonder if he's thinking… *I had sex with her yesterday. A human.*

But he doesn't say that, he says, "So what do you think?"

"About the lake?"

He just stares at me for a moment and I swear to God, I hear him thinking, *Stupid. Naïve. Cute.* But I'm not sure which one he chooses today. Everything feels different for some reason. Yesterday he felt like my best friend but today... he's just my monster. "About the tomb, Pie. Do you think you're up to going inside?"

"Do I have a choice? I mean, if the sheriff comes back—"

"Oh, he will. He thinks he can come and go at will. He probably has no idea that he's not supposed to be able to get in. I think that's working in our favor at the moment. He's not under the impression that his ability to get inside might come with conditions."

I sit on the edge of the bed and nod, looking down at my feet.

Yesterday, I had hooves. They were pretty too.

"So."

I look back up at Pell. He's waiting for me to say something. "Yeah. Sure. I'll go inside the tomb and grab the book. But... you said I can't go in. You said I can see the doors, but only you can enter. So how do I get in?"

"I have a way. But we need to go to the greenhouse. There is a plant in there called bloodhorn that Grant used to grow so he could go inside the tombs."

"Wait. Grant used to go inside them?"

"No. He never did get it to work. But that's because he needed my help, and another, more important, ingredient. But he didn't understand that, and I never did offer up that info."

"Hmm." I walk over to the closet and peruse through my new selection of clothes, choose a pair of dark jeans and a red t-shirt that says *Come Hell or High Water* across the tits. Then I go into the bathroom, wash up, change, and when I come back out, Pell is downstairs messing around in the kitchen.

He hands me a sprinkle-covered Pop-Tart as he chews. "I love these. But for the record, I like sugar cereal for breakfast. Boo Berry is my favorite. But I like Trix too. The new ones. With marshmallows. In fact, just get all the marshmallow cereal. You can't go wrong with marshmallow cereal."

And there he is. The man I met yesterday. "You're kinda dumb, you know that?" But I'm smiling when I say it.

He just smiles back. Nods. Then, with mouth full, says, "Grant always kept a candy drawer for me too. Up in the cathedral kitchen. So next time you go shopping, get some candy."

"Should I pick up the family bag of Laffy Taffy and jawbreakers? Or the fun-sized Twix and Snickers?"

He points at me with his Pop-Tart. "I would appreciate all of those, thank you."

"I am not eating this Pop-Tart. I'm not hungry. So if you want mine—"

He grabs it. "Thanks."

Then we both sigh and look at the door. But we're really looking past it. At the cemetery. I really don't want to go inside one of those tombs, but if this will get rid of Russ Roth, I will do it. He does weird things to me. I don't like it. He makes me feel very out of control.

"Shall we go then?" I ask.

Pell nods and shoves the rest of his breakfast into his mouth.

We walk up the hill side by side, but the last time we did this, he was holding my hand. And it's hard not to compare yesterday to today.

I change the subject instead of dwelling on it. "Do you think Tomas is around?"

"Probably not," Pell answers. "He needs time to recover from that whole fire-breathing scene. I've never seen him do that before."

"Never?"

"No. I mean, he and I haven't been hanging out much for the past thousand years, so I'm no Tomas expert or anything. But just appearing in that human body takes a lot out of him."

"Should we check on him?"

We're just at the top of the hill and here Pell pauses. He actually turns and looks down the hill. And at first, I think he's looking at the caretaker cottage, but then I realize he's looking at the lake out beyond the walls. He answers my question, but it's done absently. "We'll see him soon enough, but we can't help him when he's like this. He's... beyond our help when he's in his base form. When he's not around, it's best to forget about him until he comes back."

"What if he's hurt?"

"Nothing we can do. And he can't die, so..." Pell shrugs. Then he points towards the middle of the cemetery. "Tarq's tomb is over there." We begin walking again. "I need to show you the greenhouse anyway. You're gonna need to take care of it. There's always been plenty of sunshine coming through the roof, but there is an elaborate aqueduct system for watering that needs watching."

I don't really have anything to say to that, so I say nothing.

It's all very… tedious. Everything about yesterday was easy, but today there is a strain between us.

He's having regrets, I can tell. He's thinking, *What the hell was I smoking yesterday?* Except all the sex happened before we started smoking shit.

This makes me feel worse.

But he does pull open the cathedral door for me, and then wave me through first. And I am reminded about a stray thought I had that first day I came here. When I saw Tomas on the second-story balcony and I thought he was a hot guy with manners.

"What's so funny?"

"I was thinking about Tomas."

"Oh." Pell nods, then looks straight ahead again with his too-serious face.

"Not like that," I say quickly. "I mean—" I stop and sigh. "Pell?"

He turns to me.

"What's going on?"

"What do you mean?"

"You regret yesterday, don't you?"

"No. Not at all. Why?" He makes a face at me. "Do you?"

"You're acting weird. Why are you acting weird?"

"You didn't answer my question. Do you regret yesterday?"

I shake my head slowly, then look up the stairs instead of him. "No. But everything feels off." Now I look back at him. "And I don't like it. We're a team, right?"

He nods. Then he blows out a breath and his words come rushing out. "OK. I'm gonna tell you something. This book, Pie." He pauses and shakes his head again. "There is nothing in there that can break our curse. But this is a powerful book with powerful spells. And one of them is a banishment spell. But banishment uses very negative energy. It's a dark spell and it has a price."

"What kind of price? And whose book is this?"

"The price is always a sacrifice."

"Like a… virgin?"

He laughs. And I'm so relieved to see this laughing Pell, my whole body relaxes. "What is it with you and virgins?"

"Well, what kind of sacrifice are they looking for? I think this is important, don't you?"

"Of course I do. Especially since you not only have to go inside Tarq's tomb to get the book, but you're the one who has to work the spell. But as far as sacrifices go, I don't know. I'm not a witch or an alchemist. That's something between you and the spirits where you get your power." He points to me before I can object. "Don't tell me you're not a witch or an alchemist. I saw you, Pie. You saw what you did. Those moths? They come from somewhere. Where do they come from?"

"I don't know. It's not like I ever did any magic before I came here."

"What do you think that bird of yours is?"

"What do you mean? She's not even real."

"Isn't she?"

"She's not here. She conveniently disappeared."

"And what took her place?"

I throw up my hands. "Nothing took her place."

"Moths, Pie. They took her place. That's your magic. You did some high-level shit last night on the sheriff. It comes from somewhere. That's how magic works. You ask the powers to help you and if you say the right things, and offer up something they want, it gets done. So… who did you ask for help when you did that moth magic last night?"

I shake my head. "No one. I didn't ask anyone."

He sighs. Then takes my hand and we start up the stairs.

We don't pause at the top, just head across the great hall towards a door I have yet to go through.

"This is the greenhouse," Pell says as he shoves the massive double doors open. "This is where we get what we need." Then he mutters under his breath, "I really hope it still fucking grows here."

I am unable to follow him in, so when he moves forward into the room, my feet stay planted on the marble tiles just outside. And the reason I'm unable to follow him isn't because there's some magic holding me back, but because I am paralyzed with *wonder*.

"What the actual fuck?" is what I manage to say as I gaze up at the three-story walls of glass. "This isn't even possible. This… this place can't exist!" I turn and look out the front windows. Picture myself walking up to the sanctuary that first day last week. See Tomas on the second-story balcony. Then I look back inside the greenhouse. Look up, where that balcony should be, but isn't. "This… this…"

"Pie." Pell shakes me by the shoulders. "We don't have time for this. It doesn't need to make sense. It's *magic*."

"But… where is that balcony that I see from the outside?"

"Who cares?"

"I care!"

Pell huffs at me. "It's…" He looks up. "I don't know. It doesn't matter. It's like the hallways upstairs. I need to find the plant I'm looking for. Stay here while I look. And don't touch anything. Some of these plants have anger issues."

"Anger issues?"

But he's already pushing his way past some overgrown branches down the center aisle.

I stay right where I am. I do not go into the greenhouse. I think I can feel those anger issues and I think that anger is directed at me because these plants are part of my job and I've been neglecting them.

And as if this place couldn't get any creepier, there is a great rumble underneath my feet. The whole building… *thrums*. It's not a shake, like an earthquake. It's a… tone. It's a wave of deep sound. Like the sound of those humming monks that people like to meditate to.

"Don't panic!" Pell calls. "That's just Tomas. We're gonna need to go down there next. You can panic then."

"What?" But my voice is just a squeak.

Pell is deep inside the greenhouse now. His voice sounds far away. I don't quite understand the dimensions of this place, but it's three stories tall and I can't even see the other side. It looks like the forest we were running through in the rooms, that's how big some of the trees are. But there are aisles and aisles of other plants too.

"I am not cut out for this." Saying that out loud feels very necessary. "I'm not cut out for any of this. I can't do it. I don't know what these plants are, I don't know how to work a spell, I don't have any higher power guiding me or whatnot. I'm not a witch! I'm not an alchemist!"

Pell suddenly appears, pushing his way through the aisle towards me. "I got it," he says, holding up several large, bright red flowers.

"What are those?"

"These are how you can get inside the tombs." He pauses to lift his chin up, like he's proud of himself. "I have never shown this to a caretaker before. Grant used to ask me about it all the time."

"It's a secret?" I ask. Pell nods. "Maybe I don't need to know?"

"You do. You need to go in the tomb and you can't do that, only I can. But I can't see the doors. So this is a substitute for me." He smiles now. Like this is great fun. "Well"—he holds up one finger—"we need one more thing."

I look down at my feet. "Tomas?"

"Yep." He pauses. "No. We don't actually need Tomas for you to enter the tombs. We just need a few of his scales."

"Dragon's scales? This spell calls for dragon's scales?"

"And bloodhorn." He points to the flower.

"Wait. How come you can't just go get this book? Tarq is your friend. You seem to know what you're doing and—"

"I can't see the doors."

"But I can't walk through them!"

"You can't walk through them without *me*." Once again, he points to the flowers. "This is how you do that. And the scales."

"So why can't you just use that stuff and go in yourself?"

He shoots me a look that says, *Yesterday I thought you were cute, but today I think you're being slow on purpose.* "It's not a spell to *see* doors, Pie. It's a spell to walk *through* them. How can I walk through them if I can't see them?"

I want to keep this fight going and insist this makes no sense, but unfortunately for me, it kinda does. "Well, this sucks. Why isn't there a spell to see doors?"

"Take it up with whoever makes the rules around here. When you find that asshole, let me know. I have a few complaints myself. Now, let's go. We need to have this spell ready before the sheriff comes back."

Pell leads me towards the back of this side of the sanctuary. It's the same direction as the dining room and the kitchen, but we end up at the top of a winding spiral stairwell made up of stone.

It leads to a dungeon.

The rumble under my feet is stronger here at the entrance to Tomas's lair. But that's not even the most concerning thing about this little dragon scale hunt.

It's the smell.

I have to stop breathing, that's how bad it is.

Pell pauses at the top of the stairs and looks over his shoulder at me. "Are you OK?"

I'm covering my mouth with my hand, trying my best not to breathe through my nose. I just nod. Because I can't even lie. I'm not ready for this, I decide. I'm not ready for what Tomas really is.

Pell puts a hand on my shoulder. "Don't think of it as him. It's not him. He will not recognize you. And he won't even remember this when we see him again."

I swallow hard. "OK."

"I would go down and get them myself, but this is a two-person job."

I nearly piss myself when I realize he needs my help here. Because up until this very moment I had figured that I'd just be here for moral support.

"Pie?"

"Pell."

"Did you hear me?"

I nod.

"I'm gonna need you to distract him so I can get close enough to grab the scales."

This is when I notice he's holding a giant pair of... "What are those?" I point to the tool he's holding.

"Scale extractors."

"Mmm-hmm." I just nod. Because I got nothing for that.

"Don't worry." He holds them up in front of me and snicks them open and closed a few times. "I got this part."

My composure breaks. "You'd better, Pell! Because what the actual fuck is happening right now? I'm supposed to distract a dragon while you yank out its scales! It breathes fire, right? It's gonna fry me, isn't it? And oh, my fucking God, that smell! What is it?"

"It's old eggs," Pell says.

I actually gag on his words. Pell pats me on the back. "Just... breathe through your mouth. We can get this done, Pie. I'm pretty sure we got this."

"Pretty sure?"

"Come on. We'll be fine." Then he grabs a torch off the wall and we begin our descent.

What we're doing is a very bad idea.

And that thought just keeps running through my mind as we go down, down, down into the depths of the sanctuary. The smell is freaking bad and I spend most of the trip holding my breath, so that by the time we pause on the bottom, I'm lightheaded from lack of oxygen.

But that rumble—no. That growl….

I let my breath out and for a moment I can't even remember how to breathe in.

Then, the next thing I know, flames are shooting out towards us.

Pell throws his torch and yells, "Pick it up! Distract it! I'm going on the—"

But I can no longer hear his words. Because the monster in front of me right now is no hot guy working out on a balcony. He's no dragon chimera getting high with us and playing truth or dare. He's not the man who showed me how to use Grant's kitchen spells, or the friend who made steaks for dinner.

He's not *him*.

That's what sinks in as Pell disappears. And suddenly I understand why all those old fairy tales and storybooks make the dragon out to be the evil monster.

Because the dragon *is* the evil monster.

Tomas is red. I'm not talking some reddish-brown color. I'm not talking some bright valentine-heart color. I'm talking hellfire red with a healthy dose of orange and yellow. I'm talking rivers of lava flowing over brimstone. That's what color he is.

His eyes are black. And then, suddenly, they're not. They're yellow. Not some sunshine yellow, either. They are sickly green-yellow. The color of a disease.

He opens his mouth and that stench… it's not just the den of filth he lives in. It's not just the nest that reeks of demons. It's *him*.

He exhales poison.

And his teeth. Yellow-orange and blue-gray. Sharp. So fucking sharp. Like shark teeth.

I'm stuck in place. My feet have no chance of moving. Ever again. So when he opens his mouth, this is all I see. And it's like… 4-K fucking ultra-sharpness and clarity. Because this isn't some sci-fi special effects going on here, this is fucking real.

The fire. His mouth is wide open, so I see it. It lives inside him. I watch the tiny flame as it ebbs back in his throat, and then I move. Because it grows.

I truck up those stairs so fast, I take four steps at a time and get around three bends before the flames catch up with me. They shoot up the wall and this is when I notice that the walls are black. They are charred with dragon fire.

But even so, the fire licks at my clothes and then… I am on *fire*.

I scream and pat at my back, but it's no good. I have to rub up against the stone walls to smother it.

The dragon roars down below and the entire stairwell shakes. It's not some deep-bass rumble. It's fucking shaking. Parts of the walls actually begin to crumble.

I'm in shock. I can't even move. I just press myself up against the stones and look straight ahead at the opposite wall, waiting for the next barrage of fire.

It doesn't come. In fact, things calm down a little and I can take a few breaths. I no longer care about the stench. To hell with the stench, my mind is only on the fire.

Then, from down below, I hear Pell calling for me. "Pie! Pie!"

Shit. "I'm still here!"

"Come down a little. Let him see you so I can get past him. I'm done. I have the scales. But I need to sneak past."

"He's going to fry you!"

"No. He's not. He can't. I'm made of fire too. But he can eat me. And I'd rather not be eaten today, Pie! So distract him!"

I'm burned. I know this for sure because my back is screaming in pain.

"On three," Pell yells. "Let him see you. Ready?"

"No!"

And then all I hear is, "Two!" Like where the fuck did one go? And something comes over me. I have to do this or Pell will be eaten. So on three, I actually find myself back down at the bottom of the stairs, waving my arms around and yelling at the dragon, who is not looking at me, but behind him where Pell must be.

"Hey! You disgusting smelly shitbag! I'm over here! Look at me! Come get me!"

At first, I think, *Well, that's not gonna work.* Because the dragon doesn't move. But then its head—that massive, armored, spiky head—slowly, like ever so fucking slowly, turns in my direction.

And I see it again.

That tiny flame that will unleash the fires of hell.

And I scream like a stupid teenager in one of those predictable horror movies. It's shrill and, yeah,

I'm embarrassed. But I do not freeze, so I don't care what I sound like. I run. And again, I take those steps four at a time and even though my legs are burning with effort, I go fast and I get one spiral further up than I did last time.

But even so, the flames catch up with me. Lick at me. Tease me. Taunt me.

And then they burn me.

Pell comes rushing up through them and grabs my hand. Pulling me up more and more twists of the stone staircase until the fire is gone and the heat is mostly tolerable.

And then I pass out.

When I wake I'm lying on my stomach, topless, on the lounger inside the apothecary, and Pell is rubbing that cooling lotion from the steam cave pots all over my back.

"You're gonna be OK," he says, his fingers gentle as he applies the cream. "He got you good, but this will take care of it."

I don't want to look. I really don't. But it's impossible not to see the burned flesh covering my right shoulder.

"Does it hurt?" Pell asks.

I manage to croak out a, "No."

"Good. Then I got the cream on in time. It'll heal up." He pauses, then lets out a long breath. "I'm sorry. I'm sorry I made you do that. It was—"

"Necessary," I finish before he can. "You got what we need?"

He nods. Then he gets up, walks over to the closest apothecary benches, and picks up three giant red things, which I'm going to assume are scales.

Pell walks back over to me, bends down, setting them on the floor just below my eyes so I can get a good look at them. And then he resumes his care of my back.

I just stare at them for a little while, enjoying his attention as I study all the different colors in the red. There is silver in there. And yellow. And green. Even some blue. "Wow. They're pretty."

"They are. These things are worth like…" He pauses to think. "Fuck. These days? I don't really know. Millions, possibly billions of dollars. That book we're gonna get, this is why it's so special. Everything in that book runs on dragon scales. And he's the last one. Tomas is the last living dragon. So even if other magical people have these spells, we're the only ones who can use them."

"Pell, why couldn't Grant break the curse?" I have to turn over a little to see him. But my back really feels great from the lotion, so it doesn't hurt. "If the spellbook is that powerful, surely there is something in there that can free you."

"Grant never got a look at that book. It's inside Tarq's tomb, remember? You still have to go get it."

"Shit, I forgot about that."

"I never trusted Grant. I never trusted any of them, actually. But especially Grant. He was way too nice when he came here. Way too eager to please me. And that's not how it's supposed to be."

"How's it supposed to be?"

"Me trying to please him. Eros, remember?"

I think about that for a few moments. My brain isn't a hundred percent yet, but finally I catch up. "Wait. You didn't act like that with me. You hated me immediately."

"Yeah." He breathes out a little sigh. "I've been thinking about that myself."

I sit up a little, self-consciously rearranging my hair so it covers my breasts. "So"—I pause again—"you should've acted with me the way I acted around the sheriff?"

Pell and I stare into each other's eyes for a moment. His are yellow, the color of lava, and they are asking the same question. "Yeah," he finally says. "I should've... *loved* you."

"And you didn't."

"I mean"—he pauses—"I just wasn't prepared to wake up that night and find Grant gone. It was a shock."

"But that doesn't explain why you didn't swoon over me. If I'm an eros, you should've swooned." My mind doesn't even need to be a hundred percent to take this idea to the next level. It's just kind of obvious. "And if I was an eros, then I should not have swooned for the sheriff."

It takes him several beats, but finally Pell nods. "Yep."

"So. What am I?"

"I don't know." Pell has a look of 'uh-oh' on his face. Like he's expecting some big freakout from me.

But I'm not freaking out. I nod. "I'm not an eros." And then I smile. "I'm a human."

Again, he pauses.

"What?" I ask.

"Maybe?"

"Maybe? There's no maybe. I was born a human so I'm just human."

"With magic moths and a talking bird." He smiles. "Pie. I don't care either way. I'm swooning over you now. Whatever you end up being, I love it."

It's a nice response. But it doesn't answer any questions. "So why are you trusting me with this information now?"

"Well. The simple answer is, I don't think you're going to fuck me over. I think we're on the same side."

"OK." I like this answer.

"And I'm telling you, the answer to my curse is not in that book, or I would've taken my chances at one point. It's not in there. That book holds the spells of all the gods and it belongs to the great alchemist, Ostanes. But she didn't put this curse on me. Juno did."

"Juno?"

"The goddess. Saturn's wife? They had a nasty divorce—"

"What?" I huff. "This curse is some kind of settlement issue?"

"Not quite. But a little bit, yeah. Saturn and Juno sponsored the chimera breeding program. Ostanes was the alchemist who did the work. This is her book and it holds a lot of secrets. Not just how to make chimera monsters, other secrets too. She belonged to all the gods—but Saturn and Juno head up the pantheon, so they were kind of her bosses."

"And she didn't want to take sides."

He points at me. "That. And, well, you can't ever trust a god, ya know? They have enough powers already. It needs to be spread around a little more fairly. Ostanes was the balance."

"What happened to her?"

"I think they killed her. But I don't actually know. She's certainly not in here with us."

"How did you get in here?"

"Juno. Well, it started with Ostanes banishing the gods from the sanctuary. Then Saturn got the eros involved and made sure they could get inside—that's how I got caretakers. But then Juno countered with a spell to lock up the tombs so only I could get inside. Then Saturn hid the doors from me."

"Oh." It suddenly makes sense.

"Right. So we got ourselves a paradox." He picks up the dragon scale and the flower. "This is the only way around that curse."

I run his explanation back and forth in my mind for a few moments, then decide I have one more question. "Where does the Book of Debt fit in? And all those pleasure tasks?"

"Juno cursed the caretakers and came up with the Book of Debt to fuck them up."

"That was her doing?"

"That was all her. That's how I know that Book of Debt is real."

"And the pleasure stuff?"

He shrugs. "I really don't know. Payment? For me being stuck here?"

"Or"—I point at him—"a way to bond you to the caretaker?"

"Why would Juno want that? It makes it more likely that I would help the caretaker get inside the tomb, not less."

"But that's not what happened. You never liked them."

"They were just not my type." He's grinning when he says this. So I know he's making a joke. But he's missing the most obvious part of this whole thing.

"Pell?"

"Hmm?"

"Don't you think it's odd that I show up? A woman. A woman you like. You don't swoon over me, you get angry. Then, over the course of a week or so, we do bond. We bond so well, we have sex. And then, right after that, you're ready to hand over your secret."

He lets out a long breath. "I know."

"So. Maybe this is a bad idea? Maybe I was sent here to steal this secret from you, only we don't know that yet."

"Here are our choices, Pie. We do nothing and hope the sheriff doesn't come back—"

"That's not likely."

"Nope," he agrees. "Or we could go into town and kill the sheriff, I guess."

"If there's a secret family of eros living in Granite Springs, don't you think they'd retaliate?"

"I do. So our only choice is for me to send you into the tomb to get the book from Tarq and we banish him."

I reluctantly agree. But then I have another thought. "What happened to them?"

"Who?

"The gods. After the whole battle of Saint Mark's."

Pell shrugs. "I don't know. I was in here, remember? I'm sure more happened."

"They *are* gods," I say.

"Vengeful ones too. It's highly unlikely that they just gave up. Maybe Saturn gave his caretakers more power? And that's why Grant didn't age when he left? But I'm not buying it. Every caretaker before him left, right? And they all got old and died. So. That's new."

I sigh and lie back down. "I don't have any room in my head for that stuff. It's confusing me."

"That's OK. I'm gonna let you rest while I cook up the spell."

"Don't you need my help?"

"It's not that hard, actually. Boil the flower, extract the oil, rub it over a scale, then you put the scale on and wear it like armor and boom. You can walk into the tombs."

"I'm having mixed feelings about that."

Pell chuckles. "This is the easy part. Tarq's a cool dude. You're gonna like him. And you're so cute. He loves cute. He's gonna help. I know he will. Then we'll ward off the sanctuary, none of those townie assholes will be able to get in, and then…" He sighs. "Then."

"Then what?" I look over my shoulder so I can see him.

"Then… back to normal, I guess."

"Normal?" I snort. "OK." It's not normal. Nothing about this place is normal. But… on the other hand, it's not *bad*, either. I don't mind it here. Hell, who am I kidding? I had a chance to leave yesterday and I put the damn ring back on.

The truth is, I don't have a home. Have never had a home.

Until now.

And maybe, just maybe, this place is worth all this trouble. And I get it. Pell and I aren't even the same species, but there are forests and party rooms upstairs that kinda smooth out all those wrinkles.

We could make this work. Couldn't we?

I must fall asleep after that because the next thing I know Pell is shaking me by the shoulder. "Wake up, Pie. It's time to go."

I sit up. I'm topless—and don't have all the extra hair I did in my wood nymph chimera form to cover my tits—and Pell is handing me a new shirt. It's not the red one that said *Come Hell or High Water.* That one must've burned up. This one is a too-big baseball jersey that I bought to wear to bed.

I make a face at the shirt, but put it on without making a big deal.

Then Pell hands me the scale. It's big. Big enough to actually wear like a plate of armor. And he's attached a silver chain to it, so I just put on like a necklace and the scale hangs down my front. "It smells good," I say, picking it up and putting it to my nose.

"That's the bloodhorn oil." Then he's pulling me to my feet and leading me out the door.

"Whoa. We're not gonna, like… discuss this first?"

"There's not much to discuss. Just go in there, talk to Tarq, explain the situation, and get out as quick as you can. Make any promise he asks of you. Just get that book and come straight back. I'm anxious to get this part over with because we still need to make the spell."

We're already walking down the stairs and for some odd reason, the bottom is coming very quickly. Every other time I go up and down these stairs it feels like it takes forever. But the next thing I know, we're nearly to the bottom.

Pell stops, looking out the massive windows at the tombs. Then he points. "Do you see that tomb right there? The one in the middle? With the dome?"

I see it. But I don't say anything.

Pell just continues. "That's the one." We resume walking down the stairs and soon enough, we're walking across the hall and he's pulling the cathedral door open for me. "Just walk right up to it and go in."

"Those are your final instructions?"

He smiles at me. "You're gonna be fine. I swear. Tarq is a good guy."

My face crinkles up into a dubious expression. "When was the last time you saw him?"

"It doesn't matter. He's Tarq. We're tight."

"Pell—"

"Two thousand years, but—"

I stop listening. I'm gonna die in there. And if I don't, that's OK too. Because then I'll just get pitchforked by the townies.

I start walking. But when I look back, Pell isn't following.

"I can't come," he explains. "Or you won't be able to see the door."

I sigh, giving in. Because what choice do I have? It's not like I could come up with a better plan.

So I give him a little wave, turn to the cemetery, and start weaving my way through the tombs. I try not to look at all the monster statues, but it's kinda hard not to notice that they are all chimeras. Almost all of them look like satyrs, their oversized dicks a dead giveaway. But some of them are four-legged, like a... centaur, and some of them have wings.

When I finally find the tomb with the gold dome, I pause and take in the statue of the monster called Tarq.

He's sleek. Nothing about him is shaggy. He is jet black from head to toe and his horns are definitely those of the infamous Minotaur. They are thick and span out and upward over the top of his head. He's holding a whip in one hand and some kind of plant or flower in the other. This might be a crocus bulb. It's hard to tell, since it's been carved out of black marble, so maybe it's an onion. Could go either way.

Against my better judgment, I glance over at the dark shadow that is the door to his tomb and stop breathing for a moment, so I can listen for sound.

But there's nothing there.

Slight variations of light tell me that's not true, though.

There is definitely something inside that tomb.

I take one more look over my shoulder in the direction of the cathedral and spy Pell hanging off one of the gas lampposts. He salutes me.

And with that, I turn away and step through the door.

CHAPTER TWENTY-SEVEN – PELL

I don't realize that I've been holding my breath, watching her, until she disappears—just disappears in front of my eyes—and then I let it out in a rush. Really, really hoping that this won't somehow backfire on me.

It won't. I say that again in my head. *It won't.*

Pie will come back with the book, we will get knowledge, we will banish the sheriff, and she will bring news of Tarq. This thought alone is enough to make me hope. Because I want to talk to that bastard again so bad. I don't mind Tomas. And lately, I sorta like the dude. But he's got issues that will always stand in the way of a closer friendship. I can't trust him. And it's not just his dragon form, either. He's opportunistic. Always has been. And hey, isn't everyone? Aren't we all?

To a degree, yeah. We think of ourselves first.

But trusting Tomas comes with… consequences. It's like making a deal with the devil. You know you can't trust him, but you want to. So bad. Because the devil has what you need.

And in Tomas's case, it's friendship. It's company.

But I know better.

My point is, it was me and Tarq. And I know he's probably thinking, *That fuckface Pell left me here in this tomb to rot.* And he'll have feelings about that if Pie and I can find a way to get him out. But I actually crave that fight. I want that argument. I just want something from my old, real life to come back.

I want him, in his natural satyr chimera form. Because he is like me.

I want to be with my own people.

The rooms upstairs are great. Without them, I'd be insane by now. But it's fake. It's all fake and it's all been fake the entire time I've been in this curse.

Just give me something real, ya know? I don't care if it's an argument. In fact, an argument would be just fine with me. Arguments are overflowing with feelings. I want those emotions again.

I want to see my friend.

I also want to go down that that tomb and pace in front of it until Pie comes back, but I'm afraid that my presence there will block her exit.

But I do walk down the hill a little, just until I'm at that rise that allows me to see over the wall and the caretaker's cottage, and find the lake. I sit down on my favorite crumbling tomb base and just breathe. Trying my best not to look over my shoulder in the direction of Tarq's tomb to see if Pie is on her way back yet.

Time might be different in there, I don't know anything about Tarq's tomb.

Time is not different in my tomb, but that's not saying much.

So I just gaze out at the lake.

When I first got here in the New World, I used to come to this spot and sit on this tomb every single morning and every single night. I wanted to go out to that lake so bad, but my caretaker at the time was a dick of a man called Ignacious. He never let me leave the sanctuary. If I tried to follow him out the gate, he'd just refuse to leave. So there were no lake trips and by the time he left and Michael took his place, I had forgotten that I even wanted to go out to the lake.

Tomas joined me once in this lake trip planning though. His imagination came up with a whole day out there. We were gonna go swimming, and have a picnic, which was a big deal back in those days. And we were gonna make a canoe and paddle around. Then just lie on the shore and soak up the sun. Tomas always did like the sun.

This makes me chuckle.

And this chuckle makes me realize that I'm... happy.

How did that happen?

Pie, I think. And that trip upstairs. Seeing her as a wood nymph chimera. God, she was pretty. And even though I was convinced up there that she was some kind of goddess, I realize now that I was just drunk on hallway doors.

Something moves out by the lake. A deer, maybe? It's skulking through the woods on the north side of the water. But it's too far away for me to really get a good look at it.

That would be nice though. To see a deer today.

A deer. Like Pie was.

I get up off the tomb, take one look over my shoulder just to make sure Pie didn't come out of the tomb—she didn't—and then start walking down the hill. I'm going to go up to Pie's second-story window and look out at the lake until she comes back.

When I enter her cottage, the scent almost overwhelms me in the best way.

I like her. I like her a lot.

I'm glad she's stuck here with me. I could live in this curse forever if she had to be stuck here with me.

I take the stairs two at a time and then cross the room, throw the curtains aside, lift the sash, and breathe in the lake air.

It's got to be the same air as I breathe inside the sanctuary, but it feels fresher. Crisper. The November day is both cool and warm. The sun is out and it hits the lake at such an angle that it shimmers gold.

I am caught up in this shimmer when the figure steps out of the woods to the left of the lake.

I just... stare at him for a moment. Unable to speak. And then he's walking towards the sanctuary.

Then he's there. Just below me in the parking lot. "Hello, Pell."

Grant is young again, just like Pie described. So fucking mid-century perfect. Slicked-back hair. Khaki pants, a style from decades ago. Plain, white t-shirt with a button-down, not buttoned down, over it. Plaid, of course. In light blue and gray. His shoes are loafers, his face clean-shaven.

He is something out of the past but wholly here in the present too. He is my Grant. Not the old man he should be after fifty years inside this curse. Especially since he had fifty years of debt when he left.

I narrow my eyes at him and call down from the window, "What do you want?"

He shoots me one of those aw-shucks shrugs, his shoulders high, his smile broad, his hands doing a mea culpa. And there it is. He did this. It was a plan. He knew, probably from the very moment he walked into my curse, that he was somehow... *immune*.

"I knew she would come," Grant says.

"Who? Pie?"

"Who else?"

I huff. "You couldn't have known that. The bloodline—"

Grant chuckles, cutting me off. "The bloodline? How are you so stupid? After all these years, Pell? How?" His laughter is bigger now. Louder. "You've had two thousand years to figure it out, and still—here you are!" Now he guffaws. "I mean, dude! Get a fucking clue!"

This is where I would usually say, *What are you talking about? Please explain.* But I don't need to. Because for some reason I cannot fathom, this is the moment when I realize I'm wearing a veil.

Not a literal one, of course. A magical one.

Someone—maybe Grant, maybe not—has put a spell on me the way he put a spell on the town.

I have been made to forget things. Or unsee things. Or maybe just not know things.

And this conversation with Grant—who is most definitely not a human boy called Grant—has broken the spell.

So I already know what he's talking about when he starts explaining it.

"You're a joke, Pell. Don't you get it? Satyrs? Are you fucking kidding me? No one takes you seriously. You're entertainment. We made you for *parties*. So we could parade you around with your giant, always-erect cocks to amuse guests. That's all you are. Just a fucking *joke*. Do you really think I need your help to get that book?" He nods his head towards the cemetery. "Pie is getting it for *me* right now. And the best part of that? You sent her in there!"

"You." I don't say it, I growl it. "You did not make me."

His face goes still. And suddenly, all of the sunlight in the sky is gone. There is nothing but darkness over the lake. His voice booms with anger. "I made *her*. She made *you*. Therefore, *I* made *you*."

"I see the logic," I say. Because he's talking about Ostanes. "Saturn." I snarl the old god's name. "That's who you are, right? And that's fine. I give no fucks at all who made me." I hike my thumb over my shoulder and his eyes once more dart to the cemetery. "And you might be in charge of shit outside, but this place? This place belongs to *me*."

The sun is still shining very bright in the sanctuary sky.

He has no power here.

And now it's my turn to laugh. "I didn't figure it out. So maybe I am stupid. Maybe I am a joke. But you spent fifty fucking years in here and still you had to finally walk out with nothing."

"Nothing?" He guffaws again. "I didn't walk out with nothing. I took what was mine. And in my stead, I left *Pie*. She is mine too, didn't ya know?"

I don't answer him. Of course I didn't know. There was a magic veil over my eyes. But I should've seen this coming. Especially after that romp in the hallway forests.

A wood nymph chimera.

My type. Hell, I practically spelled it out for her that day in the apothecary.

I've always been partial to the nymphs. Willowy girls with evil intentions lurking in the forest.

You like bad girls?

I do.

I'm not bad enough for you?

Not even close.

And there it is. Well, she's bad enough now, I guess.

"Sorry for that," Grant says. Saturn. Whoever the fuck he is. He shrugs again, another mea culpa. "If it makes you feel any better, she doesn't know what she's doing. She really does think she's some poor, crazy girl from Philly who conjures up imaginary friends and stumbles into monsters and curses because of one bad decision to party on Halloween."

"Wait." I think I stop breathing. "*What*?"

Grant sighs. Then frowns. "She's not real. She *thinks* she's real. She *thinks* she lived that life. She *thinks* she is that girl. But her life started the moment she woke up in the Grotto Our Lady of Lourdes at Mount Aloysius College. She's a phantom, Pell. Just one of my magical ghosts sent in to do *a job*." He nods his head in the direction of the cemetery. "And that's exactly what she's doing."

My own words come back to me again.

It's a paradox.

I can enter, but can't see the doors.

You can see the doors, but you can't enter.

And none of them can come out. Trust me. I've been here two thousand years and not a single monster has found his way out of those tombs.

He sent her here to trick me. To make me send her into Tarq's tomb to get that book.

The book he needs.

The book that will redistribute power and change everything.

But not just the book.

He needs more than that book.

He needs *Tarq*.

Did I just create a hole in the paradox that could allow Tarq to escape?

CHAPTER TWENTY-EIGHT – PIE

For a moment, I am confused.

I look over my shoulder. Nope. That's all how it should be. The cemetery. The daylight. The top of the cathedral just over the hill.

But when I look forward—yeah. That's where things stop making sense. Because I'm not in a tomb. I just walked into the lower level of the cathedral. Except this is not *my* cathedral.

There are dozens, possibly hundreds, of people walking around. Going up steps that look familiar, going down steps that don't exist, passing by me and going into other rooms on either side of the lower great hall that are not supposed to be there.

But here's where it really gets interesting. None of these people are *Tarq*. They are not even monsters. They're just… people. Like… office workers. In fact, this place looks like it could be the interior of a downtown Philly office building. And in the space between the many, many, *many* people bustling about, I can even see a reception desk.

"What the actual fuck?"

There's a man at the desk. A very well-dressed young man. Neat, dark hair. Clean-shaven face. He's slight. Slim, but not skinny. Just one of those naturally trim people who can wear anything and look amazing.

Right now, he's wearing a black suit. Not just any black suit, but the kind they call *bespoke*.

He spots me through the crowd as well, and his smile becomes even bigger and brighter, if that's even possible. He swiftly comes out from behind the reception desk and the crowd almost parts for him. So he's right up in front of me before I can properly prepare myself for what comes next.

"Hello!" He beams. He clasps his hands behind his back and rocks on his heels a little. "You're a new face. How can I help you?"

"Um." Yeah. I don't have a plan for this. "Well." I sigh. "OK. I'm looking for a mon—a *man*," I correct, thanking my lucky stars I didn't just blurt out the word 'monster.' "A man called Tarq." I look around, doubtful. "You don't happen to know him, do you?"

The slim guy smiles at me. But it's not beaming anymore. It's a little tight-lipped. "Of course, ma'am." He chuckles. "Tarq is…" He pans his arms wide. "The *boss*."

"Right. Yes. I knew that. So… so I'm here to see him. I have a message from a mutual friend called Pell. Can you point me to Tarq so I can deliver this message?"

I am an idiot. This whole thing is stupid. I have to be stuck in a dream. Or maybe I really did die the morning after Halloween? Nothing in my life makes sense anymore.

Did it ever?

I don't know.

"First, let's introduce ourselves. Then we can get to the bottom of this."

"Sure. I'm Pie," I say. He makes that face everyone makes when they hear my name. But I just keep going. "Pie Vita. Nice to meet you…"

"Luciano." He shakes my hand. "Luciano Giordano. And do you mind if I say your name is quite lovely?" Then he kisses my hand.

I might blush a little at that gesture. But I quickly pull myself together. "Luciano Giordano. That's… interesting. In a nice way," I add quickly. Because I know what it's like to have someone say your name is… *interesting*. But his is very *mob*. And I don't get it. "It was just a little… unexpected."

"We all love the unexpected, don't we?"

"Do we?" I don't, I can say that for sure. But right now, I just want to play the game, get what I need, and get the fuck out of here. I feel like I just walked into an alternate reality and I don't like it. Of all the things that have happened to me over the past week or so, this is the most unsettling. Not even the orgy room or realizing I have horns and hooves shook me the way this place does.

Luciano smiles at me like he might be following my internal monologue. "You say you have a message. And I don't mean to pry. But, pray tell, can you give me more than that? It's none of my business, so I don't need details, but Tarq likes a heads up when people like you show up."

"People like me?"

"Oh, I'm terribly sorry. That came out wrong. People who come from…" He nods his head towards the back door. And when I look over my shoulder, the tomb is gone and in its place is just a city. Like… all those tombs that should be there are now buildings in a bustling downtown.

My mouth just drops open. "Where did it go? The door? Where did it go? How do I get back!"

I'm panicking. It's not a good look for me.

"Calm down, calm down. You came from the tomb, right?"

I nod. Swallow.

"It's there. But it's glamoured. You're one of them? The monsters?"

"No! Do I look like a monster?" And that's when I look down and realize I am. My hooves! My fur! My... no pants or shirt. I quickly rearrange my hair to make double sure this well-spoken mobster can't get a peek at my nipples. Then I reach up, and sure enough, there they are. My horns. "Shit," I say.

"It's OK," Luciano says. "We see lots of confused people come through the tombs. They get over it after their first time, but I've never seen you here before, have I? Because you, my dear"—he takes both of my hands, then steps back so he can see all of me at once—"you are ravishing!"

But now he's patting my shoulder and I realize that these words are platitudes. And we're walking, so he's trying to get me out of here without any more fanfare. No one seems to be paying attention to us, even though my hooves are clip-clopping across the black marble floors. And it echoes.

"Tarq is this way, Pie." I can hear the smile when he says my name. "Let's get the two of you reunited so you can stop feeling so unsettled."

He's got manners, I'll give him that. And I do feel better having him take care of things. That realization isn't very empowering. But. Whatever. I'm losing it. Like seriously losing it. And if I have to work out a single detail about this trip into the tomb that is not a tomb, I might not recover.

Luciano ushers me through a door, then down a hallway, then through another door, a room, another hallway and I lose track. I suddenly wonder if this place is the twenty-first-century version of the Labyrinth and I'm about to meet the urban Minotaur.

We stop in front of a glass-walled office and there he is. Right on the other side.

And he *looks* like the urban Minotaur. He is sleek, jet-black fur. Glossy hooves. Brown skin. Long, silky black hair flowing over his hard, muscular shoulders and tied loosely at the nape of his neck. And his horns. Cheese and fucking rice, those horns. They are the horns you picture when you think *monster*. Nothing like the ones on my head. They scream power. And they are sharp and polished. His horns look like obsidian. Smooth and lustrous. Like this man gets a hornjob *daily*.

He's in profile when we walk up to the glass door and pause, but his mouth is moving like he's in the middle of a conversation. I can't hear a word. The glass is thick. His office looks like any billionaire's corner glass office. Massive wooden desk. A view to die for—and how did we get up in the air? I don't know. We didn't go up any stairs or take any elevators, but we are like a hundred stories up. Large birds are floating past, circling out over an ocean like we're in New York. But none of the buildings are the iconic ones even poor people like me could recognize.

This is not New York.

There are no billionaire monster CEO's in New York.

Well. They are all probably monsters. But not in the literal sense.

Tarq turns, sees us, then smiles. And good fucking God. That smile is... wow. Even his sharp fangs are sexy.

I don't know what to make of this guy. He's nothing like Pell. And while I can appreciate this stunning, god-like, A-type personality, corporate-raider monster that is Tarq—this dude's attention scares the shit out of me and we haven't even spoken yet.

Nope. I like my Pell. I like him shaggy. I like his tousled fur, and his striped hooves, and his glowing horns that don't look like they were made to knock giants into another universe. Pell's horns are just... nice. He's just nice. This guy?

He's still smiling at me.

I need to leave. He's going to eat me. Or attack me. Or something worse.

But then he's walking towards us and a glass door that was not there a moment ago is now opening right in front of my face.

"Sorry to bother you, Tarq," Luciano says. "This is Pie Vita. She came through the tomb a few minutes ago."

Tarq looks me up and down slowly. Like, I'm talking his eyes take their sweet-ass time traveling down my body to the tips of my hooves, and then back up—briefly resting on my mostly hidden breasts—before they find my face again. "Of course she did. Pie. Vita." He says my name like it is two words. And his voice is deep and... wow. There's a vibration there. It's distracting. "I have been wondering when you'd show up."

"What?" I want to appear as in control as this monster man in front of me, but there is no chance. And even though all I did was utter a single word, my voice trembles and I suddenly have a stomach ache. "What do you mean? When I'd show up?"

"Oh." Tarq glances at Luciano. "She doesn't…"

"Yeah," Luciano says. "Yep. Nope. She's got no clue."

"Wait." I put up a shaky hand. "What are we talking about here?"

"How did you get here?" Tarq is studying me again. God, I wish he would stop doing that. "Hmm? Do you remember?"

"Yes." I squint at him. Because I feel like I'm just about to fall into a trap. But I'm here. There's no going back. I might as well just get what I need as quickly as possible and go the hell back where I belong. "Pell and I made—well, he mostly did all the work. But I did help him get the dragon's scales from Tomas—"

"Pell!" Tarq's entire face lights up at the mention of my new better half. "Pell!" He's even more delighted the second time he says the name. Then it's like I caught him off guard. Of all the things I could've came here to say, the name of his old friend wasn't in the top billion. His mouth actually drops open.

"So, we got the scales, the blood… blood… what the fuck was it called again? Oh." I snap my fingers. "Bloodhorn. We got that flower, and then Pell did some magic shit. And, well"—I look down, look back up while pointing to my chest—"my lucky charm dragon's bloodhorn scale is supposed to be right here. But it's not, so… I don't know what to tell you. I walked into your tomb and boom." I look around and sigh. "I feel like I just fell into that old Michael

Douglas movie. You know that one where he's playing a game and shit goes all crazy?"

Tarq points at me, chuckling. "You are delightful."

"Thank you. So. I'm just gonna get to the point because I'm feeling uncomfortable here. I don't really look like this." I pan my hand down my body. "I'm just a human on the other side of that tomb door. Though I've been told I'm a cute human. I don't normally walk around naked except for my fur. And I never—*almost* never—have hooves and horns. So. I would just like to make that clear so we're all on the same page. I am not actually a wood nymph chimera. I'm just a girl with an imaginary friend who spent a lot of time with crazy people until I learned how to lie."

Why did I just say that?

Tarq looks at Luciano, who is once again beaming a smile, hands clasped behind his back, rocking on his feet. Tarq points at him and laughs. "You did well, my friend."

"What? What did he do? I'm so confused."

"What did I tell you?" Luciano says. Then he and Tarq high-five each other.

Tarq turns his attention to me. "You answered the ad."

I cock my head in confusion. "Well." Then I hold up a finger. "I answered *an* ad. Yes. But, it has nothing to do with *here*." I make a little circle in front of me with my pointer finger.

Once again, Tarq looks back at Luciano. "She really doesn't know anything, does she?"

"It's amazing, isn't it."

"OK, that's enough!" I yell this. "Stop talking about me like I'm not here. I have a purpose, OK?" I clap my hands for each of those syllables. "I'm here to get the book. Pell said you would know which one I was talking about. It's a super-powerful, fucking whatever book. And I need it to banish the sheriff of Granite Springs because he's a cupid, or a bloodline person. I don't know what the hell his problem is, but he's suddenly gained the ability to enter our sanctuary and this will not do. I will get you out of here. Or something. Pell's real sorry you got stuck inside the tomb and he was on the outside, so he said to..."

Tarq is staring at me so hard, I swallow down my words and shut up.

"Luciano," Tarq says. But he's not looking at Luciano, he's looking at me. "I'll take it from here. I'll send her down when I'm done with her."

"What? Done with me? What... what are we doing, exactly?"

"Yes, sir," Luciano croons. Then he turns and walks out of the office. I watch him through the glass walls until he's out of my sight.

Tarq clears his throat. "So. You're here for the book?"

I force myself to turn and look up at the sleek, jet-black monster in front of me. I try not to look him in the eyes. It's too much. And I can't look down at his feet or I might accidentally see his package. So I concentrate on his horns. "I'm here for the book. We need a banishing spell."

Tarq makes a noise that might be a huff or an actual laugh. I'm not sure. "That's so... wow. It's just... it's been a really long time, Pie, since anyone has said the words 'banishing spell' in front of me. And"—he shrugs—"it was just a simpler time, I guess."

I have no idea what he's talking about.

"Let's have a drink and sit down."

"I can't. I need that spell. There's… there's… there's a time constraint. And, and, and… the townie people and shit. And Tomas!" Man, I am not handling this well. At all. "I need to get back. Quickly."

"Pell is waiting for you?"

"Yes! Exactly." I let out a breath of relief. "Yes, he's watching for me. He's waiting a safe distance from your tomb. So I can find the door out, obviously."

Tarq is silent for a moment. Then he leans back and sits on the edge of his massive desk and crosses his arms. I don't like this posture. He's thinking, I can tell. His mind is a whirlwind of possibilities. And he's a little bit frowny. Finally, he says, "I can't give you the book."

"Why not?"

"I can't just hand over the source code, Pie. It's… the fucking *source code*. It's the secrets of the universe."

"Oh." I feel defeated.

"But I can give you the page you need."

"Oh!" This time it's brighter. "Thank you."

"It is my pleasure. Any girl of Pell's is a girl of mine." His smile is *wide*. Like… big bad wolf wide.

"Mmm-hmm. I'm not sure about that last part there, but thank you again for the page. And I don't want to appear ungrateful, but—"

"Oh, let me stop you there." He puts up a hand. "You don't need to be grateful, Pie."

"No?" I swallow again. Because here it comes. The catch.

"No. It all evens out in the wash." He winks at me.

I suck in a deep breath. "It can. Even out in the wash, that is. But I'm still very grateful."

He just looks at me for a moment, still smiling. "I'm sure you are. Well." He stands up, rubs his hands together, and looks over at a bookshelf. "Let's find that book, shall we?"

I don't move. But Tarq walks over to the bookshelf. There are no books on it, so for a moment, I'm confused. But he does something. I can't see what, because his massive, sexy, muscled back is in my way. And damn. This monster here has some breeding behind him. Like his genetic stock is top-notch.

He chuckles from across the room, and then the bookcase begins to turn on a pivot point, leading to a chamber on the other side. Tarq glances over his shoulder at me. "I'll be right back. Don't you go anywhere, Pie Vita."

I can't even talk at this point. So I just nod.

He's gone for several minutes. I want to walk over there and peek inside that chamber. Kinda get a feel for what he's up to. But I don't dare. I feel the need to be on the other side of the room when he comes back out.

And just a few seconds later, out he comes. Holding a page.

It's a very pretty page. Like this page belongs in the Vatican library or something. It's all handwritten calligraphy with gold foil illumination along the edges. It's even got an illustration. He brings it over to his desk and puts it down. Then he points. "This is the side you want here. Banishing. The other side is something else." He makes a point to look me in the eyes for this next part. "I would not mess with that side."

"OK. But… should you have ripped it out of the book? I mean, maybe you should just make a copy of it. I'm not the most responsible person, ya know? I'm probably gonna ruin that page. It's practically inevitable."

He chuckles. "I like you."

"Good." I try to smile.

"But the pages regenerate. I made sure it duplicated before I came back. This one is yours to keep. You have your own book?"

"My own book? Of… spells? No. I'm new."

He laughs again. "OK. And you're honest. I like that. So you're gonna wanna start a book. Keep all your spells in one place."

"Oh. Like Grant did."

"Grant." His voice lowers a little. It's almost growly.

"He was Pell's last caretaker. I'm his replacement. He kept lots of books. But he took the good ones with him when he left. And all the shit he left me is stupid. Like… backwards-working love charm stupid."

Tarq blinks at me. "Hmm. I have to say, Pie, this is the most interesting day I've had in almost two thousand years."

"Um. Thanks. I think."

"At any rate, the page is yours. Keep it safe, use it well, and…" He pauses to smile. "Tell Pell that now that I know where he is, I'll come visit."

"Wait. You can do that? Just… leave here?"

"Here?"

"Your… tomb."

He tilts his head at me. "Does this look like a tomb?"

"No. But"—I shrug—"the hallways do weird shit. I figured that's what's happening here. The hallways."

He leans over, presses a button on his desk phone, and says, "Miss Vita is done. I'm sending her down. Can you meet us at the elevator?"

"Yes, sir," Luciano responds.

Tarq looks back at me. "Your world sounds… intriguing. But since you're on a tight timeline, we can discuss the rest at a later date. Sound good?"

I nod enthusiastically. I just want to get the fuck out of here.

"I'll walk you to the elevator." He walks up to me and extends his arm.

I do not want to take his arm. Like… I cannot even stress how much I do not want to touch this monster. But there is no polite way to avoid his offer. So I place my hand on his muscled forearm and let him guide me down the hallways.

Everything is different this time, though. Luciano and I did not come up in an elevator. But Tarq leads me to one, and when the doors open, there Luciano is. Waiting for me.

I start to enter the elevator, but Tarq grabs my hand before I can fully remove it from his arm, and I have to stop and look at him.

He studies me for several long, awkward moments. Then he brings my hand up to his lips and kisses my knuckles, just like Luciano did down in the lower hall. Tarq's eyes never leave mine as he does this. And I suddenly feel faint. Like, I'm one hundred percent certain that I am about to fall over.

But then Tarq lets go and I'm free and my head clears immediately. "Until next time, Miss Vita."

"Yep. Thank you so much. Pell and I really appreciate this." I hold up the page. Then I turn and make my escape.

Luciano says nothing as we descend, but I can feel his smile.

Delightful. They think I'm delightful.

And there are definitely worse things to be, but I get the feeling that 'delightful' is Tarq's replacement for Pell's 'naïve.'

Luciano walks me out into the lower hall, which is now empty of people and looks very much the way I would expect it to look if I were back in my own sanctuary.

We stop at the large glass doors that now lead out into the cemetery.

"Thank you," I tell him.

"It was our pleasure to help you today, Miss Vita."

I don't let him take my hand because I know he's going to kiss my knuckles and I just can't do it again. So I wave. Then turn to the glass door, open them, and…

… walk out of the tomb I entered earlier.

I'm very disoriented when this change happens and I have to look up the hill at the cathedral to get my bearings. But when I look back at the tomb, there is no door. Just that giant statue of Tarq.

Which, now that I've met him, doesn't even begin to do him justice.

But then I look down and see hooves.

Not black hooves. Not Tarq's hooves.

My hooves.

CHAPTER TWENTY-NINE – PELL

"You're lying." I say this to Grant with conviction because I don't believe him. "You've been lying since the day you arrived here."

Grant—Saturn—whoever the fuck he is—smiles up at me. "You never had a chance, Pell. You've been here for two thousand years. This isn't a curse. It's fate. You're never getting out. Pie works for me, Tarq works for me—"

I turn away. I will not listen to his lies. I will not let him poison my mind with this shit. He told Pie a whole bunch of things in town too. And that was bullshit.

She's not his. She's real. We did the phone call. She talked to her friend. We have already proved this.

The moment I realize that, I feel… not defeated. Not better, either. There is still a bunch of shit happening that I don't understand. And I don't really know which part of what he's saying is true or false, but that doesn't matter. He can't be trusted. He's lying about something. And if he needs to lie, that means he has a weakness.

I will find that weakness and I will destroy this god, once and for all.

I go outside and start hoofing it up the hill.

Grant calls after me from the other side of the gate. "You know I'm right! You know there's something wrong with her!"

But he can't get in. When he walked out, he forfeited his right to enter Saint Mark's Sanctuary.

I'm almost at the top of the hill when Pie steps out from between some tombs. I am so stunned by her appearance, I stop in my tracks.

Behind me, Grant cackles. "See!" he yells. "See! Look at her! *Look at her!* She is a creature of magic. She is a creature of me!"

Pie is crying. Shaking her head, and pointing to her feet, and trying to cover herself with crossed arms, because she's naked.

Well, she's got fur, so not really. But she feels naked. I don't know what just happened inside that tomb, but it doesn't matter. I walk up to her, put my arms around her and hold her close. "It's OK," I murmur. "It's going to be OK."

She lets out a long breath. "I don't understand what's happening." Then she pulls back. Grant is still screaming at us from outside the walls, so she's momentarily distracted by this. "Why's he here?"

"It doesn't matter. He can't get in."

Pie looks up at me. She doesn't have a book, but she is holding a page that looks like it came out of the book I'm looking for. "Things are getting weird, Pell." She looks over her shoulder in the direction of Tarq's tomb, then back at me. "That was not what I expected."

"Did you get the spell?"

She holds up the page. "He said this is it. And he said to tell you hi. But…" She waves a hand in the air. "What do we do now?" She looks down at herself. "I

398

need a shirt, I guess. But I don't want to go down to the cottage. So. Whatever."

I arrange her hair so she's properly covered. "I promise not to look."

This makes her smile, at least. "It's not like you haven't seen it all before." She pauses to sigh heavily. "Well. Should we go do this spell and get rid of that jerk?" She nods her head in the direction of still-screaming Grant. "I just want the outside world to go away for a little bit. I need to think."

I want the outside world to go away as well. Because I'm starting to worry that Grant might not have been lying about all of it.

Pie made the phone call. That's our proof she had a real life outside of Saint Mark's.

But something else is going on here too. Obviously. Since she has horns and hooves right now.

I take her hand. "Yeah, let's do it."

We go inside and up to the apothecary. Pie sets the page down on the alchemy bench and then smiles. "Holy shit. My flannel." She walks over to a table on the far side of the room and picks up the flannel she was wearing the day she arrived. She holds it up. "It's a little bit bloody and it's ripped down the back. Remember? I fell out of your freeze and hit my nose."

"Oh. Shit. I feel terrible about that."

"Don't. That was like… lifetimes ago. Bygones." She slips the flannel on with a sigh. And even though she's still a wood nymph chimera, and nothing about this day is normal, I can tell this one piece of clothing from her past is enough to ground her for now. "OK. Let's do this shit."

I shouldn't say anything. I should just let it go. But I can't help myself. "You're handling this whole thing"—I move a finger up and down in her direction to indicate her body—"very calmly."

Pie shrugs. "What can I do about it?" Then she looks down at herself. "I mean, I hope I don't stay like this forever, but I'm not going to worry about it." Her eyes meet mine and they are suddenly serious. "Now we're the same." She grins at me. "Now I'm your dream girl."

"I actually... love that. But." I hold up a finger. "If there's a way to get you back to your natural body, I'll do everything I can to make it happen. If that's what you want."

"We'll see." She sighs. "One thing at a time."

"Agreed. Let's take a look at that spell."

"It's this side," Pie says.

I take the page from her and start reading, then frown. "What the fuck?"

"What's wrong?"

"This can't be it."

"Why not?"

"It's the same spell we just did to get you in the tomb." I turn it over, checking the back of the page, just in case Pie got them mixed up. But the back says something about wings. So that's not it.

"What's wrong?" Pie comes over to me and her new wood nymph scent comes with her. It's intoxicating. But not in a magical, bad way. A good way. She smells like the forest. She smells like home. She takes the page and looks at it. "Hmm. You're right. Only two ingredients. Bloodhorn and a dragon scale."

"Hey, what happened to *your* dragon scale?"

"It disappeared when I went through the tomb door. We have a lot to unpack about that trip, but let's just do this spell first."

"What's there to do? It's the same ingredients. How can it banish something? There aren't even magic words. It's a fucking amulet."

"Stupid amulets. That's what got us into this trouble, ya know."

I walk over to the bench I was working at earlier. There's a vial of bloodhorn and the two remaining scales. I paint some oil on the scale with a brush, then hold it up and shrug. "There. It's done."

"How would we even know if it works?"

"I'll go look for Grant and see, but I'm not feeling hopeful."

She shoots me a look that says she's not either.

I carry the anointed dragon scale out to the great hall with me and I'm just about to turn towards the stairs when I glance at the front windows and see Grant on the other side of the gate. "Well." I huff. "Obviously, it doesn't work. He's right fucking there."

Pie comes out and joins me. And we both watch as Grant paces back and forth. Pie tsks her tongue. "Yeah, this spell sucks. I don't think we did it right."

"What are we missing? I mean, it's two ingredients. Bloodhorn and a dragon scale."

"Maybe it's not the oil? Maybe you need the actual flower?"

"No. That's not how it works. The flower is OK, but the oil is the essence. It's way more powerful."

"But it's not working, so…?"

I'm just about to open my mouth to agree when flashing lights appear outside.

"Oh. Shit," Pie says. "I really hope you have another idea about this spell, because we're about to be fucked. Russ Roth is here and he's going to let Grant in."

She's right. We are fucked. A whole scenario plays out in my head whereby Russ lets Grant in, the entire world finds out about this place, and then Saint Mark's stops being a sanctuary and starts being a lab where we are kept in cages like rats while some opportunistic corporate asshole sells tickets to our upstairs hallways like this place is an amusement park.

Pie must see the same thing in her mind, because she turns to me, clutching my arm, her eyes filled with panic. Maybe before today she wouldn't have fared so bad if we were ever discovered. Her magic, up until now, has been invisible. But there is no way to hide... *this*. She is not an insane human with a personal hallucination. She is not even an eros from the caretaker bloodline. She is a wood nymph chimera.

"What do we do, Pell? Should we go upstairs and hide in the hallways?"

I consider it, but reject it. "No. That won't work. They'll just come in after us eventually and it's more likely than not they'll find us. Just like Tomas found us. And anyway, the hallways will just spit us out at some point. These people must not enter Saint Mark's. They must not come in here."

"So what do we do?"

"We're missing something. This bloodhorn, I think. Because dragon scales, they're not complicated. We have dragon scales. But bloodhorn—"

I stop.

"Bloodhorn what?" Pie is shaking me.

I point to my horns. "This is a bloodhorn too."

"What?"

"My horns. Remember when you were massaging them and they got hot? That's the blood in them."

"We have to cut off our horns?" She touches hers gingerly. Like this is akin to shaving her head bald.

"Not yours. Mine." And suddenly, I know this is the way forward. This is what I was missing. This is the actual fucking secret to everything. And all this time, it was inside me. I have been carrying the magic ingredient in my fucking horns! "I need a saw and I need it right now!"

Pie shoots me another frantic look. "Where do you keep the saws? I don't know where we keep saws! Do we even have saws? Why would we need a saw?"

"Firewood! There's an ax outside the kitchen for the firewood."

"Ax?"

I grab her hand and start pulling her towards the kitchen. We weave through the hallways and as we pass the one that leads down into the dungeon, we must disturb Tomas the dragon, because there is a deep moaning beneath our feet.

We ignore that. There is no time to worry about Tomas right now. He's obviously not in any position to help us.

I drag Pie outside the kitchen to the pile of firewood. Grant was into firewood. He was always out here chopping wood for fires. Not to cook, obviously, since all his food was poison magic. That still pisses me off. But I don't have time to care what he was doing with the firewood. I just need the ax and I'm glad it's here.

I grab it and hold it out for Pie.

She looks appalled. "Why are you handing it to me?"

"I can't chop off my own horns, Pie. You need to—"

"Nope. No way. I'm not chopping off your horns with a fucking ax! That's crazy! I've never even held an ax! I will chop off your head!"

"I'm immortal, who cares? As long as you get the horn."

"First of all, I care! And second, I can't do this spell! You have to do it!"

"I highly doubt that's how it works. I'm the ingredient, Pie. You're the alchemist."

"But I'm not! I'm not magical at all." She has to realize this is stupid. She's standing in front of me as a wood nymph chimera. And something is squirming inside her flannel pocket.

"Pia!" Pie reaches down and plucks out a tiny sparrow. "Oh, I am so pissed at you! Where have you been? In my pocket this whole time?" Pie pouts her lips as the bird chirps.

And I'm not gonna lie, those pouty lips are very fucking cute, but we don't have time for this. I grab the bird, stuff it back inside her pocket, and shove the ax at Pie. "Do it."

"No! I can't—"

"Helloooooo!"

Pie and I hold our breath as we turn and look in the direction of the open kitchen door.

They're inside.

"Hellooooooooo!" Grant calls again.

"Pie?" That's the sheriff. "Pie, are you here?"

I take Pie's hand, wrap it around the ax handle, and point to her. "Chop it off right now. And then dribble the blood on the scale and tell them to get the fuck out of our home! Do you hear me?"

"Helloooooo!" Grant calls again.

Pie looks absolutely shell-shocked. But she swallows hard, and nods. "OK."

I kneel down in front of the chopping block, place my face against the scarred wood so my left horn is in the center, and then say, "Do it. Now!"

Pie grunts as she lifts the ax. And then, the next thing I know, it falls. And for a sick moment I think that it's not enough. The force won't be enough.

And then my mind goes black.

CHAPTER THIRTY – PIE

Pell slumps to the side of the stump, then to the ground, his body limp and heavy.

I just stare at the undulating knob of flesh and bone that is the stub of his left horn. It's like lava and it begins to flow. Like he really is made of fire. I can't take my eyes off it. "Pell?"

He doesn't answer me. And he doesn't move, either. Horn blood is pouring out of him. The tree stump chopping block hisses and smokes when the river of monster blood makes contact, immediately burning it. I reach for the chopped-off horn, then pull back. What if it burns me too?

But then, from behind me, a voice. "Pie."

Not the sheriff.

Grant.

I stiffen, then lean down and, without hesitation, I pick up the horn in my hand. It burns me. Like hellfire. Like nothing I have ever felt before. It sears into my flesh and for a moment, I can see the damage—the dead muscles, and the snapping tendons, and the charred bone.

But then I blink and it's gone. The pain remains, but the damage is invisible.

Magic?

Maybe. Because so far the only magic I've done comes from my hands.

I whirl around, my empty palm forward to ward Grant off, my other hand clutching Pell's horn to my chest. It hurts my heart—sizzling and searing me. Burning a hole through my flannel. But then Pia flies up.

Grant is distracted. He has never seen her. Has no idea who she is. He looks up and I use that moment to grab the dragon scale at my feet and tilt the horn filled with Pell's monster blood until the thick, viscous fire drips over the surface, covering it in a syrup of flames.

Grant turns back, smiling. His teeth are no longer human. But they aren't anything like Pell's wolf-like canines. They are like the rows of shark teeth inside the dragon's mouth.

"Who are you?" I ask, taking a step back. I don't want to look weak and afraid, but that's how I feel. This isn't Grant. Or… maybe this is Grant. But Grant is not a human. Grant is something else.

"Say the words. Do the spell." Pell's words are barely a whisper. And they are immediately lost because Grant speaks in almost the same moment.

"Do you know," he says, "how I knew you would end up here?"

"What?" I swallow hard. "What are you talking about? Who are you?"

"Don't you know, Pie? Don't you remember me?"

"No. I don't know you!"

"The spell, Pie," Pell mutters again. "Order him to leave! Banish him! Now!"

I hold up the scale, but then Grant says, "You're not even *real*, girl."

"What?"

"Don't listen to him!" Pell is getting up on his hands and knees. But he's so weak, I don't think he's going to be able to help me. "He's lying. Don't listen!"

"You wish I was lying," Grant snaps. He narrows his eyes on Pell, sneering. "I told you before." Now Grant looks at me. "And now I'm going to say it to you. You're not *real*, Pie. You do not exist. You are a bit of my magic and nothing more. You are here at my request, to do my bidding, to give me *that*." He nods his head at the bloodhorn-covered dragon scale in my hand. "And then I will go inside Tarq's tomb and get that book myself. And when I come back out, this world will once again be mine."

"Who the fuck *are you*?"

Grant laughs, throwing his head back. "I am the only god who matters, *slave*."

"Saturn," I whisper.

"Hmmmm. I guess you're not as stupid as you look."

"Fuck you. Get out! Get out of our sanctuary!" I thrust the scale in front of me, pointing it at him. But he lifts up his hand, palm out, and then…

I am pushed backwards with such force I feel like I slip through the fabric of time and space itself. I land hard onto a bare, cracked linoleum floor, skidding to a stop, banging my head on the frame of an iron bed. But it is not until I try to get up that I realize I am in a straitjacket, my arms pinned to my sides. And there are nurses holding syringes, and orderlies holding me down, and doctors pronouncing me insane…

Something flutters inside the straitjacket. Pushing against the tight fabric. And I watch this. I watch the creature pressed against my bare flesh as it wriggles and writhes until a tiny head crowned with red feathers pops out and says, "You're not crazy, Pie. You're real and so am I."

But I hate myself in this moment. Because I remember this day. This really happened to me. They did put me in a straitjacket. They did push me down onto the floor. They did stand over me with their needles and drugs and threaten to leave me like this. Drugged-up and stupid. Insane and alone. Because they had permission from my mother to do these things.

"Say it," the doctor is ordering me. "Say it, Pie! She's. Not. Real. You're not real, either. *Say it*!"

And I *want* to say it. I want to say it so bad. Because I know what comes next if I don't.

The drugs. The therapy. The names, the stigma, the insanity. The abandonment. The loneliness. The loss.

And I *did* say it. This has already happened. I said it when I was twelve and they left me alone.

This isn't real. Maybe it was never real. Maybe it was always magic?

Because real is the monsters of Saint Mark's. Real are my horns and my hooves. Real is Pia. Because Pia is me and I am her.

And we are… *monster.*

We have *always* been monster.

I open my eyes and I'm on the ground next to the chopping block, no longer stuck inside my delusion. Grant is bending down, reaching for my dragon scale.

I put up a single palm and from the center emerges *millions* of moths. They fly out and up in a swarm, swirling around Grant just like they did the sheriff yesterday, engulfing him in a dusty cloud of wings.

I scramble over to the scale, pick it up, get to my feet and thrust it at Grant. "Out!" I don't know what else to say. So I just say it again. "Out!"

Grant becomes a pillar of fire and I'm just about to think it worked—it's over!—when the moths just shatter into thin air like they are nothing to him.

He's hunched over, but he straightens now. And he directs all his attention to me. Then he laughs and puts his hands up, like he's going to send that spell I just did right back at me.

And it's going to be bad.

I close my eyes, cover my face with my arm, thrust the scale out in front of me and then—

The whole world rumbles in a very familiar way.

Not an earthquake.

A *dragon*.

The ground splits, the sanctuary walls crumble, the sky goes dark, and the air goes cold.

And then there he is. The blood dragon of Saint Mark's Sanctuary is loose.

His mouth opens, aiming right at us, and I can see the smoldering fire inside him. The pool of lava burbles and spits and everything suddenly reeks of sulfur and brimstone.

Several things happen at once.

My moths are back, surrounding *me* this time, their dusty wings beating against my bare arms and cheeks.

Pell grabs the dragon scale and steps out in front of me, holding his severed horn in the other hand. The moths surround him, putting us into a protective cocoon.

And then, in that same moment, Tomas releases his hellfire and the whole world goes up in flames.

CHAPTER THIRTY-ONE – PELL

I put my arms around Pie just as the flames wash over us from above. The stench of dragon fills the air and then... then it is nothing but flames, and fire, and heat, and molten stone as the world we know turns into a pool of bubbling brimstone.

Pie and I stand there, gripping each other, horn blood covering one side of my body.

Grant... Saturn... whoever he is—*screams.*

We fall to our knees from the power of that scream, but nothing can touch us. Not here. Not like this. Not when we're together.

We do not burn. We do not shrivel into dust. We are not incinerated.

We stay whole. We stay together.

We are the moth and the flame.

Everything goes quiet when I say these words in my head.

Then Pie's voice. "A horn, a hoof, an eye, a bone."

Before I can even think about it, I'm reciting the next line. "A man, a girl, a place of stone."

"A tick of time."

"A last mistake."

"Keep them safe behind the gate." She sighs. "I think I get it."

"Get what?"

"The curse, Pell. It's in the poem. I think it's you and me. You're the man and I'm the girl."

We think about this as the earth stills and the stench of dragon fades. There are no flames, no fire, and the molten stone that used to be the wall of the sanctuary is hard, and cold, and black as night.

Finally, I stand, pull her to her feet, and then we look around at the destruction.

But it's not the destitution of moments ago. It's the ruins of a battle that took place thousands of years before. It's something from the future and the past all at once.

It is the magic of Saint Mark's.

"Tomas!" I yell. "Tomas!"

"What the hell... What the hell am I lookin' at?"

Pie and I turn to find Sheriff Russ Roth standing in the middle of the great entrance hall. But there are no longer walls between there and here because they have been destroyed by the breath of a blood dragon.

"What the fuck is happening out here?" He says it calmly. He doesn't even shout. In fact, I'm not even sure he's talking to us. He might just be thinking out loud.

"What do we do?" Pie whispers.

"Banish him," I say. "Banish him now!"

The sheriff is not that close. He's maybe a hundred feet away. But he must hear me because he pulls his damn gun and points it at us. "You're under arrest for—"

Pie grabs the dragon scale from my hand and raises it and this motion kicks off his trigger-happy instinct because once again, he fires his gun.

Everything goes slow. Each moment becomes an eternity as the bullet flies towards Pie, the scale still too low, and this time there's nothing to break the momentum. It hits her right in the chest and she goes flying backwards and in that instant two more things happen. Pie Vita croaks out the words, "Be gone!" and I use one of my few innate magical powers to freeze her in place.

When Pie actually stops falling mid-air and it hits me that she cannot die as long as I hold her there, I breathe out a sigh of relief and turn back to the sheriff. Because he is now a dead man as far as I'm concerned.

But he is gone. Pie's last words were just enough to finish the job.

Then I look back at Pie and realize that she is gonna die. She is gonna die before we even get started because her chest is a mangled mess of flesh. "Help!" I call. I don't even know who I'm calling to. Tomas? The gods who deserted me? The little sparrow? Hell, I'd let the sheriff back in if he could save Pie from her now-certain death.

But there is no help.

Tomas is gone.

Pie is frozen.

Grant… dead?

Sheriff Roth… banished?

And now there's only me.

Standing alone in the blood dragon debris field feeling as cursed as I've ever been.

I glance down and see my chopped-off horn. Still dripping blood over the ground. Bubbling, and sizzling, and turning everything it touches to black obsidian.

I reach down to pick it up out of instinct. But the moment my fingertips touch the horn, the whole world goes black.

CHAPTER THIRTY-TWO – PIE

I am running. Breathless running. Exuberant running. The kind of running that only happens in a wood. That can only happen to creatures with hooves and hind legs.

Pell is next to me and he, like me, is overflowing with joy, his breaths coming hard and fast in perfect rhythm with my own.

We leap over fallen trees. Jump from rock to rock on a steep cliff edge. We make the orange leaves on the white-bark trees shudder as we pass.

It is the best moment of my life.

And this thought is still lingering in my mind— still echoing off the sweet happiness filling me up— when it all changes. When it all goes from bright to dusk.

I am alone. Not running. Standing.

Breathing hard, though. Like I *was* running. Like that was real. Pell, and me, and the woods. It was real.

It just isn't anymore.

The air is crisp and cool enough that tendrils of steam billow out from my mouth with each exhale. "Hello?"

And now panic begins to build. Because I am me. This is not a dream. This is real. I am *real.*

And I am not supposed to be here. This is not a place for creatures like me.

This is a place for the old gods.

The damaged gods.

The vengeful gods.

This is where *they* live, not us.

This is their wood, not ours.

And I am trespassing.

"Are you dead or alive, girl?"

The voice comes from nowhere and everywhere at the same time. It's thick, and deep, but feminine too.

"I don't know," I answer truthfully.

"Which one do you want to be?" the voice asks. And then there is a woman attached to it, standing in front of me with her hands clasped in front of her. She is tall with brown skin and wise eyes. Her robes are bright gold and orange, like the leaves in the woods around me. She reminds me of one those brightly colored Hindu women who wear those sarong things. And she jingles when she moves. Little strings of tiny bells hang around her wrists, and ankles, and neck. A bejeweled headpiece drapes pearls and crystals across her forehead. Her eyes are dark and wide and so is her smile. "This question shouldn't be so hard, Pie Vita. Which do you want to be?"

I have to take a deep breath, because I know her. "Ostanes."

"Quick! There is no time left for reunions, child. You need to decide. Do you want to be alive or dead? Do you want to be a monster or a human? Do you want to be cursed or not?"

"I get a choice?"

"No," she says. "Not really." I screw up my face in confusion. "You're *dying*, girl. The sheriff's weapon hit you in the chest. You are, in this very moment, still alive only because Pell froze you before most of the damage could be done. But he can't stop it, Pie. He can only put it off. You will die today, one way or another, because you are not eros. You are not the caretaker of Saint Mark's Sanctuary."

"What?" I look down at my hand and the ring is still there.

"That's not the same ring. You know this. You saw Grant's ring. What did it look like?"

The urgency in her voice is gone now, so I take a moment to think back. "It had... a face." I nod, looking up at her.

"Whose face?"

I'm about to say I don't know, but I do. It was the same face above the doors in the sanctuary. Which isn't some generic mythological Green Man. It is someone very specific. "Saturn's face."

Ostanes rewards me with a gentle smile. She has a very calming nature to her. I like it. "He is old now, Pie. He has almost no power left. Gods can only rule with permission. They need humans to give them power and this world's humans left Saturn behind centuries ago. This sanctuary is mine. He has no power here. But..." She pauses to make sure I'm listening. This must be the important part. "Neither do I. He made sure of that in the last battle. That's why there is a curse. He wants my power. *Everyone*"—she whispers this part, leaning forward a little—"wants my power."

"The book," I say.

She nods and straightens up. "That book does not belong to Tarq and eventually you will have to get it back."

"What?" I huff, annoyed. "Why do I have to do it?"

"You can choose to stop, if you're done."

"Done? I don't even understand what you're talking about now."

"Do you want to be a monster, Pie? Do you want to live in the curse with Pell? Do you want to continue? Do you want to try and make a difference and fix things? Or do you want to quit?"

I look down at my monster body. I like it. I do. But… "This is not me," I say.

"Isn't it?" Ostanes chuckles a little. "Are you sure?"

"It's not me. I'm Pie. I'm—"

"You are *this*, girl. You are chimera. You are nymph. You are gorgon. You are minotaur."

"What?" I almost choke out the word.

"You are *monster*."

Now, I am annoyed. "Well, last week I wasn't a monster. Last week I was just a girl. I had a past. It wasn't a good one, but it was mine. I'm real. And I'm not this…" I look down at myself. Did she use the word *gorgon*? Wasn't Medusa a gorgon? I am suddenly very confused, and tired, and I have an overwhelming feeling of defeat. "I don't think I can deal with this right now."

She tsks her tongue at me. "That's too bad." Then she sighs. "You did all this work. All this magic to get me here. To save the sanctuary from falling into the hands of these damaged and broken gods. One is as bad as the other. They were banished for a reason. And now you pretend that you're just… what? Just this girl called Pie who stumbled into the cursed monsters of Saint Mark's?"

"I did though. I literally did! I answered an ad—"

"Whose ad?"

"What?"

"Whose ad was it?"

"It was… Grant's ad. He called me here. And when I got here, he left. And I don't know his whole fucking story, so I guess there's more to it than that"—she actually guffaws at this—"but my point is, I was someone else before I got here."

"Grant? You think that ad belonged to Grant?"

I pause. "Didn't it? He told me it did."

"Don't believe everything you're told."

I'm about to scream at her for all this cryptic nonsense when I remember that weird conversation with Tarq and Luciano. *You answered the ad*, Tarq said. He was amazed at my confusion.

I narrow my eyes, thinking. "It was Tarq's ad." I feel confident about this conclusion.

But Ostanes sighs. "You're going to make this hard, aren't you?"

"I'm not making anything hard! All I want is…"

She raises an eyebrow when I don't finish my sentence. "Well?" she finally asks. "What do you want, Pie Vita?"

"I want these people to stay the fuck out of my sanctuary. I want to break Pell's curse. And save Tomas. I want him to be saved, and I want—"

"Stop." She puts up a hand. And this hand has power. Just like Pell's hand has power. "Stop it right now. That's not what you want. That's what you want to *do*. What do you *want*, Pie?"

What do I want?

"It should roll off the tongue, child. That's how long you've been wishing for it. Say it. You know what you want."

"I want to be normal."

"You want to walk away from Pia?"

"Where is she?" I whirl around, searching for my friend. And there, there on a low branch, full and heavy with bright yellow leaves, Pia sits with her crown of bright red feathers in stark contrast against the foliage.

She morphs before my eyes. Her body disintegrates, but instead of collapsing into billions of dust particles, every single feather becomes a moth. They swarm, circle each other like a cyclone. And then... they hover there. Waiting.

I turn back to Ostanes.

I know her.

"You *know* me." Her words echo my thoughts. "And you know yourself too. Who *are* you, Pie?"

I want to say, *I am that girl from Philly.* Then I want to say, *I don't know.*

But it's just all lies, and there's no way to hide from it anymore.

So I give in. I say, "I am yours."

And this earns me a wide smile. "Yes, child. You are mine. I called you to Saint Mark's. Pell is mine. Tarq is mine and Tomas is mine. And I put you all here for this one moment when you could confront that bastard Saturn and take back what belongs to us."

"Is he gone, then?" I ask. "Is Saturn dead?"

"He is gone for now." She huffs. "But he'll be back. We're not to concern ourselves with him just yet. Let him lick his wounds. We have bigger, better things to do with the monsters of Saint Mark's. Like set them free. But first, you have to choose, Pie. Because Pell's magic is only temporary. He has already been holding you in this freeze for longer than he should. Just a little bit longer and you will fall out of it on your own. And if you do not make a choice, you *will* die. You will not come back from this. You are not the caretaker of Saint Mark's Sanctuary. Grant was able to leave because you brought your magic with you. And Saturn was able to take over his aging body and make him young again—use him to do his bidding—because his curse was still in place. But you were not the replacement and if you die, you will be dead. You will not come back. Not tomorrow, not next year, not next century. And Pell will live on. Forever, and ever, and ever inside his curse. Knowing that his one chance to be with you the way you were meant to be together is over."

There is a part of me that wants to ask a lot of questions about setting the monsters free. Like… are we sure the world is ready for that? And other such important things.

But Ostanes keeps spilling out information that seems critical, and I just can't keep up. "Wait," I say, putting up a hand. "I don't understand."

"Oh, you do." Ostanes holds out her hand, palm up, and the moths that I thought were mine swarm to her. Cover her from head to toe, so that she is nothing but fluttering wings. She speaks and even her words come out with wings. "I made you four to keep my magic safe. Tarq to hold the book. Pell to hold the tombs. Tomas to hold the sanctuary."

I blink at her. Because that actually kinda does make sense. "But what about me?"

"You hold them all, dear Pie. You hold them all. But they hold you as well. The curse has not been lifted, but it has shifted. Pell knows what to do, but he needs a sign from you that this is what you want. And then the two of you can find the new boundaries together. Tell him, Pie. Tell him what you want."

What I want is to make her explain this shit in tiny little baby words. But it's just a distraction. I understand what she's saying. "He needs to know that I want to be a monster."

Ostanes' smile is sad. "You have *always* been monster. But I put you here to hide you from them. Don't listen to Saturn when he says you belong to him. You do not. I made you. You are mine."

"So… he's right then. I'm not real."

"Do you feel not real?"

"No, but—"

"You are as real as you want to be." She smiles at me. "Listen carefully now. We are getting dangerously close to the end and there are things you must understand. Your human soul is gone. The moment that bullet hit your chest, it died. It cannot be recovered."

"Then what the fuck? Why are we even having this conversation?"

"Because your soul has two halves, Pie. All of my monsters have one soul with two halves." Suddenly, the moths around her body converge once more and turn back into Pia. She chirps. Flies over to me. Snuggles into the front pocket of my flannel. And everything in this moment feels… inevitable.

"She is your other half. Your *monster* half."

"You want me to say this is me. This girl with hind legs and hooves. This girl with horns and hide. This *is* me."

"Yes. This is who you are. So you will say it again," Ostanes whispers. "Say it again, Pie. And this time… you will *mean it*. And then, dear girl, you will take all the power you were always meant to have."

I still want to deny it.

I want to hold on to my humanity for dear life.

But I'm having trouble remembering what it was like to be Pie. My past is fading as I stand here. Everything that came before Pell and Tomas seems… irrelevant.

There is still a small part of me though. A tiny part that want to deny this new me. Guilt, maybe? Fear? That lingering question in the back of my head about Pell.

Is he evil? Is that what horns mean? And if so, am I evil?

I am not evil. I do not require a single moment to debate that.

It's settled.

I straighten up. Feel the muscles in my legs. My fingertips absently brush along the side of my thigh. Against fur, not skin. The horns are heavy on my head.

And somehow, it all fits. It all feels right.

So when I say, "This is me," I really do mean it.

The woods disappear.

Ostanes is gone.

And then… I am alone.

And this is not what I was expecting.

I was expecting to return to the sanctuary. To wake up in Pell's arms. Or find Tomas's handsome face hovering over me with a look of concern.

But I am in the nowhere. The in-between. Not in the gray, something worse than the gray.

There is no air here, so I cannot breathe.

There is no light here, so I cannot see.

This is darkness.

This is emptiness.

And then I get it.

I am done and this is the end.

I have one last breath inside me.

The breath that Pell gave me that night of my date.

I use it now to call his name.

"Pell," I whisper.

But the darkness swallows it up.

CHAPTER THIRTY-THREE – PELL

"Hello?" I call out to the dark emptiness.

Where the hell am I? And what happened to the sanctuary?

"Tomas?" I call. "Hey! Can you hear me? Pie?"

I don't know how long I stand here doing nothing but listening, but I think it's a while. Because something has changed. There is a sudden blankness to me. Like… like I'm about to be erased.

I have heard caretakers complain about the gray over the centuries. When they step outside without that ring, that's always the wake-up call. It's the one thing I can count on to wipe away their disbelief and force them to pay attention to my rules and expectations.

But I am unable to walk through the gates without my caretaker, so I have never experienced it myself. Even if I had, it would not matter now. Because this is not gray, this is *black*.

It is the absence of everything.

"Why am I here?" I yell.

I do not expect an answer, nor do I get one. But if those damned gods are going to abandon me here in this new hellish purgatory, then questions are all I have left.

"Who is in charge? What do you want?" My voice is loud and booming and my words bounce back. Like there are walls somewhere in the distance.

And they stop.

And there is just... nothing.

I let out a long sigh, ready for this curse to be over. So done with this bullshit life. What is the fucking point of living when you're just a toy to them? Nothing more than entertainment. Just a fucking joke.

But something happens to my breath when I sigh. It glows a little. Lighting up the space around me.

And then I'm back in the dungeon with Tomas, holding that torch above my head, thinking, *This is not how light works.*

Light rules dark. Light needs only to exist to banish darkness. The dark has no such power over light.

Except when it's not really darkness, but something else altogether.

I am in the something else.

"Tomas?" I call again. Only this time, it comes out in a small, hesitant whisper.

And again, with my breath comes the light.

Am I the dragon?

I breathe harder, but it does not get brighter. No fire comes out of me, even though I am, like Tomas, made of fire. So I am not a dragon.

I am just me.

The worthless Pell.

Joke of jokes.

The entertainment.

But just as I think those words, I catch a whisper in the dark. "Pell?" the whisper asks. Just a few letters on the wind. And I am alert again.

"Pie!" I yell as loud as I can. "Pie!" I call her name over and over as I stumble forward into the blackness. Because that whisper belonged to her. "Pie!"

She does not answer me back.

She's going to die here. She's going to die here and I will be stuck in the cursed dark for all eternity.

No. "Think! *Think*! She's here! You're here! How do you find her?"

I don't know.

I'm a formidable enough monster in the real world. But I'm not in the real world. I'm in the magic of Saint Mark's. And my magic is very limited. I can slam doors. I can freeze the caretaker. I can put my claim on them with a breath. I can chop off a horn and collect the blood and make a magic dragon scale.

I've done all that and I'm still here.

So what more can I do?

I sigh again. And again, the breath comes out as a tiny bit of light.

Light rules dark.

I am fire.

Fire is light.

I am light.

And I know what to do.

I bend down, feeling on the ground beneath my feet for the horn I know is there. I grab it, hold it up in front of me like a torch.

At first, it does nothing. I can't even see it. But I breathe. I make just enough wind to blow the light inside me onto the horn and the blood glows. I send another breath of encouragement and it glows again. Brighter this time. Little flecks of potential fire appear.

One more breath and the tiny embers catch and sputter into life.

I have a torch.

And I walk forward into the dark emptiness calling her name.

Because she is the moth and I am the flame.

And if she can't come to me, I will go to her.

CHAPTER THIRTY-FOUR – PIE

Somewhere, a bell is ringing. It's calling me.

A wave of panic rushes through me as I consider who is summoning me now. Grant? Saturn? Sheriff Roth? What asshole is looking for me now?

The darkness is so absolute that even if I wanted to find that bell, there is no way I could. It's not possible. I am immersed in a void of nonexistence.

You're not real, Pie. That's the new voice in my head.

Before Saint Mark's it was always, *You're crazy, Pie.* I thought that was pretty bad. But nope. This is worse.

Because I am alone, I am afraid, and no one is coming to rescue me.

I have been forsaken.

No. No. There's a better word for that. It's called 'abandoned.'

But just as I think those words, there is a spark in the distance.

I lean forward and take a step, my feet suddenly underneath me. But they are not feet. They are hooves. And when I brush my hands against my hips, there is fur there. The horns are heavy on my head.

"You will say it again," Ostanes whispers into the nothingness. "Say it again, Pie. And this time… you will really mean it."

I don't say it. Because I don't need to say it.

I feel it in my half-dead monster soul—this is me.

The woods appear. Dark, still, but not empty.

The torch in the distance floats in and out through the shadows of the leaves. Bobbing up and down. This way and that.

And then there he is.

Pell.

Running towards me.

Lighting the way.

CHAPTER THIRTY-FIVE – PELL

My light grows, the darkness fades, and then, suddenly, I am in the woods. *My* woods. No. *Our* woods.

I run with my horn torch held high. Looking for her. Calling for her.

At first the crashing of my hooves in the underbrush drowns it out, but then I hear it. I hear *her*. The small tinkling of tiny bells around her neck, and her wrists, and braided into her hair.

She is running towards me. Leaping over long-dead trees, leaves smacking her face.

We race towards each other. But when we meet up, we change. Become small. Become kids.

I look over at Pie, no longer holding my horn torch, no longer needing it. The sun is shining above the forest canopy and little pillars of light find their way through the web of leaves, illuminating her face with golden light.

She laughs. We both laugh. And I take her hand so we can run together.

We run through our forest of white-trunked trees and bright-yellow leaves.

And we still pause when we get to the boundary of the flower meadow.

We still consider our options.

But this time, when she calls her moths and sends them forward, I do not let her go without me.

I take her hand and we step into the clearing together.

Grown up now, we look at each other one more time, just to make sure.

"Yes?" I ask.

"The curse won't be broken," Pie says. "But the boundaries will shift."

We stop walking in the middle of the meadow and I pull her towards me. "That could mean anything, Pie."

"I'm ready for all of it," she says.

I kiss her.

She kisses me.

I gaze into her wood-nymph blue eyes and she searches my satyr-yellow ones. And then, finally, we really are ready for what comes next.

There are more monsters caught in this curse than us. And when we turn back to the woods, they are there. Waiting. Monsters of every shape and size. Horns, and hooves, and wings, and tails peek out from behind the burnt-orange leaves of the temple woods.

We stop at the edge of the trees. And one by one they come forward, some angry, some sad, some just beaten down and tired.

But they come and they follow us across the meadow. They run with us through the woods.

We take them back through the darkness, my horns—whole again—lighting the way.

And when we step out of the darkness and back into the light, we walk back into the sanctuary.

And we bring all the monsters of Saint Mark's with us.

EPILOGUE – PIE

TWO WEEKS LATER

So many things have changed around Saint Mark's Sanctuary.

First and foremost for me, it was the new look. But getting used to being a full-time monster didn't take as long as I thought it would. In fact, I pretty much settled right in. And the best part? I'm not the caretaker anymore. The entire Book of Debt has disappeared. We looked everywhere for it and it is just gone.

At first, I figured maybe Tomas burned it up with half the walls and ceilings. But the walls and ceilings have repaired themselves. You can't even tell that a blood dragon did his best to turn this place to ashes a few weeks ago. And still that dumb book never came back. Besides, Pell's little pleasure cave wasn't affected by the burn at all. None of the magical rooms were. So the book should still be in there, and it isn't.

Pell was a little worried about this for a few days. He muttered some concerns regarding the balance sheet of the universe, but even he had to admit that it's not our fault the book disappeared, and let it go.

Tomas is another huge change at Saint Mark's. First and foremost for him, there is no dragon version of himself in the dungeon. That smelly beast is gone. In fact, the smell is gone too. Everything that was down there is all gone.

And not only does Tomas get to be the hot dragon chimera he was always meant to be, one hundred percent of the time, but when he and Pell leave the sanctuary to go get provisions, he gets his hot-guy human body back too.

It's crazy good luck.

First and foremost for Pell, he's not the only monster. This place is crawling with them now. And he's got me, his dreamy wood-nymph better half. And when he leaves the sanctuary with Tomas, he turns human! So does Tomas! Though Pell isn't as excited about it as Tomas is. And they still have their curfew or whatever. Can't stay gone longer than a few hours. So there are no nightclub trips to Pittsburgh in Tomas's future, but there are still plenty of things out here in the sticks for him to explore.

Pia is back. She's not the same as she was. She doesn't talk to me anymore. I think this is because I'm her now. Or she is me. But she stays near me the same way she used to, so maybe it's more natural this way? None of the other monsters can see her—not even Pell or Tomas—so she's still my fluffy little personal hallucination.

One day, perhaps, I will find a spell to make a bird talk and we will have another conversation. But it's just as likely that she stays this way forever. She sings a lot, something she never did before. So I think she's happy with the new arrangement.

I haven't seen the moths again. But that makes sense. I never really learned to control them, they just appeared when things got stressful and magic was my last resort. I actually hope they stay gone forever. I am satisfied with who I am at the moment so if they never come back, I'll get over it.

Almost everything about Saint Mark's feels… easier now.

There are a few small snags that we're still getting used to. For me, it's that I can't leave the sanctuary boundary at all because my human form died. I have horns, and hooves, and hind legs at all times. So whatever magic is being used to glamour Pell and Tomas, it decided to skip me, even when I have my ring on. I will not be running errands for the monsters any time soon. I'm OK with this. I have no desire to see Sheriff Russ Roth again. And yes, he's still there. When I banished him, or whatever, it knocked him back into town and put some kind of memory spell on him. Because Pell and Tomas have been to Granite Springs and bumped into him twice now and he just smiles and tips his hat as he passes. No clue who or what they are.

But if I were to be in front of him, there's no telling how that magic might go wrong.

Better safe than sorry.

As far as Grant goes—no one has seen or heard from him since Dragon Day.

"What are you thinking so hard about?"

I look over at Pell, smiling. We're lying on a blanket down by the lake. It's a nice late November afternoon and the sun is warm on my bare back. "Us." It's my standard answer because he's always asking me this question. But I like the question and it's a true answer too. "I'm just so… content these days. It's like a dream, Pell."

We're both on our stomachs, shoulder to shoulder. He bumps me a little. "Are you worried about waking up?"

I was. Maybe for a day. But what's the point? So I shake my head. "Nah. I'm not worried about anything. I'm just... counting my blessings. I feel like a princess who was rescued from the tower and now I'm living the full-on happily ever after."

Pell kisses me, then he flops onto his back and sighs with his eyes closed. Agreeing with me about my conclusions.

There's some good-natured yelling a little way down the lake shore. A group of monsters are playing Frisbee and one with wings just made a good catch. For whatever reason, all the monsters are allowed to walk through the back gate now. So the lake and the woods are part of their curse. They can't find the country road that runs past the front of Saint Mark's, but they don't seem to care. They like it down here by the lake. They like to wander the forests. They like the hallways in the cathedral too. Lots of them spend time up there. But they do not like the tombs.

Most of the monsters who came out of the dark wood with us hang out here instead of inside the sanctuary walls because even though everything is pretty great, there is still one more mystery: None of the monsters who came back with us were from the tombs. Those are all still locked. Only now, I can't see the doors. No one can see the doors. It's like we were banished from the tombs.

I dunno. It's weird.

And Tarq didn't come out of the dark wood with us, so he's still in his tomb.

And here's another kinda fucked-up thing that's weird. In fact, there's maybe a lot of things about Saint Mark's that are still weird—but this one's the kicker.

There are no girls. None. I'm talkin' a zero number of those monsters are female.

And it's OK now because it's only been a couple weeks. But eventually—what will they do? I mean, not even Pell was celibate this whole time. He went looking for human women.

One day their satisfaction with freedom and their hesitation about the outside world will wear off at the same time and they will go looking for the out clause the same way I did.

Which leads me to the final snag: The ring.

It's still here on my finger. Oh, heck yeah, it's still here and it's snugger than ever. No way is this thing coming off.

But now there is one for every single monster in this place.

We know this. We counted them.

When we went looking for the Book of Debt, we found a bag of ancient silver rings in its place. This is how Tomas and Pell are able to walk out the gates and go to town. Everyone gets a magic ring.

Which is kinda cool. In theory. Because the whole point of freedom is to be free, right?

But they are *monsters*. So we didn't give them the rings.

It's one thing for Pell and Tomas to leave. They've been living in this modern world the whole time. They kinda get it. At the very least, they understand that human society has rules.

But do we really want to set fifty-seven chimera monsters loose in the world?

Can you imagine Old Lady Blue down at MoMack's Towin' coming face to face with the monsters of Saint Mark's?

And here's another weird thing. None of those rings are the same. They are all different.

Tomas thinks this means they belong to different gods. And once the right monster is paired up with the right ring, there's no telling what will happen. They could get super-magical powers, they could turn into maniacal evil beasts, or they could die, for all we know.

Pell isn't as sure about that god theory. He insists there were only twenty old gods involved in the chimera breeding program, so it must have some other meaning. Cults, maybe.

There's *that* word again.

And even though I understand it better now—a cult is more like a club in the eyes of the ancient gods—it's still unnerving.

Then there are the doors.

The poem over every door in the sanctuary went like this:

A horn, a hoof, an eye, a bone.
A man, a girl, a place of stone.
A tick of time, a last mistake.
Keep them safe behind the gate.

But now they all say this:

A horn, a hoof, an eye, a bone.
A man, a girl, a place of stone.
They fight, they fall, they rise again.
A brand-new dawn, a new domain.

What's *that* about? Sounds a bit ominous if you ask me. Like perhaps there's some kind of war brewing.

But hey, what do I know? I've been a monster for a grand total of two weeks.

"I'm hungry," Pell says, lazily rolling back over onto his stomach. "Wanna go grab a Pop-Tart with me?" He waggles his eyebrows, like we're just going to mess around when we get in my cottage kitchen.

And I'm up for that. So I say, "Sounds delicious."

We get up and he folds our blanket, then takes my hand and leads me along the lake shore. I admire the bright autumn colors of the leaves as we enter the parking lot and then pass through the gate.

I'm still looking up at the trees when Pell suddenly stops on the path. I'm just about to ask him what's up when I look up the hill towards the cathedral and see a huge, imposing dark monster standing at the top.

"Oh, shit," I say, just as Pell says, "Tarq!" He drops my hand and the blanket and then he's practically running up the hill towards his friend.

I follow, but with a lot less enthusiasm.

They are hugging, and slapping each other on the back, and talking excitedly as I approach. "Look!" Pell beams. "Tarq!" Then he points at me. "You remember Pie, right, Tarq?"

Tarq—still looking very much like the urban minotaur—nods his head and smiles. "Oh, I sure do."

"Hi," I say, waving my hand a little. There are fifty-nine monsters in this sanctuary—sixty, if you include me—and none of them unsettle me the way this guy does. Not even the ones that have a healthy dose of Cyclops in their pedigree make me want to hide the way Tarq does.

"What's that?" Pell says, pointing to Tarq's hand. And that's when I see the book.

Tarq doesn't answer Pell. He just smiles at me.

"Tarq?" Pell asks, maybe a little bit nervous. Like he's starting to get the feeling that something is off here.

I'm not starting to get that feeling, it's already overwhelming me. Because Tarq isn't holding just any old book.

It's *the* book.

My book.

The Book of Debt.

"Like I told you, Pie," Tarq finally says, "it all evens out in the wash." He flips the book open and I don't need to read the name at the top of the page to know what it says, but I look anyway.

And it says, *PIE*.

END OF BOOK SHIT

Welcome to the End of Book Shit. This is the last chapter in all my books where I get to have an opinion about what you just read. It's never edited, I write them last minute... blah, blah blah. You know the drill.

But I've been thinking about these EOBS's lately because of all the crazy shit that's happening in the world and how in like fifty years, or whatever, people might want to read journals about people who lived through this time in history. Maybe? For historical context? And I have always wanted to write a journal or have a diary but I'm just so not that... what's the word?

Reliable?

Dependable?

Responsible?

I think all of these words fit.

I like the idea of having a journal but I just don't have the ability to follow through. Nor do I have the time to just casually ponder the day's events each evening and then spend hours making pretty bullet-journal pages. If you do that, I wish I was you. I would love to be that kind of person, I'm just not.

I once took part in this study in college. This woman was doing her master's on blah, blah and she put an ad out on the college board or wherever the fuck it was I saw this ad, looking for women who "fit this certain profile" and I fit the certain profile and my life was a shit show of epic proportions at the time, so I contacted her. And she wrote her fucking master's thesis about me. lol

I'm literally laughing out loud as I type that this actually happened.

I had a copy of it and everything. It was a serious hardcover book. Of course, I was anonymous. And I never read her thesis. Just... fuck that. But when we first met in person, she asked me to keep a journal so she could "get my honest thoughts" about things. And I told her to fuck right off. I do not journal.

So I've known for a long time that future generations would never get my personal slant on things. I came to terms with it.

But then, I started thinking, well, these End of Book Shits are kinda like personal essays. And I've got a shit ton of them by now. This is book number who-the-fuck-knows. And all but the very first couple of Junco books have an EOBS because I started writing these in March of 2013.

So I guess the joke is on me, eh?

Anyway.

Here's my point. My EOBS is about writing. Because this Damaged Gods book is a first.

My very first paranormal romance.

Junco was not paranormal romance. I could lie and say it was, but when I wrote Junco I didn't even know what a genre was. That's why that series has no real genre.

Is it a romance? Not exactly.

Is it paranormal? Not exactly.

Is it sci-fi? Yeah. Mostly it is. Except for those "angels" right?

So I guess it's a sci-fi thriller. That's what RJ, my one and only editor for almost ten years now, called it at the time. And she would know better than me. She has an actual degree in shit like that and I went to school to be a veterinarian then ended up with a masters in forensic toxicology. So I actually know nothing about the "serious world of publishing".

So after Junco I just went full-on sexy romantic suspense until the Anarchy supervillain series in 2016-ish. And then I got super bored in 2019 and decided to write the Harem Station series. I set out to write the most ridiculous sci-fi romance I could because have you seen the state of sci-fi romance lately? lol Yeah. It's… a unique genre. And I figured, hell—let's just give those boys two dicks. It felt like a really funny idea at the time. But that series got serious and… long.

Harem Station was not paranormal. It really was a full-on sci-fi alien romance so this is why I got the KC Cross pen name. I didn't want a pen name, but I could see the reviews in my future. And listen, while I generally give no fucks about reviews, I do like to meet expectations of readers. I didn't want any of my one-click fans to one-click Booty Hunter and be like—what is this alien with two-dicks shit?

So I gave myself a pen name and made that name the most prominent text on the cover so long-time readers would pause before they clicked and actually make sure this was a story they wanted.

That worked, BTW. If I got any reviews complaining that readers were "tricked" I didn't see them.

I thought maybe I'd write three or four books in that series. But it turned into seven.

And then, because I am always plotting six or seven stories in my head as I'm writing my current work in progress, I figured I was gonna write some vampires. I have a really cool "new take" on vampires. And that's coming. I've been thinking about that story for about three or four years now and I'm just about to the point where I'm ready to get to work.

But then I came up with this monster romance idea last summer. I had the actual Damaged Gods title for about two years now. So I had been thinking about that story—meaning, the story that went with that title. And it was always one girl who got stuck with monsters, but I couldn't quite pull together how this whole scenario came to be until I stumbled into the subtitle, The Monsters of Saint Mark's.

I don't think I've ever said this before in any other EOBS, but I always have a title for the story first and then I build the story off the title. Sometimes this doesn't work. Sometimes the title gets tossed because the story went a different way. But most of the time it does work. Because once I get a title, or in this case, a subtitle, I have a direction.

So this is how I ended up with this story of Pie, Pell, and Tomas.

And I had the first scene. I had the gas station, the flyer on the bulletin board, and her first encounter with the sanctuary and the three people inside it.

But I didn't have anything after that. Nothing. I literally pulled this story out of my brain one page at a time once I sat down to seriously write it in January 2021. I didn't even have the fucking bird. I think I added Pia about a week after I started writing.

Writing Damaged Gods was exciting for me. I had just come off polishing up Sick Heart which is a very… I mean, it's dark. But it's also sweet. But it's very serious. Very serious.

So Damaged Gods was going to be my **fun** book.

And I needed a fun book in the worst way—not because of Sick Heart. Though, that was part of it. But because I just spent two fucking years writing **TWO** seven-book series.

Oh. *My god.*

I don't think people understand how hard it is to write a long series like Harem Station and Bossy Brothers, both of which have a stupid-complicated mystery running through all seven books, and then have to pull all those threads together in one final story.

It's pretty stressful. The time between Harem Station book six (Veiled Vixen) and Harem Station book seven (Uncrossed) was almost a year and a half. And every day when I woke up to write both Uncrossed and the last Bossy book, Luke, I was soooooooooo unmotivated. I wanted to do anything BUT write those two books.

I am fully aware that I do this to myself because I always write these twisted plots. It's so hard for me to write a straight-forward plot. My story brain just doesn't work that way. And every single time, without fail, there I am on the last book going why the fuck did I write all that complicated shit?

I get stuck every time. I would not call this writer's block. It's just ending block. lol

And this has always happened for as long as I've been writing because in order to have a perfect ending it must be "inevitable, but unexpected". That's a direct quote from Larry Brooks, author of Story Engineering. And Story Engineering was one of two books that taught me how to plot a story back in 2011.

So even back in 2013 when I writing the last Junco book (again, six-book series, stupid-complicated plot) I had to stop writing the last book to figure out how Junco was going to save the world. I had the very last scene—I had that last scene from the very first day I started writing that series. But I didn't have anything else. The story kind of wrote itself. So I had to stop writing the last book for about a week because my climax scene wasn't right. And then, BAM. The scene came to me while I was in the shower. And I sat down that day and wrote the rest of the book in one sitting.

This happened in Manic, Rook & Ronin book two. And that was only book TWO. That manuscript was due to my editor at 5 AM (she's on UK time) and I was literally writing the end at 4:30. This was back in the day when RJ didn't just drop everything to help me out, we were both really new. She needed time to get the edits done. So this was a serious deadline. And I could not find the epilogue for Rook in Manic until I figured out what Spencer was painting on her body at Sturgis.

This happened in The Company. Don't get me started on the stress of ending that series. It was so bad. It happened in Meet me in the Dark. It happened in Mr. Match. I thought I was going to die writing that book five.

But there's a pattern here. And a point.

And the point is: Book One is **easy**.

Standalone books are easy too.

But last book in series?

That is the definition of SUCKS.

I hated every moment of writing Uncrossed and Bossy Luke. And part of it was just 2020. Every day people were talking about new crazy shit. I don't even know how I got any writing done but I released five books in 2020. It was a very difficult time to be creative. Especially when you MUST end your book with a happily ever after. (#1 Rule of Romance.) That's why Sick Heart took me six months to write. Though Sick Heart is way up there with Ford and Junco as far as my own personal favorites go.

And of course I love both Bossy Luke and uncrossed *now*. I have listened to the audiobook of Uncrossed so many times, I lost count. It's such a good audiobook. I love it. And the ending of Bossy Luke made that whole struggle worth it. Just… Nick Tate, man. I love that guy. (And he's coming back in Gorgeous Misery and Lovely Darkness!) And I got a LOT of satisfaction when I tied the little girls in Luke to the same little girls in Wasted Lust. Seriously, I'm not gonna lie. That was the best moment in the entire series for me. And I think a lot of readers who went on the full Rook & Ronin/Company/Bossy journey got that same satisfaction. Someone wrote something like, "Why didn't I wonder where those little girls came from in Wasted Lust?" I didn't wonder either. Not until the ending of Luke and then those scenes with Posie and the girls turned into the only scenes that mattered as far as I was concerned.

Ending a series is **very** satisfying. (Once it's done).

But starting a series—that's the BEST of all worlds in my opinion. You don't have to worry about all those stray plot points or how *old* everyone is.

Oh. My God. Let me just tell you about ages. I just finished the Vicious book and this is in the Rook & Ronin world. Specifically in Spencer and Veronica's world. And they have all those damn kids. I wanted to kill myself every time I needed to know how old these kids were. I had to go searching through six years of emails to actually find where I wrote it down. Now you know why I never delete emails and have hundreds of thousands of them just hanging out in my inbox. And now you also know why I can't journal. I am just not that organized.

Anyway. Damaged Gods is book one and I loved it. I loved this whole story.

And I'm not saying writing it was easy or that it's perfect, or anything like that. But I surprised myself several times as I pulled this story together. It was a fun escape for me.

And I LOVE the cover. I made the Damaged Gods cover months ago and when I was done I just sat and looked at it for like a week and then immediately started making magnets and stickers to celebrate. ☺

I'm very happy that there will be a book two and hopefully it's up for pre-order right now. It's May as I write this—this book is going to narrators in a couple days—so I won't even have the cover reveal for another month.

So my plan is to have book two, SAVAGE SAINTS, up for pre-order when Damaged Gods releases. I love that cover too. I just made it like a week ago and wow. I don't usually get to make covers like that (and when you see it, you'll understand) because covers for romance need to look a certain way and covers for paranormal or fantasy need to look another certain way. So doing these covers was amazing.

I am planning on a March 2022 release for Savage Saints and I know that feels like a long gap between the two books but listen. I learned my lesson in 2020. I don't want to wake up dreading my job the way I did last year. I am not interested in the stress of deadlines anymore.

Why write fun books like this if I can't enjoy them?

When I started Damaged Gods I wasn't even sure I wanted to do a series but when the interior of Tarq's tomb popped up out of nowhere my excitement level for a book two became very, very high. I had originally planned something more frightening and suspenseful for Pie's tomb trip. But I love the way Tarq turned out. And I especially love that Tarq now owns Pie's debt.

So many smiles coming up with Tarq and Pie.

And Tomas. Oh, the fun I will have with virgin Tomas out in the real world. Maybe not in book two, we'll see if I can fit him in. But he was an unexpected delight.

If you're wondering if this is a reverse harem, I'm not sure yet. I don't know. I like all these characters. And Pie is a fun girl. And when Pie is uncomfortable, she's the best. I plan on making her squirm and blush like crazy in book two.

I set this series up so that Pie has many choices. The sheriff will be back as well. I kinda went in to Monsters thinking it might be a little bit like the Sookie Stackhouse series (True Blood show on HBO, if you're not familiar with the books). But Sookie

Stackhouse was always solving mysteries, and Monsters won't be a "mystery" series. Still, Sookie had lots of love interests and I want Pie to have the "full experience" too.

Also, another interesting note. I am an avid YA reader. I love young-adult fantasy/urban fantasy and science fiction. And there has been a rise in popularity in ancient Roman gods and goddesses in the YA world recently. I didn't really plan on making Pell from Ancient Rome, it just kinda happened. But now that it's part of the story, I'm excited to see what the old gods and goddesses are up to.

So I guess that's it for this End of Book Shit. I hope you enjoyed this new story. I hope it didn't stress you out. :) It wasn't meant to stress you out. It's just fun.

My next book releases August 31, 2021 – Vic Vaughn is Vicious. Yes, that Vic Vaughn of Sick Boyz Inc. fame. It's so fun. So cute. And I know I do not normally write cute—my books are a lesson in mind-fucking almost every single time. But there is no mind-fuck in Vicious. It's just a sexy rom-com.

I'm also writing two "vellas" for Amazon Vella. Have you heard of it? It's serialized fiction like the stories on platforms such as Radish and Wattpad. I don't expect any of you to give a single fuck about these two serials BUT if you're curious – that's where that "Vampire Story" will end up. And I have Cyborg Romance I'm going to put up on there too. (No, he will not have two dicks.)

I don't know when that whole "Vella" thing will go live—Amazon tells us nothing. We are but mere content creators. But I think it might be live by the time this book releases.

Who knows? Just wanted to let you know that was coming if you're interested.

Also, I'm only writing stories for Vella for fun.

That's my new goal in life.

Have fun.

You might want to make it your goal too.

Thank you for reading, thank you for reviewing, and I'll see you in the next book!

Julie
JA Huss
May 18, 2021

ABOUT THE AUTHOR

ABOUT THE AUTHOR

JA Huss is a New York Times Bestselling author and has been on the USA Today Bestseller's list 21 times. She writes characters with heart, plots with twists, and perfect endings.

Her books have sold millions of copies all over the world. Her book, Eighteen, was nominated for a Voice Arts Award and an Audie Award in 2016 and 2017 respectively. Her audiobook, Mr. Perfect, was nominated for a Voice Arts Award in 2017. Her audiobook, Taking Turns, was nominated for an Audie Award in 2018. Her book, Total Exposure, was nominated for a RITA Award in 2019.

She writes Sci-Fi Romance and Paranormal Romance under the name KC Cross.

Made in the USA
Monee, IL
15 November 2022

17818795R00268